Catch of the Day
(1973)

Phillip Legard

Dedication

For my dad.

Prologue: The Four Gangs

A cold easterly breeze skipped in from the North Sea, biting hard, chilling the rickety forts of No-Man's Land and freezing the fluttering flags of the Four Gangs. Fat banks of sea fog clung to the ground, swirling in corpulent eddies, numb fingers prying into every cranny, sucking the life from all that they touched. With the delicate spring sun obscured from view, it fell to the myriad of buzzing streetlamps that surrounded the vast expanse of derelict earth to guide the way. All they could muster was a sickly orange glow that turned the cold, thick mist into tangerine candyfloss.

A shrill whistle sounded. It was answered by another. A torchlight danced, picking out shallow trenches, treacherous barricades and tall wooden walls. It flashed downwards, upwards, then, with a *clatter*, fell to the ground.

"Ruddy divots!" exclaimed a man. "Yer can't see owt through this damn fret."

"Halt!" shouted a boy. "Ooo goes there?"

"It's yer dad. It's past yer teatime."

"Wot's the password?"

"Come 'ome this instant, or yer'll get a thick ear!"

"Aw, Dad. Just tell uz the password."

"*Up the Mariners*! Now 'ome with yer. And bring yer bruvver."

Pogsy laughed. You could always trust a grown-up to ruin the atmosphere. His nostrils flared. He caught a brief whiff of brine. Then it was gone. They were perhaps a couple of miles inland, but even so their lives depended on the sea. Everyone's lives depended on the sea. There it was again. Just a hint of salt spray. And with it, the stink of freshly gutted fish. Possibly it was his vivid imagination adding in the smell of the docks and the tang of the waves, as they lashed angrily at the North Wall. He pulled up the collar of his jacket around his ears and warmed his hands on a crackling fire. They were supposed to be cooking bangers on sticks, but Bigzy's cousin hadn't turned up with the sausages. It wasn't a surprise. You could hardly see beyond the end of your nose. It was a shame though. Bangers on sticks always looked extra yummy, even though Mum claimed sticks were chock full of nasty diseases.

Pogsy looked at his imaginary watch.

It was a hair past a freckle.

They'd have to pack up before too long and head home for their own teas. The gang had been leaving in dribs and drabs for a while now and there were only three of them left. Even the older boys from the other gangs wouldn't last long in weather like this. The dens were snug, but they weren't as warm as a roaring hearth fire.

"Giz 'and with the flag," said Pogsy.

Bigzy nodded enthusiastically, grinning cheekily from ear to ear. "Sure thing, boss," he said. He was the titchiest boy in the whole year, which made his nickname kind of ironic.

Between the two of them, they soon had the banner down from the flagpole. Red Top, who was supposed to be on guard duty, offered to help fold it in four. His assistance wasn't strictly necessary, but it was understandable that he didn't want to be left out. Although none of the Four Gangs would ever steal a flag from a fellow gang, there were other less trustworthy gangs in town who might. They didn't usually roam as far as No-Man's Land but there was no point in taking a chance with something as valuable as the gang flag.

The three pals saluted their banner and packed it away neatly in its cloth bag. Pogsy felt his chest swell with pride. "Here," he said, handing it on to Reddy. "It's your turn."

"Thanks," said Red Top. "I won't let uz down. Honest." Pogsy thought he saw a tear form in the corner of his friend's eye. He didn't say anything, mainly because Reddy was funny about that sort of thing and might lash out. The boy who was Pogsy's secret best friend was as skinny as a rake with a tangled mop of unwashed brown hair. Ever since his mam and dad had gone to war with each other, he'd been wearing a permanent frown that didn't suit him.

The flag had been Dad's idea. He'd said that if a gang didn't have a flag, they weren't a proper gang. Granny Green had helped to sew it. She was a demon with fabric, scissors, and a needle and thread. She'd stabbed her fingers so many times that they were as hard as leather. As soon as Granny had finished her work and Pogsy had his hands on the flag, the gang had set about constructing a flagpole. That was when all the other gangs had decided to make their own flags too. This was how it was with the gangs. When one boy invented something really good that no-one else had, the others had to try to improve it.

"Anyone there?" shouted a voice. It was impossible to see its owner through the clammy tendrils of pea-soup.

Red Top grabbed his guard-stick from where he'd leaned it against a wall and jumped to attention. "Halt!" he shouted, prodding into the pall beyond the entry gate. "Who goes there? Friend or foe?"

"Friend," said the voice, all a quiver. "It's Bingo. Please don't stab me."

"You div!" Red Top let the new arrival into camp. "We're packing up. What *are* you doing here?"

"I heard you might be going on a mission." The words came out as a stammer. Bingo pushed his square-rimmed glasses up his tiny round nose. "There's a rumour that the Old Clee lot have sided with the Daleks."

"We think one of them is a German spy," replied Pogsy. "But we don't know who it is yet. We can't have a mission until we're sure. When we do, I'll let you know."

"Thanks," said Bingo. "I've never been on a real mission before. I'm dying to know what it's like."

"Dangerous," said Bigzy, flashing his gnashers and showing the gaps at the front where two of his milk teeth had recently fallen out. "There's angry misters and sometimes dogs."

"Oh, my," said Bingo. "How do you cope?"

"By running away as fast as we can," said Bigzy.

"By getting stuck in," said Red Top, putting up his fists.

"I'm not very good at either of those things," said Bingo, all of a fluster.

"Don't worry," said Pogsy. "We'll show you the ropes." It was a lie. Much as Pogsy really liked Bingo, who was easily the brainiest boy in class, he had no intention of asking him along on a mission. The most important attribute a boy could have, when trespassing in gardens or crawling on his belly through dangerous underground pipes, was the ability to lie about it afterwards. Bingo, unfortunately, was just too honest to be trusted.

"Our next mission is at Easter," said Bigzy. "We're going to see *Batman* at the cinema. You can come on that."

"Thanks," said Bingo. "It doesn't help with my balance though. I almost came a cropper in the trenches with all this fog."

Pogsy laughed.

He still remembered the day the first trench had appeared like it was yesterday. Initially, when they'd started playing on No-Man's Land, there had been many small groups of lads. One day someone had erected a tent. Soon everyone had one. When a group of dads had dug a trench around their boys' tent, all the other groups had pestered their dads and older brothers to dig deeper trenches around their tents. Two dads had decided to go one better and had brought along the remains of an old patched-up potting shed with a hatch in the roof for a lookout post. The next Sunday afternoon, after the boozer, some of the other dads had made plans for a wooden hut with a lookout post *and* secret hatches for catapults. By the next weekend it was built, along with the first of the moats. In response, some of the groups of lads had asked if they could join forces with the hut builders, thus creating the first two gangs. Not wanting to be outnumbered, the remaining groups had formed two gangs of their own. Pester power ensured that it wasn't long before everyone had a fort, although, if the boys were honest, they were really just jazzed up huts with big ideas. They were all solid and waterproof though, even if some of them smelt of mould and damp and had fungus instead of timbers.

None of the gangs had proper names back then. They were called things like the *Garden Shed Gang*. Or the *Bunker Gang*, who'd got their name because they had a secret underground bunker which a pair of dads had dug out. Although they'd called it a bunker, it was really just a pit covered over with corrugated iron. When the Bunker Gang had revealed their secret, everyone was extremely envious. In response, someone's uncle had borrowed an excavator to dig a deeper hole, then lined it with bricks and mortar to prevent a cave-in.

That had been the start of the earthworks.

It was so exciting, rushing home from school every night with Reddy to find out who'd spent the day twagging it and building dens. When a gang finished something new, they always had a proper unveiling ceremony where everyone else was invited over to have a good neb and express their envy. When boys and their dads and their brothers and cousins set their minds to construction, there was no end to what they could achieve.

Once the gangs had finished burrowing holes and digging trenches, the stockades arrived. They needed teams of lads to help with the construction. In the end, everyone had helped everyone else. Some trenches were widened into full-scale moats; others were abandoned.

After the dens were completed, the dads had celebrated their achievements around a bonfire, with beer and a good old-fashioned singsong, where they decided that there was only one rule they were going to impose on their boys: all fires must be lit outside.

Pogsy smirked to himself.

The Old Clee lot had discovered the hard way that silly old dad rules weren't so stupid after all. They'd nearly smoked themselves to death in their bunker finding out. Everyone had called their leader *Sooty* after that. He hated it. His Second-in-Command hated being called *Sweep* even more.

Pogsy, who was also Second-in-Command, was convinced that this was actually the most important position in any gang, far more important than the leader, whose only job was to be gobby. He reminded himself that he'd been responsible for persuading groups of boys from three different streets to come together. The Patrick Street boys and the Torrington Street boys were historically bitter rivals, but he'd managed to stop all the name calling by getting everyone to work together on designing the fort complex, which, when it came down to it, was Bingo's idea. They'd needed the Legsby Avenue boys though, to help with the stockade and the flagpole. The one thing they'd argued about a lot was the gang's name. The joshing had gone on for what seemed like a year, but was in reality less than a week. In the end, they'd voted unanimously to call themselves *The Kings*, because it sounded like they were the kings of all the castles.

Each of the gang HQs had its own character. It was generally agreed that The Kings had the tallest fort, but they also had the smallest bunker. The Old Clee lot, who called themselves the *Wheelers* were forever repairing their stockade, due to issues with the foundations which led to a collapsing wall. The dads had gathered round one day to problem solve. They concluded that a busted sewer pipe was pumping out effluence that was causing sodden timbers in one corner. Busted pipework was council business, and council business was best left to the council to sort out. Not that anyone thought to report the problem. The Convamore Road lot, who'd voted to call themselves the *Hard Nuts*, had the largest stockade. Everyone knew that, because all of the stockades had been competitively measured to the nearest inch. The Welholme Road lot, who'd named themselves the *Wingmen* had the deepest moat with the most water. When it had frozen over last winter, all the other gangs and their brothers and sisters had used if for ice skating. Later, when everything thawed out, they'd found they had an expanse of bog mud that was capable of sucking off a pair of wellies in under three strides.

In early spring, the snow had fallen so thickly the dens were impossible to find. Dads had had to dig everything out, leaving piles and piles of white stuff everywhere, which had in turn provided enough material for four gigantic snowmen and more ammunition than anyone knew what to do with. The ensuing fight had gone on for days. Projectiles were whizzing everywhere. The sky was thick with them for hours on end, in what had become known as the Siege of the Snowballs.

Overall, thought Pogsy, the last year had been brilliant fun. They'd built a fantastic den and had some really good fights. They'd learned how to make fires and, true to their word, the grown-ups had left them alone. Just like today, there had been days when it was Baltic. Your breath froze and, if you weren't wearing a hat and a scarf, your ears and nose turned bright red. In shorts, everyone's knees knocked, especially when the school heating didn't work. It was on days like these that the icicles on the sides of the trawlers out at sea were ten feet long. The fronts of the boats were covered in ice and snow and the gales howled and tried to tear the oilskins from the fishermen's backs. Ships were tossed from side to side and everyone on board was soaking wet and frozen to the bone, unable to feel their fingers or toes. Yet they still carried on doing their jobs, hauling in fish and gutting it on deck, forever chipping away at the ice to prevent their boats from capsizing.

One of The Kings' boys had a dad who worked on the trawlers. He'd often be away for weeks at a time, then home for a few days to get roaring drunk before heading off back to sea. Pogsy was glad that his dad didn't do that job. He'd never know for sure whether he was safe, not until he returned home. He'd heard stories of dads coming home with missing fingers and toes, and sometimes missing arms. It was a hard life being a fisherman. It wasn't for everyone. Although Pogsy's dad didn't work on the boats, he was still involved with fish. Everyone was. Pogsy didn't know a single person who wasn't involved with fish in one way or another. It was an inescapable fact of life.

"Goodnight, den. Sleep tight." Pogsy gave a salute. It was his traditional goodbye.

"Nighty night," said Bigzy, his trademark smirk in evidence.

"Night," said Red Top, waving his spear above his head.

"It seems a bit silly to say goodnight to a den," said Bingo. "It's not like it's going anywhere."

Pogsy prodded his friend. "You have to say it. Those are the rules for last one out. Otherwise, it'll bring bad luck."

Bingo mumbled something under his breath.

Pogsy had decided long ago that the dens were definitely the best thing that had ever happened. He found it difficult to imagine a time without them, or the gangs that had built them. Come the summer, when the weather was better, they planned on playing *Capture the Flag*. Everyone was going to be armed to the teeth with eggs and flour bombs and water bombs and water pistols and catapults. Then they'd all attack each other's dens to find out once and for all which one had the best defences. It wouldn't be long now. It was only a few weeks until Easter.

"I'm off home to listen to the Top Twenty on the radio," he said. "There's this new band called T. Rex at Number One. They're brilliant."

"I doubt it," said Bigzy, moving away to a safe distance. "Your taste in music is rubbish!"

"Never heard of them," said Red Top. "My dad likes Neil Diamond. 'Sweet Caroline' was pretty good."

"I quite like that one by Dad's Army," said Bingo. "The one about grandads."

"That's the worst pop song ever, in the history of pop songs," said Pogsy.

"You're right there," said Bigzy. "Loads of me little cousins bought it for me grandad for his birthday and now he's got fifty copies and he never wants to hear it ever again. If I catch you singing it, I'll kick you in the goolies."

"Can I hum it?"

"If you want," said Bigzy, readying his foot.

"I'll give it a miss."

That night, Pogsy dreamed of dens built on top of other dens. It was all he could think about these days. It didn't matter whether he was awake or asleep. Everything revolved around dens. Sam, his brother, said he was obsessed. He was probably right. If his schoolwork was suffering, then Mum would have had a word by now. But it wasn't. As long as he kept up in class, being obsessed with dens was fine. Pogsy wasn't the top of his class, but he was close, apart from maths and English. As with every class in his school, there was a group of girls who were the real clever clogs. Between them, they were the best at everything except football, fighting and building dens.

It was a well-known fact that, although girls had Wendy houses to play in, they loved to try to take over boys' dens. They'd always try to add curtains and cushions, and, if you didn't watch it, picnic sets and chairs would suddenly appear from nowhere along with plastic ponies. Once they had a bridgehead into your den, hundreds of dolls would mysteriously teleport in overnight. This was why all dens had a sign that read: No Girls Allowed. There were no exceptions.

Such signs only worked with girls who were old enough to read. If you had a secret den in your back garden, it was going to get invaded at some point by your little sister and her friends. If this happened, it was impossible to get them out again. This was why all the best secret dens were built on disused land. The gangs all pretended that the moats and stockades were there to keep other gangs out. Really though, they were there to keep girls out. Especially little sisters.

Pogsy hurried home from school after a long day of hard lessons, his head full of plans. He changed out of his school uniform as fast as he could, while Red Top waited downstairs. The pair then headed over to No-Man's Land, where they discovered a gaggle of boys gathered together, staring at a hastily erected barbed-wire fence with Keep Out signs everywhere.

Pogsy felt his face contort into a grimace. "What's going on?"

"Innit obvious?" said Red Top, his perma-frown turning into a scowl. "We've been done."

A bunch of men dressed in donkey jackets were busy feeding timbers into a smouldering bonfire. Piles of ash littered the muddy site, where several other smaller fires had already burnt themselves out. Bulldozer tracks criss-crossed the ground. To Pogsy's eye, they looked more like evidence of tanks. The bright yellow vehicle that was responsible for all the destruction roared its approval. It was definitely a Panzer.

Pogsy rubbed his eyes. "It's the Germans..."

"Worse than that," retorted one of the group of boys, "it's the council."

Briefly, the wind changed direction and blew smoke directly at the group. Everyone coughed and covered their eyes and mouths. Pogsy did likewise. He gasped for breath and spat out a gob of phlegm in disgust. As the smoke drifted off, he rubbed his eyes again.

"Where are the forts?" he stammered.

"Told you it's the council," said one of the rival gang members. "They sold the land. Everything's got to come down."

"The misters say they're gonna build a cold store," said someone else.

Pogsy felt all wobbly at the knees. It was like he was living in the worst nightmare imaginable. He covered his eyes and wished as hard as he could for things to be different. Slowly, he moved his fingers aside and peeked out. Nothing had changed. The forts were gone, levelled by heavy machines. The trenches and moats they'd spent so long digging were completely filled in with earth. All of the underground bunkers had had their roofs ripped off, leaving a series of sorry-looking craters. Everything flammable had either been burnt or else was on fire right now.

"This is illegal!" he screamed.

"You're a bunch of horrible misters!" yelled Red Top. He turned to Pogsy. "We've got to fight them."

"They're the council," said one of the boys. "No-one can fight the council."

"Council does what it wants," said another.

Red Top shook his fist at the group of lads. "Cowards, the lot of you."

"We're just boys," said one of the boys. "They're big, strong, mean council misters."

Pogsy felt his eyes fill with tears. "The dens."

"At least we've got our flags," said one of the Welholme boys.

"We can't let them get away with it!" Pogsy wanted to curl up and cry, but he was determined not to, not in front of the other boys.

"We don't have a choice," said one of the boys. "It's the council."

"The council can bog off!" shouted Pogsy. "Every last one of them."

"Nowt we can do 'ere," said another boy. "Might as well go."

Eyes downcast, a group of lads drifted away.

"I hate you!" screamed Pogsy. "I hate you all!"

One of the men looked up. He shrugged his shoulders and chucked another bit of den on the fire. Sparks flew. The fire crackled, gobbling up the fuel.

"That was our flagpole!" Reddy ran up to the barbed-wire fence and shook his fists.

"Son," shouted a mister from the cab of a bulldozer, "go 'ome. It's dangerous 'ere."

"We can't," said Pogsy. "This *is* our home. And you lot destroyed it."

One of the remaining boys touched Pogsy on the shoulder. "They're council. They don't care. It's like talking to a seaweed monster. You're wastin' your time. It can't understand you."

"I'll get you for this!" shouted Pogsy. "I'll get you all!"

"They're not worth it," said one of the boys.

"We'll come back later when they've gone," said another boy.

The wind changed direction again, blowing a stream of grey and yellow smoke directly at the group. Pogsy coughed and retreated to a safe distance. His hair was going to stink for days. And he wasn't due a bath for nearly a week. He rubbed his eyes once more and, feeling crushed inside, shuffled off.

It wasn't fair.

The misters were horrible and heartless and stupid, and they didn't care what they'd done.

Boys were like fleas to them. Summut to be itched and scratched and popped between their fingernails.

Red Top put his arm around Pogsy. "We'll make another den," he said. "Me dad says I'm nearly old enough to start helping him on the milk floats. I'll find uz somewhere."

"It won't be the same."

"It'll be better."

Pogsy turned to look at the workmen. "I hope you all get the worst lurgy ever and your willies drop off!" he shouted at the top of his voice. "And I hope your dogs get to them first and eat them!"

Pogsy was eight and a bit. It was the *worstest* day of his life.

1973

One: Kevin Keegan

"You can't have a girl in the gang!" Steve folded his arms and leaned against the lamppost under which a small group of boys were gathered. "You know the rules. You shouldn't have brought her."

"But Ali's different," said Pogsy, folding his own arms and facing Steve.

"She's a girl." Steve turned his attention to Ali. "Girls are *yeuch*. Everyone knows that. And they're always crying and moaning and doing stupid girl stuff."

Ali glared at Steve like she was going to kick him, or scream in his face, or pull his hair, but thankfully she fumed in silence. Pogsy breathed a sigh of relief. He'd gone to great lengths to explain the gang rules to Ali. At least she'd listened.

Steve glared back. He was nearly eleven and the biggest boy in class. He stood a couple of inches taller than Pogsy. Everyone said he took after his dad, which, if true, meant he was going to be ginormous one day. Like the rest of the gang, Steve had been growing his hair for the last year, keeping up with current trends. His blond locks were well below his ears now, but still not a patch on Pogsy's curls, which reached all the way down to his shoulders.

Pogsy weighed up the expression on his friend's face. He'd known Steve since before they started school, and when his pal was cross-your-heart-dead-set on having his own way, he folded his tongue over in his mouth. He couldn't help it; he'd been doing it for years. For now, his tongue was straight.

Over the years, the pair had had numerous tussles, including a topless wrestle in the summer. The self-proclaimed leader of the gang had won every time. In a boxing match, Pogsy knew he'd come out on top, but playground fights were never like that. He'd punched Steve on the end of his conk once out of annoyance, but Steve had just laughed and used his superior strength to put Pogsy in a headlock and administer a monkey-scrub.

At the thought of having his head rubbed raw again, Pogsy felt his ears redden. He bit his tongue. He couldn't afford to blow up and throw a strop because, if he did, Steve would win. But although Steve was bigger than him, he wasn't cleverer.

"Ali's not like all the other girls." Pogsy stared Steve down, feeling comfy in the red and white chequered teddy-bear jacket he'd chosen for the coming winter. "She does climbing and stuff. Ask Reddy. He's seen her."

"S'true," said Red Top, scratting at the side of his head and pulling at a strand of tangled brown hair which fell all the way down his face. "I saw her get higher up the climbing tree in the park than anyone else has ever gone. I'm dying to see her have a go on Mister Mortis's apple tree."

"I'm the leader of The Kings." Steve scowled, resting his outsized front teeth on his plump bottom lip. "And the rules are simps: no girls."

Pogsy recognised the tell. *The Beaver*, he called it. Whenever Steve was unsure about something, he prepared to gnaw wood, as if he was going to build a massive dam with a secret underwater entrance, just like the Beaver Family Robinson on *Survival*.

Steve turned to the one member of the gang who had yet to have his say. "What do you think, Bigzy?"

"S'true that she got higher up the climbing tree than I've ever been," said the little lad after some consideration. "But then she don't have no balls to bust if she falls."

Reddy burst out laughing and had to steady himself against a set of railings protruding from a low wall.

"Ah got up that tree real easy, because Ah've had more practice than any of you," said Ali pointedly, breaking her silence. "In America, we have trees twice the size of that one. Your climbing tree is kinda cute. It's more of a shrub."

Damn, thought Pogsy. *Ali shouldn't have said owt.*

Except she wasn't like that. He really liked the fact that she had an opinion on almost everything and didn't keep it to herself. He liked the fact that she was from America, and was now everyone's favourite in class, exactly as he thought she would be the first day he'd met her. He liked the fact that she lived four doors down from him and that he'd made friends with her before anyone else. Finally, he liked all the great stuff she had. This was the secret trick up her sleeve, one which he knew would get her in the gang, provided he could make all the other boys double-excited about it first. Unfortunately, that option was about to go the way of the dodo. All because of her big mouth, framed by perfect lips, which, if he was honest, he hoped one day to kiss. Not that he'd ever snogged a girl on the lips before.

He had to act quickly.

"Betsies," said Pogsy. "I bet Ali can get higher up the Mortis tree than Bigzy and get more apples. That's what we're here for: to harvest as many apples as poss."

"So Pogs wants a bet." Steve flicked his bottom lip repeatedly against his jutty-out teeth. "OK. Let's have a vote. Who wants to see Ali climb?"

Three hands shot up in the air.

"What do you think, Bam?" asked Steve.

Bam, like Ali, was also new to school. And just like Ali, this was the first time he'd been out with the gang on a mission. He was a boy with masses of curly blond hair and twinkling blue eyes that suggested mischief. His school clothes were always immaculate. The rumour was his dad was loaded and his family were too posh to do hand-me-downs.

"Well," said Bam, shuffling about, "where I come from, girls do sewing and cooking and cleaning. So really, she shouldn't be climbing at all."

Everyone laughed, apart from Ali, who seethed.

"Righto." Steve rubbed his hands together. "Everyone, gather round. As the greatest Steve in the world and the leader of this gang, I've made my decision. I'm changing the rules for tonight. Ali, you can come on the scrump with us, but you have to get at least twenty-five apples and more than Bigzy. Then you have to bake uz an apple pie. If you can do that, you're on the first step to becoming a member of the gang. If you don't get to twenty-five, or Bigzy beats you, or you can't cook, then you can't ever be in the gang and Pogsy has to do a forfeit, and it's my choice what it is. Agreed?"

"Agreed," said Pogsy. His answer came out as a growl.

"Shake on it."

Both Steve and Pogsy stuck out their right hands, but prior to contact stretched their fingers as wide as they could go, moved their hands to their faces, touched thumbs to noses, and loudly blew a raspberry at each other while wiggling their hands like crazy.

"Pogs," said Steve, "if Ali doesn't make it to the top of the tree and get her full twenty-five apples – no maggotsies – or Bigzy tops her, or her oven doesn't work, then tomorrow morning in the playground at

---

first break everyone's gonna hold you down and Gas-tank Gaz will fart in your face."

Bigzy pretended to boke, imaginary spew dripping between his fingers, gathering in congealed puddles on the pavement. Pogsy felt nauseous at the thought. When Gas-tank let one off, never mind a classroom, he could clear an entire school.

He crossed his fingers and prayed for Ali to succeed.

The gang walked briskly along a wide, tree-lined road, chatting away to each other about what had happened in school that day. They were oblivious to the slow trickle of traffic and the constant honking of horns. Darkness was descending, which was a major requirement for going on the scrump. One by one, along both sides of the road, streetlights flickered into life. Some of the passing cars switched on their headlamps. Most didn't bother. A youth on a bike came barrelling past at a hundred miles an hour and, as he shot by, he shouted an obscenity. The gang members all gave him two fingers in unison. The rider turned left, ran a red light, then shot up the pavement and into a large, walled car park that bordered the only pub in that part of town. Panting, he leaned his bike against the wall and disappeared inside. In the few seconds that the door was open, Pogsy heard the sound of many men talking loudly. When the door shut, it pushed a cloud of cigarette smoke outwards, which made it look like the pub was blowing smoke rings. Pogsy hankered to be inside. He'd never set foot inside a boozer before. He'd heard from his classmates that there were country pubs roundabout that had gardens with swings for children. Town pubs didn't welcome children at all. Most of them didn't even allow mums. Dad said there were boozers on the docks that let anyone in. But the women had to drink pints of beer and be able to fight using proper punches, just like Dad had taught him to do.

Red Top hummed the tune to "Ernie", a song about the fastest milkman in the West. Pogsy recognised it immediately. It was his friend's favourite tune, even if it was yonkers old now. It was his way of reminding everyone that he was a milkie in training.

Pogsy glanced over at Bam and saw he was wearing checked flares and a pair of roundies, which were both the height of fashion. The rest of the gang – who were old hands at the art of garden creeping – were all wearing plimsoles. Even Ali was wearing plimsoles, although hers came up all the way over her ankles and she called them sneakers.

They looked really great, with their blue stars and red stripes. Pogsy
wondered whether he should try to hold Ali's hand. If he did that
though, Steve would never let her in the gang. You had to hold a girl's
hand before you could kiss her. Those were the rules. Except snogging
girls was for puffs. Or so Steve said. And Pogsy was pretty sure he
wasn't a puff.

So why was he dying to kiss Ali?

It was all a bit odd.

The only time he'd kissed a girl before was on the cheek, at a
birthday party, when you had to because that's what girls' mums made
you do.

The gang crossed the road at the traffic lights. Ahead, the road
dipped, heading underneath a railway bridge. Later in the month,
ignoring the Keep Out signs, they'd climb through the fence and head
along the track, away from town to an allotment where some of the best
apple trees they knew were located. Bigzy had already checked it out
and reported back that the apples were sour. Hence tonight they were
going to pay Mister Mortis a visit. He had earlies. He lived straight on,
third left, near the end of a cul-de-sac in one of the newer, better-off
parts of town where the houses were spread out and not crammed tightly
together like books on a library bookshelf. It was possible to creep into
his back yard via the side gate to his house, but if he was in the kitchen,
he'd likely hear the latch click or the gate bang. Then he'd come out and
they'd have to leg it. Pogsy remembered their first mission last year.
They'd not even reached Mortis's bins before they were discovered.

The houses they walked past were all semi-detached, built in
roughly the same block style, with a single bay window, a grassy front
garden, a short drive and a wide, tiled porch. For all Pogsy knew, the
houses might have been built a hundred years ago, or just yesterday. He
didn't pay attention to details like that. It was enough to know that the
people who lived here had loads of space to themselves, both inside and
out. He'd been in a few houses in this part of town and they all had
curtains, and wallpaper and carpets. Where there were hedges, they
were well-trimmed. Rose bushes were loved and properly shaped. The
grass on display was short and luscious. Flower borders didn't have any
stray weeds muscling in, trying to take over. The houses themselves
were always spick and span and their paintwork wasn't cracked or tired.
There were no broken windowpanes or missing roof tiles. Each house

had a single, fully functional television aerial, with the cable hidden away around the back. Everything was neat, tidy, and orderly.

And, if he was honest, *very* safe and *very* boring.

Reddy stopped his humming.

Bigzy pulled up the collar of his tracksuit top to partially cover his face.

In the distance, a car door banged shut.

Pogsy removed a packet of sweet cigarettes from an inside pocket and pretended to light one. He offered them around. Everyone followed his lead and pretended to light up too, except for Bigzy, who ate his and asked for another.

Pogsy felt his heart beat a little faster. His vision became brighter. His nose picked up the sleezy stench of burnt plastic from a nearby rubbish bin, which some youths had recently set on fire.

Not far now.

"Who's seen the new James Bond?" asked Steve.

"Me dad sez the new mister is rubbish compared to the old one," said Red Top.

"But have you seen it?"

"Naw."

"Me and Pogs went," said Bigzy.

Pogsy nodded. "It was brilliant. It had car chases and boat chases and Voodoo."

"I saw it in London," said Bam, "in Leicester Square."

"Ah saw it back home in Texas," said Ali. "Roger Moore is real good."

"Me mam sez he was crap," said Red Top insistently. "She likes the other one. James Bonds are like Doctor Whos. If you change them, they're never as good."

"We're here," said Steve. "Captain Crane to crew: periscope down. Rig for silent running. Reddy, you're up."

"Roger," said Red Top, ushering the gang into single file behind him. Ever since he'd started working on the floats, he'd been expanding his milk-knowledge of the local area, which included an inventory of secret shortcuts. "Have I ever said that the Wilsons have been delivering milk every day since 1855?"

"Only every mission," said Bigzy.

"Shush," said Steve, putting his finger to his lips.

Pogsy let Ali in front of him and took up the rear. The gang carried on past the Mortis house and after fifty yards turned left, wriggling underneath a line of bushes that marked the boundary to a set of school playing fields, which were shared between two schools. Lisle Marsden Junior School lay straight ahead. It was surrounded by a tall, wire fence. Its entrance consisted of a great steel gate that shuttered off access like a medieval portcullis and which had double-secure padlocks, just to make sure no-one crept in after hours. It looked impressive but Bigzy could scale it like a capuchin monkey and be over in less than ten seconds. Pogsy had timed him once when they'd had a bet. In the distance, to their right, was Wintringham Secondary School for teenagers.

The gang moved slowly, their eyes adjusting to the dark. Where the edge of the playing fields butted up against the wooden fences of the residential properties, patches of weeds and long grass had sprung up. It was impossible to tell whether there were any stinging nettles present, so everyone kept a safe distance. Pogsy counted the number of steps they'd taken. When he reached fifteen, Reddy gave the signal. Bigzy was over the stout wooden fence in seconds. Red Top cupped his hands together and gave Steve a leg-up. Pogsy glanced over his shoulder then followed. He and Steve straddled the fence, pulling up Reddy, leaving Bam as the guard. They scanned around for Ali. She was nowhere to be seen.

"Scared off," whispered Steve. "Girls don't have the guts for this sort of work." He turned to the new boy. "Tonight's codeword is *Kevin Keegan*. Only shout it if you're sure the coppers are onto us."

Bam nodded and kicked his heels.

Pogsy and Red Top kept pace with each other. They sped across the first garden, jumped a stern-looking gnome with a fishing rod and, in the eerie half-light, clambered over a second fence, which was somewhat lower than the first. Steve followed. One after another, they tumbled into a densely planted flowerbed. Moving quickly on their hands and knees, they ducked under a window. Although the room beyond was dark, the dull light of a glowing television screen peppered the inner walls with splashes of colour. Pogsy thought, at a guess, that the clueless residents were watching *Spy Trap*. If only they knew. One by one the three pals skirted around a goldfish pond. Finally, they reached the side of Mister Mortis's garden. Thanks to a low bench, it was really easy to climb up onto the flat roof of Mortis's potting shed, which was slightly angled, being higher at the back.

Steve and Pogsy climbed up and joined Bigzy on the shed roof while Red Top scaled the fence into Mister Mortis's garden, on a mission to pick up any good-looking windfalls.

"It's a ruddy big tree," said Bigzy. "I'd swear it's grown double since last year."

Pogsy caught his breath. "Have you seen Ali?"

"Up there," said Bigzy, pointing.

Against the night sky, Pogsy could just make out Ali's lithe figure. From previous escapades, he knew the route she was taking to the top of the tree. Muscle memory kicked in. Hand high to the left; other hand mid-way to the right, and twist. One leg up. Second leg up. Another twist. Crouch. Lean slightly left. Extend arms. Pull up. Zigzag straight up the middle.

"Wow," whispered Red Top, rattling a door, "she's good. Anderson shelter's still locked Pogsy."

"One day," said Pogsy. According to his dad, nearly every house in the world had had an Anderson shelter at one time. Most of them were gone now. This was the only one still standing that Pogsy knew of, and he was desperate to see inside. He wished his own house had an Anderson shelter. It would make a cracking den.

Bigzy reached out for the tree trunk and pulled himself up, intent on following Ali all the way to the top.

With Ali and Bigzy up the tree, Pogsy felt like a spare engine at a stock-car rally. It had always been him and Bigzy doing the climbing until now. Not that he minded too much. Not if it got Ali in the gang. She was already far higher up the tree than he dared to go. It wasn't that he was scared of heights, it was more to do with getting back down again. With enough practice, any idiot could climb a tree. The trick was to know which branches would support your weight before standing on them, and apple trees were notorious for having rotten branches that were chock full of apples. This was the downfall of many a boy at this time of the year, as the casualty department at the hospital knew only too well. Pogsy crossed his fingers, hoping that Ali knew what he knew. He hoped she was better at getting down than he was. It would be horrible if she got stuck. The higher you went, the more exposed it became and the less options you had with handholds and footholds coming back down. All it took was one slip. One miscalculation. Not that it bothered Bigzy. He was fearless. But then he wasn't wired right.

Steve opened up his backpack and removed a tightly rolled bundle. Pogsy helped him straighten it out. Once the two climbers had filled their tracksuit tops – which were tucked into their tracksuit bottoms – with scrumped apples, they'd start throwing down anything they could grab hold of and, without a catching net, there was a good chance they'd lose a ton of apples. In previous years, apples had gone everywhere and, although Mister Mortis wasn't particularly quick, it only took a single stray apple to alert a dog or a neighbour.

From up the tree someone whistled. Instinctively, Steve and Pogsy grabbed a corner of the net with each hand and, after a brief bout of confusion regarding who was taking which end of the shed roof, moved into position and waited for the hailstorm to begin.

The first apple landed squarely in the middle of the net. It was followed by another. And another. Thirteen apples in, a stray came zooming in from the side and struck Steve on the shoulder.

"Soz," whispered Bigzy.

Pogsy counted in his head as more apples landed on target. Seventeen. Eighteen. Nineteen.

A light went on upstairs in the Mortis house, illuminating the back bedroom and showing off the lurid purple walls. Mister Mortis strode into full view, his grey knitted cardigan buttoned all the way up to his neck, crooked nose protruding from his face like the chimney of a witch's house.

Steve and Pogsy hit the deck, not daring to move.

An apple, already in flight, landed in the net, which was no longer taut. It bounced. Pogsy tried to grab it and missed. He checked the bounce and tried again, but it vanished out of sight.

"Got it!" Red Top stood in the shadows, beneath the lip of the shed roof, grinning.

"Thanks."

Unfortunately for Pogsy, he realised too late that in trying to save one little apple he'd let go of the net.

Apples rolled.

One.

Two.

Three.

Crash

Tinkle

Mister Mortis, who was busy drawing closed the curtains, stopped what he was doing and pressed his face to the window.

"Kevin Keegan!" bellowed Steve. Then again, for good measure. "Keegan! Keegan! Keegan!"

Pogsy gathered up the net the best he could, saving around a dozen apples, and slipped off the roof into the neighbouring garden, behind his friends who were already crawling past the picture window. On the TV there was some sort of car chase taking place. Pogsy heard Mister Mortis open the back door. It was followed by an excited yap.

Ruddy hell.

Mister Mortis had only gone and got hissen a dog.

Without warning, the Mortis garden lit up like Blundell Park on a match day in the middle of winter.

Double ruddy hell.

After last year, he'd only gone and installed floodlights.

"Come back here, you little bleeders!" bellowed Mister Mortis. "You ruddy hear me?"

Pogsy's heart thumped in his chest. His legs wobbled. He felt a blast of juice flow into his arms and legs and, slinging the net over his shoulder, he ran for it. Steve and Reddy saw him shoot past, abandoned their commando-shuffling and legged it too. The three of them vaulted the low fence together. Seconds later they were passed by Bigzy, who shot past like a runaway rocket train, legs pumping frantically.

Ali was on her own.

"You're a ruddy idiot," said Red Top, poking Steve in the chest.

"He was onto us," retorted Steve.

"If you hadn't yelled, we coulda stayed 'idden. He'd never 'ave seen us."

"You're kidding, right?" Steve shook his head. "The Clangers could see those lights from the moon!"

"He only put 'em on after you shouted." Reddy stamped his feet.

"He'd have put them on anyway," said Steve, resting his front teeth on his lip.

"You should have let Pogsy lead," said Red Top, shaking his head.

Bigzy grinned, his smile filling up his face. "That was magic. Who wants to do it again?"

The flight from Mister Mortis's garden had been pretty straightforward. Once they were over the tall fence at the end, they'd kept on running across the playing fields. They'd trotted along for ages, following the markings of a football pitch before Mister Mortis's lights were extinguished. Soon after that the fields had given way to tarmac, which marked the perimeter of Wintringham school. Unlike Lisle Marsden, the school for seniors was fenceless. The boys stood just inside the main gates, where they could see in all directions. Pogsy huffed. Based on experience, grown-ups only ever gave chase down their own streets. If the coppers did come, they'd only search near the Mortis house, and not very thoroughly at that. Not for scrumpers. And anyway, now they were two streets away from the crime scene, they were innocent lads. If any torches did appear over the field, they could easily leg it out of the gate and onto the railway line, which was home turf. The coppers never came on the railway line. Like all sensible grown-ups, they assumed that no boys in their right minds would hang about there because of the warning signs. And if a train hit a bunch of boys in their wrong minds, well, that would improve the crime figures for the month.

Pogsy removed an apple from the net and took a bite. It was crisp and juicy. He wiped his mouth and handed an apple to Steve and another to Bam. The others all had their own supplies, although judging by the swearing during the escape, Bigzy had lost a few along the way. Pogsy sniggered. Standing there in the shadows with his rotund apple-laden belly, Bigzy looked just like the Penguin out of *Batman*.

"Wah, wah, wah, wah..." said Pogsy, waddling up and down, puffing away on an imaginary cigarette in a long, thin holder.

Red Top caught on and did the same, following behind.

Pretty soon, they were all parading around in a line, doing the penguin waddle, Bigzy included.

"Hey, guys," said a voice from the heart of the darkness.

Pogsy jumped out of his skin.

Ali.

"Thanks for waiting for me," she said sarcastically.

"My pleasure," replied Steve, assuming an air of authority, while everyone else fell about laughing. "What's your score?"

"Twenty-eight," said Ali.

Pogsy opened the neck of the net and, one by one, Ali emptied her tracksuit top of contraband. Steve made a point of counting loudly. Pogsy thought he heard a tinge of disappointment at twenty-five.

Bigzy confirmed that he'd only managed twenty-three.

"Well done," said Steve. "Very impressive. Now, before I give you your new nickname, how did you get out of that?"

It turned out that Ali's escape was easy. The boys had made so much noise that Mister Mortis had focused solely on them. His dog, which was a little grey Scottie with a tartan collar, had made an awful racket, which had, in turn, set off every other dog for miles around, creating a *bark-chain*. The gang had a theory that once a bark-chain had started it could easily travel across town, sometimes going as far as Lincoln. While this remained unproven, the Mortis bark-chain was certainly epic, reverberating long into the night. With his dog yapping for Jesus, Mister Mortis had ambled over to what remained of his cold frame, removed three apples, tutted and returned inside, dragging his enthusiastic pooch with him. Although the lights had remained on for a full five minutes, not once had he thought to look up.

"You're a jam tart with extra jam on," said Bigzy. "That's how jammy you are."

"Her nickname should be *Strawberry* then," said Red Top. "You can't beat strawberry jam."

"It could be," said Steve. "Except giving out nicknames is *my* superpower, along with being the greatest model-maker ever." He motioned for silence, then put his fists to his temples, as was customary when receiving a new nickname from the heavens. "I'm Steve King, the King of all the Steves in Grimsby and the Greatest Steve in the whole wide world," he said. "Do you take me to be your lawful leader, until death us do part?"

Pogsy whispered in Ali's ear, "Say 'I do'."

"Ah do," said Ali.

"From this day forth, you'll be known as *Chimpy*."

"Excuse me?" said Ali.

"Chimpy. You can climb better than anyone else we know. That's your superpower. If you want to be in my gang, my gang, that's your nickname, because I'm the leader of the gang, I am. But you can't be a full gang member until we have a vote, and sometimes that takes ages. If you do anything stupes in the meantime, you're out."

The gang divided the haul of apples and headed out the school gates. They crossed the road and cut through the allotments opposite as planned, scaling the rickety entrance gate with ease, talking avidly about the night's adventures. Steve took credit for setting off the longest bark-chain they'd ever heard, which was still going strong. Pogsy realised he was out of sweet cigarettes, so broke open a pouch of coconut chewing tobacco, which he shared around. He pretended to be a cowboy from *The Virginian*, rounding up cattle, pretend spitting pretend tobacco across a pretend prairie. After a few minutes, they reached a chain-link fence. Red Top located the secret escape hole they used for transit and everyone slipped through in single file. The gravel embankment up to the railway line was overgrown with weeds. Even so, it gave a satisfying *scrunch* underfoot. Skipping along the sleepers made the least amount of noise, but at night it was difficult to see the random spots of tar that, once stepped on, got everywhere, ruining clothes in seconds. The only way to be sure of avoiding complications was to walk on the rails, which was fine over short distances. Within thirty seconds, everyone had forgotten about the muck and grime and moved on to playing rude *I Spy* instead.

Pogsy sniffed the air and tried not to breathe in through his nose. The wooden slats underfoot stunk of creosote. It was a smell he particularly loathed.

After a quarter of a mile, the gang reached the railway bridge they'd walked under earlier. They slid down the stony embankment and entered a thicket of gorse bushes. Reddy led the way along a rough dirt path which looked like it didn't go anywhere, ducking down onto his hands and knees to squeeze through a narrow gap. The gang followed one by one. On the other side of the bushes, Red Top was holding onto a gnarly old branch covered in sharp spikes. Once everyone was through, he let it go with a satisfying *twang*.

The route forward was blocked by a solid wooden fence. Red Top located a plank marked with a blue circle, which stood slightly proud of the planks on either side, stuck his index finger through a knothole set at knee-height and swivelled the board about a single gigantic nail set a third of the way down. Once everyone was out, he closed the secret entrance behind him.

As one, the gang said, "Close Sesame."

"You're not to tell anyone about this," said Red Top, looking at Ali, then at Bam. "Milk-knowledge."

Ali nodded.

Bam stuck his hand up. "May I make an observation?"

"Go on," said Steve.

"If we'd just knocked on Mister Mortis's door and offered to pick all his apples for him, we'd be much better off. We could have asked him for, say, a quarter of all the apples as our picker's fee."

"Impressive," said Steve. "We'd never thought of that."

"Except then it wouldn't be scrumping," said Pogsy.

"It all depends on what your objective is," said Bam. "If you want apples, my idea's best. If you want to skin your knees and get in trouble, then carry on."

"That's the sort of thinking we need from new gang members," said Steve. "Why don't you organise a trial run?"

"Will do," said Bam.

"Right. I'm off that way." Steve pointed towards a long avenue lined by trees. "Bam?"

"I'll come with," answered the rich boy.

"Me too," said Bigzy. "See you all tomoz."

"Tomoz," said Pogsy.

The trio tronked off at right angles, talking about TV. Pogsy couldn't wait to see *Star Trek* in colour. The new television set was due to turn up any day. For Ali, colour TV was old news. Casually, she told the boys that with colour it was easy to see who was going to get killed that week, because the security team always wore red.

On a black and white TV, Pogsy mused, *it was inposs to know who was who.*

But for his collection of comics, he wouldn't even know that Kirk dressed in yellow and Spock and McCoy wore blue. Bam had had a colour TV for over a year, or so he'd said. But he wasn't allowed to have any friends over, so his claim remained unverified.

Reddy was the next to peel off. He lived in a semi-detached house at the very edge of the school catchment area. Pogsy knew the estate as the new houses, because that's what the neighbours called them, even though they were over twenty years old now. Every house had a private drive and a garage, although as far as Pogsy could tell, garages weren't actually used by grown-ups for keeping cars in, but rather to store junk.

The new-build estate soon gave way to rows of terraces. This was home territory. After a couple of streets, he and Ali turned right.

They both lived at the far end of a row of red-brick houses. Each house was three-up, three-down, with an inside bathroom and an outside loo, fronted by a wide bay window and a small, rectangular front garden. According to his dad, a block of six streets had been constructed around the turn of the century, laid out in a grid pattern. The grid was bisected by a pair of grand old avenues. Houses on the avenues were laid out the same as the terraces inside but with larger rooms and bigger front gardens. Around the back, out of sight, their gardens were identical. At regular intervals, passageways cut through the terrace blocks, giving access to a back alley that ran the length of the street. The back alleys and their interconnecting passages were how the gang moved about, unseen by grown-ups. Most of the back passages were uniform, but there were one or two that were unique and worth investigating. More importantly, some of them were dead ends. Knowing the lay of the land mattered, because if you got chased and took the wrong alley, it could easily become a matter of life or death.

While they walked, Pogsy talked nonsense at a hundred miles an hour. Reddy had been right. Steve *had* ruined the mission by panicking.

"Why didn't you tell him?" asked Ali.

"He already knew," said Pogsy. "And besides, I'm his Second. Seconds don't question Leaders in front of everyone."

"In girl gangs, everyone questions everything all the time. It's the only way to be sure we reach the right decision."

"Well, I wish Steve hadn't brought Bam along. He didn't do owt but come up with a stupid idea that Steve loved."

"Ah thought it was very entrepreneurial."

Pogsy had no idea what *anti-prime-audible* meant and he was surprised to hear Ali use such a long and complicated word. He felt his ears turn red.

"It was still stupes. Bam's gonna get in the gang, I just know it. When he does, he'll come up with more and more silly ideas, and Steve will listen to all of them. Hopefully, you'll get in too. Between uz, we might be able to talk Steve out of going loopy."

"If Steve is so stoopid and he makes real bad decisions, why don't you become leader?"

"Because..." Pogsy bit his lip. "There are reasons..." He looked down at the pavement and wondered what might happen when word got out that The Kings had two new members, and one of them wasn't a

boy. Steve was going to get his leg pulled. They all were. Fortunately,
they could look out for themselves.

Ali had to get in the gang.

It was that simps.

She wasn't like any other girl he'd ever met. She was
interesting, with some great toys, and he could listen to her accent all
day long and never get bored.

"Do you like your new gang name?" he asked.

"It's kinda okay."

"If I was in charge, I'd never have called you Chimpy. Cheetah
would be better. Or Jane even. Or Judy. If you've seen *Daktari*."

"Ah don't want to be a *Jane* or a *Judy* or a *Cheetah*," said Ali,
raising her voice. "Chimpy is kinda cute. Ah can make it my own."

"But..." Pogsy left the thought hanging.

If Ali was okay with being called Chimpy, then he supposed he
was too. It wasn't Ali he was mad at, it was Steve. Out of spite, he'd
given her a nasty nickname. The only other boy that Steve had done that
to was Donut. Pogsy ground his teeth. Donut had been his best mate. Or
rather Pogsy had been Donut's best mate, and when a boy claimed best
mates, that was it. You were stuck with it. Donut had left to go to
boarding school at the end of the summer, which meant he was best
mateless. Perhaps Ali could be his new best friend.

Could boys have girls as their best friends?

Pogsy realised he was putting off the inevitable. It was time to
reach out and hold Ali's hand. He'd taken an age to get around to it. But
he'd had to be sure first. As he brushed arms, pretending not to brush
arms, Ali turned around and punched him on the shoulder.

"What's that?" she pointed.

"What's what?"

"The flashing blue lights at the end of the street. How did you
not see them?"

"That's the coppers." Pogsy laughed to himself. "I was busy
thinking about summut else. I'll bet the Petherbridges have been out on
the rob again."

"Where do they live?"

"Er... Over there."

"So the wrong side of the street. It looks to me like they're at
your house."

"My house?" Pogsy felt all the colour drain from his face, followed by all his freckles sliding off. "It must be yours. It's gotta be. You were the one up the tree. Mister Mortis has never seen uz, except from behind. He must have hidden cameras that link to the police station."

"Don't be crazy." Ali shook her head, her mouth breaking into a smile, showing off the dimples in her cheeks. "They're definitely at your place. Look, there's your pop."

"They can't know it was me." The words came out as a whine. "It's inposs."

"There's only one way to find out." Ali headed towards her front door. "Go face the music, Patrick Green. Ah'll see you tomoz on the way to school."

Pogsy straightened his back, looked dead ahead and thought about his happy place. The sandpit was where he used to build Tracy Islands when he was little and play *Thunderbirds*. Periodically, the Hood would come along and destroy everything, as baddies were wont to do. Then the Tracy brothers, assisted by Brains, would have to rebuild their island from scratch. Fortunately, they had pods full of diggers and cranes, and a Mole, which was perfect for adding extra secret tunnels and new levels. Once his sister Ellie had come along, it had all changed for the Tracy Boys. She wasn't the Hood, rather she was an escaped child from *The Land of the Giants*. The Thunderbirds weren't built for tackling monsters like the Elliesaurus. She'd throw Thunderbird Two around and, if she could, grab Thunderbird Four and chew its engines. The worst part of dealing with the Ellie monster was the time she'd wee'd a lake and dropped Gordon in it. He'd nearly died from radioactive poisoning.

You haven't done owt wrong, thought Pogsy. *Act normal.*

He reached his house, located at the very end of the row. A couple of the neighbours were out in their front gardens watching events unfold, transfixed by the flashing lights. Missis de Ville from across the road, who was an avid curtain-twitcher, was twitching away like her life depended on it. She'd be tittle-tattling with her friends over tea and biscuits for weeks. Dad was standing on the pavement flapping his arms in wild circles, shout-talking to one of the coppers, who, helmet in hand, was doing that thing that all coppers do in an arrest situation: lifting his heels off the ground and plonking them back down again. For a Tuesday night it was all a bit wild.

"What's happening, Dad?" asked Pogsy, trying to act as casually as possible, all the while expecting the constable to reach out and grab him by the collar.

"Go inside, Pat," said Dad.

"Your youngest's looking a little tubby these days, Mr Green," said the copper with a wink.

"Did you hear me?" Dad waved his arms and pushed Pogsy towards the door.

"Look," said the copper, "we don't want to cause any trouble. You do a great job keeping the telexes at the station ticking over. You're well liked. Just show us what's inside your shed and that'll be the end of it."

"What the ruddy hell is it with you lot and sheds?" Foam was starting to fleck around Dad's lips. "You're not going in mine without a warrant and that's final. I know my rights. Pat! Go inside!"

"Yes, Dad."

Pogsy's felt his legs wobble like a giant strawberry jelly. He wanted to hear what was being said, but at the same time he was filled with a desperate need for safety. Once inside his house, he was protected. He craned an ear to listen to the conversation, inching closer to the front door, one half-step at a time.

"That's a shame, Mr Green. I didn't want to make it official. One last time: it'll take thirty seconds at most."

"It's nothing personal," said Dad. "It would be easy to say *yes*. But given that you've got nothing on my lad and you're only acting on behalf of that cretin across the road who's never liked me, you can stuff your request where the sun don't shine. Pat! I'm only going to say this one more time!"

Pogsy slunk through the front door and stepped into his living room, amazed he'd made it in in one piece. He felt his shoulders sag. The living room, with its great stone fireplace, was the third-safest room in the house, mainly because that's where his parents usually sat. The upstairs bathroom, with its locking door, was the second-safest room, but the safest space by far was the airing cupboard, which wasn't really a room at all. It was, however, the last place a burglar would think to look for a frightened boy.

His thoughts collided as he tried to form a plan.

The coppers might try to take him down the station yet, but before they did he had to hide the evidence stuffed inside his jacket. The copper had made a point of noticing. But then *coppers notice everything.*

It's what they're paid to do, he reminded himself.

He had an idea but he'd need to get past the guard first.

Mum was sat at the end of their new sofa, smoking a cigarette and keeping an eye on the Elliesaurus, who was busy playing with her dolls, trying in vain to swap their heads. She should have been in bed by now. Pogsy counted two butts in the ash tray. This was serious. Mum never smoked near Ellie. One thing he'd learned over the years was never to say his mum smoked fags or tabs, because she didn't. Fags were for grown-ups who worked in the factory or down the docks. His mum smoked cigarettes. The other thing he'd learned was not to cross his mum when she was rooting through her handbag, lighter in hand, with a determined look on her face.

"Where have *you* been?" Mum asked, pointedly.

"Out and stuff."

"Stuff?" Mum drummed her fingers on the sofa's pale mustard-coloured arm and fixed her stare. "What sort of stuff?"

"I was round Steve's playing *Cluedo*. It went on a bit. Sorry I'm late back but I've got to go to the loo." Pogsy crossed his legs to make the point.

"If I phone Steve's mum now, she'll corroborate your story?"

Pogsy had no idea what *cobolorate* meant. Mum was an English teacher. If he asked her, she'd explode at him. It was one of the games she played: use big words and then tease him for not knowing what they meant. He decided to play it safe.

"She wasn't there. You'll have to talk to his dad."

"Have you seen your brother?"

"Not since tea-time. Look, I gotta go. Before you-know-what happens." Pogsy waited a half-second to see whether Mum was going to fight him, and when he saw she wasn't, he walked past her and through to the kitchen as calmly as he could, shutting the door behind him. To the left was an eating area with a table and bench seats, large enough for the whole family. To the right, was a run of blue cabinets, laid out in a long galley, stuffed with packets of dried food and cereals in the lower cupboards and tins of fruit and vegetables in the upper cupboards. Halfway along, a cooker and a tall white fridge with a mini-freezer compartment at the top broke the run. At the far end of the room, a porcelain utility sink with a constantly dripping tap was mounted beneath a double window, which looked out onto the back yard. Opposite that lived a washing machine, concealed within a false cupboard. Heart pounding, Pogsy wandered over to the cupboard that housed the washing machine, opened the cupboard door, clicked the latch to the front-loader and emptied the contents of his jacket into the enticing hole.

Ker-thunk... thunk... thunk...

"Wot'cha."

Pogsy jumped out of his skin. It was Sam, his older brother, sneaking in the back door.

"What *are* you doing?" asked Sam.

"Nowt."

"You've been on the scrump, you little tyke. Giz one."

Pogsy handed his brother an apple. "Eat it quick, it's evidence. And you're not to tell where the rest are hidden."

"Evidence?" Sam screwed up his face and shook his head, tossing his tousled hair everywhere. He spat a strand from his mouth. "You're mad. Have you been eating lead gum drops again?"

"No. And I'm not mad, you are."

"No, you're the mad one," smiled Sam. "I've got a letter from the loony bin and it's addressed to you."

"Only because you scribbled your name out and wrote mine in instead," said Pogsy.

"It's not my fault Mum dropped you on your head when you were a baby."

Suddenly, the penny dropped. Sam was swerving, trying to divert attention away from the mud on his shoes, which suggested he'd crept in over the back fence.

"I'm starving," said Sam, tossing the apple from hand to hand. "Man cannot survive on fruit alone. You want a 'wich?"

"The coppers are out the front," said Pogsy, closing the washing-machine door. With the outer cupboard sealed, he was sure the police would never think to look there.

"The cops are *here*?" Sam removed his coat and, with a wry grin, hung it on a hook by its hood. "Have the Petherbridges been stealing cash tills again?"

"They're here for uz," said Pogsy, the words blurting out like Acme daggers in search of a speedy Roadrunner. The tears welled in his eyes. He'd tried so hard to hold them back, but they were coming whether he liked it or not. Crying wasn't something he did, not out in the world. If he cried, it was usually in the airing cupboard.

"I'm scared, Sam," he blubbed. "I've never been arrested before."

As best he could figure it, based on what his dad had said, Mister Armstrong from across the road had called the coppers. He was a retired police sergeant who still had contacts at the cop shop. His dad had sat him and Sam down one day, shortly after Mister Armstrong moved in, and told them both in no uncertain terms that they were to stay away from him. He'd made them both repeat back, word for word, *There's no such thing as a retired copper.* The other words of wisdom that he'd offered that day were, *Coppers are like vampires, son. Never invite them into your house, because if you do, you'll never get rid of them.*

Mister Armstrong obviously knew Mister Mortis. Mister Mortis had phoned him and asked for help with troublesome scrumpers. Mortis had mentioned a boy in a teddy-bear jacket, with apples for a belly. Mister Armstrong had seen him leave earlier in the evening and put two and two together.

There's no such thing as a retired copper.

Coppers notice everything.

If only he'd paid more attention to the cretin across the road, none of this would be happening.

Sam put his arm around Pogsy's shoulder and let him cry. "I've never been arrested either. What did you do exactly?"

"It's that... Mister Arm... strong," sobbed Pogsy, barely able to draw breath. "He dobbed... me and... and me mates in... for... for scrumping round Mister Mortis's."

"Armstrong? The not-so-ex-copper?" Sam withdrew his arm. "Balls."

The kitchen door flung open with a sharp bang, releasing a veritable *clap* of thunder. Mum stood in the doorway, her hair billowing out like angry storm clouds. Pogsy swore he could see forks of lightning where her eyeballs should be.

"Samuel *Green!*" she said sternly, blocking all escape routes. "Would you care to explain *what* you've been up to this time? I've a good mind to bend you over my knee."

"Me?" said Sam, in astonishment. "I thought it was Pat who was in trouble."

"Usually, it is. But not this time."

Pogsy took a deep breath and rolled his eyes at his brother. Against the odds, he was off the hook. Mum wouldn't let Sam go until she'd given him the full nag, and sometimes that could take up a whole day. In comparison, the coppers would be a delight. However things played out, it was going to be a long night.

Dad continued to simmer away while Mum put Ellie to bed. Although Sam wasn't formally under arrest, it was still an extremely embarrassing situation in which the Green family found themselves. The official line was *helping with enquiries*. Pogsy was just glad it wasn't him. Dad had had a few run-ins with the coppers before, so he knew what he was doing; as Pogsy recalled, he had been stopped twice for a bald tyre and once for a busted back light on his car. But they'd never been round the house before, and they'd certainly never taken an interest in his shed.

"Ruddy coppers," mumbled Dad at regular intervals.

Pogsy had to admit, he was rather interested in what was inside Dad's shed too. Dad kept the keys to himself. Neither he nor Sam were allowed in without asking first. He'd been in when he was still little, but all he could recall were assorted paint cans and a strong smell of turps. Sam had been in more recently, but said he was sworn to secrecy. Pogsy had tried many times to get a good look, but it was difficult. The shed had no windows and only one door with a Yale lock and an massive padlock that was impossible to pick. The gaps between the wood panels were too small to see between. He'd thought about drilling a hole, but the lack of an internal light source made that option a non-starter. Getting round the back was difficult too, due to all the junk that was piled up between the shed and the fence to the allotments behind, and an allotment shed behind that. Finally, the roof was no good either. He'd climbed on it once to be sure but, apart from being a great point to jump from, there was no reason to go back up there again.

In his imagination, Dad's shed contained a collection of Second World War Tommy guns, some ammunition belts, a shelf full of helmets and a British officer uniform from Colditz. There was a rack of Jeep parts at the back and some jerry cans to keep them company. When he thought about it, the potential inventory was endless, and every time he discovered something new related to the war and small enough to fit inside Dad's shed, he added it to the list. As far as sheds went, Dad's was bigger than most. Bigger than Mister Mortis's potting shed, for sure. Bigger than Steve's dad's shed by four feet one way and two feet the other. He knew that because they'd measured them for a bet.

He still didn't know why Sam had been summoned to the station for an interview with Grimsby's finest. Mum and Dad knew but they weren't saying. When something bad happened, Mum had a belief that, if you didn't talk about it, it would go away. Dad's point of view was completely the opposite: in order to deal with something bad, you had to first understand it, and that meant talking about it a lot, usually to the exclusion of everything else. By his standards, he was doing a very good job of keeping quiet.

"Patrick," said Mum, "it's way past your bedtime."

Reluctantly, Pogsy headed upstairs to change into his pyjamas and brush his teeth. It was while he was in the bathroom with a mouth full of foam that he heard the doorbell ring. He crept to the top of the stairs, toothbrush in hand. He recognised the voice. It was Mister Payne, Dad's friend from over the road. He lived next door to Mister Armstrong.

Pogsy couldn't hear much from where he was standing but Mister Payne definitely mentioned No-Man's Land. His ears pricked up. He knew the patch of derelict land well. Most of it was now occupied by an enormous, grey cold store. What remained was a rectangular plot of fenced-off earth reached by three access gates that were never locked. Some grown-ups said it belonged to the cold store and they hadn't got around to building on it yet. Others claimed it belonged to the council. Regardless of who the owner was, the Four Gangs had been squabbling over it ever since that fateful day two-and-a-bit years ago when the bulldozers had moved in.

Pogsy sighed, remembering the best of times when everyone used to get on.

Technically speaking, most of the land that was left belonged to The Kings, as it was where they'd built their trenches. There was a small patch at the far end, near the third gate, that the Old Clee lot could lay claim to. The other two gangs, however, had lost everything. There were calls to divide what was left into equal quarters, but the four parcels of land would never be big enough to build four forts. Not that anyone wanted to. The thought of seeing their dens destroyed again was too much for the boys to bear. Rather than uniting and finding a common enemy in the cold store, the Four Gangs had taken to joshing with each other and riling each other up.

Pogsy's ears pricked up when he heard the word *explosion*. Quietly, he crept halfway down the stairs to listen in, hanging back in the shadows where he was sure he couldn't be seen.

Mister Payne said that the first bang had occurred on Saturday. It sounded like a banger. There were two similar explosions on Sunday night and three on Monday. Tonight, there'd been a further two bangs but they were seriously loud. Mister Payne had thought the first one was a petrol tank going off. He'd looked out of his back window to be sure. As the bangs had continued night after night, Mister Armstrong's dog had gone from excitable to frantic to scared out of her wits. As a result, the not-so-ex-copper had set up camp in his back garden with some equipment he'd borrowed from his pals on the force, determined to discover who the culprit was. When he'd seen Sam run away from the scene of the last explosion, he'd decided enough was enough and he'd called the police. Because he was one of them, they'd decided to give him the full show, lights, sirens, the lot.

Dad fumed. "Bloody idiot. How many times have I told him, *not in your own backyard*?"

"Strictly speaking, Al," said Mister Payne, "it's not in his own backyard."

"It's that friend of his," said Mum.

"I'm going to give him a thick ruddy ear!" retorted Dad. "Bonfire Night's still weeks away. What *is* he thinking? With the Paddies bombing railway stations now, it's no wonder he's got himself noticed. And the ruddy fool's gone and got me noticed too."

Mum tutted.

"What did the coppers say?" asked Mister Payne.

"The one I was talking to on the doorstep said they'd not press charges if I let them see inside my shed."

"Ah," said Mister Payne. "That's what all the arm flapping was about."

Dad laughed. "They clearly haven't heard that an Englishman's shed is his castle."

"So you told him to stick his request up his arse?"

"I didn't put it quite like that." Dad chuckled. "If you swear at coppers, as I well know, it sends them funny in the head."

"I'm off to bed," said Mum.

Pogsy crept quietly back up the stairs and into the bathroom. Once there, he washed out his mouth with cold water, replaced his toothbrush in the rack and headed along the hallway to the back of the house and the bedroom he shared with his older brother.

"Patrick," shouted Mum from down the corridor, "you've left toothpaste everywhere."

"Sorry, Mum," he shouted back. "I won't do it again. I promise."

Pogsy's mind was racing. If there were explosions, then Sam had bangers. Except he hadn't said anything, and he was always gobby when he had fireworks. Therefore, his mate Jimbo had bangers. And something else that was louder than a banger. Pogsy wracked his brain, trying to think what it might be. The only thing he could come up with was a hand grenade. Not that he'd ever heard a hand grenade in real life. They let hand grenades off in *Combat* all the time and they were pretty loud. The real thing must be amazing. He drifted off to sleep wondering where Jimbo Jones, the pyromaniac from the end of the road, could possibly have got some real-life hand grenades from.

Pogsy was awoken in the middle of the night by the front door banging shut. He'd been having a great dream that involved him and Ali finding a secret hidden bunker in No-Man's Land that the council had missed, with loads of rooms that kept on going forever. He knew one of them contained a crate of hand grenades, but they couldn't seem to find it. He heard footsteps come up the stairs, then along the hallway. Although the voices were muffled, he counted two people. When the bedroom light was switched on, he blinked, covering his eyes. Sam staggered into the room. He looked tired. He was followed by Dad. Pogsy closed his eyes, pretending to be sound asleep.

"You could at least sound grateful," said Dad. "I didn't have to come and get you."

"Can't we talk about it in the morning?" said Sam irately.

"We need to talk about it now," said Dad, barging into the room behind him. "Is Pat asleep?"

"I think so." Pogsy felt Sam broggle his big toe. He froze. "Yes."

"The coppers believe you had bangers?"

"That's what I said. I stuck to my story. I told them we were just messing about."

"Good. Except I know different. How many did you have?"

"Bangers? A packet."

"Don't mess me about."

"Two." Sam's voice came across as a defeated whine. "That's all. I promise."

Pogsy opened an eye, just a titchy bit. His brother was busy getting undressed, throwing his clothes all over the floor instead of hanging them up properly. He tossed a rolled-up dirty sock at the clothes basket and missed.

"Are you sure about that?"

"OK, it was three. We let them all off though."

"Those things are ruddy dangerous. Where did you get them?"

"Dad! I've got school in the morning."

"And I've got work. Come on. Spit it out."

"Jimbo's dad went shopping for us. I told him what to get. Look, I'm tired. I want me bed."

"Have you any idea of the trouble you've caused? The coppers want to see inside my shed. The sarcastic one down the station who asked if we have any Irish relatives suggested that I might be running an illegal explosives factory."

"That's just stupes. He was fishing, like coppers do. You told me to look out for that."

"I know that. Your mum knows that. And you know that." Dad laughed. "But still, I can't afford to have the coppers nosing around."

"I'm not an idiot," said Sam defensively.

"You went back to the scene of your first crime two nights running and then got caught."

"It's No-Man's Land. That's what it's for."

Dad inhaled loudly. "You're sure you haven't said anything to anyone?"

"Please. I need my beauty sleep."

"What's done is done," said Dad. "The matter's closed. Unless the cops get a warrant, then we'll need to come up with a new plan."

"Night, Dad."

"One more thing. And I'm deadly serious. No more crow scarers until firework night. And if you're unable to resist, let them off round Jimbo's house."

"We can't. His grandad lives with him now and it sends him shell-shock bonkers. It takes a week to get him back out from under the bed."

"Go down the woods then. Anywhere but No-Man's Land."

"I get it. Night, Dad."

"Goodnight, Sam."

Pogsy lay there with his eyes closed, waiting for his brother to climb up into the upper bunkbed and get settled. Once Sam had had a good shuffle, the light went out. That was the moment to strike.

"Sam," whispered Pogsy, "what's a crow scarer?"

"Go to sleep, Pat."

"I can't. Is it like a hand grenade?"

Sam yawned. "You remember that time we went to Potty Gran's farm and there were all those loud bangs that got the birds excited? Those were crow scarers. Farmers use them to scare away crows."

"Do they have swan scarers and sparrow scarers as well?"

"Not that I know of."

"What about eagle scarers?"

"Go to sleep, Pat."

"What about *German* eagle scarers?"

"They only make crow scarers."

"Could you use them on German eagles?"

"They're only guaranteed to work on German crows."

"Have you got any more?"

"They come in tens, Pat. Do the maths. I'm sure Dad has. He started it, after all. He gave me and Jimbo a string of them the week before Bommie Night last year and told us what to do with them. That's how we know about them. He's just annoyed I worked out how to get someone else to buy some for me instead of going through him. He's funny like that."

"Oh. Do you think he'll give me a string if I ask?"

"You're too young. Night, Pat."

"Night, Sam."

Pogsy tried to remember where he'd got to in his bunker dream, but when he closed his eyes, he found that the Daleks had got there first. He was fed up with fighting the Daleks. They were a menace. They were even worse than the Germans. But still not as bad as vampires. He nodded off to sleep, wondering what might happen if Daleks had German vampires inside. Then he heard noises from down the garden and wasn't sure whether he'd imagined them or the Daleks really were invading. He made a mental note to reinforce the airing cupboard, just in case.

Three: Dog Trouble

The morning ritual in the Green household on a school day was one that was mirrored up and down the land. Dad had first dibs on the bathroom. Pogsy heard him having a wee. He didn't ever shut the door. Then he let one off and gave his customary morning greeting: *missed him!* Pogsy heard the creaking of floorboards, followed by a door sliding shut. The lock clicked. That was Mum. He drifted off, thinking about what a great scrump they'd had. After Mum had finished, she'd head downstairs with Ellie and fuss over her, making sure she was dressed ready for Missis Darnell from three doors down, who would look after her for the day.

"Pat! Sam!" shouted Mum from the bottom of the stairs. "Time to get up!"

Groggily, Pogsy opened his eyes. He lay there, extracting the maximum amount of warmth from his pyjamas. Mum would shout another two times before it was really time to move. He imagined her applying her lipstick and playing with her hair, styling it into place. He heard the second shout. It had an increased sense of urgency.

Just one more to go.

He turned over and rubbed his eyes. He had long enough to read a story from *TV21* before the next yell came. It was an old comic that he'd read many times, from before it had been combined with *Valiant*. The new comic wasn't anywhere near as good. It was horrible when the grown-ups in charge changed your favourite comic for no good reason.

"Pat! Sam!"

It was time. Maybe just one more quick story.

Pogsy skipped the text and looked quickly through the pictures. Oh, no! Spock was in massive trouble! He needed the next comic from the pile. The sound of hurried footsteps came closer, followed by a bang on the bedroom door. Normally, this was the cue to get up and fight with Sam for the bathroom. Except today, Sam was still snoring his head off. Pogsy had a quick wash behind the ears, pulled on his school uniform and shot downstairs. Mum was busy issuing instructions to Missis Darnell.

"Morning, Missis D," muttered Pogsy. Comic in hand, he rushed through to the kitchen and grabbed a box of his favourite cereal, determined to find out how Spock had wriggled out of the mess Kirk had left him in.

"I'll see you all later," said Mum. "Pat, make sure your brother gets up. And comb your hair."

Pogsy looked up from his bowl of Crunchy Nuggets and nodded. He had just enough time to fit in another story before Dad went to work. He crunched and slurped away, expecting Sam to appear any moment. Once he'd eaten, he had a quick play with his little sister, then went back upstairs to brush his teeth. Having left it until the last possible moment, he then paid Sam a visit, tweaking each of his brother's big toes in turn, followed by his ears. It was only when he held Sam's nose that he finally woke up.

"Urgh," spluttered Sam. "What time is it?"

"Late," said Pogsy.

"How late?"

"Twenty past eight."

"Oh, God... Oh, God..."

"I'm off," said Pogsy. "See you later."

He left Sam in a panic, trying to pull on socks and keks at the same time. He pushed Ellie's little button nose with his finger for luck, eliciting a squeal of delight, while Missis D wiped the side of his mouth with a damp cloth and pulled a comb through his hair. Grabbing his satchel from the coat hook in the kitchen, Pogsy stormed out the door and walked swiftly along the terrace, keeping an eye out for dog poo, whistling "Angel Fingers" by Wizzard. It was a good Number One, but *not* his favourite song of the year. Ali waved from her front room and joined him, saying goodbye to her nan. Further down the street, they were met by Chip and his little sister, who the family called "Rosie" on account of her rose-red cheeks. Ali's nose, which had a cute little upturn near the end, twitched. Pogsy chortled to himself. Chip and his sister always smelt slightly of day-old fish. Their house was ten times worse. Even from the front gate, you could catch a whiff. It was common knowledge that, if you wanted black-market fish, Chip's dad was the one to see. He dealt mainly in haddock, kippers and crab, with the odd stone of flatfish when he could get hold of it. Chip said it all depended on what his mam was filleting on the line the night before. Cod was a definite *no-no*. Anyone knocking on Chip's door and asking his dad for cod was in for an earful of abuse and a kick up the backside. Chip's dad prided himself on being a supplier of top-quality gear, which didn't include cod. Cod was for soft southerners and Yorkies. True Grimbarians were raised on haddock alone and wouldn't consider a lesser fish.

"Wot'cha," said Chip. "I 'ear the nee-naws wuz roun' yers las' ni'."

Somehow, thought Pogsy, no matter how new his clothes were, Chip always managed to look scruffy. It was probably due to his hair, which hung straight down to his shoulders like a pair of greasy, blond curtains.

"It was me bruv," replied Pogsy. "He tried to blow up Mister Armstrong's dog."

"That's horrible," said Ali. "It sounds like Sam deserved it."

"Patch goes *BOOM!*" giggled Rosie.

"He wasn't actually *trying* to blow Patch up." Pogsy shrugged his shoulders emphatically. "He's not like that. That's what Mister Armstrong said to the coppers."

"Meks sense," said Chip, his bright blue eyes flashing from side to side. "Ol' pigs never 'ang up their truncheons. So me dad sez."

The gang turned right at the crossroads, where a main road bisected the terraced side-street, and met up with Reddy and his two brothers, who were deliberately dawdling. In grey school shorts, Red Top's knees, which were located halfway up a pair of matchstick legs, looked ridiculously knobbly. His brothers' legs were identical. The air was chill but not yet biting cold. Even in the middle of winter, they'd still be wearing shorts. Those were the rules.

"Wot'cha, Reddy," said Chip. "'Ave u 'eard? Pogsy's bruvver's a dog-mangler."

"That's not true," said Pogsy defensively. "He loves dogs."

"E's bin tyin' fireworks te Mister Armstrong's dog's tail an' the nee-naws 'ad te cum an pu' 'er ow'," said Chip, waving his hands around his head. "Nee naw, nee naw..."

"He has *not*," said Pogsy.

A block later they were joined by Bingo and Sparksy. Bingo's uniform was perfect as always. His hair was neatly combed and parted at the side.

"Sixty-three times thirty-nine," said Pogsy.

"Two thousand, four hundred and fifty-seven," grinned Bingo, pushing his glasses up his nose.

Pogsy knew the answer was right. He'd done the maths on paper and memorised the result. Everyone else had stopped at their twelve times table, but Bingo had carried on all the way up to a hundred.

"'Ave y'eard Pogsy's bruv stuck a banger up Mister Armstrong's dog's bum'ole?" said Chip.

Sparksy snorted. He was a quiet boy with tiny, sticky-out ears, who kept himself to himself.

"Ee's bin blowin' up a dog a nigh'," said Chip. "A' this ra'e, there won' be no dogs lef' be Bommie Nigh'. Race yers. Las' one te the ga'es 'as the lurg."

As was traditional when a gang of fourth-year boys were charging around, any stray lads from years one, two and three got out of the way before they were mown over. Only the fifth years stood their ground, growling while the gang surged past, racing to be the first one to the tag-post.

Pogsy won by a fingernail.

The best thing about Wednesday, thought Pogsy, was that it was swimming class in the morning. If you couldn't swim or were scared of water, then it was probably the worst day of the week.

Pogsy loved the swimming bit. He didn't much care for the long wait, while a bunch of rowdy boys and girls were counted on the bus at school, counted off again and then counted for a third time before they were allowed inside *Scaffa Baffs*. He didn't much care for the excessive quantity of chlorine in the water as it made his eyes sting. But, as his mum had told him on numerous occasions, some of the children at school didn't have inside bathrooms and the swimming pool *was* their weekly bath. Pogsy had heard that, in the poorer parts of town, some houses still had tin baths, which had to be filled by boiling pans of water, while other houses in the old fisherman's quarter had washrooms and toilets out the back that were shared between houses. He'd never actually been in a proper fisherman's house but he found it hard to believe they still lived like Victorians. None of his gang lived like that. Out of all the boys he knew, Chip had the most basic house. The floorboards in his sitting room were bare and there wasn't any wallpaper

in the bathroom. But his house did have a bath, even if it was full of fish
and ice most of the time. Bigzy's bathroom, on the other hand, was full
of smelly stuff that his mum collected, which was why Bigzy always
ponged like Granny Green every Monday morning. Steve's house had
two bathrooms but only one bath, while Bam's mansion had three. Or so
he said. All in all, there was only one girl who went swimming in their
group who Pogsy suspected might not have a bath every Sunday and
that was Gerbil, so called because she'd got herself a cushy job in the
pet hut looking after the school rodents. Gerbil always smelt of hamster
cages, but that didn't mean she was dirty, it just meant she preferred
hamsters to people. Pogsy avoided her during swimming classes, just to
be on the safe side. It was well known she had fleas.

When he compared himself to everyone else, Pogsy knew he
was a good swimmer. The fastest boy over fifty meters by a long chalk,
though, was Sarge. His mum was from Jamaica and his dad was from
Grimsby. Sarge had grown up near Birmingham, but moved back to
town when he was nine. He'd been winning Sports Day ever since.
Pogsy was in a separate group from most of the other swimmers,
messing about inflating pyjama bottoms in the deep end while he trained
for his silver endurance badge. Bigzy's bottoms wouldn't stay up, and
he kept on making everyone struggle to stay afloat with his stupid
antics.

Pogsy cast his eye towards Bam, keeping tabs on him. The rich
boy claimed he was an ace swimmer but he was busy in the shallow end
messing about with foam boards. He'd been bragging about a lot of
things of late and Pogsy was convinced he was lying, as new classmates
often did, in an attempt to become popular.

Aside from Bam, the other boy who Pogsy had his eye on was
the boy from 4C with plastic bags on his feet. He was easy to spot
because of the exclusion zone and he *definitely* had fleas. Or to be more
precise, a massive crop of verrucas. When they'd done the rounds last
year, good old reliable Donut, who always caught anything going worse
than anyone else, had ended up being the source of all the verrucas in
town. At the final count he'd had sixteen, each the size of an Eccles
cake, and they'd all had to be frozen off. Donut couldn't walk for weeks
afterwards. Pogsy imagined that the hospital had used Mr Freeze's
freeze gun from *Batman* to do the removal. It made more sense than
using a *Star Trek* phaser. That would either kill you or stun you.
Certainly, Captain Kirk had never used a phaser set to "disintegrate

veruccas" on Mister Spock's feet, not in all the episodes that had been on so far, and not in the comics either. With Donut gone, there was a role open for the-boy-with-the-most-types-of-lurgy. Pogsy crossed his fingers and hoped it would be Bam.

To his surprise, Ali turned out to be really quick in the water, beating all the girls at front crawl. He shouted encouragement when she raced against Sarge, who wore a light blue swimming cap to keep his hair under control. Ali lost by a quarter of a length. On the diving-board challenge, Sarge easily got the highest in the air off the bottom springboard, but Ali beat him on the next board up by doing a forward roll in the air. It all came down to the top board. With everyone watching and screaming for their favourite – especially Steve, who had a voice like a foghorn – Sarge pulled off a clean dive. Pogsy splashed and hollered in appreciation. He'd tried diving from on high but found it impossible to stay vertical. From that height, it was scary enough jumping in feet first, stomach churning as the water raced towards you at a million miles an hour. Doing a dive and not keeping your legs straight stung your thighs like a swarm of jellyfish the second you hit the water.

Ali stood with her back to the crowd, who went silent except for a pair of boys playing *Splash-chase*. She jumped, touched her toes, then somehow did a roll and a twist, straightening out before she hit the water arms first. Even the teachers and the boys in the seating area with excuse notes from their mums made plenty of noise. Their applause bounced off the high ceiling and echoed around the baths. It reminded Pogsy of the time Sarge won three golds, representing the school.

"Nice moves," said Sarge afterwards to Ali, while they were all playing *Catch* with a rubber ball in the shallow end, surrounded by the learners and rubbish swimmers who kept on getting in the way. "Can you teach me to do that?"

"Sure," said Ali, removing her goggles to reveal a pair of flickering brown eyes. "If you don't mind getting beaten up a bit at first."

"I'm a quick learner," said Sarge with a smile. "I hear we're calling you Chimpy."

Pogsy realised that Sarge had great teeth. He wished his were as white as his friend's.

"Just the boys," said Ali. "Are you the one who can do amazing wheelies?"

Sarge nodded. "Pick any bike you like. I'll wheelie it first time."

"He even wheelied me Chopper," said Pogsy.

"It's a MKI," said Sarge. "Those things steer like a cow no matter how many wheels you're on."

Pogsy felt himself blush. The bike was a hand-me-down from his brother, who'd moved onto a racer. The bright orange Chopper looked great for riding around on and posing, and the extra-long seat was great for carrying other lads, but overall it was too easy to pedal in third gear and that made it useless for long journeys.

"Ah do gym practice on Saturday mornin'," said Ali. "Come round mine, we can go together and practice some moves."

"I'd love to," said Sarge, "but I don't know where you live."

"Four doors down from Patrick. Bring some pop. Bellamy's cream soda's ma favourite."

"Deal," said Sarge, high-fiving Ali.

Pogsy found a feeling running through his brain that he hadn't felt before. It fogged up his eyes with a putrid green mist. He tried to dismiss it. Whatever the feeling was, it was annoying him. There was only one thing for it. He dived under the water and pulled down Sarge's trunks. He surfaced a few yards away, but Sarge had already spotted him. He swam for his life but before long Sarge caught up and gave him a good ducking, which wasn't that bad really, considering they were in a swimming pool.

By afternoon break, everyone in school knew that Pogsy's brother had had a ride in a cop car. Thanks to Chip, there were hundreds of versions of the truth in circulation and Pogsy had given up trying to issue corrections. He concluded that the playground wasn't bothered about what had really happened because it wasn't as interesting as a shed full of half-burnt dogs with their tails blown off being rescued by the RSPCA. Wingnut was certainly impressed. He was a few months older than Pogsy and the leader of the Welholme Wingmen, one of the Four Gangs. Their sign was two white "W"s in a red circle, usually drawn in chalk.

"Nice going by your bruv," said Wingnut. He was a scruffy lad with ears that protruded at right-angles from his head. He was accompanied by his Second, a lanky lad with a face full of freckles called Gecko, and a short, stocky boy called Gilly who was always coughing and spitting. "Arrested for maiming fifty cocker spaniels with a flame-thrower as I 'eard it. Any time you fancy joining me gang, just say."

"Why would my Second-in-Command want to join the Wingnut Wankers?" said Steve, barging forward, fists cocked, tongue folded double.

Red Top, seeing the potential for trouble, sped over to even up the numbers, puffing out his chest to look extra tough.

"Just saying," said Wingnut. "Pogs is obviously moving up in the world and hanging about with the weakest Steve in the world might not be his thing anymore."

"I'm stronger than you are," said Steve, squaring up.

"Yeah, sure you are. But your gang are a bunch of weaklings, and calling me gang a bunch of wankers ain't very friendly, is it?"

"What you gonna do about it?" said Reddy.

"Me?" said Wingnut. "I'm not going to do nuffink. I don't beat up little kiddies. I can't guarantee the rest of me gang will feel the same way though, not once they hear what *Princess Steve* thinks of them. See ya, Pogs. Offer's open. Anytime you fancy it."

Wingnut and his Wingmen blew kisses at Steve. He let them go.

"I'll kill him," he said. "One day he'll go too far and I'll kill him. I swear I will. On my grandad's grave. Cross my heart. If the Wankers want a war, we'll give it to them."

And so it continued for the rest of the day. Pogsy had never been famous before and he soon discovered he didn't like the attention. Having Wingnut's respect felt good. He was hard, with a scar that ran all the way up his left leg to prove it. It was when girls pointed and whispered that Pogsy winced. It felt like he had beetles crawling under his skin. During afternoon break, he stumbled across a gaggle of them singing a skipping song they'd made up.

How many dogs did Patrick's brother maim?
One a thousand,
Two a thousand,
Three a thousand, four.
Five a thousand,
Six a thousand,
Seven a thousand, more.

Towards the end of the day, Pogsy spied Ruth Maddox having a sneaky word with the teacher. When Missis Wainwright looked in his direction, his heart sank. He and Ruth really didn't get on and he did his best to avoid her. In the first year they'd argued about whether Goofy was a dog or a cow, even though it was obvious he was a pooch. Later on, after he'd cajoled the gang into chanting "numbskull" at her, she'd told the teacher in revenge. Even though he'd made a point of avoiding talking to her ever since, she'd still managed to tell on him and get him in trouble year after year. This year had the potential to be the worst of the lot. She was sat on his table.

As class finished for the day, Missis Wainwright took Pogsy to one side and asked him in a very roundabout way if everything was alright at home. She liked to trill her letter Ts for effect, and when she did so, she sounded like Chip's mam's budgerigar.

"Yes, Miss," he replied, shrugging his shoulders and squirming, aware that his mates were listening in from outside the classroom. They might as well have been stood across the road. You could hear those Ts loud and clear from miles away.

"Only it's not like your family to get in trouble with the police." Missis Wainwright tutted. "I used to teach with your mother, you know."

"Yes, Miss."

"You'd tell me if things weren't right?"

"Yes, Miss." Pogsy shuffled his feet. The segs in the soles of his shoes scraped across the wooden floor. When the classroom was empty, every squeaky floorboard sounded like a rabble of rats escaping from the Pied Piper; every slamming desk lid was a dangerous undersea clam from *Marine Boy*; every chair-drag a spaghetti monster, resonating from *Doctor Who*. None of them topped Missis Wainwright though. Her budgie-chat was the stuff of nightmares. "It was only a banger, Miss. Boys have been making stuff up all day. And me bruvver wasn't even cautioned. It looks far worse than it is, Miss. You should ask me mum."

"Thank you, Patrick. I think will. And I'll make sure the headmaster knows that no animals were harmed. He's been taking an active interest in this incident."

"Yes, Miss. Thank you, Miss."

Pogsy left as fast as his legs could carry him. The last thing he needed was Grizzly Greythorpe the headmaster getting involved in an imaginary incident that hadn't even happened. Bigzy and Reddy were the only members of the gang still left and they both made a point of slapping him on the back.

"It's not the first time that Chip's tales have reached the head," said Bigzy with a smirk.

"It's the first time for me though," said Pogsy. "I've never been in trouble *in* school before."

"Me dad's milk float was stolen by the Great Train Robbers," said Red Top. "They made a getaway in it, with me dad all tied up in the back. The head called uz into his office to ask if he was OK."

"I've had to see the head seven times," said Bigzy. "He knew who I was before I even started school."

Pogsy laughed out loud. "I really hope I don't get the call. The last thing anyone needs is the headmaster knowing who they are."

There was always a lull around four o'clock in the afternoon, between Pogsy and his brother getting home from school, Missis D leaving, and Dad and Mum coming home. Quite often Missis D would make sandwiches and a cuppa tea for herself while Ellie watched *Play School* and tortured her dolls with crayons. In Pogsy's opinion, Wednesday was the worst day of the week for TV, so he was laying horizontally across the floor, socks on his toes, reading comics, rather than fighting over which of the two TV channels to watch. He'd already changed into his favourite red tracksuit. Sam hadn't bothered to go upstairs yet and was lounging around on the sofa in his school uniform, tie undone, nibbling the chocolate from the edges of a Club biscuit.

There was a firm knock at the front door.

Bang... bang... bang...

Pogsy and Sam looked at each other. Their friends and all of the neighbours their parents liked knew to either ring the bell once or else come around the back. Instinctively, they both scanned the sideboard and mantlepiece for anything untoward that their dad wouldn't want a stranger to see. Those were the rules. Never let anybody see something they shouldn't. Missis D, meanwhile, did the neighbourly thing and, cup of tea in hand, answered the door.

"Afternoon, ma'am," said a gruff voice. "CID."

"C-come in," stuttered Missis D, taking a step backwards. "Please, follow me."

Sam jumped to his feet and headed straight to the door. "Excuse me. It's not her house. My dad says we're not allowed to let people in who we don't know."

"Son. We have a warrant to search your dad's shed."

Pogsy noticed the man was wearing ordinary clothes, as was the man behind him. The last one was in uniform and he definitely *was* a copper. Pogsy pulled his socks up and guiltily thought about the contraband in the washing machine. He tried his best to act normally but he felt his ears glow bright red.

The two plainclothes men and the copper barged into the lounge, scanning the orange and black walls. One of them ran a finger across Mum's favourite painting.

"Nice fireplace," said the first plainclothes. "Now, you can either cooperate with us or we'll take you down the station for resisting."

Missis D turned as white as the sheet on a fake *Scooby Doo* ghost. She hurried over to where Ellie was playing, to protect her from what she imagined was about to happen.

"My dad isn't here," said Sam defiantly. "You'll have to wait."

Pogsy nodded and joined his brother, creating a line of defence. "We're not allowed in our dad's shed."

Both the plainclothes continued poking around the lounge, lifting things up and sticking their noses where they didn't belong.

"Nice stereo," said the second plainclothes. "Does your dad have a receipt?"

"How would I know?" said Pogsy. Immediately, he wished he'd kept his mouth shut.

"Do you know where the shed keys are, son?" said the first plainclothes.

"I have an idea," said Sam. "But I'm not sure. You best wait for my dad."

"If you don't produce the keys in the next minute, we'll jammy the ruddy thing open. And it'll all be your fault. I can't imagine your dad liking that one bit. Cyril, go get the crowbar."

"OK, OK," said Sam, raising his hands. "I'll find the keys. Before I do, show me your ID and your warrant. For all we know, you might be burglars pretending to be the police."

The first plainclothes' ID looked about right. Pogsy's mind raced. He had no idea how to tell a real ID from a fake. His dad had sat them down once and told them how to deal with coppers at the door. The lesson hadn't involved identification and warrants though. He knew that Sam was making things up as he went along, doing his best to stall for time. Dad would be home any minute. He had to be. Then everything would be fine. Pogsy joined forces with his brother, asking daft questions, showing the coppers some of his best toys and finally suggesting they might like a cup of Missis D's tea, which was really, really delicious. Or so he'd heard, not being a tea drinker himself. He and Sam kept on creating obstacles, playing for time. The only problem was the coppers were wise to it and the more delay he and Sam caused, the more things they picked up and examined and made notes about in their heads. Having searched through all the drawers in the lounge for the keys, Sam led the cops through to the kitchen.

The second plainclothes opened a cupboard door.

Pogsy felt his tummy flip over.

Please, not the washing machine.

After much fiddling around in the back of a drawer, Sam found the keys to the shed. He instructed Missis D to look after Ellie and see if she could get in contact with Mum or Dad, in case they were working late. While the neighbour picked up the phone and dialled the numbers she'd been left in case of an emergency, Sam led the three men down the garden. Each of them studied the contents of the yard.

"Where did your dad get all this wood from?" asked the first plainclothes.

"Dunno," said Pogsy, hurrying after his brother. "It's nowt to do with us. We just live here."

Sam fiddled with the keyring, trying several keys in each of the locks, pretending he didn't know what he was doing. Finally, just as the first plainclothes lost his temper, the lock clicked open.

"This is a bit much for a silly little banger," said Sam.

The lead copper ran a hand through thinning hair, coming away with a palm covered in Brylcreem. "Well, son, that's what we're here to find out. We've had reports of explosives being used. There's a team examining the land across the road. Cyril, this one's all yours."

Sam opened the shed door and switched on the light. The three cops entered Dad's sanctuary, one at a time in single file, squeezing around each other, always looking, searching for anything unusual or out of place. Pogsy watched from outside, doing his best to hide his disappointment at the lack of racks and racks of Second World War goodies, aware that, had he been right about the guns, his dad would likely be in all sorts of trouble. Instead, what he saw was a shed that was about three times bigger than an average shed with about ten times the amount of stuff packed neatly away inside. Along the left-hand side, Dad had made two shelves for screws that were all filed away in neatly labelled tins, graded by size and head-type. A further two shelves were dedicated to nails, similarly labelled and graded, this time packed away in old jam jars. At the very back Dad had constructed a huge ceiling-to-floor hanging board for his tools, all neatly labelled and outlined. There were five hammers, hundreds of screwdrivers and three saws. On the opposite side to the shelves was a rack for two pairs of garden sheers and a cradle for a petrol lawnmower. A lower shelf, set alongside the mower, contained four boxes of charcoal and two boxes of grass seed plus some unopened packets of fertiliser. To the side of the door there was an old wooden workbench inset with deep grooves, with a sack of old clothes neatly filed away underneath it. Above the bench, on a high shelf that was out of his reach, Pogsy spied three rusty orange cans, each labelled with a skull and crossbones.

Cyril, who was the copper in uniform, pulled on a rubber glove and gave it a healthy *twang*. Then he reached up for one of the rusty cans. He prised off the lid with a screwdriver he'd borrowed from Dad's rack.

"That the stuff?" said the first plainclothes.

Cyril took a sniff of the tin. "It don't smell at all right."

"That's what we like to hear."

Pogsy was fascinated by the whole process. For grown-ups, coppers had a unique way of seeing things. They weren't like ordinary grown-ups such as Mister Mortis, who saw diddly squat even when you thrust it in their faces. If you wanted to become a copper, you obviously needed to be able to view the world like a little kid.

The second plainclothes went outside. Sam followed. Cyril, meanwhile, opened each of the orange cans in turn, took a sniff, then replaced the lids and dropped each tin into an individual plastic bag.

"Is that evidence?" asked Pogsy.

The first plainclothes nodded. "They're off to the lab."

"I'll just take a swab of the vice," said Cyril. He rummaged in his big black bag of cop equipment and took out what Pogsy thought was a bit of cotton wool. He swabbed the top of the vice, then opened it up and used a second swab inside the jaws. As an afterthought, he swabbed the handle with a different swab again, placing each swab in its own labelled bag.

"All done?" asked the first plainclothes.

"Yep," said Cyril, filing away the evidence in his cop bag.

The other plainclothes reappeared at the door. "There's wood piled up everywhere around the back of the shed, Bill. And some metal poles and a bedstead too. This bloke certainly likes his rubbish."

"Rubbish isn't our concern," said the first plainclothes. "Unless someone reports it stolen. Make a note of the bedstead." He turned to Sam. "Thanks for being so cooperative, son. I'll put it in my report."

"Me dad'll be home any minute," said Pogsy. "Aren't you going to wait?"

"No need, lad. You two saw what we did. You can tell him we've been. Here, take this: it's a copy of the warrant. We'll be in touch if anything interesting shows up."

Pogsy and Sam followed the coppers back to the house, ushering them down the side passage so as to prevent them tramping back through the recently decorated living room in their big cop boots. Normally, Mum made visitors take their shoes off at the front door. Pogsy wondered what would have happened if they'd insisted the coppers follow the house rules. He imagined it ending badly. By the time they returned inside, Missis D was sitting in the kitchen, on one of the dining benches, in a right tizzy. She'd been unable to get hold of Mum or Dad and was busy telling herself off.

"I'm a useless old woman," she said. "I've never had to deal with the police before."

"Me neither," said Sam. "This is all because I frightened Mister Armstrong's dog with a banger."

"Poor Patch," said Missis D. "I'm sure you didn't do it on purpose. All he had to do was knock on your door and ask you for an apology. Instead, we get all this unnecessary nonsense. I shall be having strong words with his wife."

"Thank you, Missis D."

Pogsy heard the front door open.

Mum or Dad? he wondered.

The door banged shut, its Yale lock clicking solidly into place. *That was the sound of Dad.*

"Dad, Dad!" yelled Pogsy, rushing into the lounge. "You'll never guess what?"

"Whoah," said Dad, holding up his hands. "At least let me take my shoes off. Aren't you going to ask me what kind of a day I've had?"

"You need to ask us what kind of a day *we've* had," said Sam. "Except you won't like the answer."

Dad remained silent. He took his time slipping off his shoes and finding his slippers. Then he took a set of car keys, two one-pound notes and a load of change out of his pocket and dumped everything in a bowl on the side.

"Let me guess: we've had a visit from the police." Dad smiled broadly, flashing a set of uneven, off-white teeth.

"How do you know?" asked Sam.

"Because I sat in my van around the corner waiting for them to leave."

"*Dad!*" Sam and Pogsy screamed together.

"Missis D, make us a cuppa, will you?" Dad took a seat at the end of the settee. "I need to hear from these two all about the visit we just had. Did you like it? Either of you?"

"It was horrible," said Sam. "I felt they were watching my every move."

Dad nodded. "That's coppers for you. If I'm not mistaken, they poked and prodded everything in here, had a good neb in the kitchen cupboards, asked about my collection of wood, then rummaged around inside my shed and ended up taking away three rusty cans of rock-hard baking soda as evidence. Does that sound about right, boys?"

Pogsy felt a nauseous swirl in his tummy. "They did everything you ever said they would and worse."

"Plus, I heard them say they were searching No-Man's Land," said Sam, a worried look on his face. "I knew I should have gone over there and cleared up the evidence."

"The only evidence they'll find," said Dad, "is three exploded bangers tied together with a piece of string."

"I..." Sam let the words trail off into space. "But... How..."

"They got there completely by accident," said Dad. "Some might call it planting evidence but that would be misleading the law. And we'd never do that, would we?"

"No, Dad," said Sam.

"If the cops were to take a look in the River Head, near where I drove past this morning, they might find the remains of those other bangers you had. But they won't think of that."

Sam raised his eyebrows and opened his mouth wide. "I've been a right nid."

"You have," said Dad. "I hope being busted by the cops and having to defend yourself has taught you a valuable lesson. Next time, son, don't be so ruddy stupid."

"I won't," said Sam. His grin was the width of his face.

Pogsy laughed. Everyone always thought that they had the best dad in the world, even when they didn't. In his case, though, he knew it was true. He really did have the best dad in the world. And Sam and Ellie did too.

Four: My Friend Stan

It was Sunday tea-time and Pogsy was lying on his bed listening to an old beaten-up radio, its front and back bound together with insulating tape. By its side was a cassette player with a microphone, all plugged in and ready to go. He twitched nervously and rubbed his lucky troll charm as he patiently waited to hear his current favourite song and hoped that somehow, by a miracle, in the last few days it had gone to Number One. At least he thought it was his favourite song. Truth be told, it was difficult to tell. He pressed the eject button on the cassette player and checked the tape he'd spent the afternoon preparing.

He would happily have gone out down *Freemo Street* and spent the little money he had on records by any group with long hair and platform boots that had the Glam sound. However, his dad thought that singles were a waste of money because they were a pain to put on the record player and, although you got two songs, only one of them was any good. He preferred cassette tapes, which ran for up to forty-five minutes a side. He could make compilation cassettes for free, by borrowing records from his mates at work. He encouraged both of his lads to do the same, not that Pogsy ever listened.

"Counting down the top five. And down two, it's 'Monster Mash'."

The song had been in the top ten for a few weeks now. Ellie liked it, although she preferred "The Laughing Gnome", which was at Number Six. Her eyes lit up every time she heard either of the two songs and she giggled uncontrollably, shaking her chubby little arms from side to side.

At the beginning of term, one of the girls had brought a transistor radio into class and persuaded Missis Wainwright to let her and a group of her friends listen to Johnnie Walker on Radio One on Tuesday lunchtime. Not wanting to be outdone by the girls, Steve had asked Sparksy to build a better radio with better reception. The next week, there were two competing groups listening to the same show at the same time in the same classroom, pretending to hear something that the other group had missed. It was a thing now: at 12.45, once a week, everyone would gather round in a hush to hear the countdown of the Top Twenty, culminating in the announcement of the new Number One.

"And up one at Number Four it's Ike and Tina Turner with 'Nutbush City Limits'."

Pogsy had no time for that song. It was a racket and there wasn't a single platform boot in sight. Ali was familiar with Ike and Tina Turner, who were apparently huge in America, although she wasn't a fan. Unlike Sarge, who thought they were great. The song didn't have enough sirens and that made it boring, just like some of the music Sam and his mate Jimbo were listening to. Their current favourite band was Pink Floyd, who'd just released a new record called *Dark Side of the Moon*, which Sam had borrowed the week it came out and recorded. It went on a bit too long and, although some of the voices were funny when they were going on about being mad, Pogsy had lost interest before the end of the first song.

Frantically, he rubbed his lucky troll with his thumb. If God existed and he listened to wishes, he had about ten minutes to work his magic. It would be brilliant if he did. He assumed that God was a man because all the pictures of God he'd even seen depicted him as a man, even though Mum swore blind that anyone who could bake the universe in just seven days had to be a woman.

"At Number Three this week, down one place, it's The Sweet with 'Ballroom Blitz'."

In Pogsy's opinion, The Sweet's stonking great platform boots made them a great Glam group. He had to concede that, for five weeks earlier in the year when their previous single, "Blockbuster", had been Number One, they'd been his favourite band. So much so he'd learned all their names. It was a fantastic song, with outstanding sirens, and Brian and the band always looked so happy performing it. Their current single should have been Number One and most of the Radio One DJs agreed. It was brilliant fun to shout and jump along to. Except, for the last three weeks, it had just failed to get there, kept off the top spot firstly by Wizzard, who were an OK Glam group apart from their strange singer, and then a really rubbish song that Pogsy hated so much he'd vowed never to speak its name.

"This week's Number Two..."

Extra-hard rub.

"Up two places, it's 'My Friend Stan' by Slade."

He pressed the record button on the cassette player and crossed his fingers, hoping that no-one would interrupt and ruin the recording. Last week the song had come in at Number Four and everyone had been shocked because it was supposed to go straight into the top spot. When the tape recorder had jammed and chewed up the tape, Pogsy had wondered if it was a sign. By the time he'd found a reserve tape, there was only ten seconds of the song left to memorise.

He turned up the volume to be sure the recording worked properly, then listened intently, learning all the words. Although The Sweet were a great Glam group, this was the band he'd been waiting for. It was impossible not to like Slade when they were at their stompiest. Bigzy and Gas-tank Gaz both wanted to be in Slade, and even Mum enjoyed tapping her foot to Noddy Holder and the boys on *Top of the Pops* on a Thursday night, despite Dad's obsession with Pan's People.

Every song Slade had released recently had gone straight in at Number One. "Cum On Feel the Noize" was a screamer and it had been the best song in the country for four weeks back in March. Then there was "Mama Weer All Crazee Now", which was a hit last year, and "Skweeze Uz Pleeze Uz", which had topped the charts in July, plus "Take Uz Bak 'Ome" and "Coz I Luv U", which were other ace screamers. Pogsy liked any song by his favourite band, no matter what, because those were the rules. He'd recorded cassette copies of every previous Slade hit, and by the time he'd gone out and bought the single down the shops, he'd already known all the words. Once he had a proper recording of "Stan", he'd listen to it again and again, and learn it all the way through ready for Tuesday, when he was absolutely positively sure, with the assistance of his lucky charm, that it was going to be the new Number One.

"Top of the charts, for the third week in a row, it's 'Eye Level' by the Simon Park Orchestra."

Pogsy cussed and pressed the stop button on the cassette recorder. Then he turned the radio off and rewound the cassette. How could a song that had no words and was the theme tune to an appalling detective series be the best single in the country? It was the worst Number One of the year by far. Except for perhaps "Young Love" by Donny Osmond, which had topped the charts for what seemed like an eternity over the summer. Nearly all the girls were in love with either Donny or David Cassidy, who kept on appearing in all the girls' magazines even though he hadn't had a hit for ages. The only one in class who liked "Eye Level" was Bam. He thought it was a good hummer. But then his mother and father probably listened to groups that posh people liked, like Beethoven and Brahms.

Pogsy fiddled with the cassette player, found the start of "Stan" and played it again. This time he sang along as best he could, adding sounds where he didn't know the words. Hopefully, when it did get to Number One, it would be there for ages, even longer than The Sweet. He thought about it for a moment. "Stan" or "Blitz"? He couldn't decide. Perhaps "Stan" needed sirens, although that would be copying. Wizzard had had another single, "See My Baby Jive", which had been the best-selling single for a month back in May. "Stan" was definitely better than that. One of the biggest hits of the year had been from Gary Glitter, who'd had a super massive stomper with "I'm the Leader of the Gang I Am" over the summer months. It had been played everywhere, incessantly, until the entire country was sick of it. Except for Steve, who was still mad for it and claimed it was written about him. He'd learned all the moves and proudly shown off down the park and at his friends' birthday parties for weeks afterwards. Thankfully, Donny Osmond had come along and rescued the world. Reluctantly, Pogsy concluded that "Stan" probably wasn't a six-weeker. It should do four though. And that was good enough. It was certainly going to be on *Top of the Pops* next week.

He couldn't wait.

He played "Stan" three more times, his singing improving with each listen. Come Tuesday lunchtime, he'd be prepared for when Slade finally dumped the horrible "Eye Level".

He supposed it was time to head downstairs.

Dad was spending a lot of time glued to the news these days. Ever since Egypt and Syria had attacked Israel the other day, he'd been seriously worried, and the way that the BBC was reporting it, it was like something out the Bible. Dad said it was *really bad* and Russia and America could easily get involved. The last thing anyone needed was a full-scale war in the Middle East that might spill over. Some reporters were saying the price of oil might go up even further.

"If it does," said Dad, "we'll all have to tighten our belts."

While Dad had his moment, Pogsy drifted off, thinking about Wingnut and his Wingmen. They'd frightened Sparksy in an ambush on Friday night after school. They hadn't hit him but they'd made threats and told him to tell Steve that No-Man's Land belonged to them now. Sparksy was the weakest boy in the gang, so it was important to protect him. Except, when the gang had met to talk about it, Steve had expressed no interest in going to war. "If they'd actually hit Sparksy, it would be different," he'd said. "And claiming No-Man's Land isn't the same as occupying it." Pogsy wasn't so sure. If The Kings did nothing, the threats from the Wingmen would just get worse. Eventually, there was going to be a fight. He could feel it in the air. Everyone knew that, if a fight was coming, it was better to start it than have it happen to you.

It was just plain common sense.

Five: Chimpy's Tea Party

The ritual of Saturday afternoon round Ali's had begun with just a few members of the gang. True to her word, at the first gathering, Ali had baked an enormous apple pie and, even though Steve had been critical about the flavour, he'd ended up eating three slices with custard. Pogsy didn't say anything but it looked and tasted exactly the same as one that Ali's nan had made a few weeks earlier. The next week, Bingo had come along. He'd heard that Ali had a collection of comics that weren't available in Britain, and slowly but surely he'd managed to install himself as a silent but permanent fixture. Steve had then invited Bam without asking first, and the rich boy had been very rude and rubbished all of Ali's best toys. Nan Eagle had spotted that there were suddenly a lot of boys in her lounge, so had nudged Alison into having a birthday party and inviting her girl friends. Steve christened it *Chimpy's Tea Party*. He insisted that, if Ali wanted to be in the gang, Bam had to be there.

Ali seethed at the threat but eventually agreed to make the new boy first reserve. She wrote the invites by hand at dinner time and gave them out later in the playground. When Reddy received his, the look on his face suggested his dog had just been eaten to death by crabs. Sullenly, he mumbled he was probably doing something else that day, thus opening the door to Bam. Pogsy tried unsuccessfully to remember the last time his friend had turned up to a girl's birthday party. When he saw Red Top sneak Ali's invite into a storm drain on the way home from school that night, he suspected a rumour he'd heard the previous summer was true.

Pogsy felt a wave of relief wash over him. He was glad his dad wasn't funny in the head like Red Top's dad. But then his mum hadn't run off with another milkie and wasn't likely to. Still, making your lad *RVPS* to say he was going and then banning him from leaving the house on the day of the party was not a normal thing to do.

It was just before two when Pogsy headed over to Ali's house, a big bottle of bright red cherryade pop clutched firmly in one hand, a card, a present and a collection of his best singles in the other. He skipped happily along the pavement, keeping his eyes peeled for dog droppings, having already downed a bottle of sneeze-inducing

strawberry Cresta, which was renowned as the bubbliest pop on the
shelves. He had on a new pair of Brutus jeans with super-wide flares,
roundies with segs in the raised heels and the toes, a white cheesecloth
shirt with a massive collar, and a brown and red striped tank top. His
dark ginger hair was flicking up at the ends. He'd been waiting ages for
that to happen. What he really, really wanted was wavy hair and frizzy
sideburns like Noddy from Slade but, as his hair only had a slight wave
and his sideburns refused to grow, he'd considered having his fringe cut
halfway up his forehead like Dave Hill. Mum had discovered his plan
and forbidden Mister Buzz the barber from doing anything to her son
that made him look like a silly beggar.

Pogsy knocked on Ali's door. She answered with a smile.
"Happy birthday." He handed over the card and present.

"Swell," said Ali. "You look nice."

"You don't look bad yesen."

Ali had on a pair of tight-fitting crimson pants with stand-out
pockets and wide turned-up flares. On top she wore a knitted burgundy
jumper with a pattern across the chest, and a cream shirt, but only the
cuffs and wide collar were visible. Her hair was all puffed out, like a
dandelion clock, and it looked very different to the pigtails she often
wore to school. She'd decorated around her eyes with light blue eye
shadow, which was what all the girls were wearing. It made her cow-
brown eyes look huge. Her lips were covered in bright red lip gloss the
colour of roses, and in her ears she wore a pair of silver hoop earrings.
Pogsy noticed that she was taller than usual. He bent over and lifted a
flare to reveal a calf-length platform boot with brown patterned panels
and a four-inch heel.

"What's that horrid stink?" asked Ali. "It reminds me of a dead
cat."

Pogsy blushed. "I borrowed some of me dad's Brut."

"Well, he better be careful or he'll attract flies."

Pogsy pushed Ali on the shoulder. He leaned in to kiss her but it
was too late. She'd already turned away and was headed inside. Every
time he'd tried to make a move, it had gone wrong. He was sure he was
doing it right but he didn't have anyone to ask. Sam was the best bet,
but whenever you mentioned girls in front of him, he went bright red
and ran away. Pogsy followed Ali inside and closed the door behind
him. In contrast to his own house, which had been knocked about and
redecorated earlier in the year, Ali's nan's house still had a dark brown

tiled floor in the hall, with a door to the stairs straight ahead. The front room and middle room had been knocked through to create a single gigantic room, although both original doorways were still intact. Much to his mum's ire, when his dad had done their conversion, he'd removed all the downstairs walls so that the front door led straight into the lounge.

"Hello, Nan Eagle," said Pogsy, following Ali through the door.

"Hello, Patrick. Don't you look dandy."

Pogsy flicked his hair. "Thank you, Nan."

Nan Eagle was wearing a long, grey wool dress with a vertical criss-cross pattern that she'd knitted herself. She had a brass bangle on each wrist and a gold chain around her neck. Her feet were covered by a pair of furry slippers. Pogsy had no idea how old she was, other than she was about the same age as Granny Green, who also had lots of grey hair. She was certainly younger than Mister Armstrong and Missis D. Pogsy had once thought to ask but he remembered his mum telling him that ladies didn't take kindly to such questions.

"I'll pop that pop in the fridge," said Nan, taking the bottle from Pogsy. "Do you want a glass that's already cold?"

"Yes, please, Nan. Cherryade, please."

"You brought some records," said Ali. "Great. I don't suppose you've got 'Eye Level'?"

Pogsy felt his eyes narrow and his bottom lip quiver.

"Just kidding," said Ali.

"Wot'cha, Pogs," said a voice from inside the bay window.

"Wot'cha," replied Pogsy. The words deflated like a popped party balloon as they left his mouth.

Sarge was wearing a pair of purple corduroy flares held up with a great big gold buckle shaped like a snake, and a purple and cream diamond-patterned shirt with a wide collar and big cuffs. His afro hair looked alive, like a bush on fire. He had a glass of bright green pop in his hand.

Nan Eagle went into the kitchen, which was located at the back of the house, and returned shortly with a glass of red pop. Ali picked up a glass of bright green pop from the table.

"Cheers."

"Cheers," said Pogsy and Sarge together.

Ali and Sarge were halfway through a game of *Mastermind*, so Pogsy rummaged through a pile of American comics on the sideboard.

He found the July copy of *The Amazing Spiderman*, which was new. He knew Bingo was dying to read it too. In the previous edition, the Green Goblin had killed Gwen Stacy, and Spidey wanted his revenge. Pogsy half-read the comic to find out what happened. What he really wanted was to play a game with Ali. Any game would do. But she was busy with Sarge.

These days, she was always busy with Sarge. Sarge this. Sarge that. Sarge, Sarge, Sarge. He felt sick inside at the thought of it. But at the same time, Sarge was his friend.

It was all very confusing.

The smell of freshly baked cakes drifted through the open kitchen door. Pogsy wiped the drool from around his mouth. Later on, at around four o'clock, Nan Eagle was going to serve birthday tea, consisting of sandwiches and quiches followed by sponge cakes and trifle. Unlike his mum, who would do anything to avoid it, Nan didn't seem to mind all the cooking. According to Ali, her pop was happy to pay for everything. He worked in oil, and he was spending most of his time travelling on jets between London and Texas. He had been popping by frequently but, due to the war erupting in the Middle East, things were very tense at the moment and he was stuck in Houston. Pogsy had tried really hard but he didn't fully understand what the war was about. Red Top said it was simple: everybody hated everybody else's guts and they were all having a big old barney.

That seemed about right.

For a while, all the grown-ups had said that the Egyptians and the Syrians, with help from the Ruskies, were winning. That had sent Mister Cohen, who taught Reddy's brother, frantic with worry. He'd wailed in frustration, ruminating on the end of the world until the Americans, who everyone knew had the best army in the world, had got involved to even things up. By listening to the grown-ups, Pogsy gleaned that this was a good thing. However, it had resulted in an oil *inbargo* and Dad was convinced it was going to last a very long time and end up in a petrol shortage. He'd left early that morning in a bit of a panic to undertake a secret mission with Mister Payne, which was unjust as, when he or Sam refused to say where they were going, they were given a telling-off. Some of the teachers at school thought that a third World War was just around the corner. They talked about it a lot, using code-words, so as not to alarm the children.

Their rubbish system had taken all of thirty seconds to crack.

Pogsy grumped.

If a World War happened, Slade might *never* have another Number One.

He was still livid that "Stan" hadn't made it, even with his help. Being Number Two was a horrid feeling. There was a rumour in the playground that it was because Don Powell, Slade's drummer, had been involved in a car crash over the summer and he wasn't able to play properly. The drums were perfect though, so it wasn't that. On the plus side, at least that stupid hummer was no longer at the top of the charts. On the minus side, what the girls were singing instead these days was *far* worse.

The doorbell rang.

"Get that will you, Pat," said Ali. "You're such a great doorman."

"Sure," said Pogsy, in a lilting American accent. Ali didn't appear to notice.

Pogsy answered the door to Bigzy, who offered up a bottle of bright yellow pop and a card. He was encased from head to toe in faded denim, wearing a huge pair of nearly square sunglasses with bright red frames and pink lenses atop his chubby little nose. His chunky brown hair, which had curls at the back and sides, was parted down the middle with a fringe at the front.

"Howdy," he said, clicking the heels of his cowboy boots together.

Bigzy was followed by Steve, who was wearing dark denim trousers with bell-bottoms and a white polyester shirt with a wide collar. The top three buttons were undone, showing off a gold necklace with a letter "S" hanging from it.

"And in at Number One," said Steve, "is the Greatest Steve in the World with 'The Steve Song', featuring the brilliant Band of Steves."

Pogsy laughed.

"Are Judy and her sister here yet?" asked Steve.

"I thought you didn't like girls," said Pogsy.

"Well, I'm slowly changing my mind. But don't let on, or they'll all want a turn with the best-looking Steve in the world."

Nan Eagle looked the pair up and down. "Don't you two look dandy."

"Thanks, Nan Eagle," said Steve with a massive beaver grin. He turned to Ali. "Here's your card. Bam says soz but he can't make it after all. He's gone round Mister Mortis's house to pick apples. You've got to give him a gold star for his brilliant ideas."

Ali glared derisively. "Typical."

Pogsy growled. He imagined Bam feeling smug at getting one over on Ali. Then he imagined punching the smirk off his face until it was located on the back of his head.

That felt better.

Bingo was the next to arrive. He was dressed in a white and green paisley shirt with a brown tank-top, and brown pants with a slight flare. His wavy blond hair hung down to his collar. Until he'd officially joined the gang, some of the lads used to call him *specky four-eyes*. That had stopped now.

"Has she got it?" he asked feverishly, handing over a bottle of bright yellow fizz and a birthday bag.

"Yep. And the August one."

"Don't tell me, don't tell me!" Bingo hurried through to the lounge, where Nan Eagle complimented him on his appearance. His face turned traffic-light red.

The girls all arrived together, in one big gaggle. They'd pooled their money and bought a single present between them, which they fussed over. Pogsy took one look and knew they'd all been doing each other's make-up. Judy and Shaz Davison, who were twin sisters, both had their long blonde hair in plaits. They'd been copying each other forever and were both wearing floral dresses that reached all the way to the ground and made it look like they were hovering. Lynn Pointer, who'd only joined the school in the middle of the previous year, had on a red patterned jumpsuit with bell-bottomed flares and a halter neck that showed off her freckled shoulders. Her blonde hair hung down to her bum. Some boys in class thought she was mad but a lot of the boys in the year above liked her. The rumour was she liked one of them back. Susan Grainger was dressed in blue and white polka dot; her brown hair was down for a change. Even though she looked nice, the way her mouth wrinkled up at the edges made it look like she was sucking a lemon. Ruth Maddox, the teacher's pet, came in next. Her long dark hair had recently been cut into a page-boy style and she wore a yellow hairband to keep it pinned back. Her outfit consisted of brown flared pants, roundies and a dark green jumper with a roll-neck. Pogsy

pretended she didn't exist; he was delighted when she did the same
back. Bringing up the rear was Pollyanna Delacroix, who wore yellow
and green check pants, ankle boots and a yellow and green striped roll-
neck sweater. She had more hair than anyone else that Pogsy knew. He
blushed the moment he saw her.

"Hiya, Patrick," she giggled, pursing her plump, pink lips.

"Wot'cha, Pollyanna." Pogsy knew better than to call her Polly,
mainly because he was currently sitting next to her at school. He knew
he should know a lot about her. She was always telling him what she'd
been doing, or where she'd been, or who she'd met, or what her aunties
had been up to, but he didn't pay her much attention as she didn't watch
television and knew nothing about any of the best programmes.

Last to arrive was Gas-tank Gaz, who was twenty minutes late.
He was dressed from head to toe in silver Glam gear, including a pair of
silver platform boots and silver eye shadow.

"Da, da!" he said, spreading his arms wide.

Steve guffawed and spilt pop everywhere while the girls all
screeched their approval. Pogsy felt immensely jealous. Nan tut-tutted
but offered Gas-tank a drink anyway. After the first round of pop, the
girls had all taken off their shoes and begun a game of *Twister*, which
had them giggling uncontrollably, in a tangle of limbs that looked like a
tent frame bent double by a storm.

Gas-tank wedged himself in, forcing the rest of the girls to
budge up on the sofa while Steve disappeared to the kitchen. He
reappeared carrying a tray with six glasses of brown pop on it. He
explained that they were about to play a game called *Russian Roulette*,
which he'd learned from his uncle.

"Five are Coca-Colas and one's a dandelion and burdock," he
said. "Three, two, one, down in one!"

"Yeuch!" screamed Bigzy. He followed up with a loud belch.

Steve disappeared to the kitchen and returned with seven
glasses for the girls, who adamantly refused to play his silly game. He
handed one to each of the boys and counted down again.

"Bleughh!" said everyone but Steve.

He sniggered loudly, doubling up with mirth. "Soz. I must have
poured just one cola that time."

The pop drinking continued unabated, with everyone hitting the
brightly coloured fizz hard, playing the traffic-light game with a
cherryade followed by an orangeade and a limeade. There was no

burping allowed. Ali had *Buckaroo* and *KerPlunk*, which everyone played. Even Bingo put down his comics for a bit. Bigzy and Steve both hooted with laughter, trying to outdo each other at everything, but as soon as Lynn joined in, she out-hooted everyone. There were calls for Ali to show off her gymnastic skills but she refused for fear of splitting her pants.

With the playing of games in full swing, Steve took charge of the record player and announced he was now *DJ King*, the hottest disc jockey in town. Pogsy couldn't believe it. Steve had only gone and brought along the prize-winning gold crown he'd made the previous Christmas, using gold foil and fake rubies. Steve loved his lucky crown almost as much as Pogsy hated it. DJ King borrowed Bigzy's pink glasses and played "Metal Guru" by T-Rex, followed by "Crazy Horses" by the Osmonds, because he knew Judy liked it. The girls all got up to dance. To Pogsy's absolute horror, rather than play one of his Slade singles, DJ King turned up the volume and put on the dreaded "Eye Level", prompting the girls to form a line and hum-sing along. When David Cassidy's new single, "Daydreamer", crept on next – the very song that had ensured "Stan" didn't get to Number One – Pogsy began to suspect a conspiracy.

The girls formed a line and sang along in harmony, with moves they'd copied from *Top of the Pops*. Pogsy felt his left eyelid twitch.

"Gas-tank, you're out of pop," he said, feeling a bit light-headed and unable to concentrate properly. "Let me get you one."

"Thanks," said Gas-tank. "I feel a bit of a prat. Bigzy said it was a full Glam party and everyone was getting dressed up. I'm never going to believe him again."

"Well, I like what you're wearing," said Pogsy. "Are there any flavours I should avoid?"

"Ginger beer," said Gas-tank with a wink. "We don't want a repeat of Warwick."

Pogsy laughed out loud.

Without warning, Gas-tank dropped to his knees and joined in singing with the girls, who encouraged him to finish the song, which he did with a flourish, hitting all the right notes. Gas-tank had a great voice. Probably because he was always singing in the church choir. Pogsy approved. He was glad that Gas-tank was on his table at school this year.

DJ King decided at that moment that the crowd was sufficiently warmed up and, with a wink, put on his favourite song, stomping away to the opening riff. The rest of the boys joined in.

Come on, come on...

Pogsy felt his left eyelid twitch again. He growled, then disappeared to the kitchen, fuming away while he sorted out a drink for his friend.

Gas-tank Gaz wasn't properly in the gang yet. He'd earned his nickname on a school trip to Warwick Castle to see armour from the Middle Ages. Due to a previous squabble, the school had sent a note to all the mums instructing them to pack identical lunches. Hence the whole class was packed up with orange squash, a packet of plain crisps and four smelly egg sandwiches made with white bread. Except for Gaz, who had shrimp paste on brown bread. He took great pleasure in telling everyone how eggs *did him in* and, because of what came out the other end, he wasn't allowed to have them at home. Bigzy bet him he was fibbing and offered his sandwiches in a swap. Gaz merrily chomped down the eggs, determined to prove he wasn't all hot air.

Gaz had dropped *Little Boy* in the armour room of Warwick castle at 2.33. Pogsy knew that, because that was the time the clock stopped. Gaz had walked up to Bigzy, told him to pull his finger and the rest was history. The thundercrack that came out of Gaz's bum had rattled off the shields and swords, tinkling the stained-glass windows. Bigzy gagged. Gaz coughed and giggled at the same time, his eyes streaming with tears. Steve had held his nose and run from the room. One of the teachers had remarked that the sewers clearly hadn't been cleaned since the Middle Ages. A boy from another school declared it smelt worse than his grandad's bedpan and had patted Gaz heartedly on the back.

In between bouts of hysterical laughter, Gaz had managed to communicate that he always let off in threes, and the third one was the one that peeled your eyeballs. Steve called a gang huddle. After much excitement, a plot came together and a deal was struck. Gaz had proved that he had volume, now he had to prove he had staying power. If he created a pong that lasted five minutes, he could apply to join the gang.

Fat Man was dropped in the confines of the ladies' loos at 2.47 in an operation that required two lookouts, who were instructed to shout "Ray Clemence" at the first sight of a teacher. Bigzy stood guard at the door, while Pogsy had the task of nipping inside to confirm that all the cubicles were empty. Gaz had hardly been able to walk straight, thanks to a really bad giggle fit. Once he'd staggered in, Bigzy had slammed the door shut, sealing Pogsy inside as a joke, while the gang had waited patiently outside for the clap of thunder they were sure would follow.

Nothing emerged.

Not a single tremor.

Pogsy's face soured as he remembered Gaz standing there, arms folded, tittering away in his mustard-yellow paisley-patterned shirt and apple-green trousers. Suddenly, his face had turned roughly the same colour as his shirt, then without warning changed to match the colour of his pants. Pogsy had double gagged. His brother had once created stinky rotten-egg gas with a Mark Two chemistry set he got for Christmas, and that had stunk up their bedroom a treat. What Gaz had released was far worse, in both width and depth. It was a poison-gas weapon that could turn your lungs inside out. Pogsy had taken a trip to the Army Surplus store after that, and bought a gas mask and case, but in all likelihood, even that wouldn't have been enough.

He and Gaz had taken a huge gulp of swamp gas, held their breath and banged on the door, claiming that there was nothing doing and Gaz had let off a dud. The second the door was opened, they'd yelled "SBD" and legged it, leaving a confused Steve to face the deadly onslaught alone. He'd later claimed it was the one and only time he'd had all the enamel stripped from his teeth.

The ladies' loos had soon been closed by the staff because of complaints about a broken waste pipe. Gaz had continued to ferment stinkers for the rest of the day, dropping SBD after SBD and convulsing into fits of laughter after every single one. They'd had to explain to a bunch of lads from another school that SBD meant "silent but deadly"; the Brummies took it onboard immediately and, in exchange, they'd shared the term "to honk your guts up", which was very apt.

Pogsy returned to the living room with two glasses of bright green limeade pop. He handed one to Gas-tank.

"You had any more trouble from Wingnut's lot?"

Gas-tank gulped in a lungful of air. "They're too busy letting off fireworks to bother anyone at the mo'."

"Let uz know if owt changes."

DJ King thanked the best band in the world for the best song in the world, then thanked Bigzy and Sarge for joining in. He commended Chimpy for a great party and put on some Suzi Quatro, which got the girls bopping along. Pogsy was still trying to get over his fear of dancing and looking silly, when Bigzy jumped to his feet and did some mock jiving. The DJ followed up with the Detroit Spinners, which got Sarge going. Finally, DJ King came to his senses and put on "Cum On Feel the Noize", which was the signal for Pogsy to join in. He'd been practising his dance moves in his mum's bedroom mirror for weeks. He'd even tried wearing her six-inch platform boots to get the feel right. Brimming with confidence, he headed over to grab Ali.

"Hey, Patrick," said Pollyanna, intercepting him.

Pogsy hesitated. His shoulders sagged. Once again, he'd lost out to Sarge.

Pollyanna waved her willowy arms up and down and shook her long, dark blonde hair, dancing like her ankle boots were covered in burning petrol. It was hard to keep up. Pogsy didn't try. He stuck to his own moves and made Pollyanna copy him instead. She blew a bubble and popped it, pulling in the strands of pink gum with her tongue. Then she blew another. Pogsy threw more of his best Noddy moves, enviously looking through the crowd towards Ali and Sarge, who he had to admit looked pretty good together. He just couldn't understand why Ali was dancing with Sarge and not him.

"Have you seen Ali's baseball bat?" asked Pollyanna, fluttering her eyelashes.

Pogsy nodded.

"And her catcher's mitt?"

"It's really good. Steve McQueen had one just like it in *The Great Escape*."

"I like her. She's so sophisticated, coming from Los Angeles."

"She was born in Texas," said Pogsy. "She was just living there for a bit. Until her mom went loopy or summut."

Pollyanna shook her bum. "I have a mad mum. What about you?"

"Me mum says all mums are mad. On account of their children."

"You're funny, Patrick." Pollyanna brayed loudly, like a donkey. "I like you."

"I like you too," said Pogsy. The moment he said it, he regretted it.

"Did I hear Steve call Ali *Chimpy*?" asked Pollyanna.

Pogsy nodded. "It's his new nickname for her."

"He can get stuffed!" said Pollyanna adamantly. "The girls have decided it's the most rubbish nickname in the history of nicknames, and we're never going to use it."

DJ King decided it was time to slow things down and he put on "Young Love" by Donny Osmond. All the boys instantly sat down, with the exception of Sarge, who continued to dance with Ali. The rest of the girls joined in and formed a circle, linking arms and performing a slow dance that only a bunch of soppy girls could have invented. Pogsy's heart kicked the inside of his ribcage, like the same donkey that Pollyanna had borrowed her laugh from. His lips trembled. Ali and Sarge were getting far too close. He really didn't like it.

Nan Eagle interrupted the dancing by shouting for help laying the table. The music came to an abrupt stop. The girls assisted Nan with a tablecloth while the boys had a gang huddle and plotted what they were going to do next. Steve had been quite happily dancing with Judy until Shaz pushed her out of the way. Then Judy had pushed Shaz back. Finally, they'd danced all three together. He couldn't decide who he liked more. Bigzy shrugged his shoulders. Gas-tank admitted he liked Lynn but doubted she liked him back. Sarge sat in silence, all starry-eyed. Bingo didn't even look up from his comic books.

"You and Polly," said Steve, elbowing Pogsy in the ribs. "No surprise there. Everyone knows she likes you."

"Except me," said Pogsy, playing aimlessly with the flares of his trousers.

"So, when are you going to pass the spoggy?" Steve chuckled, resting his front teeth on his bottom lip.

"That's disgust!"

The girls began to bring plates laden with grub through from the kitchen. As it was a special occasion, Nan Eagle had got her best green-wash crockery out. It was the set without any chips. Someone hummed the opening bars to "Eye Level". Within seconds, all the girls joined in, moving the plates in time with the music. Gas-tank couldn't resist and broke ranks, bobbing up and down in time with the cacophony, lending his voice to the happy throng.

Pogsy covered his ears and wailed.

"'Ere," said Bigzy, twitching one of the dark green curtains that lined the front bay window. "There's a couple of misters sat in a car over the road. They look like rozzers."

"They're probably staking out the Petherbridges," said Pogsy. "I hear they had a pally full of aluminium pots away from the pontoon down the docks."

"Me cousins deal with the Petherbridges all the time," said Bigzy. "Cousin Mick says they'll sell you stuff they nick, then dob you in for the reward. I've got an idea: get Chimpy's 'nocs. Let's spy on the spies."

Pogsy pulled out a black leather case from underneath a nearby sideboard. He flipped open the catches and withdrew a pair of field binoculars, which he raised to his eyes. He adjusted the focus and zeroed in on the car. "Ruddy hell! I recognise the one on the left. He's CID."

"Giz a gander," said Bigzy, grabbing the 'nocs. "Yeah. I recognise the mister on the right. He nicked one of me cousins for flogging fish that wasn't his off the back of a lorry. I don't think they're doing the Petherbridges, I reckon they're staking out another house out further down. Is there summut you're not telling uz, Pogs?"

"It was deffo bangers me bruv had," said Pogsy quickly. "In fact, I've got a box at home. You fancy letting them off down that back passage near you with the dead good echo?"

"I'm in," said Bigzy. "We can blow the lids off some bins as well."

"Me too," said Gas-tank, returning to the ranks. "I'll have to get changed first."

Steve shook his head. "You know what my dad's like."

"Don't look at me," said Sarge. "I get in trouble just walking down the street in most parts of town. My mum says it's best not to attract attention. Unlike you lot, I might end up in prison just for stepping on the cracks in the pavement."

"That's stupes," said Bigzy. "They can't nick you for that."

"But they do," said Sarge. "That's why I won't go anywhere near the docks."

Pogsy shook his head.

Grown-ups really could be stupid.

His mum had gone to great lengths to make sure he knew that black people and white people were the same inside. Until then, he'd never even thought about it. His friends were his friends. What mattered most was whether or not he liked someone. And he liked Sarge. Even if he was trying his best to be Ali's boyfriend.

"Food's up!" shouted Ali. "Grab a plate. Anyone for more pop?"

Pogsy awoke on Sunday morning feeling like death warmed up. He had no idea what was in all the pop he'd drunk but it had left him feeling parched with a dry mouth and overcome with cramps, indigestion, bad wind and a thumping headache. He ached all over. He remembered *Musical Chairs* going horribly wrong, and him and Bigzy going for the last chair together, then crashing to the ground when the chair had collapsed beneath them. That was funny. Then the thought he was trying to hide away from jumped out from behind a bush and shouted "*Boo!*" He groaned. He'd tried to kiss Ali on the cheek but timed it really badly and accidentally kissed Pollyanna on the lips instead. For a brief second, his lips had stuck to her lip-gloss, like a fly to a spider's web. She couldn't wait to see him Monday at school. She'd said so. He crawled out of bed, swatting away at the memory.

It was a nightmare!

He had to put things right.

The feeling of trepidation in his belly made him feel like double-honking. He had no idea what he was going to say to Ali. But he had to say something.

He pulled on his clothes and rushed downstairs into the kitchen. He felt hungry but at the same time the idea of eating made him want to retch. He scooted out the back door and around to the front, then marched down the street. Before he could stop himself, he'd rung Ali's doorbell.

"Pat," said Ali, opening the door wide. "Ah was just thinking about you."

"I was thinking about you too. Ali, I don't know what was in that pop but it made uz act all funny and weird and it messed me head up. Pollyanna said she likes uz and I said I like her back, and now everything's ruined."

Ali poked her head out the door and looked both ways. "Come in. Nan's popped out to see her friend."

Pogsy followed Ali into her living room and sat down beside her.

"I really like you, Ali." The words were out before he could stop them.

"And Ah really like you too, Pat. The thing is, Ah like Sarge as well. Ah like you both. And Sarge has a lot of stuff that needs fixin'."

"Will you accidentally kiss uz, to make up for uz accidentally kissing Pollyanna?"

Ali looked away. "What Ah really want is to be friends. Ah feel Ah can talk to you about anything and Ah really like that. You don't tell lies, at least not about the things that matter, and that's important to me."

"Aren't the girls your friends?"

"Girls are different to boys. They never tell you the truth, they tell you what they think you want to hear."

"What about uz being best friends?"

"Ah don't think Sarge would like that."

"You're right." Pogsy shook his head. "I wasn't thinking straight, it's the pop. Sarge would have a massive sulk and he might even decide he doesn't like either of uz anymore. Then everyone'll laugh at uz and I'll end up having a ton of fights. What about *secret* best friends."

"Secret besties. Ah like that."

"I still want to try kissin'," said Pogsy.

"Pat. We mustn't. You're kinda with Pollyanna and Ah like her, and Ah'm kinda with Sarge and you like him. If we kiss each other, bad things will happen."

Pogsy decided to give it his best shot. "Sometimes you just have to do stuff anyway."

"Secret best friends," said Ali firmly. "No kissing."

"I suppose. I won't stop asking though."

"To seal the deal, we have to tell each other a big secret." Ali smiled. "You first."

"Well..." Pogsy paused, thinking hard about the incident in question. It still made him cringe to this very day. "When I was about six, summut bad happened at Peterborough railway station. Me Dad took uz and Steve out for the day to see the *Flying Scotsman*, and it was cold so I was wearing me trackie bottoms."

"That doesn't sound so bad."

"It was one of those days when the station was dead busy and there were hundreds of trains coming and going, and one of the trains was full of girls in school uniform. They all had their faces pressed to the windows, staring at uz. Steve ran up behind and pulled me pants down but he got me undies as well. It only took about two secs to pull 'em up again but, in that time, every single girl on the train saw me willy and they all pointed and laughed, and I've never bin so embarrassed before or since." Pogsy stood up, wandered over to Ali's pile of comics and found her most treasured issue. Sitting back down he put the book between them. "You have to pinkie swear on *The Avengers* that you'll never ever tell anyone."

"But Steve knows."

"He was so busy runnin' away that he didn't see."

Ali joined little fingers with Pogsy. "Pat. Ah pinkie swear on Iron Man, Thor and Hulk, cross my heart and hope to die, that Ah will never reveal your big secret. So help me God."

Before Ali could stop him, Pogsy kissed her on the cheek. "Now you've got to tell uz a big secret."

Ali took a deep breath and looked him in the eye. "When Ah was nine, ma mom kidnapped me. We were on the run for a whole year until Pop tracked us down. Now Ah'm here, starting over and Ah never want to see her again."

"Wow." Pogsy put his arm around his new secret bestie. She didn't resist. "That must have been horrible."

"It was. Ah still have nightmares about it."

"Does Sarge know?"

"Sarge is lovely and he's cute and strong, and when we practice gym, he just knows what Ah want him to do. But he's real innocent and, if Ah were to tell him tales about Mom, Ah'm scared Ah'll frighten him off."

Pogsy wondered where Ali's mom was now.

He didn't like to ask.

Chip had said he'd heard a rumour that she'd got run over by a truck and had no arms, legs or head. The rest of her was on life support while the doctors found the missing pieces. It was a stupid story. It made no sense. But then Ali's big secret didn't make that much sense either.

For the first time since he'd met her, Pogsy wondered whether Ali was telling the truth.

Six: Bommie Night

Pogsy followed his dad down the street towards a dark blue Morris Marina with two men sitting in the front. It was parked six houses down, outside the Petherbridge's, two away from Mister Armstrong and three away from Mister Payne. Pogsy laughed as he walked. Whatever you said about Mister Armstrong, his house was always clean. Even the front doorstep and front path were scrubbed spotless. Missis Armstrong made sure she did it once a week, usually on a Thursday, getting down on her hands and knees with a scrubbing brush. There was never a weed in sight in their front flowerbed. In comparison, Mister Payne did the minimum he had to. His path was swept once a year. The Petherbridge's house looked like the front garden had recently been bombed with Agent Orange. They didn't bother to keep what was left tidy and their collection of upturned metal milk crates and bike frames were all welded together with rust. The yellowing paintwork around their bay window was cracked, exposing rotten wood. Mum said it was obviously a house where people who were up to no good lived. Pogsy couldn't argue with her assessment.

There were three families who lived down his street whose houses were in a similar state of disrepair. One even had a collection of dog poo in the porch. For some reason, bad families always felt it necessary to advertise their presence to the rest of the world. It was a trend that extended across town.

On the plus side, thought Pogsy, *at least it made it easy to spot the vagabombs and thieves.*

As they walked, Pogsy put a name to each of the seven cars that were parked at his end of the street. Along with his neighbours, he knew who the owners were and where they lived. The car in which the CID were sitting stood out like one of Nan Eagle's pink-iced fairy cakes on a plate of blue-iced buns. They were fooling precisely no-one with their intrusion.

Dad approached the car. The plainclothes sitting in the passenger seat wound down his window. "Morning, Alan."

"Morning, boys," replied Dad. "I'm guessing you've finished the flask you brought with you and you're ready for a refill."

"Thanks, Alan. We very much appreciate it."

Pogsy saw Mister Armstrong's front-room curtain twitch. His dad made a point of changing position, using his body as a shield to obscure Armstrong's view. He positioned Pogsy to his left, to fill in the gap. Only then did he open up the carrier bag he'd brought with him. He handed over a tall, tartan-coloured flask and a greaseproof paper package. Pogsy smelt cooked bacon. He sucked up the drool from around the edges of his mouth.

"Here you go," said Dad. "This is my youngest lad. I brought him along this morning, to teach him about police work."

"You're Patrick."

Pogsy nodded.

"Well, son. All the programmes you see on TV about the police: most of them are rubbish. Your dad here is a decent bloke. We've known each other since school. DI Moon and me, we did something to upset our Chief Inspector, who's a personal friend of Mr Armstrong. We have to sit and watch your dad go to work every day for two weeks. We make a note of the time he leaves. Then we follow him, to make sure he goes where he's supposed to go."

Pogsy's curiosity got the better of him. "I thought you were investigating me bruvver."

The copper laughed. "Son. It's almost Bommie Night. The streets of this town have been lit up like the Blitz for weeks. If we tried to nick every lad with a banger in his back pocket, the cells would be full ten times over. What your brother did wrong was to start earlier than everyone else."

Dad turned and looked down at Pogsy. "Sam bought bangers. That's allowed. He let them off on No-Man's Land. That's allowed. It was early in the evening, so no noise laws were broken. My shed was searched, just in case Sam had been making explosives as Mr Armstrong claimed. I assume nothing was found. Otherwise, I'd have been taken in for questioning."

"You know we can't comment on an ongoing investigation," said the copper.

"What it boils down to then, Pat," explained his dad, "is that Mister Armstrong thinks he's better than us and the crime that's been committed is upsetting his dog. Except that's not illegal. And your brother is underage. So instead, the police have decided to take an interest in me."

"That's how the law works," said the copper, "even though it's a waste of my time and a waste of DI Moon's time. With Bommie Night just days away and kids stuffing fireworks in post boxes, hopefully our boss will see our report, accept that your dad's a law-abiding citizen, see some sense and let the matter drop. And when that finally happens, Mr Armstrong will do what he should have done in the first place: ask for an apology."

Pogsy felt himself blush. He hadn't blown up any post boxes, but he had made some very loud bangs in the bins behind the local off licence and shattered half-a-dozen milk bottles too. Bigzy's brother had shown them how to fire rockets up drainpipes, which had kept everyone amused for days. Sam, of course, already knew all about that particular trick. He said it was for children and that crow scarers were the future.

"Let's leave these fine officers to their brekkie," said Dad, leading Pogsy back towards the house.

Pogsy waited until they were out of earshot before speaking. "Dad, I thought you said all coppers are vampires."

"They are, Pat. That's why you have to be nice to them. Show them some respect. They shouldn't be wasting their time harassing us, not when there's real crime going on down the docks and across the estates twenty-four hours a day. And they know that."

Pogsy looked up at his dad. "I was sure you were going to shout at them."

Dad shook his head. "Their boss gave them a poo sandwich and told them to smile and eat it. There's no point in making it worse than it is."

"But you shouted at that copper who came to the door."

"That's different. He was on my land. Without permission. I treated him like I'd treat a neighbour doing the same. He knew that. It's all a great big game with the coppers. You have to stand up to them where you can and be nice to them when you can't. Those are the rules. I don't particularly like them, but I didn't make them and I don't have the power to change them. That's the way it is. I hope this has been educational."

"It has." Pogsy paused and then decided now was a good a time as any to ask. "Dad?"

"Yes, Pat?"

"Can you take me and Steve to see the Ice House bommie before it gets lit?"

"Be on your best behaviour for the rest of the week and we'll see."

On the lead-up to Bommie Night, Pogsy's house and Steve's house were both a hive of competitive activity. Pogsy's dad and Mister King had been building bonfires together for years and between them, they always threw a huge party for all their friends. This year, Steve's mum was doing the toffee apples, the punch and the apple-dunking barrel, while Mum was in charge of making cinder toffee and fudge. Sneakily, she'd delegated the task to Missis D. Steve's dad had sent Steve to school with a shopping list, to pass on to everyone who was coming. Dads had been requested to donate cans of booze or a bottle and a bag of fireworks, to be delivered to Mister King's bagwash by the weekend. Of all the jobs that needed doing, Pogsy had pestered and pestered for the best one of all, and this year he'd got it, snatching it from right under Steve's nose.

It was official: he was in charge of making the Guy.

When he dropped by on a mission to collect old clothes, Ali was mystified as to what was going on. She'd been expecting everyone to go *Trick or Treating* for Halloween and was very surprised to discover no-one at school was talking about homemade fancy-dress costumes for the occasion. Pogsy explained that they had *Penny for the Guy* instead, but that you had to make one first. For the body he'd scrounged a pair of dad's old work pants, which were now tied off with string, one of Mister Stamp from two doors down's old jackets, and a flying hat he'd found in a jumble sale, which the moths had had a nibble on. Now he was shopping for an old nightshirt that Nan Eagle had promised. Nan took Pogsy's bag of rags, pulled out her sewing machine and set to stitching everything together. Ali and Pogsy sat down with a glass of pop each, looking on in fascination. Once the body and legs were joined together, they were stuffed with a mix of crumpled-up newspaper and straw from Ali's rabbit hutch. A pair of old boots, a scarf and a pair of gloves completed the look. The final addition was the head, which was made by ramming an old stocking full of scrunched-up paper balls and topping it off with the flying hat. The face was a moulded, cardboard

Guy Fawkes mask with a stonking great hooter, which was held in place with elastic.

With the Guy prepped for action, some of the gang met up the next night after school at a corner shop near to Bigzy's house. The store owner had claimed a square section of pavement outside his shop and installed two rows of moveable racks, which he'd stacked high with assorted vegetables. Somehow, no matter what was on display, be it cabbages or turnips or swedes, all Pogsy could smell was a combination of fusty onions and paraffin wax. He looked around for the offending items but found none. He reminded himself how glad he was that his mum shopped elsewhere for her fruit and veg.

The weather was miserable. It had been drizzling all day. According to the news, it was set to continue long into the evening. Every few minutes, somewhere in the distance, a firework went off with a characteristic *boom*, which was followed by a dank echo and the barking of dogs. Pogsy patted his gloves together, shaking off the rain drops. He unstrapped the completed Guy from his Chopper bike and, with Red Top's help, set it up on the pavement. Bigzy added a cardboard sign he'd made along with a flat cap for donations, then got stuck into the main job of the night: accosting anyone and everyone for dosh. He soon had two pence in the pot. A grown-up he knew stopped to have a gander. He gave the Guy a push and a prod, declared it was a great job, and with a nod and a wink dropped three bangers in the hat.

Pogsy saw they were jet black with a red logo and nearly wet himself. It was the best thing that had happened so far.

At that moment Ali and Sarge arrived dressed in old bedsheets, tied around the waist with string. Pogsy felt his tummy turn. Ali stared long and hard at the collection of vegetables and, with a look of indignation, shook her head. "Where are the pumpkins?"

"Pumpkins are horrible," said Bigzy. "They taste of vom."

"Not to eat," said Ali. "To carve. You cut out shapes and put a candle inside."

"We don't do that over here," said Pogsy.

"So Ah can see. Your quaint Old-World customs are very strange."

"What you do in America is stranger," said Sarge, sitting on the crossbar of his bike. "Dressing up, knocking on doors and asking for goodies. I feel like a right prat."

"If a strange mister I didn't know gave uz goodies, me cousins would beat 'im up and chase him out of town," said Bigzy.

"Mine too," said Sarge.

"Bommie Night's better," said Reddy. "As long as you like fireworks."

"Who wants to banger a bog?" said Bigzy.

"That's inposs," said Pogsy.

"According to me bruvver, you just need to do it right," said Bigzy, defensively. "We've already got bangers."

"Tell you what," said Pogsy, "we'll work really hard and make loads of dosh. Then we'll spend it on a bag of goodies and a box of matches and go on a mission to find out if it's true."

By the time the gang had collected enough change it was almost dark. Grown-ups were coming home from work in droves, some on foot, others by pushbike. Whenever a car driver spotted the Guy, they slowed down and honked. The gang raised their thumbs in response. Pogsy caught a whiff of smoke and soot from somewhere down the street. Although his dad had moved over to a gas fire when he'd done up their house, there were plenty of houses about in this part of town that still relied on smelly old coal. Chimneys were supposed to ensure that the soot all went up, but they didn't work. It always fell somewhere, usually in the next street, leaving a thin veil of grime on the pavements and blackening all the cars. In Cleethorpes, there was a coalman who still delivered sacks of coal using a horse-drawn cart. Pogsy had seen him out and about just the other week.

While everyone was busy choosing penny chews, Weeble and his little brother Squib turned up. Both were dressed in grey parkas with fur-lined hoods.

"Wot'cha, Weebs," said Pogsy. "We haven't seen you about for yonks."

"Mam's at bingo and me dad's finally back a' sea," said Weeble, pulling down his hood to reveal a huge, round head covered in thick, black curly hair, fronted by a stubby nose. He was about the same height as Pogsy, but broader across the shoulders with short legs that bulged with muscle.

"I heard he'd busted a rib."

"Free," said Squib. "Ee's signed off, bu' ee never does wha' the doctor sez." Facially, Squib looked nothing like his brother, having a long, thin head with a nose like a Concorde. He definitely had the family build, including the massive shovel hands, even though he was only eight.

The two brothers added their favourite goodies to the bag. As the oldest-looking boy present, Sarge was given the responsibility of buying an extra packet of bangers and a box of matches.

Bigzy dug him in the ribs. "Go on," he whispered. "Don't be shy."

"Please, mister," said Sarge, looking at his shoes.

"Listen, son," said the shopkeeper. "I'm not fussed about selling you a few fireworks. Just let them off far away from my shop."

"Thank you, sir." Sarge lightened up. "Foggy first dibs," he yelled, thrusting his hand in the goodie bag and grabbing a chocolate frog.

Everyone else dived in, ripping the bag apart. While the gang argued over who should have the last Fruit Salad, Pogsy packed up the sodden Guy and strapped it into place on his bike, all the while sucking away on the biggest gobstopper he could find.

"It's mission time," he said, tucking his sopping hair behind his ears. "To the park and cubicle two."

According to Ali, ghosts and witches were now afoot, hiding behind every bush. Weeble pretended to be frightened and that spooked Squibly. He kept very close to his brother, warily avoiding dark crevices and back passages. Even a slight rustle of leaves set him off. People's Park was a short walk away. It was circular in construction and surrounded by well-lit, posh houses. Bam lived in one of them. The middle of the park was unlit. It had one particular loo that no-one liked to use, mainly because it was always jammed. Either the handle was busted or the flush didn't work or it was blocked. Even the council had given up on it. It was the most useless loo anywhere in town. The only people who used cubicle two were either new to the park, or else very desperate. As prime agitator, Bigzy led the way along the darkened walkways, which the gang all knew like the backs of their hands. When they reached the toilet block, Bigzy struck a match and walked inside. The rest of the gang followed.

"That stinks," said Reddy, poking open the door to the wretch-inducing cubicle.

Squib ducked down and pushed his way to the front. "It's fulla bobs," he squealed, holding his nose.

"Just what the doctor ordered," said Bigzy. "Who wants to do the honours?"

"Uz!" shouted Squib, raising his hand.

Bigzy handed one of the bangers that his neighbour had dropped in the hat earlier to the little lad. "These are Blackjacks. They're the most powerful bangers ever. Bury it so the fuse is sticking out, and after you've lit it, close the lid and leg it. But leave the bog door open."

Everyone stood back and let Squib get on with the filthy job of placing the banger. The truth was no-one wanted to go anywhere near the solid block of poo and paper, let alone push something into it. Squibly wasn't at all bothered.

Pogsy was confident that they had the right banger for the job. Blackjacks were a couple of pence more than normal bangers, but they had a much louder bang and could blow a tin can higher into the air. If you needed the best, you'd chose a Blackjack every time. From the middle of October onwards they were rarer than rocking-horse teeth. Newsagents sold out in minutes, and if one did have any spares, word soon went around. Bigzy had been really jammy to get three of them.

Squib lit the match and stared at the flame for an age, transfixed by its beauty. Only when it had burnt down almost to his fingers did he light the firework's fuse. He closed the lid as instructed and legged it, joining the rest of the gang at the entrance to the loos. The banger fizzed away, throwing out a cloud of smoke.

BOOM!

The toilet bowl shattered into a thousand pieces and debris flew everywhere, splattering the walls of the cubicle, the walls opposite the cubicle, and the floor and ceiling around it with a mix of pottery and soiled, soggy paper.

The aroma of spent gunpowder drifted lazily by.

Bigzy doubled over with laughter, tears streaming down his cheeks. He struggled to catch his breath. Weeble collapsed to the floor, pounding the soggy earth with his fists. The laughter was contagious. Pogsy caught it too. When they checked, the only thing left of the loo was the lid, which hung forlornly on its hinges. After that, there was no holding back. They became a ten-legged mirth machine without an off button.

"I'm off," said Sarge, jumping on his push-iron. "You should all do the same."

Ali's face was a picture. A mix of astonishment and mild disgust, although Pogsy was sure he saw the edges of her mouth turn up in a supressed smile. She climbed on the seat behind Sarge. "Bye, boys. We're going haunting. In future I think I'll stick to asking strangers for sweets."

"Parkie!" shouted Red Top suddenly, staggering to his feet.

"I... can't... move..." said Bigzy. "I... really... can't..."

"Me... neither..." said Pogsy, slapping his thighs.

"F... f... f... frig us," spluttered Weeble, "tha' were ace. Now runnnn!"

The gang scarpered in different directions. Pogsy pedalled hard, praying that the Guy held firm.

"Gizza pag!" shouted Reddy, running after him.

"Be quick." The best thing about a Chopper was that you could carry two lads at a time, provided they weren't fatties. Or a lad and a Guy, as long as you didn't mind people staring at you disapprovingly all the way home. It didn't help that his bike didn't have lights. But given the stealthy nature of the mission, he wouldn't have switched them on anyway.

The next day, word of the gang's exploits shot around the playground faster than Billy Whiz on a snort of sherbet. As it was one of Chip's stories, everyone took it with a pinch of salt. After school, a procession of lads paid a visit to the park loos on their bikes, to see the supposed mess for themselves. The area was taped off, with "Do Not Enter" signs at both ends of the loos. Not that it stopped anyone. Everyone who saw the results of Squib's handiwork agreed it was an impressive job. Within a day, Bigzy had earned himself a reputation as an explosives expert, which in turn prompted Steve to give him a new nickname. Henceforth, on the run up to Bommie Night, he was to be known as *Blaster Bogs*.

Historically speaking, there was a difference of opinion around town as to when Bommie Night was celebrated. Dad was a traditionalist and insisted it had to be held on the November 5th no matter what day it fell on, which by coincidence also happened to be Mum's birthday. The bonfire down Meggies' seafront was always lit on the nearest Saturday to the actual day, whereas the one on the playing fields down *Scaffa* was always lit on the nearest Friday. The biggest, most impressive bonfire of them all was located up near the docks on a piece of wasteland surrounding the old Ice House. This bonfire was a law unto itself. Nobody but the builders knew when it was going up.

As promised, but mainly due to consistent pester power, Dad took a drive with Pogsy, Steve and the Guy on the Saturday morning, two days before the big day. To begin with, Pogsy wasn't sure what to say. He and Steve had been riling each other up in the playground of late, for no good reason. It took less than a minute for them to share a joke and that broke the ice. Looking out for bonfires was something they had in common. They'd been doing it together for years. This year, for the first time ever, Pogsy was conscious of the lack of seatbelts in the back of Dad's old MG Magnette, due to a campaign on the TV imploring everyone to *Clunk Click Every Trip*. Steve noticed it too. He strapped in with an imaginary seatbelt. Pogsy nodded and did likewise.

Dad's car trundled around town, its engine burbling away. Every time he turned hard left, the exhaust pipe *bonked* from side to side. That was more or less normal. Periodically, there was a *pop* from somewhere under the bonnet. Dad paid it no attention, even though it was a new gripe from the ageing car. After a ten-minute drive down terraced streets that Pogsy only vaguely recognised, they reached a huge expanse of open ground, where the houses around the edges were being demolished row by row. It was desolate. A scar across the face of town. Mum said it was necessary. The old fisherman's quarter had to come down. The council said so. The houses were either too old to be sanitary, or else were too structurally unsafe to be lived in.

Every time he saw wanton destruction on such a large scale, Pogsy felt all contorted inside. It was as if his favourite pet had just died. His thoughts turned to No-Man's Land and the death throes of the dens. It still hurt to think about that day. He'd never really had the chance to say a proper goodbye, not in the way he'd wanted to. Then he saw the bonfire.

"Wow." He stared up at a Guy perched atop a single plank of wood at the apex of a towering structure built from old pallys, floorboards and roofing timbers. "It's dead huge. It's the most emassive bommie I've ever seen."

"It's a hundred-footer," said Steve, biting down on his bottom lip.

"A hundred and fifty," said Pogsy in amazement. "It's gotta be at least two hundred across."

"Three hundred," said Steve.

The Guy in the back nodded his approval.

Behind the bonfire loomed the old Ice House. Once, it had been used to store blocks of ice for the fishing trade. Now it was derelict, just a shell of a building, but with an ominous reputation across town. Supposedly it was the meeting place for the notorious Ice House Gang, who were the hardest gang in town. Dad slowed down. Pogsy felt the hairs on the back of his neck stand up. He stared at the building silhouetted against the cold November sky. None of the original windows were intact, having fallen out long ago. The rectangular holes that were left were covered by rough planks of wood. The cast-iron gates at the front were padlocked shut with yards and yards of thick chain. In places, the three-storey concrete structure had been struck by a demolition ball, which had gouged great chunks from the walls. There were blackened patches all around the ground floor and the edges of many of the windows, where fires had been lit. It was impossible to tell if the roof had collapsed, not without getting up close, and this was something Pogsy had sworn never to do. He wondered if the Ice House had a secret underground cellar. That would be it. That would be where the gang met. When they weren't scrapping with the Nunsthorpe Gypos, or the Bradley Boot Boys, or the Park Street Mafia, or the Scaffa Skins.

"I don't reckon the Ice House Gang are real," said Steve.

"Reddy says they are," replied Pogsy. "His dad knows them."

"Say they are real. Which I doubt. Our gang could have them."

"They're all teenagers." Pogsy screwed up his face in contempt. "That's what Reddy says. Anyways, we need to sort out the Wingmen and the Hard Nuts first. Smiffy threatened to threaten Bingo the other day."

"The Convamorons couldn't hurt a fly," said Steve. "All you gotta do is say *Boo*! and they'll run a mile."

"Maybe," said Pogsy. "But we should bash one of them in, just to be sure."

"Are you two having gang trouble again?" asked Dad.

"Please, Mister Green," said Steve. "It's not been right since the council destroyed No-Man's Land and took away our dens."

"Then find somewhere else."

"But there isn't anywhere," said Pogsy, his voice coming out as a whine. "No-Man's Land is rubbish now. If we had somewhere like the Ice House it would be different."

"Steve," said Dad, changing the subject, "how's the firework collection coming on?"

"Brilliant, Mister Green! We've got loads."

"We're doing another *Penny for the Guy* tomorrow," said Pogsy. "There's some new shops that we haven't been to before."

"I wish I could be there," said Steve, "but you know what my dad's like. Especially on Sundays."

As it turned out, the *new shops* claim wasn't quite true. Bigzy's plan was so off-the-wall that Pogsy thought it best to go over it first. While they talked, Weeble and Squib bickered over who was going to be first in the bath later.

"This is Wingmen territory," said Red Top, pointing to the gang's Battle Map, which was one of his prized possessions. "They own Convamore Road down to Pasture Street, then across to Hainton Avenue and back to Welholme Road. This bit here – Ladysmith Road down to Fiveways, then down Carr Lane to Clee Road and Weelsby Road, and back to Ladysmith Road – that's divided up between the Hard Nuts and the Old Clee Wheelers. We don't know exactly where their boundaries run because we don't go there. Clee playing fields is neutral. I shouldn't need to tell you that."

"That puts Bigzy's church right on the boundary between the Wingmen and the Hard Nuts," said Pogsy, stabbing the page with his finger. "Smack bang in the middle of enemy territory. That makes it more than a simple *Penny for the Guy*. It's a raid."

"Bet'cha they won't dare attack uz though," said Bigzy. "Weeble's the hardest kid in our year. The plan is simps: we set the Guy up on a barrow, wheel it in five minutes before the service ends and bingo! We've got a captive audience. As soon as everyone comes out, I'll give it the old song-and-dance routine with me sad eyes, while you lot run around with hats collecting change. It's perfect. We're in and out in less than ten minutes. Fifteen tops. Trust uz – nowt can go wrong."

The following evening, Pogsy rushed home from school, desperate to get the bonfire lit. Although he wasn't certain, he expected it was in the same place as last year and the year before: Mister Morton's yard, which was somewhere near the Pyewipe Industrial Estate, located due west of the docks. Pogsy was so excited, he could hardly concentrate when Dad gave Mum her birthday present and card. All he was bothered about was his Guy. The Guy they'd almost lost, thanks to Bigzy's idiotic plan. He'd had to abandon his best homemade go-kart and that was bad enough. If he'd taken Dad's wheelbarrow, which was the original plan, he'd be in massive trouble. He rubbed the knuckles on his right hand. He'd skinned them in a ruck the previous night. He was sure he'd hit the other boy hard, but a metal fence had got in the way when they'd tussled with each other. There were scrapes on his knees where he'd fallen to the ground. Thankfully, he didn't have a black eye. He was convinced it was going to swell where the lad had lamped him good and proper.

While Mum dressed Ellie up warm, Sam gave Pogsy a handful of jumping jacks for the Guy's pockets. He soon forgot about his injuries. Between them they added four Roman Candles to help keep the arms and legs straight, and chuckling madly installed an air-bomb for a willy.

The family drove through town in Dad's old MG, Mum sitting up front. All the while, they watched the sky for rockets and listened out for explosions. Pogsy sat in the middle of the back seat, holding Ellie tightly on his knee, Sam to one side, Ali to the other. The Guy, along with all the food, was relegated to the boot. Dad turned into the Nunsthorpe Estate. It was an area of town that Pogsy had never actually been to before. He knew it by reputation though.

"Where *are* you going?" asked Mum.

Dad ignored her and kept on driving.

"This is like the fourth of July," said Ali, pointing at a front garden with a broken-down fence where multiple Catherine Wheels were spinning away and shooting out trails of sparks.

"What's that?" asked Pogsy, bouncing his sister up and down.

"It's the day the Yanks celebrate beating the Brits and winning their country," said Sam.

"With the best fireworks ever." Ali poked Pogsy in the ribs.

A fizzing banger bounced off the bonnet of Dad's car. Pogsy looked behind but he didn't see it detonate. Instead, he heard a soft *pop*. It was too pathetic to be a Blackjack. On all sides, they were surrounded by terraces of houses built from red and brown brick. Most of them had tatty curtains; some had no curtains at all. Others had their windows boarded up, or panes of glass with cracks running across them, which showed up clearly every time a firework went off. Multiple explosions ripped through the twilight on either side, throwing coloured fragments of light high up into the air. A Screecher echoed off the walls and pavement, sounding like the death throes of an impaled alien. It was soon joined by another. A rocket shot horizontally down the street, orange fire spitting from its tailpipe. It exploded in a cacophony of colour.

"Alan!" Mum's scream was almost the same pitch as the aliens outside.

"Right," said Dad, "that's enough of demolition alley. Who wants to see the bommie?"

"Me!" shouted Pogsy. Involuntarily, he ducked to avoid a barrage of fireworks that skittered over the car. Two neighbours who lived opposite each other were engaged in a war of traffic lights, shooting coloured fountains of fire over the road at each other. For a moment, Pogsy wished he lived in a street like this. Then he saw a three-legged dog looking quizzically at a lamp post and changed his mind.

As they drove onwards to Mister Morton's yard, memories of the previous evening flooded back. Quite how the other gang had known they were going to be outside the church remained a mystery. The ambush, when it happened, was sudden. Five boys had rushed at them from a dark passageway and demanded all their money. Weeble had instantly seen red and charged, striking the biggest lad in the belly, while the rest of the gang took up a defensive position around the go-kart. When the lads' resolve wavered, Pogsy and Reddy had broken ranks and gone for them, drawing blood. The assailants soon panicked and fled, inviting chase.

Pogsy pushed the memory back into its box. Dad pulled his car into Mister Morton's yard and parked up near the edge of a well-lit stockade, just next to an old petrol tanker that had had its wheels removed. It was surrounded by a collection of rusty old car parts. The bonfire was located roughly in the middle of the yard, away from the surrounding fences. It was constructed from palettes and broken timbers, harvested from the streets of partly demolished houses that littered this area of town, which was, for the most part, an extension of the fishermen's quarter. A circle of silver balls, glistening like futuristic ostrich eggs, marked the bonfire's perimeter. Each package contained a tater, to be cracked open once the fire had done its work.

Pogsy jumped out of the car holding his nose. The nearby Pyewipe Estate was renowned for its fertiliser factory, which converted fish guts into plant food. It was always surrounded by screaming gulls, even when the factory was closed, and the whole area had a sickly stench about it. He was determined not to sniff the poisoned air, which reminded him of burning fish poo. Breathing through his mouth was even worse. It left him with the horrible taste of dog vom. The Guy had the right idea. He'd thought to bring a mask.

Steve and his sister were busy chasing each other around with sparklers. Pogsy pestered his dad for one, then his mum. He was shooed away. Uncle Peter, Steve's dad, helped with unloading the grub from the boot of the car. Steve looked a lot like him, right down to the tombstone front teeth. Barging in, Pogsy took possession of the Guy, but not before Steve had had a chance to check the needlework.

"Not bad," he said, "but not up to my standard, obviously. You've used a machine. That means Aunt Elizabeth did it."

"It was deffo uz," grinned Pogsy. With Sam's assistance, he manoeuvred the Guy into pride of place, making sure it was secured with bits of string.

Aunt Susan, Steve's mum, gave Pogsy's mum a birthday present and card. She was a jolly missis with a voice like liquid honey. Mum thanked her then, with a glass of punch in one hand and a cigarette in the other, supervised Ellie, who was busy chasing Steve's sister with a sparkler. She was too old now to try to eat the flames but there was no shortage of divots to trip up in.

Pogsy finally got his hands on a sparkler. He made sure Ali had one too. They grabbed a couple of glasses of orange squash and ran around laughing and squealing, ducking amongst the other children. The fiery metal sticks spluttered out. With all the twirling about, they'd lost their shapes. Pogsy begged a couple more and the dance began anew.

Chip, his sister and his dad were the next to arrive. Pogsy watched Mister Flowers put a box in Dad's car boot. Dad gave him a different box in return.

"What do you think about our frigates coming home and leaving our lads defenceless up north?" asked Dad.

"Them damn Icicles'll tek the pish, Al," said Mister Flowers, "an' tha' in' good fer business."

Dad nodded in agreement. "We lost the last cod war. Before our time, eh? We can't afford to lose this one too. If you ask me, there's something bad brewing. My money's on Heath selling us out."

"Meks sense. Never trusted tha' bloke."

Mister Flowers sent Chip and his sister off to play then headed straight for the beer keg, pouring himself a pint. He leaned back against the tanker, slicked-back hair glistening in the torch light, pulled up the collar on his jacket and lit a fag.

Red Top arrived in an old banger of a car with one busted headlamp. Pogsy heard it spluttering down the road long before it came into sight. Red Top's younger brothers, who Steve had nicknamed Blue Top and Silver Top, got out first. Reddy followed. They all wore matching parkas. Mister Wilson climbed out and kicked the wheel of his car with a steelie. He was going bald on top and he always tried to hide it with a flat cap. He half-smiled and half-frowned, exposing his front teeth, which were made for opening bottles of beer. On his top lip lived a really thin tash no thicker than a caterpillar.

Pogsy sat down on an empty wooden crate with Ali beside him. It was the first time they'd spent any real time together since the day after Ali's party. "What do you think of Bommie Night?" he asked.

"It's really great. Thanks so much for inviting me."

"It's the second most important day of the year, after Christmas, so I thought you should see."

"How are you getting on with Pollyanna?"

Pogsy shrugged his shoulders. "OK. I suppose. She made me buy Mud's new single even though I don't like it that much."

"What happened to your chin?" asked Ali.

"Nowt," said Pogsy.

"Were you fighting?"

In the poor light, Pogsy found it difficult to tell what Ali was thinking. The lines on her face were solid and hard; she wasn't laughing.

"Only a bit."

"Ah wish you wouldn't."

It wasn't clear to Pogsy why Ali didn't like scrapping. She'd once said that her mom was a fighter. He'd seen an old picture of her near the Statue of Liberty and she was tiny with lots of hair and a popstar smile. He doubted she'd stand a chance against any of the fishwives who worked down on the docks. According to Mister Flowers, they regularly beat seven shades of slop out of each other, usually over a drunken husband who'd put his hands in the wrong place. Pogsy had blushed when he heard that story. He'd seen a few girl fights in the playground and they were nothing like boy fights. It was all biting and scratching and pulling hair. He wondered if Ali's mom was a hair-puller like the girls, or a punch-in-the-facer like the fishwives of Grimsby.

Ali's face suddenly lit up. "Ah spoke to Pop earlier," she said. "He says that, even though the war's nearly done, oil production's still been cut and there's a crisis coming."

"You've told me so much about him, I really want to meet him."

"He says he's needed over in the States. He might not be back before Christmas." Ali's previous burst of light vanished and became a sudden outpouring of tears. "Pat. What if Ah don't ever see him again?"

It was the first time Pogsy had seen Ali cry. He put his arm around her. She pushed him away, but not hard. Hopefully, if there was a crisis, it would come soon. Anything that stopped David Cassidy from being Number One for another week had to be a good thing.

"Hey, Chimpy," said Steve, arriving with typical impeccable timing to destroy the moment. "I bet you can't climb that fence over there and stand on the top."

"Watch me," said Ali, drying her eyes and regaining her composure. Seconds later, she was off. Pogsy watched her go, making a conscious effort to hide his disappointment in front of Steve.

For the next hour, grown-ups who Pogsy didn't know that well kept on arriving. There were people that Uncle Peter knew and people Dad worked with. A few teachers from Mum's school came armed with cards and presents. Bingo's dad dropped him off, said hello to Dad and took a box out of the car boot but didn't stay. By the time the gates were closed, there were cars parked all the way down the street. Pogsy estimated there were a hundred guests. Steve reckoned two hundred. They settled on two hundred and fifty.

With the gates shut, Uncle Peter called for silence.

In the distance a hungry gull cried out, mocking him.

"What are we here for?" he shouted.

"Bommie Night!" yelled all the boys and girls together.

"What do we want?"

"Bommie!"

"What did you say?"

"Bommie!" yelled all boys and girls, louder than before.

"I can't hear you."

"Bommie! Bommie!" yelled all the boys and girls and grown-ups together. The little kids finally got the hang of it and joined in too.

While the shouting was going on, Dad circled around the pile of wood with a can of petrol, pouring it around the edges, making sure it splashed all over the strategically placed newspaper and cardboard that poked out between gaps in the framework of wood.

"Stand back, everyone!" shouted Uncle Peter.

Dad struck a match and used it to set fire to a rag wrapped around a big stick, which he then lobbed at the bonfire. A ball of flame erupted with a *whoosh*, licking away at the Guy. Everyone stepped back. As Pogsy watched, the fire died down a bit. Dad had taught him and Sam never to throw petrol on a bin fire because petrol and turps were both very dangerous in a confined space. Petrol was only to be used to light bonfires. And even then, you had to stand well back and make sure you hadn't splashed any on you.

Respect the fire.

Pogsy rubbed his hands together and watched the Guy. It wasn't long for the world now. Steve joined him.

"Between us," said Steve with a wink, "we make a really good Guy."

"The best," said Pogsy. For the first time that evening he felt warm.

Mister Morton's yard had everything that was required for an outstanding Bommie Night party. The seagulls certainly thought so, and they kept their beady eyes on proceedings from the fence line, forever on the lookout for unattended food. The focus of their attention was an old oil drum that had been sawn in half to create a pair of makeshift grills, which were set up side by side. Dad speared bangers on one grill while Uncle Peter flipped burgers on the other. Between the two cooks stood a camping stove with a pot of steaming onions, slow-frying in butter. On a table to the side of the cooking area lay a mountain of shaped buns, along with a pile of paper napkins and six squeezy bottles of mustard and tomato sauce.

Ten minutes after the eating started, the table looked like it had recently hosted a dogfight.

Pogsy and Steve had a sausage-eating competition. Red Top boasted he could eat three burgers in a bun, but then couldn't fit his creation in his gob. Chip claimed he'd once done fifty but was too full to try it that night.

Mum's fudge stall did a roaring trade with the little kids, while Aunt Susan's drink stall kept everyone from going thirsty.

From time to time an empty can of hairspray hidden in the depths of the bonfire would detonate, catching the grown-ups unawares and making them spill their drinks. Ellie, along with all the other little kids, shrieked loudly with every *boom*.

Eventually, the moment that Pogsy had been waiting for arrived. The Guy atop the fire caught alight, exploding in a fury of colour, flames leaping from all its appendages. Everyone roared. Then came the chant:

Remember, remember the Fifth of November,
Gunpowder, treason and plot.
I see no reason why gunpowder treason,
Should ever be forgot!

The air-bomb exploded right on cue, blowing the Guy's mask clean off his head. A loud cheer went up.

Dad called everyone's attention to the far end of the yard, where a great metal trunk loaded with fireworks was located. Sam's mate Jimbo, who'd appeared sometime after the bommie was lit, assisted Sam with the rockets, while Dad and Uncle Peter lit all the fireworks that required ramming into the ground, except they used bricks instead to hold them in place.

There were pops and crackles and whistles and bangs, rainbow plumes and showers of sparks in red, white, green and blue. It took ages to light everything. Not that the crowd minded.

Pogsy breathed in deeply. He loved the smell of burning gunpowder. There were clouds of the stuff. Along with the smoke from the fire, you'd be able to smell it on your clothes and your hair for days.

It was a good smell.

The smell of a successful Bommie Night.

With the fireworks done for the year Pogsy beckoned to Steve and Reddy.

"What is it?" asked Steve.

"Show him," said Pogsy.

Red Top unzipped his parka and lifted up his jumper, to show a raised red mark flanked by blisters.

"Nasty," said Steve. "Looks like a firework wound."

"We woz jumped," said Red Top. "Last night."

"Why didn't you say something at school?" asked Steve.

"I did," said Red Top. "Except you weren't there. You were twaggin' it, building bonfires."

"Oh, yeah." Steve sniggered to himself. "Miss thinks it was a doctor's appointment."

Pogsy picked up the reigns of the story. "We did a church service with the Guy. It was Bigzy's idea. He said that we'd make loads of money, but unfortunately everyone kept on saying they'd given all their change away already. In the end we made about three pence, a bottle top and a button. Then we were attacked. Against Weebs, the lads didn't stand a chance. They ran off and we followed them, tugging the Guy behind uz on our best soapbox racer."

"It's a good racer, that," said Steve. "I own half of it."

"When we got to No-Man's Land, that's when the real ambush happened," said Red Top. "Lads appeared out of the dark and blocked off all the entrances."

"We made a defence ring around the kart," said Pogsy. "Just in case they were after the Guy."

"It was pitch black," said Red Top. "We had no idea how many we were up against."

"They let off a rocket along the ground," said Pogsy. "It ended up stuck in the fence behind uz, where it exploded."

"They had Roman Candles," said Red Top. "They were at the far end of No-Man's Land, waving them about and calling uz names."

Steve screwed up his face in disbelief, gnawing away at his bottom lip. "How many?"

"Twenty at least," said Pogsy.

"Plus five at each of the entrances," added Red Top.

"Are you absolutely poz?" said Steve.

"I'm your *Second*." Pogsy shook his head.

"One of their gang got a length of drainpipe out, which had a shield attached," said Red Top. "He mounted it on his shoulder, like a bazooka, and aimed it at us. Another lad stuffed a rocket into the tube from behind."

"It hit Reddy in the ribs, bounced off and exploded," said Pogsy. "It could have taken his eye out."

"So who was it?" said Steve. "I'm guessing the Convamorons *and* Wingnut's Wankers together."

"Nope," said Pogsy. "It was the Old Clee Wheelers."

Steve scratched his head. "But after last time they're the weakest gang of all. Are you sure it wasn't the Wankers or the Convamorons *pretending* to be the Wheelers?"

"Poz," said Red Top. "They had the Wheeler's banner. The strange thing is, they weren't chanting 'Wheelers', they were chanting 'Tramps!'"

"That's my nickname for them," said Steve with a toothy grin. "Sooty hates it."

Red Top nodded. "That's why it dun't make no sense."

"After they hit Reddy, we hid behind the kart," said Pogsy. "But they kept on firing rockets at uz. Squib was beeling his eyes out. Weeble went funny like he does. He was all for fighting the lot of them. In the end we waited until the lad with the bazooka was reloading then charged at the weakest-looking guards."

"We had to abandon the racer," said Red Top. "Soz about that."

"I went back this morning for a looksee," said Pogsy. "They'd bloomin' well torched it."

"At least we gave their guards a good pasting," said Red Top, rubbing his lip. "They tried to hold out while the rest of their gang got there but we were too strong for them. Weeble has to take most of the credit. He's a steamroller. But Pogsy did good as well."

"And you," said Pogsy. "The Wheelers kicking off again changes everything. For starters, Clee playing fields aren't safe anymore."

"We don't use them that much anyway," said Steve. "The park's better. Maybe it's finally time to move our base and give up on No-Man's Land."

"No!" shrieked Pogsy. "We can't do that! It's ours. We'll look like puffs."

Steve hopped from one leg to the other, like he was busting for a wee. "I'll talk to everyone tomoz. Work out what to do next."

"Somehow," huffed Pogsy, "the Wheelers have risen from the grave like a demented Dracula. This time they're stronger than ever and it looks like they're out for revenge."

Seven: The Cold Store

It was a shock to discover that the Old Clee Wheelers were back to full strength so quickly after their last defeat. Pogsy remembered how they'd tried it on the previous summer when Sooty, their leader, had laid full claim to No-Man's Land because he was riled up after someone had wee'd on his dog and no-one would tell him who'd done it. All the other gangs had got together and challenged him to a scrap, which the Wheelers conclusively lost. They'd retreated in shame to lick their wounds. When a gang was thoroughly beaten and their leader forced to submit, they often broke up afterwards. Because the Wheelers had been quiet for so long, Pogsy had assumed that this was what had happened to them. If he was honest, he hadn't expected to hear from them ever again. It wasn't possible to know for sure though, as the Wheelers went to a different school. This was also true of the Hard Nuts. Only the Wingmen shared the same playground.

The next morning, Red Top had feedback from the milk-vine that confirmed the Old Clee Wheelers were no more. They'd finally given up the ghost on Halloween. The Tramps had risen from their ashes. The word was they were trying it on everywhere. That night after school, Smiffy, the leader of the Convamore Hard Nuts was waiting by the school gates with his Second, Mopey Joe, who had a birthmark shaped like bloody bogie on the side of his face. They stood under a flag of truce, which was more of a snot-encrusted hanky than a banner. Smiffy was a stout lad with eyebrows that looked like hairy caterpillars. He had a wart on the knuckle of one thumb. Pogsy had heard that if he poked you with it, you'd get wart disease, so he kept his eye on it at all times.

"Them Bike Tramps is outta order," said Smiffy, waving his thumb about. "They shifted their markers. We need 'elp getting uz old territory back."

"We need help getting No-Man's Land back," said Pogsy. "They've taken that over as well."

"That patch of wasteland ain't no good to no-one," said Smiffy, "and I ain't goin' over the top for it."

"Meks sense," said Mopey Joe.

"Then we aren't going over the top to help you," said Steve.

"'Ave a word wi' Wingnut, will ya?" said Smiffy. "See what 'e sez. He ain't talking to uz since I fretened to wart 'im in the peepers."

Pogsy tried again to engage the Hard Nuts over No-Man's Land. He argued that it was an agreed neutral space, available to everyone, and it was just a coincidence that it happened to be located within The Kings' boundaries. Except the link-mesh fence surrounding the chunk of communal ground was now marked with a sign saying "Tramp Land Keep Out!"

The response from the Hard Nuts was the same.

"It's nowt to do wiv uz."

Everyone went their separate ways. Pogsy felt dejected. Steve tromped off in the direction of his house, a look of defeat on his face. Red Top cursed. He went home to redraw the lines on the Battle Map.

The following morning during break, Steve, Pogsy and Red Top stood in the middle of the school netball court, in the *parlay circle*, waiting for Wingnut to arrive. The north wind was blowing Baltic hard, scattering withered leaves across the playground. Pogsy's knees knocked together. Steve made a quip about Wingnut's ears and the dangers of him taking off if his gang didn't hold him down. Pogsy and Red Top laughed nervously.

"Wot'cha," said Wingnut, stepping into the circle flanked by two of his Wingmen.

"Wot'cha," said Steve.

"Alright, Pogs," said Wingnut.

"Alright, Wingy," said Pogsy.

"We've got some stuff to discuss," said Steve.

"Don't tell uz: Bike Tramps."

"They ambushed uz and took No-Man's Land," said Red Top.

"I 'eard," said Wingnut. "They brought ordinance."

Pogsy didn't know what *ornidance* meant, so he took a guess. "They shot uz up with rockets and bangers. It's a good job there's a worldwide shortage of Blackjacks."

"We need your help," said Steve. "No-Man's Land belongs to all of us. We have to take it back."

Wingnut turned, chuckling, to Gecko. "'Ear that? The greatest Steve in the world needs our help."

"Nowt to do wiv uz," said Gecko.

Pogsy stared at Gecko's freckles like they were a page in a join-the-dots book. He smirked when he saw a willy. Gecko frowned back.

"There's nowt there but muck," said Wingnut. "Why should we fight for a pile of old muck?"

"Not so long ago you said it was yours," said Pogsy.

"We only said that to rile you lot up," said Greebo, the second Wingman. He was a small boy with a mop of greasy black hair and eyes that looked like ping-pong balls.

"It's *all* of ours," said Pogsy. "It's where our dens were."

"*Were*," said Gecko. "They're no' there now."

"Aye," said Wingnut. "We're officially out. No-Man's Land is useless to uz. Plus, it can't be defended. Soz, mate, you're on your own."

"The Hard Nuts have lost out too," said Pogsy. "They've asked for our help."

"Not 'appening," said Wingnut. "I'd rather stick me nuts in a mangle."

The three Wingmen turned and left the parlay circle, sniggering away like a trio of Mutleys in search of a medal.

That evening, Pogsy and Reddy walked home via No-Man's Land, looking for stray Bike Tramps to bash. Even though they kept their wits about them, it still felt like they were trespassers on their own land. Pogsy chuntered away, talking more at Red Top than to him, saying everything that came into his head out loud. Every few seconds, Reddy looked over his shoulder.

"If we take it on the chin," said Pogsy, "their raids are just gonna get worse. They're gonna grab land in all directions until they run up against the Wingmen."

"You heard what Wingy said. Not 'is prob. Cuts both ways."

"We have to make an alliance," said Pogsy. "Otherwise we're all finished."

"I can't see it mesen," said Red Top, "not now Wingy and Smiffy hate each other's guts. I gotta go, Pogs."

"Before you do, there's summut I've been meaning to ask you. Since Donut left, I haven't got an official best mate. How's about it?"

"Yeah?" said Red Top, puffing out his chest. "Of course. We've been secret best mates for ages. It's long overdue."

"One day, when I have me own gang, you'll be me Second," said Pogsy. "We've done loads of scraps together over the years. You've never let uz down."

"Yeah. You're right," said Red Top, holding his head high. "I've never legged it from a fight in me life."

"Official best mates," said Pogsy, holding out his hand.

Red Top nearly fell for the prank, only pulling away at the last and raising his hand to his nose, to sign the pact with a raspberry.

For the next few days, Pogsy mulled things over. Despite three good sleeps, nothing came to him. Steve had said he was going to formulate a plan, but instead he'd gone into hiding, claiming that his dad had told him he had to help out at the bagwash. Bingo, whose braininess was legendary, suggested building a Trojan Horse, towing it to Old Clee, climbing inside and waiting. The only flaw in the plan was that they didn't have the materials to construct a massive wooden horse, and even if they did, based on recent experience, the Tramps would likely set fire to it and then wee on the remains. The next best option was to steal a radioactive serum from a research lab located on the Humber Bank where Pogsy's Grandad worked on the gate as a security guard. However, the outcome was far from guaranteed. If one of them turned uncontrollably green, the situation might end up far worse than it already was.

Bam suggested coming to an agreement with the Tramps whereby they rented back No-Man's Land. Pogsy knew what happened when you paid bullies: the next time, the price went up. And so on, until you had nothing left. That was how bullies worked, and it was the reason they had a gang in the first place. Bigzy was keen to airlift his cousins in but that wasn't really an option. If his family got involved in their troubles, then it wouldn't be long before Uncle Fagin took over and turned the gang into a profitable criminal enterprise.

While Pogsy continued to tear his hair out, things took a turn for the better on the home front. An enormous weight was lifted from Dad's chest when Mister Armstrong called to demand Sam apologise to his pooch. Dad argued with the not-so-ex-copper on the doorstep, as he always did when anyone came to the house telling him what he should do. Eventually, he relented and asked Sam to do the right thing. Sam said he was very sorry and promised not to do it again. After miserable

Mister Armstrong with the jowly fizzog had left, pulling his sorry-looking jowly-faced pooch behind him, Dad punched the air.

"Yes!" he shouted. "Up yours, Armstrong!"

Pogsy and Sam gurned at each other. Mum tutted and continued to thumb her way through a fashion magazine. Ellie made "up yours" her new phrase of the day and kept on saying it out loud. Mum shook her head in despair.

"Mum?" said Pogsy. "What would you do if you were in a gang and you had trouble with a bigger gang?"

"Gangs should be banned," said Mum. "They are at my school."

"That's not fair," said Pogsy.

"You should persuade the bigger gang to split up," said Mum. "If they won't, then the right thing to do is to split up yourself. Problem solved. Once the bigger gang no longer has any enemies, *ipso facto*, they'll split up too."

Pogsy didn't know what an *ipsoid factor* was exactly, other than it was a film starring Michael Caine which involved taking people's brains out, washing them in detergent and then putting them back in again. He knew better than to grill his mum for details though.

That evening the news headlines were all about the Second Cod War officially coming to an end. The announcer on the BBC used his sternest voice to declare that the United Kingdom had formally agreed to limit its catch to a hundred and thirty thousand tons of fish a year. This caused Dad to explode like a volcano full of swear words.

"Damn Scrobs!" he shouted, shaking his fist at the TV screen. "What's our government thinking? I swear, they'll be the death of this town."

"Alan!" said Mum, wagging her telling-off finger back and forth. "Don't use that word in front of the children."

"Damn?" said Dad. "They've heard that plenty."

"The other one. I don't want them using it at school."

That very second, Pogsy knew he had a new swear word. It was funny how his hearing never quite worked properly with words he hadn't heard before unless they were rude. Then he managed to hear them perfectly first time.

By the time the weekend arrived there were only four people in his immediate circle of friends that Pogsy hadn't sought advice from. Ellie was too young to come up anything sensible that didn't involve dolls and teddies, Missis D was too old and Nan Eagle was too nice. Which left Ali, who he'd dismissed as being a girl with girl views on gangs and fighting. In desperation he'd tried to tell her on the way home from school how the Old Clee Wheelers, who'd always been the biggest gang by far, had tried to take over the whole of No-Man's Land a few years back, and the only way to stop them had been an alliance of gangs, which had kept the peace for ages until the building of the cold store had marmalised everything.

"*Marmalised*?" she'd said. "That's so quaint."

Pogsy couldn't remember exactly what he'd said after that. There was something about the Wheelers getting gobby every six months and needing shutting up, except the other gangs wouldn't join forces this time, all because Smiffy had grown a wart and Wingy hated his guts. Then he'd talked about scrapping and his best fight ever, and Ali had stuck her fingers in her ears and said "Abracadabra" over and over until he'd finished.

The last thing Ali had said was, "Why don't you persuade everyone to build a den together."

Which was easier said than done.

Pogsy slithered through a narrow gap in the chain-link fence that ran around the perimeter of the electricity company located next to his house, near to the lamppost opposite his front door. It bathed the world in a hue of pale apricot. He'd first scouted the electricity board's yard for likely dens two years ago, and in that time nothing had changed. It was still as useless as ever. Between him and Red Top, they'd looked everywhere.

At least twice.

He removed his lucky troll from his pocket and in desperation gave it a rub and made two wishes, the first being that his troll would work this time.

Something landed by his foot.

He looked up to see what he thought was someone standing a good twenty feet away, dressed in a black tracksuit.

"Who's there?" he said suspiciously. "Is that you Bigzy?"

Whoever it was, they were moving around a lot, never keeping still, not even for a second, looking and listening intently to every sound. Without warning, the figure performed a backflip, landing cleanly on both feet.

"I wish I could do that," said Pogsy to the stranger. "Who are you?"

The figure turned and moved swiftly in the opposite direction.

Slowly and cautiously, but without fear, he gave chase across No-Man's Land, keeping an eye out for Tramps. He passed the remains of his old box racer, pummelled into the mud. The kart had been viciously smashed to bits, its wheels ripped off, then the whole lot set on fire. He clenched his fists and stared into the dark, daring any Tramp observers to issue a challenge. All was quiet on the Western front. On the other side of No-Man's Land, the figure turned right and crossed a badly maintained car park covered in loose gravel. The tarmac surface had disintegrated, leaving a minefield of potholes. It was a clone of every other car park in town. The figure made a beeline for a tall, imposing concrete wall topped with barbed wire, stopping by one of its corners. Pogsy walked slowly, trying his best to ignore the walls of the cold store and shuddering at the thought of what those horrible council men had done to the dens.

Under the watchful pale orange glow of a pair of sodium streetlights, Pogsy saw that in one direction the wall ran for miles in a straight line. His view was partially obscured by a tall bush, but the wall was taller still, seemingly reaching to the sky. In the other direction the wall ran straight for perhaps two hundred feet before turning away from them, creating a huge concrete rectangle. Just beyond the nearest corner, set back from the car park, was an electricity sub-station marked out by warning signs and claims of instant death. He'd been in such a sub-station once before, shortly after Sparksy had developed an unhealthy obsession with generators. That was the night Georgie Porgie had had his willy blown off. Everyone had hollered at him not to stand on the wall and wee on the power supply, but he took no notice whatsoever until a crackling blue spark had leapt up and zapped him clean between the legs. The poor lad had been in hospital for weeks. The rumour from Chip was that he'd have to wee out of a plastic tube forever.

The figure moved on gracefully, its movements fluid and dynamic, following the wall until it reached the tall bush. It squeezed behind. Up close, Pogsy saw the bush was made up of a number of tall, interwoven strands of gorse. He followed and carelessly snagged his trackie bottoms on the spiky plant, allowing the figure to get quite a lead on him. He disentangled himself, accidentally pricked his forefinger and squealed in pain. Behind the bush was a ten-foot-high wire fence. He scaled the obstacle by using its diagonal concrete support beam for leverage. At the top, he squeezed through a gap in the barbed wire and flipped down, landing on a bed of gravel with a satisfying *crunch*. It was a short walk to a second fence, similar to the first. On the other side, grown-ups had thoughtfully installed a flat-topped wooden hut, which came to just below the level of the barbed wire. The figure, who Pogsy assessed to be a lad about his own age with the agility of a monkey, beckoned him to follow.

Too easy.

He clambered up and over the second fence, landing on the shed's asphalt roof. From there, he saw the figure get a leg up onto the first of a series of long, exposed steel bolts that acted as handholds and footholds, extending in a run all the way up to the top of the wall. It looked scary and, in Pogsy's estimation, the climb was impossible. And besides, it was the cold store. After the death of the dens, he'd sworn never to have anything to do with it. The thought of breaking his word filled him with dread.

He'd stay here.

He had to.

The figure reached the top of the wall, where it stood with its hands on its hips, looking down at him.

Pogsy gulped.

He wasn't about to be bettered by a stranger.

He bigged himself up until his confidence overflowed, then climbed, ignoring the jelly in his legs. It took all his willpower to remain calm and not look down. Finally, he reached the top and hauled himself upright. From on high he saw the compound in all its glory. A series of concrete posts that were angled inwards at about forty-five degrees ran all the way around the top of the wall. The posts supported three runs of barbed wire, each set a foot apart, which protected the entire yard. It was easy to slip between them and climb down. The only problem was the fifty-foot drop to the ground. At least it looked like fifty boys' feet laid end to end. In grown-up feet, it was probably less.

The lad moved away from him. Pogsy saw he was wearing some sort of face covering, so only his eyes were visible. He sat down, dangling his legs into the void, and shook his head in amazement, wondering how on earth the figure had found its way up here, and bemused as to why he'd never considered the climb himself. He scanned the enclosure, concluding it was easily the size of a football pitch. What was most astonishing were the piles and piles of sawn timber. It was more wood than he'd ever seen in his life, arranged in four long lines that went on forever. Between each line was a gap, the width of a road. In the distance, under floodlights, he saw a forklift truck speeding up and down the furthest line. At the very end of the lot, he spied a workman's hut. Behind the hut, cutting across the yard, was a chain-link fence with two massive gates to the right of the shed, topped with barbed wire. He looked at each of the columns of wood more closely. They were made up of thousands and thousands of wooden planks, all neatly packaged together in bundles and laid out end to end. Each of the planks was possibly fifteen feet long. Every thirty feet there was a gap. Wide enough for a boy to squeeze between, but not wide enough for a grown-up.

Pogsy's brain-cogs switched up a gear.

"This is a brilliant discovery," he whispered softly, mouthing the words. "I simply gotta find a way in." He felt his cogs switch up another gear. In his head, he performed a little jig.

We need a secret mission. And it has to include Bingo. He'll tell uz what we can and can't build. This is brill. The ultimate revenge against those horrible council misters.

We'll build a den right under their noses.

The figure slid between the barbed wire, into the compound. Pogsy declined to follow in case it was a trap and instead climbed back down the wall. On the way out, he hooked the barbed wire atop the fence around itself to create a secret opening and make it easier to get in and out the next time. Then he headed off to get changed for his first ever visit to a brand-new youth club that was opening that night.

"What a find," he said to himself. "No matter how good this new youth club is, all I'm gonna be thinking about all night is dens, dens and more dens, with dens on top, underneath and to either side."

Pogsy had concluded a long time ago that Sunday was the best day of the week to get up to mischief, mainly because it really was the day of rest. All the shops were shut, including Woolies. Apart from men fishing off the North Wall for free food, the docks were always deserted.

Even the coppers put their massive cop feet up for a bit, while their wives washed their smelly old cop socks. Factory workers nipped off down the boozer the second it opened, then stumbled home for Sunday dinner and a snooze in front of the radio. Mams did knitting and darning while their young kids played them up. Girls either sewed, repairing torn clothes for their dads, or they helped their mams peel spuds. Grans and grandads went to church to pray that the fishing boats came home safe and sound. Some days they went twice. Boys were made to stay at home, where they tore their hair out through boredom, or else, if their mams trusted them to come home in time for dinner, went to the park to play football. Or, in Pogsy's case, pretended to be down the park playing football.

It was another cold, grey November morning. Low cloud tumbled in from the North Sea, filtering out the sun, creating a world that was listless and washed out. Up and down the street, chimneys pumped out columns of dark smoke, adding charcoal paint to the pale sky. Pogsy hurried on his way, barely able to contain his excitement. When he reached Reddy's house, he explained that it was vital that they went on a secret recon mission immediately to prepare the way for a full secret mission later in the day. While they raided Reddy's dad's toolbox for a pair of bolt-cutters, Pogsy babbled away at a thousand miles an hour. Red Top stopped him on multiple occasions for clarification but was still unable to understand what Pogsy was trying to say. It was only when they reached the top of the first fence that everything fell into place.

"Are we going where I think we're going, Pogs?"

"You'll see." Pogsy used the bolt-cutters to cut a hole in the barbed wire and then replaced it with a length of string, which was spray painted silver. The added knots, which had been stiffened with glue looked just like real barbs, and from a distance the trickery was hard to spot. Pogsy made sure he always had plenty of fake barbed wire to hand, hidden away in an old shoe box in his wardrobe. You never knew when you might need it.

He repeated the trick with the barbed wire on the second fence.

"What are you doing?" said Reddy with a scowl capable of warping a battleship. "Don't you remember what we all swore? We saluted what was left of the dens and promised we were gonna punish the council misters by pretending that the cold store they were buildin' don't exist."

"That was before. Follow uz. You gotta see what I've found."

"I can't climb a wall that don't exist, that would be stupes."

Pogsy cracked on anyway, giving his pal a running commentary on how to scale the wall while Red Top covered his ears and looked away. Once up on top, Pogsy lay down and offered his hand, just as the figure he'd met previously had done. It took a full ten minutes to talk Reddy out of his monk-on and into the climb, and even then he looked uncomfortable all the way up.

"OK. I'm here," he said. "But I'm not looking."

"You've got to." Pogsy produced a goodie from his tracksuit pocket. "It's worth a Mars Bar."

"I want two. One for each eye. You owe uz t'other."

"Deal," said Pogsy, sticking out his hand.

Red Top grinned and beat him to the Raspberry. Grabbing the goodie, he took a very quick look over the wall, whistled, then took a much longer look, his eyes sucked into the woodyard.

"I need you," said Pogsy. "If we're to build uz a den in here, then we gotta have your milk-knowledge. I'm counting on you to ask around and find out everything you can about this place. Whatever we do – and we don't even know we *can* build a den in here yet – we can't do it without you. You're our *lunchpin*. When it comes to scouting stuff out, you're world-class."

"Yeah?" Red Top puffed out his chest and thumped his heart with his fist. "I suppose I am."

With help from Pogsy, Reddy counted out the streetlamps in the distance and used them as markers to work out the rough dimensions of the woodyard. The pair then tronked their way around the perimeter of the cold store, noticing it for the first time, all the while watching out for stray Tramps. They spotted a likely looking lad and gave him abuse. He hurried on his way.

"This store specialises in freezing fish," said Red Top. Then, as an afterthought, he tapped his temple with his finger. "Milk-knowledge."

The building was a monster.

Around the front, a large coloured sign with three-foot high letters proudly proclaimed that it was owned and operated by *Christian Salvation*, which sort of made sense with Peter being a fisherman. The grey metal-clad factory reminded Pogsy of an aircraft hangar. At a hundred and twenty feet tall, he estimated it could house a whole squadron of Spities. The entrance was offset slightly from the centre, and was the width and height of a lorry. Entry to the site was controlled by security fences and a guard post with a swing barrier. Pogsy ran up and tapped on the glass as a dare, then legged it. No-one gave chase. By the righthand side of the building he spotted the gate to the woodyard, which, according to Reddy, occupied approximately one-third of the entire complex. The pair set off once more, passing the edge of the woodyard, where they ducked under a hedge and sneaked into an office complex, also owned by the Christians.

One of Pogsy's favourite pastimes was *garden creeping*, which by a happy coincidence involved the same set of skills required to locate the flat-topped wooden shed from the main road. After a brief stop to remove a jagged splinter from Red Top's thumb, they found what they were looking for. Although the shed was part of the cold store complex, it was situated outside the main wall, alongside the woodyard in its own fenced-off area, accessed via a sturdy metal gate. Between the locked gate and the hut was a long, straight path constructed from gravel and slabs, peppered with the corpses of dead weeds.

Pogsy scratched his head, wondering what on earth the shed was used for.

"Got it," said Red Top with a glint in his eye. "Look at the fag butts and the empty milk bottles by the door."

"Go on," said Pogsy.

"It's a skiving shed. When workmisters don't want to do any real work, they need somewhere they can go where the bosses can't see them. That's what this is. Me dad delivers milk to one on his rounds. I'll bet it's got a radio, a fridge and a kettle. It might even have its own bog."

"How much is it used?" asked Pogsy.

"According to the milk-knowledge, skiving sheds are in use all week. If there's overtime on a Saturday, then it'll be packed with workmisters sitting around drinking tea, listening to the football on the radio. Ooo. Do you see what I see?"

"You mean the skiving ladder," beamed Pogsy.

The ladder was mounted horizontally to the front of the shed, just below the edge of the roof, making it invisible from above. Pogsy and Red Top unhooked it and used it to climb up onto the shed, hauling it up after them. From now on, it was going to be a lot easier to scale the wall, especially for the weaker lads who couldn't climb. Pogsy went first. The ladder proved to be both sturdy and stable. He bounced on the rungs halfway up to be sure.

"Looks good," shouted Red Top from down below.

Pogsy gave the thumbs up.

Later, once they'd both wolfed down their dinners at breakneck speed, they returned to the yard with Bingo in tow. It was a well-known rule of the playground that boys could be brainy or good at sports, but not both, and Bingo was no exception to the rule. To his credit, he didn't moan once during the first fence climb, although his eyes did give away a deep-seated fear he had of accidentally tearing his clothes and having to face his mum.

"I'm rubbish at lying," he said, as Pogsy pulled him up from above and Reddy pushed from below.

"It's like riding a bike," said Pogsy. "The more you do it, the better you get."

"It's easier to not start." Bingo wiped his forehead then bundled through the gap in the barbed wire. "I'm glad you've finally admitted the cold store exists."

The trio approached the second fence in the same manner as the first, helping each other with the climb, until all three were on the shed roof.

Bingo breathed in and out rapidly, catching his breath. "Thanks for inviting me," he said excitedly. "I can't believe I'm finally taking part in a secret mission.

"You know you're not allowed to say owt to no-one," said Pogsy. "Not ever."

"I'll keep my trap shut," said Bingo. "I promise."

While Pogsy jostled the ladder into position, Red Top produced the gang's Battle Map, which he'd updated while he'd had his dinner. He proudly pointed out the perimeter of the compound. "There's summut I don't quite get, Pogs. What made you break your promise and climb a wall that don't exist?"

"This is gonna sound mad." Pogsy screwed up his mouth at the edges. "I chased this mystery lad who moves like a monkey the other night. He led uz 'ere."

"You're right," said Reddy. "It does sound mad. What's he look like, this monkey boy? Is he blond or dark?"

"I've no idea," said Pogsy, rubbing his chin. "He was wearing a mask."

"So he could be a Tramp leading uz into an ambush?"

"That's what we have fists for."

The three pals shimmied up the rungs, one after another, with Bingo in the middle. The boy with the brains made a nest for himself atop the wall, then from out of his knapsack produced a set of binoculars and a notebook. Pogsy and Red Top left him working away, while they tied a knotted climbing rope to one of the angled pillars and shimmied down the wall using their legs. At first they proceeded with caution, mindful of other lads in hiding. The corner of the yard that they found themselves in was a vast dumping ground for broken palettes and empty cable drums. It smelt strongly of bitumen and tar. Pogsy located a burner and an oil drum full of viscous black liquid. Both were cold to the touch. He counted the cable drums, which came in various shapes and sizes, stopping at eighteen. The solution to the problem of getting in and out was obvious.

Red Top saw it too.

"We have to make the steps look random," said Pogsy. "To throw any guardmisters off the scent."

Between them, they tried to move the drums. The smaller ones rolled easily but the larger ones were far too heavy.

"This is a job for Weebs," said Reddy, beads of sweat breaking on his forehead.

Pogsy wiped his face. "Let's plan for next Wednesday. That gives Bingo ages to work on the design. It's Steve's birthday in a few weeks. Let's keep our discovery secret for now and surprise him."

In truth, Pogsy didn't want Steve to know about his discovery at all. Ever since "I Love You Love Me Love" had come straight in at Number One, which Steve attributed to his lucky crown, he'd become the most pompous, idiotic, self-obsessed bum-hole in the entire world. It was worse than last summer when the power of his crown had caused "Leader of the Gang" to gang up with Peters and Lee (whose records needed lobbing in front of a steamroller) and David Bowie (who Sam said had invented Glam with Marc Bolan) to displace "Skweeze Uz Pleeze Uz" from the top spot.

By the time Pogsy and Reddy returned up top and hid their rope, Bingo had completed his calculations.

"They're using the wood to build pallets," he said, looking up from his beautifully crafted notes. "I've done the maths and there's enough timber to make approximately two hundred thousand of them."

"That'll reach to the moon," said Red Top.

Bingo's eyes shot from side to side, shuttering away like a mechanical calculator.

"At four feet per palette, it should cover a distance of one hundred and fifty-one point five two miles," he said. "It'll certainly reach orbit, but not to the moon. Which is two hundred and thirty-nine thousand miles away. To get to the moon you'd need three hundred and fifteen million, four hundred and eighty thousand pallets."

"Show off," said Reddy.

Bingo continued, "Let's assume the misters work eight hours a day, six days a week. That's three hundred and twelve working days a year, excluding holidays. Let's say three hundred. If they were to make ten palettes an hour, it'll take them eight years to use up all that wood."

"I like where this is going," said Pogsy, his voice full of admiration. "If we were to build a den in the woodpile that's furthest away from the main gate, it will take the misters until forever to discover it."

"Correct," said Bingo.

"What a peach of a find," said Red Top. "Good going, Pogs."

"It's all thanks to the monkey boy," said Pogsy.

Reddy shook his head. "Are you sure this lad's not you?"

The following Wednesday was a special bank holiday, due to Princess Anne marrying Captain Mark Phillips in Westminster Abbey. News of the wedding was on all three TV channels and in every paper. It was even broadcast live. Everyone at school received a free mug, although some of the boys in Class 4C smashed theirs up on the way home. Most of the grown-ups were delighted to have something to celebrate for once, and even the news presenters promised not to mention the state of the country for the day. Down Pogsy's end of the street, Nan Eagle was the only one who had a colour TV, even though she hardly ever watched it. She hung bunting and Union Jack pennants around the outside of her house, making sure it matched the other nan houses up and down the street, then invited all the neighbours over to watch the wedding, but accidentally forgot the Petherbridges. They didn't care and were spotted mid-morning in their party hats, pushing a trolley full of booze down the street. Many grown-ups dressed in a combination of red, white and blue. Missis Armstrong had even sewn a special Union Jack jacket for her dog and had made sure to scrub her steps a day early.

Pogsy was desperate to get going, but he also fancied a pikelet and he'd had his eye on them ever since they'd appeared in the bread bin a few days earlier. He watched his dad scoff one down, slathered in melted butter, all the while griping on and on about the unfair end to the Cod War, which had been signed into law the previous day.

"If only Heath had had the balls to send a few more frigates, we'd be having victory celebrations," he said wistfully.

In Pogsy opinion, the price of fish was far less interesting than the pikelet making its way towards Dad's gob, and he soon noticed he wasn't the only one tracking its progress. Sam and Mum stood there transfixed and, even though Ellie was inexperienced in the art of eating Northern delicacies, she soon got the hang of looking longingly at Dad's plate. Eventually, he twigged.

"You lot," he laughed. "You'll eat me out of house and home."

The packet of pikelets was soon grilled and served, and everyone sat down to eat. What no-one had realised was that the entry fee to the great pikelet scoff-up was a full ear-bending about the Prime Minister's latest outrage.

"What's a state of emergency?" Pogsy whispered in Sam's ear, his mouth stuffed full to bursting.

"The Prime Mister's throwing an eppy," mumbled Sam, his lips glistening with butter, "because he's not getting his own way with the miners."

"More *pikeleck*," said Ellie, her eyes lighting up.

Mum cut up one of the pikelets into eighths and passed a piece on. "If you paid more attention, Patrick, you'd know it's all to do with what's going on in the Middle East."

"But..." Pogsy spat out the word through a mouthful of bready delight. "The oil crisis is over."

"Patrick. Don't speak with your mouth full," said Mum.

Pogsy swallowed hard. "But Ellie does."

"She doesn't know any better."

"Even though the war's over," explained Sam, "petrol's still going up. It cost Jimbo's dad nearly fifty pence to fill his motorbike the other day. More expensive petrol means more expensive transport costs, which means more expensive everything."

Pogsy shook his head. It used to be two pence for an eighth of apple drops. They were now two and a half pence. If this continued, he wondered how boys and girls would make ends meet.

"If you followed the news," said Sam, "you'd know that the miners can't feed their families because of all the price rises and they need more money—"

"For goodies and petrol," said Pogsy. "That makes sense."

"But the misters who run the banks say that the country doesn't have any spare dosh, so the miners are on strike until the government finds some." Sam grabbed the second-to-last half-pikelet.

"I'm sure I heard Dad say that the ones on strike don't get paid."

"That's right," said Dad. "Not all the miners are on strike though. Thankfully, some of them saw sense and stayed on at work, doing overtime. The unions then decided to ban overtime, and guess what? The country's running out of coal—"

"Which we need to make electricity," said Mum.

"And that's why the emergency." Sam looked pleased with himself.

"That's just stupes." Pogsy had known for ages that grown-ups in charge behaved like loonies if they didn't get what they wanted, and once that happened, they'd refuse to see sense for much longer than was good for them. Usually, according to Bingo, they did something called "doubling down", which involved trying something that hadn't worked previously but doing it twice as hard. When that didn't work, they'd try twice as hard again. When they eventually reached fifty times as hard and it still hadn't worked, they'd do what they should have done in the first place: find someone innocent and blame them.

Dad continued talking about how the country was going to have to adjust. Pogsy learned that the use of electricity for floodlights was now banned. Which meant evening football games had to be played in the afternoons when the fans were all at work, which was extra-double stupes. And then there were extra new rules preventing the use of heating in shops, offices and restaurants.

Pogsy chewed it over for a few seconds.

None of the changes his dad was talking about had a direct effect on him, so it wasn't a problem. What was a problem was that none of these measures did anything to address the problem at the top of the charts.

"Mum," he said, "if the country needs to save money on electricity, then they should ban rubbish Glam songs from being played."

"That's a great idea," said Mum with a wry smile. "Why don't you write a letter to Mister Heath to suggest it?"

"Will you help?"

"Of course."

Pogsy felt his mood lift. He'd soon get the country back on its feet. While he was at it, he'd get "Eye Level" banned too. Followed by Cassidy and little Jimmy Osmond. Then Slade could rule the airwaves forever, unopposed.

While the grown-ups celebrated the wedding, Pogsy snuck out and headed to the woodyard, where he met up with his pals, letting Bigzy and Weeble into the big secret. Bigzy feigned surprise at the sudden appearance of a cold store that didn't used to be there, but Weeble wasn't at all bothered. With their help, the access steps from the wall to the ground quickly took shape. By the time they'd finished, even Bingo was able to descend and ascend unassisted. He'd arrived armed with a school notebook, a set of coloured pencils, a sharpener and a tape measure, and was soon engrossed in calculus.

"The entrance is here," he said, pointing at a dark corridor running between two towers of wood. "It's easily the best spot."

Bigzy nodded in agreement. "Good choice. It's invisible from the workmisters' hut and miles from the gate."

"The only thing I can't figure out how is how to remove the wood from the middle. We can't take any from the sides or the top or it'll be too obvious."

Bigzy laughed. "Leave the burrowing to uz. I come from a family of termites. If I read your plan right, the first room is about fifteen feet long and six feet high, with two feet of planks for the ceiling and a second room on top."

"For stage one," said Bingo, fiddling with his glasses. "Stage two is more ambitious."

"Sounds good," said Pogsy. "What are we waiting for?"

"Well, there is *one* complication," said Bingo. "I've run the calculations a couple of times. If we have five boys doing this for a couple of hours every Sunday, as planned, then it's going to take us a year to build the den you want."

"OK," said Pogsy. "What if we multiply the number of boys by three and work four hours a day?"

Bingo's eyes moved up and down as he did the calculations in his head. "If we do that, then we'll have the shell completed in thirty-one days."

"Except," said Bigzy, "we don't have fifteen boys."

"Not yet," said Pogsy. "But we will."

"I'm gonna go explore down there," said Red Top, pointing towards the hut.

"I'm gonna climb up top," said Bigzy, searching for a handhold.

"I gotta go get Squib," said Weeble. "'E'll be chewin' the carpe' be now. If 'e ant se' fire to i'.""

Pogsy waited until the gang had dispersed before addressing Bingo: "How are you with contracts?" he said, keeping his voice low.

"I've read some of my dad's," said Bingo, pushing a pencil behind his ear.

"What I need," said Pogsy, "is a treaty. Not a playground treaty like we used to write in the back of our exercise books, but a proper one. One that'll hold up a court of law, that's fully legal, that's been signed in blood and everything. The sort of contract that Churchill signed with the Yanks and the Ruskies when we went to war against Hitler. Can you do that?"

"Absolutely!" grinned Bingo. "An actual real honest-to-God Second World War treaty? Thank you, Pat. I've been waiting my whole life for an opportunity like this. I think you might just be my new best friend."

"Pogs!" shouted Reddy, running to meet his pal. "Quick. It's the monkey boy."

"Where?" said Pogsy, his senses alert.

"Someone snuck up behind Weebs, flicked his lughole then shot off up one of the woodpiles. Bigzy's the only one wot saw 'im like. He's givin' chase."

"What are we waiting for?" said Pogsy. "I'm dying to meet him properly. At the very least, we need to know his name and what school he's at. That'll tell uz if he's our friend or our foe."

Eight: Voyage to the Land of the Giants in Space

Finally, the day he'd been waiting for was here. Pogsy waved a hurried set of goodbyes to his friends and rushed home from school, unable to contain his excitement. There was only one thing he'd been able to think about all day and pretty much only one thing he'd been able to talk about too. Which was a relief, as it helped to blot out the horrors of dinner-time radio. The Osmonds had put in a solid performance and come so very close; then their sister Marie had waded in, but ultimately neither of them, even with the help of Mud's "Dyna-mite", were able to displace the self-proclaimed god of Glam Rock from the pinnacle of the charts. Which meant the unthinkable had happened: Steve's wish had come true and his idol was Number One for his birthday. Pogsy decided he'd deal with the fallout later. For now, none of it mattered. What did matter was that there was a colour TV in his house.

Bam regularly boasted that he'd had a set for ages and Steve's dad was supposed to be getting one any day. As for the rest of the gang, they were all still stuck with black and white. Pogsy supposed it made him a bit spesh. As long as the TV was actually there and not stuck in Dover. Or wherever it was that TVs came from. He panicked at the thought and ran faster, tearing through the front door like he was trying to evade a swarm of angry bees on fire, almost upending an engineer in blue overalls who was busy supping away on a cup of tea. Hot liquid splashed everywhere. The engineer growled. Dad glared.

"Soz," said Pogsy.

He quickly scanned the room. The old TV was lying on its side in the middle of the lounge, surrounded by a sea of red and orange carpet. It looked like it had kicked the bucket. In its usual spot was a brand-new set with an array of shiny buttons instead of a warped plastic dial. In comparison to the old set, it was a monster. Pogsy stood transfixed. The latest addition to the lounge was housed in a polished wooden cabinet, supported by a leg at each corner. There were no crayon marks where Ellie had tried to colour in the picture to make the *Blue Peter* logo blue rather than mid-grey. There were no scorch marks out the back where it had overheated and singed the curtains. There were no cup rings on top where Dad had left a drink standing instead of using a saucer.

"Wow," said Pogsy, the words drooling from his lips. "It's beautiful."

"It's rubbish," said Dad sternly. "We're sending it back."

"What? No!" Pogsy felt all the colour drain away from his face. Tears welled in his eyes.

"He's kidding," said the engineer. "I need to adjust one of the boards. It won't take long."

"How long is long?" asked Pogsy.

"As long as it takes to drink a cup of tea plus ten minutes," said Dad. "Why don't you go get changed?"

Pogsy froze. At the moment, he had first dibs on what channel to watch. If his brother came home while he was upstairs, that was it. He was done for.

"What are you waiting for?" asked Dad.

"I was here first," said Pogsy, thinking on his feet. "I get first choice of what to watch. Fogs, bags, no changes."

"He's got you there," said the engineer. "You can't un-foggy a fogs, bags."

"Alright. Off you go," laughed Dad.

By the time the engineer had finished fiddling around in the back of the set making adjustments, he had an audience of five. Missis D should really have gone home but she was determined to be there for the grand switch-on. For Sam it was no big shakes. Or so he said. He was sat fidgeting from side to side, moving his left leg up and down, which meant he was ever so excited really . Ellie wanted *Play School* but caught only the last few seconds of the show.

"Humpty!" she said, reaching out in wide-eyed delight to touch the great green egg, who wore green and white checked pants.

With Humpty gone until tomorrow, the first TV programme they all watched together was *Huckleberry Hound*. Pogsy was amazed. He'd no idea Huckleberry was light blue. Mum, who'd just come in, commented that he was the colour of squished huckleberries, thus putting the matter to rest. Nobody moved from the screen until after *Animal Magic* had finished. It might not have included any huckleberry-coloured dogs, but seeing the real-life animals in their real-life colours caught the attention of the entire family. Missis D made her excuses and left, gazing longingly at the colour picture as she headed out the door.

Pogsy breathed a sigh of relief. Thankfully, they'd managed to avoid *Romper Room*, which Ellie loved to run around to, screaming at the top of her lungs.

In his head, Pogsy composed a list of all the TV shows he couldn't wait to watch in colour. Top of the list by far was *Star Trek*. By a happy coincidence, it was on later that night. Pogsy already knew that the crew wore different coloured tops but, apart from Spock, Kirk, Scotty and McCoy, most of them remained a mystery. Sam wouldn't fight him over this choice, and Dad rather liked a bit of Captain Kirk, especially if he was giving the Klingons a good pasting. *Doctor Who* was next on the list, but it wasn't on at the moment. Pogsy couldn't wait to see the TARDIS in colour. So much so, he'd considered borrowing Ellie's crayons to do the job himself. In order of preference, the next three shows on the list were *Voyage to the Bottom of the Sea*, *Land of the Giants* and *Lost in Space*.

It was common knowledge in the playground that, when shows weren't on TV, the characters were on holiday. Pogsy had heard that Butlins near Scarborough was pretty swanky, so he assumed that this was where the Doctor was taking a well-earned break from blowing up Daleks. Instead of voyaging around, Admiral Nelson and Captain Crane had probably left the *SSRN Seaview* in dry dock and taken the flying sub to Butlins in Hawaii, away from the werewolves and the ghostly *Flying Dutchman*. Captain Steve Burton and his co-pilot Dan Erickson were having an adventure exploring Giant Butlins, trying to discover a power source for their spaceship, the *Spindrift*, so they could escape the giant's planet forever. Finally, the *Lost in Space* Family Robinson were no doubt enjoying themselves at Space Butlins, leaving Dr Zachary Smith to annoy aliens, insult the robot and be a right cowardly custard, just like he was every week.

The five big shows were what the gang used to play every break. It was great fun mixing them up, having the *Seaview* invaded by Daleks, or pretending to be titchy and avoiding giant *Doctor Who* monsters such as the Yetis. Donut was the boy with the wild imagination. He'd been the driving force behind make-believe. Now he was gone, the boys were playing all sorts of team games instead, usually involving a tennis ball, which was either lobbed or kicked.

The best thing about not playing so much make-believe was that the arguments about who was who had stopped. In any make-believe game, Steve was in charge. For *Land of the Giants*, the captain happened to be called Steve, which made things easy. Pogsy had quite happily played the role of Dan the co-pilot, until Donut had received the *Giants* annual for Christmas and discovered that Dan was black. As Sarge's first name was Daniel, it was an easy swap. Pogsy had ended up playing Mark Wilson, the annoying millionaire. Eventually, Sarge had tired of taking orders from Steve and quit the game.

They'd been forced to play *Voyage* after that and it quickly became a firm favourite. On the TV show, Admiral Nelson was in charge, and this was Pogsy's character. However, Steve insisted it was his character, Captain Crane, who was really the boss. They'd split the difference. Steve had taken command of the main submarine and Pogsy had command of the flying sub. He easily had the best missions, especially with Donut onboard. Sparksy's favourite character was Sparks, the radio operator, who was always getting electrocuted. He was chuffed when Steve had made his nickname official.

Tuesday evening came and went. Pogsy spent all of the next day talking about *Trek*. On the Wednesday, he watched *Dad's Army* and later that night *The World at War*, which was all about the Battle of Britain. It was a show that he couldn't get enough of, even though, ironically, most of the footage was shot in black and white. On Thursday he had to confront the nightmare scenario of *Top of the Pops*. The Number One song, in colour, seared itself into his brain. The more he heard it, the more he thought of Steve's toothy beaver-like grin and the more he disliked it, to the point where he began to wonder whether he might prefer the Osmonds. Dad enjoyed Pan's People much more than usual.

Friday night was the first time that week Pogsy didn't get his fix of colour TV shows. It didn't matter though because Dad was having friends over to watch *Miss World* and, more importantly, Pogsy had a date down the youth club. Steve's dad had hired it for the night, for Steve's birthday party. As Second, he couldn't miss it. He had a gold-embossed invite telling him to be there.

Pogsy gulped. The hollowing out of the woodpile had progressed much faster than expected and everyone involved was ready to explode. It was a wonder no-one had accidentally said something to Steve already. Pogsy hated keeping secrets, especially to someone's face, which was why he'd been avoiding the leader of the gang of late. With all the clandestine goings-on, he had to admit that it might look like he'd formed a breakaway gang. This was never his intention. The

Kings *had* to stay together, more than ever. Steve was their leader and the best hope they had of coming out on top in a gang war. Pogsy crossed his fingers and hoped that his friend would see it the same way.

Pogsy stared at the circular, brass-framed clock that hung on the great stone fireplace that ran the length of his living room and wrung his hands. Tonight was the night. His tummy ached. It felt like it was tied in knots and giving birth to *flutterbies*, as Ellie liked to call them. Sam waved goodbye. He was wrapped up against the cold in a thick jacket and scarf, heading out to see his mate Jimbo, to engage in a spot of sky watching. Apparently, Comet Kohoutek was visible in the night sky if you knew where to look. Pogsy remembered there'd been a big song and dance about it months ago. It was supposed to be the brightest comet ever seen, brighter even than the moon. Instead, it was speeding towards the sun at thousands of miles an hour and it was no larger than a space-pea. Even Mister Spock, with all scanners set to full, wouldn't be able to detect it. Dad, for his part, had been out buying beer. He'd purchased two-dozen tins of Double Diamond and Worthington E, proudly lining them up on the kitchen table. He was expecting a big turnout for what Mum described as "a good old ogle at the goggle box".

"It's degrading," she said. "Being made to parade around in swimsuits and answer daft questions from leery old men."

"Nonsense," said Dad, taking a crisp from a green glass bowl and crunching it loudly. "They get paid for it. And they're on TV."

"That's not the point," snapped Mum. "How would you like it if that was Ellie up there, being poked and prodded and slapped on the bum for entertainment?"

"You know what I think," said Dad. "If you don't like it, don't watch it. When Ellie is old enough, I plan on teaching her to fight, just like I did with the boys. Then, if anyone get frisky with her, she'll know where to punch them."

"I'm *not* staying in to watch you undress a bunch of scantily clad girls with your eyes." Mum took a glug of vodka and orange squash then set to with a can of hairspray, fixing her hair in place.

Pogsy covered his nose and mouth with his hands and encouraged his sister to do the same. The spray came out in a great sticky cloud, filling one end of the living room, and hung about like an alien life-form from Gamma Five. He knew from previous experience that, if you didn't watch it, it could easily stick all the hairs in your nose together. Any flies that accidentally found their way in didn't stand a chance. From the glares that Mum periodically shot at Dad, she was obviously miffed. He just didn't know why. It wasn't unusual for her to make a special effort when other grown-ups were coming over, so he wasn't surprised that she was all dressed up in a blouse and a plaid yellow skirt with matching jacket. By the side of her make-up area lay a pair of monster yellow platform boots.

The doorbell rang.

"Get that will you, Pat," said Dad. "It'll be Mr Stamp."

Except it wasn't.

Pogsy had to look twice to be sure who it was. The lady in front of him was tall and thin, with stomping white PVC platform boots that went well past her knees, ending in one of the shortest skirts he'd ever seen in his life. If, indeed, it was a skirt. He searched his brain for the word.

Hotpants.

Up top she wore a white fluffy jumper and a long white coat, trimmed with white fur that tumbled around her, falling all the way to the ground. Atop her platinum-blonde hair sat a black and white striped turban, with a big purple jewel set in the front. The look was completed by a pair of star-shaped glasses with purple frames and lenses.

"Aunt Lorna!" said Pogsy, grabbing hold of his favourite aunt around the waist and giving her a big hug.

"Alright, ar Pat," said Aunt Lorna. "You look dead smart, you. You gonna invite uz in or wot?"

"Come in," said Pogsy, making way. "You look like a film star."

"That's 'cos I am. Din't yer dad tell yer?"

"Tell uz wot?"

"I'm in *Corro* now! Except it ant bin shown yet." Aunt Lorna moved her thumb and forefinger across her mouth in a zipping motion. "Can't talk about it. But I will. Later, when I've 'ad a few."

Pogsy turned to his dad, whose face looked like Cleethorpes beach when the tide was out: unhappy and covered in dead crabs.

"I won't be a minute," said Mum, handing her drink to Aunt Lorna, who slurped it straight down. "Pat. Give me a hand with my boots, please."

Pogsy hurried over to help his mum with her zips. Ellie joined him. She didn't have the strength to tug a zipper all by herself, but she still tried. Pogsy helped his sister finish both boots off. Although Mum could get her feet in okay, she was rubbish at the bending over bit. He didn't mind helping though. It was good practice for when Slade needed assistance getting into their boots.

"Sandra," said Dad. "What are you doing here?"

"It's Lorna," said Aunt Lorna, peering into the empty glass in case she'd missed a bit. "Lorna Diamond. It's me stage name, but I'm makin' it all official, like. If ar Pat 'ere can remember, so can you."

"I thought you were in Manchester," said Dad, defensively.

"Come 'ere ar Al," said Aunt Lorna, "and give uz a kiss. 'Onest, the way you's carryin' on, anyone ud think me own bruvver want 'appy to see uz."

"I'm not," said Dad, giving his sister a tepid hug.

"Nice telly," said Aunt Lorna. "So what else 'as bin 'appening? On second thoughts, don't tell uz now, tell uz tomorra. Taxi's waitin' an me an Liz are goin' on the razz down Meggies, then to Tiffs to pick up fellas. I know the bouncers, me. They'll let uz in for nowt."

Dad pulled away from his sister and looked sternly at Mum. "You're *not* going out with Sandra dressed like that!"

"Says who?" said Mum. "Enjoy taking the mick out of the beauty parade with your mates. You might want to watch the *Black and White Minstrel Show* first, and take the mick out them too. I've got my key. Make sure Ellie goes to bed nice and early. I'll see you later, Pat."

With which Mum and Aunt Lorna disappeared out the door, cackling like a pair of witches on their way to a bring-your-own toad-licking party.

Dad's face continued to look like Cleethorpes beach, except now he was imitating the end nearest the docks when the tide had just come in, and everything was coated in toxic slurry. He took a can of beer from the kitchen table and opened it. Foam bubbled everywhere, which just made things even more realistic.

Pogsy felt a smirk begin to form. He quickly made his excuses, donned his teddy-bear jacket, grabbed Steve's card and present, and followed his mum and Aunt Lorna. It was unusual for Mum to be going out on a Friday night without giving at least a month's notice, and doubly unusual for her to be going out with his aunt. Something was afoot, but he had no idea what.

Ali was waiting by her gate. She was dressed in orange flared pants and a red jumper, with a brown floor-length, fur-trimmed coat to keep out the cold. Her eye make-up glittered underneath the streetlights.

"Hiya," she said, watching the taxi depart and smiling at Aunt Lorna's nose pressed firmly against the window.

"Wot'cha," said Pogsy. "Did you hear from your pop?"

"Kind of." Ali pursed her lips. "He's workin' on something called *crisis management*. He says that the oil situation is gonna get much worse before it gets better. Ah have no idea what that means for us. All Ah know is that Ah'm not gonna see him for a while."

"Me dad's dead worried there might be petrol shortages," said Pogsy. "He says that whenever the government tries to control summut, they always end up making it ten times worse. If there's a petrol shortage, then it'll be because the papers make people panic and rush out to fill every container they have, not because we're actually running out."

"Your cars are half the size of ours!" Ali laughed. "Imagine what it's like in the States, tryin' to tell folk they have to cut down on going places. Pop's working on a proposal that's going to the President. He says that if the government folk aren't real careful about what they say and how they say it, there might be riots."

The idea of smashing everything up and taking what you wanted sounded ace, until Pogsy considered the Petherbridges. He gulped. They'd be in everyone's houses in seconds and the rumour was they'd just moved into nicking colour televisions. He quickly amended "ace" to "ace as long as the rioting was confined to someone else's street".

"What will we do if there's no more oil ever?" said Ali. "Ah might never see ma pop again."

"No more oil?" Pogsy stopped dead. Plastic was made from oil. No more plastic meant no more Action Men and no more models or toys. "Do you know summut I don't?"

"The look on your face!" Ali poked him in the ribs. "There'll always be oil. Pop says there's still plenty of dinosaurs buried all over the world that we haven't discovered yet."

"Phew! I was about to panic. The oil crisis has been pretty good for uz so far. They've had to shut the guard's office in the woodpile I told you about. Bingo says it's to do with the new heating laws. And the yard's dark at night now. There's never any security."

"So you keep on sayin'," said Ali.

"When are you gonna come pay a visit?" Pogsy half smiled. "You should see it."

"From what you've said your woodyard is owned by the cold store and that makes what you're doin' trespassing," said Ali with a look of bemusement. "Isn't that illegal?"

"Only if we get caught. Which we won't."

Friday night youth club was now a regular occurrence and it was all thanks to Gas-tank, whose dad was a vicar at one of the local churches. Following the cancellation of a long-term booking, the church hall had become available for use, and Gas-tank's mum had asked him to ask around to see if there was any interest in a youth club. Everyone thought it was a fantastic idea, even though there was an entry fee of ten pence a week for lighting and heating. Tonight, everything was free. Music was being provided by Gas-tank's sister's boyfriend, who fancied himself as a DJ. He'd brought along his record decks and his collection of pop singles the previous week. After just three songs, everyone had agreed he did a great job.

Pogsy and Ali arrived to discover that Steve's mum had spent the afternoon decorating the hall with party banners and brightly coloured balloons. With help from Gas-tank's mum and Bam's mother, they'd assembled an incredible spread of food, which was laid out on three trestle tables at the back of the main hall. In pride of place was a cake shaped like a football pitch, covered in light green icing, with white markings, two corner posts and a goal. Steve had a vomit-inducing self-congratulatory grin installed and was busy telling anyone who'd listen that he'd had to hire the hall this year because he was so popular it wasn't possible to fit everyone in his house. Pogsy thought it was more likely related to the jelly-and-ice-cream fight that had broken out the previous year. Steve's mum had turned purple with all the yelling, causing Susan Grainger to burst into tears and wet herself.

Missis King had gone silent after that.

Just inside the door was a small wooden table on which a pile of presents and cards had begun to accumulate. Pogsy and Ali added their offerings and skipped inside. The long, rectangular hall had a musty smell about it, which reminded Pogsy of the old hardcover books both his grandmas liked to collect. The cut-block wooden floor had clearly seen a lot of action over the years and its surface was scuffed up. There was a patch near the outside door that had been worn away completely and around the steps up to the stage an indent had formed. Condensation gathered on all of the windows. Pogsy noticed the chill immediately and opted to keep his coat on for a while longer. He tested one of the radiators, which was painted in a thick coat of blue gloss that matched the walls. It was too hot to touch. He supposed that, unlike the security guards in the woodyard, Gas-tank's dad had done a special deal with God to keep everything warm, which was funny really, as everyone knew it was the Devil who was in charge of heating. Pogsy looked around. A couple of his classmates were swinging their arms from side to side, urging the hall to heat up. Every noise they made, no matter how small, bounced around leaving a trail of echoes all the way up to the roof. He hung up his jacket and started a game of tag, encouraging everyone else to join in.

One by one the pile of presents grew and, with each body added to the inside space, the temperature steadily rose. Soon, nearly the entire school year was present. The pile of birthday goodies was more than the table could handle, and they were now stacked on the floor as well. All the available coat hooks were full. Lads were bombing around like crazy, enjoying themselves.

Missis King called everyone's attention by ringing a bell, just like they did at school. Steve took to the stage.

Pogsy felt a knot in his tummy. He hated it when everyone looked at him. How Steve could stand there and be gawped at was beyond him. In a similar position, he'd just curl up and die.

"Thanks for coming, everyone!" shouted Steve at the top of his foghorn voice. "Thanks for all the cards and presents. It's the biggest pile ever. Just so you all know, I'm the most magnanimous Steve in the whole of history. That's why we've got nosh and music and everything."

Pogsy had no idea what *magmaminous* meant. He suspected Steve didn't know either.

Missis King glared hard at her son. Pogsy smirked. It wasn't as powerful as Mum's *peel-your-head-to-expose-your-skull* stare, but Steve got the message.

"Just one more thing. A massive, huge thanks to my mum for organising my party. Thanks, Mum. And a big thanks to Missis Marsden and Reverend Marsden for letting us use the hall. And thanks to Bam and his mother for helping with the grub, especially the sausage rolls. They're delicious! Have a great time, everyone. And help yourselves to food."

DJ Popeye, as he liked to be known, had his record decks and banks of flashing lights arranged on the stage and this was his cue to start the first set, which was played at low volume as background music. Pogsy rushed to be first to the food, but only managed third. On his plate he piled a couple of fat sausage rolls, three mini-bangers on sticks, some cocktail sticks containing cheese and pineapple, and a great big handful of beef crisps from a wooden bowl. Usually, when crisps were on offer, you had to guess the flavours, but one of the mums had written out some very neat labels, which made it easy to avoid the nasty ones like salt and vinegar, which for some reason were always soggy. Once everyone had food, Pogsy sneaked another sausage roll. He thought about taking a fourth one but decided to leave space for cake and had another handful of beef crisps instead.

Steve opened his cards and arranged them along the walls. Footballers with the number 11 on their backs were well represented; there was a splendid collection of cars, a few Glam rockers, two dogs, a cat, and a picture of a vase of flowers from his gran. The girls, led by the twins, had got together and made their own card, which was four feet tall and two feet wide. The picture on the front was a collage of pop stars cut from *Popster* and *Music Star* magazines, with a blurred photograph of Steve's smiling face stuck on one of the bodies. Steve loved it to bits. He made sure he gave everyone involved a kiss on the cheek. Pogsy, meanwhile, had to take Bingo to one side to calm him down.

"They vandalised comics!" he muttered to the heavens, expecting God to somehow intervene, as they were in his house.

"It's only girl comics," said Pogsy.

"S'not the point," wailed Bingo. "You wouldn't vandalise the Bible. Girls just have no respect."

Suddenly, the speakers shook as "Jailhouse Rock" by Elvis Presley came on at full volume. Bigzy took to the floor and strutted his stuff, engaging in an Elvis-off with all comers. Pogsy thought he did a really good impersonation, getting the legs just right. Other boys joined in. Bam looked immaculate in a silver suit with wide lapels, wide cuffs and flares. It was complemented by a scarlet polyester shirt. He'd had his blond hair styled into a tight quiff for the night and was showing off his moves like he was a rock 'n' roll legend. Pogsy tittered and nudged Reddy, who was watching on with envy. Bigzy's Elvis stomped over to the girls, who did their very best to ignore him and focus on Ali instead, who was teaching them how to jive. The twins invited Steve to give it a try, while Ruth Maddox, who Pogsy didn't trust even for a second, kept an eye on proceedings, noting everyone's interactions, probably so she could tell on them all in her weekly report to Miss.

Pogsy tutted and wandered over to join the boys, cursing at the teacher's pet for always being on duty. He tried shaking his legs, but he hadn't got the hang of it the way Bigzy had. He knew from hours practising in front of the mirror that he had one of Elvis's trademark moves off to a tee, and it was one that no-one else could do. He let his Elvis lip-tremor loose on Bigzy, who fell about laughing. Pogsy did it again. Other boys laughed too and tried to match him, but no-one else could get it quite right. Within a few seconds, Pollyanna left the rest of the girls and boogied over, shaking her bum from side to side. She was dressed in a white shirt, a brown suede top edged with tassels, and a long, flowing skirt. Her hair was held back from her face by a bandana made from an American flag.

Pogsy chuckled. This was exactly how Aunt Lorna used to dress when she was still Aunt Sandy.

The next single the DJ played was "My Coo-Cha-Choo", which was performed by an Elvis look-a-like called Alvin Stardust who was new on the charts. Steve stopped dancing and signalled Pogsy to join him by the remains of the food.

"Wot'cha, Pogs," he said, adjusting his lucky crown. "Did you get a card for the best-looking Steve in the world? Because if you did, he doesn't remember seeing it."

"Of course," said Pogsy, encouraging willowy Pollyanna to go dance with Gas-tank instead. "I've been keeping it back. I wanted to give it to you mesen."

He led Steve to the coat racks, where he handed him his card. It was yet another footballer with number 11 on his shirt, which Mum had bought from Woolies. She was convinced no-one else would think of it. Pogsy had replaced the footballer's head with that of Captain Steve Burton from *Land of the Giants*, an idea he'd borrowed from the girls. It was important that Bingo didn't ever get to see the defaced comic book as there was no telling what he might do.

With a big, toothy grin, Steve opened his card. A photograph with a wide white border fell out. "What's this?" he asked, picking it up.

"Ali has this dead ace camera that takes pictures that develop instantly, before your eyes," said Pogsy. "She lent uz it. That's a picture of your special birthday present."

"You got me a pile of wood?" Steve screwed up his face, causing his eyebrows to knit together.

"No." Pogsy felt beads of sweat form along his hairline. He pointed at a dark recess on the picture. "It's a den. And not just any old den. It's a secret den and everything."

"Really?" said Steve, his eyes widening like a pair of fried eggs. "Because it sure looks like a pile of wood to me."

"Me and a few of the gang have been working on it for a while. Soz about keeping it secret but we wanted it to be a surprise for your birthday, seen as you're the most *mamnagimous* Steve in the world."

"Wow." Steve's body shook from top to bottom. "That's brilliant. When do I get to see it?"

"Sunday," said Pogsy nervously. "Come round mine about nine. And wear your best climbing gear."

It was Saturday morning and there was a peculiar atmosphere in the Green household. Pogsy couldn't quite put his finger on it but, whatever *it* was, it was doing a really good job of ruining children's TV, although Ellie's insistence on splashing her spoon into a bowl of Coco Krispies to turn the milk chocolatey brown wasn't helping much either. Dad was hiding away in his shed and had been since just after he'd got up. Mum was still in bed, which was unusual. This left Pogsy and Sam in charge of their little sister, which was why they were lounging on the pale cream sofa in a line, in their pyjamas, eating cereal in front of the telly rather than sitting in the kitchen.

"Did you see it?" asked Pogs, chomping away on a bowl of Shreddies.

"No chance," said Sam, prodding at a soggy Weetabix. "It's the most useless comet in the history of comets. We spent ages on Jimbo's garage roof with his telescope. The only thing we saw that was even a bit interesting was Joanne Dowling getting undressed."

"I know her bruvver," said Pogsy. "He's in remedial and he isn't right in the head. In fact, that whole family isn't right. You've been dilly-watching."

"I have not!" said Sam loudly.

"You watch dillies in the nude." Pogsy smirked, pleased with himself for getting one over on his brother.

"Well, you go out with one," said Sam.

"I do not!"

"I've heard from Jimbo's sister that you've got a girlfriend."

"I HAVE NOT!" Pogsy felt his cheeks turn scarlet.

"Polly – someone from your class. In school they call you *Pollypog*."

Pogsy felt his ears glow red. "Take that back."

"Will not," said Sam. "Pollypog! Pollypog!"

"You tug-off to nude dillies," said Pogsy, the anger rising inside.

"You don't even know what that means," said Sam. "Pollypog!"

Pogsy couldn't stand being taunted a second longer. He dropped his empty bowl and spoon and flew through the air at his brother. Pretty soon, the two of them were wrestling on the sheepskin rug in front of the fireplace. Ellie thought it would be fun to join in so, cereal in hand, walked over and tipped damp Krispies on Pogsy's head. Pogsy screamed. Half a second later, the door at the bottom of the stairs flew open and Mum appeared in her dressing gown, clutching her forehead. Her hair looked like she'd just stuck a finger in an electrical socket. Pogsy caught a whiff of stale cigarettes.

She took one look at her daughter and bellowed out loudly, "Elspeth *Green*! What do you *think* you're doing!"

Pogsy and Sam froze. Tears formed in Ellie's eyes.

"And you two!" Mum grimaced. "What sort of an example are you setting your sister?"

"He called me a 'dilly-watcher'," said Sam, letting go of his brother.

"Well, you are," said Pogsy.

"Patrick," growled Mum, "clean yourself up this instant. Samuel, you should know better. Get dressed, both of you. Aunt Lorna's due round soon. I need coffee. And aspirin. And a time machine."

One thing Pogsy had learned over the years was that, whatever his aunt was called, her superpower was definitely not keeping appointments. Her arrival varied between ten minutes early and three weeks late. He was not surprised in the slightest when she turned up as they were sitting down to dinner at the American-style diner table in the kitchen, tackling beans and fish fingers on toast, burnt five different ways.

"Now then, ar Al," said Aunt Lorna, breezing in the back door without knocking, "don't mind uz, I'll just stand over 'ere and wait. Who won then?"

"Evidently, you did," said Dad, pointing at his sister's leopard-spot jumpsuit with his fork. "In the fight with the big cat. Bite it in the neck, did you? Or did it bite you and die of alcohol poisoning?"

"You're a cheeky bugger, you are," said Aunt Lorna. "You know what I mean. *Miss World.*"

"Cheeky bugger," said Ellie, stabbing a fish finger.

Mum glared at Aunt Lorna.

"Soz. I'm not good with kids, me. I ferget mesen."

"Marjorie Wallace," said Dad with a wry grin. "Miss USA. If you ask me, it won't be long before she's dating George Best."

"Less of that, you. I've met 'im. He's a smashin' fella."

"So you keep saying." Dad smirked.

Pogsy and Sam looked at each other across the table and copied Dad's facial expression.

"Get uz his autograph," said Pogsy. "You said you would. It'll be worth thousands."

"Next time I see 'im," said Aunt Lorna. "You're a little tyke, you. Talking of tykes, I 'ear ar Sam 'ad a run-in with the rozzers."

Sam slunk backwards in his seat and hid behind Dad.

"You go' your Auntie Lorna to thank for sortin' it out. As soon as I 'eard, I 'ad a word, I did, with some people wot I know. Say thank you."

"Thank you, Aunt Lorna," said Sam, doing his best not to sneer.

"That's better. Now we'll 'ave none of that blowin' things up nonsense in future."

Pogsy shot a glance at his mum, then at his dad. Whatever bad blood there had been between them earlier had sorted itself out. He wasn't sure if it was because Dad had spent hours locked in the shed alone, doing dad stuff, or because Mum looked the same colour as Morticia Addams and had spent a good hour locked in the bathroom, calling for God. Dad had definitely been annoyed with Mum last night. Pogsy was convinced it was because Mum had gone out with Aunt Lorna. Sam wasn't so sure. He'd overhead something earlier in the day and he thought it was to do with dad having his mates over. All Pogsy knew for sure was that his mum and dad weren't getting divorced this time, so the argument hadn't been as bad as the previous one.

Once dinner was over, Dad set to washing the dishes. Aunt Lorna sat down and lit up a fag. Mum produced an ashtray and joined her. That was coded language for "the grown-ups need to talk, please leave the room – and take Ellie with you." Sam was as inquisitive as Pogsy, and equally determined to listen into the conversation. They took it in turns to stand on the other side of the closed kitchen door, one listening in while the other entertained their little sister, making sure that any mischief she got up to was contained. Later on, once Aunt Lorna had gone on her way with promises to see them all again soon, they compared notes in their bedroom, away from the ears of their parents.

"What's a 'scally'?" asked Pogsy.

"I'm not sure," said Sam. "I think it's the same as a scallywag."

"Then whatever a scallywag is, Aunt Lorna knows some. And they've got a van."

"Ah," said Sam. "That makes sense. Dad was talking about transport and how the car won't do. If it's anything illegal that's being plotted, we shouldn't know about it."

"Why not?" asked Pogsy.

"Because if the police question you, and you let on you knew and kept your gob shut, it makes you an accomplice."

"Even though I'm only ten?"

"That's what Jimbo says."

"Then I'd lie." Pogsy nodded his head.

Sam snorted. "Imagine lying to the coppers who came round to search Dad's shed. Do you think you could do that?"

In his mind's eye, Pogsy looked DI Moon straight in the eye and told the biggest whopper he could think of. Santa Claus was really Guy Fawkes's dad.

Coppers notice everything.

Pogsy squirmed all over, like his body was full of angry, wriggly woggums instead of veins. "I've decided I'd rather not know what Dad's up to," he said, after a lengthy pause. "Me mate Bigzy says his cousins lie to the coppers all the time and get away with it, but that's one of their family superpowers. That and legging it. Fibbing to the cops isn't a hobby I want to get into. I think I'll stick to playing togger."

Whilst Pogsy hadn't done any fibbing to the coppers, he *had* done fibbing to Steve. He felt bad about it, but he was sure that the consequences of telling the truth, the whole truth and nothing but the truth from the very outset would have been far worse in the long run. In with fibbing to Steve he'd also fibbed to most of the gang. In fact, out of the group standing around the electricity sub-station next to the woodyard that Sunday morning, the only person he hadn't fibbed to was Bingo.

The four members of The Kings, plus Squib and Bam, were restless and joshing with Pogsy over his constant delaying when Smiffy and Wingnut arrived unexpectedly, along with their Seconds. Upon spotting his rivals, Steve immediately assumed his favoured battle-stance. Red Top and Weeble joined him.

"Wot'cha, Steve," said Smiffy. "Wot'cha, Wingy."

"Wot'cha," said Wingnut, looking at Smiffy with barely concealed contempt. "Wot'cha, Steve."

"What's going on?" said Steve, staring at Pogsy.

Pogsy held his lucky troll tightly and cleared his throat. Twice. His legs felt wobbly. His tummy flipped over, like a greasy beefburger on a fat-encrusted griddle. He could feel his nerve slipping away. "Listen, everyone," he croaked, talking quickly, forcing out the words. "We need to gang up against the Tramps. If we don't, they'll wipe uz all out. What we need most of all is dens. For all of uz. For our protection."

"All fine an' dandy, like," said Smiffy, "but what's to stop the council from comin' along and destroyin' owt we build?"

"No-one can fight the council," said Wingnut.

"Last time our dens were too obvious and we made it too easy for the council to discover them. Which was why they got flattened. If we had *secret* dens that no-one knew about but uz, then that couldn't happen. Some of our gang discovered the perfect site for a secret den. In fact, we've been building it for a few weeks now. But if the Tramps discover it, they'll kick uz out and take over. It's as simps as that. We don't have the numbers. Another of our gang has done the calculations and there's room for two more secret dens alongside ours. If we all have secret dens together, we're invincible. The Tramps won't dare attack."

Weeble nodded. "Pogs is righ'."

"This den is the best den I've ever seen," said Reddy. "I'd hate to lose it to the Tramps."

"OK," said Smiffy. "You've got uz attention."

"Uz too," said Wingnut. "But what's to stop uz just takin' this den for uzselves?"

"You need to know where it is first," said Pogsy. "But before we show you, we're all going to sign a treaty."

Bingo fumbled in his backpack and produced three sheets of stiff paper, each entitled *The Treaty of the Three Gangs* and all inscribed with identical wording. "They took me ages to make. I wrote them all by hand in my best writing."

"So we sign a treaty?" said Smiffy. "And that's i'?"

"It's not just any old treaty," said Pogsy, nervously. "First off, we're all gonna sign it in our own blood. Second, we're all gonna give our word to each other to abide by the laws of the Treaty."

"All treaties start with the word of those signing it," said Bingo. "When it comes down to it, the only thing of value any of us have is our word. If we make a promise and we break it, then we're nothing. So we all have to give our word, in front of each other and in front of God as our witness."

"That's some serious shit you're proposin'," said Wingnut. "Me dad works down the docks. Always 'as. His word is his bond. If you break your word to your mates, it's unforgiveable. They'll shave your head and make you stick your willy in a bucket of nipper crabs, then they'll send you off to Coventry."

"Agreed," said Smiffy. "Me old man's a cranie. Same fing. Anyone wot breaks their word is utter scum and can never be trusted again. Even if they survive the crabs, everyone teks it in turns to piss in their flask and dump in their lunchbox for the next month."

"Wot dock?" asked Wingnut.

"Royal," said Smiffy.

"Same as mine," said Wingnut. "If uz dad's can work together, mebbe we *can* too. I'm willin' to give it a try. Jus' keep your wart to yesen."

Smiffy held his warty knuckle aloft and shook his fist. Everyone took a small step backwards.

"Brilliant!" Steve narrowed his eyes and laughed heartily. "And who gets to be in charge of this new gang?"

"You do," said Pogsy.

"Really?" Steve rubbed his eyes in disbelief.

"The rulers of this new super-gang are known as the *Triumvirate*," said Bingo. "The Treaty is based on a three-way alliance made in ancient Rome between Julius Caesar, Pompey and Crassus. All three leaders have to give the OK on really important matters, but each gang leader is still in charge of their own gang. The leader of the Triumvirate gets to give speeches and receive tributes. And he wears a special crown so everyone knows who he is. There's a lot of prestige goes with being the Leader of the Three Gangs."

Steve looked at Smiffy, then Wingnut. "And you two are okay with this?"

"Yep," said Smiffy.

"Good by uz," said Wingnut. "What do we do next? Slash our palms with a penknife or summut?"

"Heavens, no!" said Bingo. "My mum's a nurse. I borrowed one of her blood-testing kits. You prick your thumb and then use a quill pen. Let me show you."

Pogsy took a step back and let the three leaders get on with leading. He'd done his bit. At least for now. He chanced a quick look in Bam's direction. He wasn't particularly happy that Steve had brought the rich boy along but, seeing as Squib wasn't formally in the gang either, he couldn't really argue. While the leaders took it in turns being brave and getting their fingers pricked, Bam snuck a look at the Treaty. Pogsy watched him out the corner of his eye, scanning down the page. When he reached the end, he stuck his bottom lip out and nodded. Pogsy heard him whisper in Bingo's ear. It sounded like *great job*. He scowled. He'd half expected the new boy to pick the words to pieces and find fault in everything. In a way, he was annoyed he hadn't.

Once the formalities of bloodletting and applying sticking plasters were over, and everyone had declared they would honour the Treaty, cross their hearts, hope to die, so help them God, Pogsy led the way over the two outer fences, then with a bit of help, erected the ladder and climbed up onto the wall that ran around the woodyard.

"Just one thing," said Wingnut to the group gathered atop the skiving shed. "I remember uz lot deciding the cold store don't exist, as revenge for what the council misters did to our dens."

"Wingy 'as a point," said Smiffy. "We did swear until the end of time and all tha'."

"What do you say to that, Pogs?" glared Steve.

"We tried ignoring what they did to uz and it didn't achieve owt." Pogsy laughed nervously. "If you ask uz, buildin' a secret den right under their noses is the best revenge ever. Three dens right under their noses is the ultimate – it'll be the best revenge in the history of revenges."

"Sold," said Wingnut.

"Same 'ere," said Smiffy. "Let's ge' on wi i'."

One by one the three leaders climbed the wall.

"Wow!" gasped Steve, looking into the enclosure. "You'd never know any of this was here."

"We'd no idea," said Smiffy, his jaw hanging open.

Over the last few weeks, Pogsy and his hand-picked crew had worked tirelessly to make significant changes to the route in and out of the woodyard. They'd piled up the cable drums as planned, to create a series of steps, but stacked them in such a way as to make them look treacherous. If you were a grown-up, they would likely collapse when you reached the top. But to a boy who knew where to put his feet, they were perfectly stable. They'd all learned to scale the wall using ropes, just in case the steps were taken away. Climbing in and out was a cinch now.

"'Ooo's that?" said Wingnut, pointing at a figure in black stood with its legs apart and its hands on its hips on the roof of the furthest woodpile.

Pogsy coughed. "We don't know exactly. I saw 'im one day on the wall and gave chase. That's how I discovered the woodyard."

"We've seen 'im a few times," said Reddy. "He's 'armless but even our best climber can't catch 'im. Talkin' of Bigzy, where is he?"

"Docks with 'is cousin," said Pogsy. "I think that lad might live here. Or at least nearby. He guards the place when no-one's about."

"Great," said Smiffy. "So 'e's like Stig o' the Dump or summut?"

Everyone laughed.

As if on cue, the figure ran along the top of the woodpile and performed a series of flips in a single, fluid motion, landing on its feet.

"An acrobat," said Wingnut. "Impressive. Our gang could do with one of them."

"We saw 'im first," said Smiffy.

"Actually, we did," said Steve. "If anyone's having him, it's The Kings."

The gang of lads made their way into the woodyard and gathered in a circle between the second and third columns of wood.

"Until heating was banned, there used to a guard mister who'd sit in that hut over there watching telly all day." Red Top pointed down the concrete road that ran the length of the yard between the columns of wood, towards a large wooden building with double windows. "Now, the misters all scarper at five thirty on the dot. Sunday the yard's empty. We've got it to uzselves. Saturday you just gotta keep your wits about you."

"I've watched the forklift misters driving about," said Bingo, "and like most grown-ups, they take the easy option and use wood from the far end. When any new wood arrives, that's where they stack it. I've only ever seen two misters come down this end, and they were both smoking cigarettes and talking about football. One was a grandad. He's the one to watch, he's the security guard. They both stopped to have a Jimmy Riddle. They had no idea we were hiding just a few feet away."

Wingnut shook his head. "Amazin'."

"My gang are the best inventors and the greatest builders ever," said Steve, his voice full of pride.

"I've revised my discovery calculations," said Bingo. "Initially, I said it would take five years for the misters to work their way down the yard. Now I know how lazy they are, I'm certain it'll take nearer ten."

"Bet you can't find the den," said Bigzy.

"If it was down to me," said Steve, his front teeth perched firmly on his bottom lip, "I'd choose the furthest place from that hut."

"Me too," said Wingnut.

"Meks sense," said Smiffy. "Fourth column, far corner."

Steve set off first. Everyone else followed. The four columns of wood that ran the length of the yard stopped some fifteen feet before the end wall, allowing enough space for a forklift truck. The layout of the columns created a mini-wind tunnel and all kinds of litter had accumulated on the ground at the end of the compound. There were sweet wrappers, crisp bags and fallen leaves, all gathered together in piles. In one area, the concrete was noticeably decayed, allowing a massive puddle to form. Red Top picked up the remains of a kite. Its frame was broken and the tatty old tail was frayed and covered in mud. Its flying days were well behind it.

Steve took his birthday photograph from out of his jacket pocket and compared it to the column of wood, looking for a match. "What a rubbish photo," he said, scratching his head.

"Follow uz," said Red Top.

The squeeze between the woodpiles was narrow for the first eight feet or so, and had to be approached sideways on. After that, the space opened up into a dark rectangle. Red Top fumbled in his pocket, produced a torch and switched it on. The room they entered was around fifteen feet long, with planks stacked on each side to form benches that ran nearly its entire length. At the far end, set in the middle of the roof, a dark square beckoned. A set of handholds and footholds ran up the wall for access.

"Ruddy hell," said Steve. "You've been busy."

"Stick your 'ead up the 'atch," said Red Top, pointing with his torch. "There's another room as big as this one."

Bingo produced a plan from his knapsack, along with another torch. "In total, we can fit six rooms into this pile. That's what we're planning on building at least. If you use our plans you can do exactly the same in two of the other piles."

"Steve," said Smiffy, "we bow down to you. This is ace. By the time uz lot 'ave finished, this'll be the best bunch o' dens ever."

Wingnut nodded. "That time I called you *Princess Steve*. I tek it all back."

The three leaders faced each other, then performed a three-way handshake, which ended in one excruciatingly long raspberry.

"We got climbing holds," said Pogsy, shooting halfway up the gap where the gang had gained entry to the den.

"Nice," said Mopey Joe, rocketing past him towards the top of the woodpile. "I'm gonna see if I can't catch mesen an acrobat."

Pogsy returned to the ground.

All in all, bringing the three gangs together had been a very good day's work. The work wasn't finished though. And neither was the fibbing to Steve. He knew that in all likelihood he was going to have to meet up with the other Seconds on an ongoing basis, to keep everything ticking along. It had taken a lot of back-and-forth secret diplomacy to persuade everyone to let Steve be the leader of the *triumph-a-bet*. Or whatever that word was that only Bingo could pronounce. The extra photographs he'd taken using Ali's camera had helped. Along with assurances that, whilst Steve made loads of noise and did plenty of barking, he didn't actually do much biting.

But that was for later.

For now, it was time to take a back seat and let Steve bask in the glory of being the best Steve in the world.

"Pogs," said Steve, breaking the spell. "You got a sec? Outside."

"Sure," said Pogsy, leading the way back out the woodpile. He turned to face his leader, expecting praise and adulation.

"This sneaking around behind my back is an outrage," said Steve angrily. "I can't have a Second I can't trust."

"What you on about?" said Pogsy, taken aback. "I've never let you down. And I've just given you the best den ever."

"You could have told me straightaway. That's the right thing for a Second to do."

"Then it wouldn't have been a birthday surprise."

"Pogs. I've decided to put you on secret probation." Steve growled the words out. "One more step out of line and I'll get Weeble to kick your head in and then I'll chuck you out the gang forever, until the end of time. Got it?"

"Yes... Steve..." the words dribbled out slowly.

"What a div, trying to get one over on *me*." Steve slapped his palms together like he was dusting a coating of sherbet from his hands, turned and headed back to the den. "I sometimes wonder why I bother to have a Second who thinks that Slade are the best group in the world. If my Second can't even get the basics right, I have to wonder what else he's got wrong."

"Nowt!" said Pogsy firmly.

"We'll see about that. Seen as I'm in charge of all the gangs now, I'm gonna go make my first rule. Guess what? In these dens, just like the good old days, there's gonna be a big sign that says 'No Girls Allowed'. Even though I quite like girls now. And I've even snogged one or two, which is more than you've ever done."

Ten: Swapsies

Fish was something that Pogsy had been surrounded by in abundance his entire life, and as a consequence he hadn't dedicated much time to thinking about it. As a youngster, he'd nip down the North Wall with Sam and his dad and watch the fisherman going about their business. If the boats were in, No. 1 and No. 3 docks were a hive of activity. Fish was either being unloaded, or else the boats were being prepared for the next dangerous voyage north. On a busy day, when the boats had just come in, the Pontoon was where all the action happened. Brusque captains and their crews, dock hands and fish buyers all moved about like tiny figures on a grand clockwork toy. Everyone was always in motion and they all somehow knew where everyone else was supposed to be. Boxes flew through the air and looked like they were going to land awkwardly, smashing to smithereens, only to be caught by a man who wasn't even in the right spot when they were thrown. And the noise! The clamour of cargo unloading, cranes and joists straining under the weight, popping and groaning, all accompanied by harsh yelling and plenty of joshing back and forth. *Clonk, clonk, clonk,* went the barrow boys' clogs as they whizzed along the harbourside at full speed, shouting at everyone and everything to get out the ruddy way.

Dad loved to buy cooked shrimps straight off the boats and then stand there nonchalantly shelling them into the harbour. They were a bit fiddly for large fingers and Dad usually squashed a few before he handed the bag on. That was where the smaller hands of a child came in useful. Pogsy could peel a thousand shrimps a minute when he was up to full speed, which was more shrimps than anyone else he knew. Dad referred to him as "The demon peeler of Fish Docks Road", a title of which Pogsy was immensely proud.

The number of ways in which fish from the docks was served was almost limitless. Fish and chips from the chippie came as either haddock or skate wings. Unless you were down Meggies, in which case there was plenty of cod for the tourists. On a Friday, Dad brought home lemon sole or Dover sole or plaice, with the occasional halibut, which mum cooked up with a creamy, white parsley sauce. Then there were kippers and smoked haddock, which sometime came as finnan haddock. Pogsy didn't care much for kippers, because they gave him terrible wind, but Sam and Dad happily gobbled down platefuls of the stuff. He preferred fish fingers and fish cakes, which were all made locally by the *Christians*, then shipped up and down the country on palettes constructed from the piles of wood around the dens in the woodyard.

The only stuff from the sea that Pogsy didn't get on with were cockles, mussels and whelks, which he considered to be relatives of the slug and therefore chewy and horrible. Eels were his mortal enemy, especially the electric kind, which he'd never encountered, but feared nonetheless. Weeble's dad loved them. Between trips to Iceland, he'd quite happily spend an entire day fishing for eels in Tetney Lock, then cook his catch in a large aluminium pan, simmering the water until it turned to jelly. He'd spend the next week eating them every day for his dinner. Pogsy had only been fishing with Weebs and his dad once, and that was the day when he and eels fell out. He could map the moment to a precise second in time, which occurred when Weeble had tried to stuff what amounted to a slimy, wriggly sea-snake down his trousers as a joke. Electrocution didn't happen but Pogsy had vowed never to touch an eel again, and that included eating one with a knife and fork. Squib had run around quite happily with a sea-snake stuffed down each of his trouser legs until one bit him on the thigh. That was when Mister Pearce had stepped in and clubbed both eels to death with a cricket bat. It was no surprise to Pogsy that eels didn't appear on the fish counter at *Freemo Market* or on the menu at the chippie. Neither was he concerned about the lack of delicious breadcrumb-covered eel bites in the freezer drawer at the supermarket. There was no such thing as a snake sausage, so why on earth would there be sea-snake cakes or sea-snake fingers? The only person who'd eat any of those things anyway was the Devil. Or possibly Mister Pearce.

Pogsy first noticed that something had changed in the world of fish when he realised that Dad had stopped bringing home white paper packages that went straight in the freezer. When he checked, out of interest, the freezer drawers were only half-full. The second indicator that all was not right came that Friday when, for the first time in living memory, there was no fish and chips at dinner time. Instead, the dinner ladies served up chewy meat balls in lumpy gravy, with tasteless mash and mushy peas. It was a meal that somehow didn't quite work. Unless your name was Gas-tank, in which case it worked far too well. Even Missis Wainwright noticed and changed the scheduled afternoon lesson, sending the class to the school library to research Adrian's Wall. Pogsy heard her whisper to one of the other teachers that even Roman engineering at its finest wouldn't have been able to contain Gary Marsden's bottom.

When Pogsy came in from school that night, Sam was already home and was busy watching Ellie watching *Deputy Dawg*. His brother's primary job was to make sure that the Lego in his sister's hands didn't find its way up her nose or into her ears.

"Wot'cha, pipsqueak."

"Wot'cha, bellend," said Pogsy. "You know there's going to be a dead bad petrol shortage, right?"

"I know Dad's got a book of petrol coupons just in case," said Sam. "It's the same with all my mates' dads. They all rushed out to get them yesterday. Apparently, it was chaos at all the post offices in town. And the garages have been crazy all week."

"I saw the petrol queues when we went swimming," said Pogsy. "They were round the block."

"That's grown-ups for you: they always panic at the thought of shortages."

"Ali says it's much worse in America than it is here. But it doesn't affect uz anyway – we've got our bikes. And we can always give a pag to anyone that don't have one." Pogsy took a deep breath. "Sam. Is there going to be a dead bad fish shortage too?"

"I've no idea." Sam took a red Lego one-er brick from Ellie and attached it in the middle of two white one-ers. "Why don't you ask Dad?"

"Because fish is summut he won't talk about. He used to sneak fish home nearly every night. But he hasn't had any for ages. And the fish drawer's nearly empty. I looked."

"Ah." A light switched on in Sam's eyes. Pogsy saw it happen. "It's to do with how they ended the Cod War with Iceland."

"You mean the Scrobs," said Pogsy, pleased he was able to correct his brother.

"Technically speaking," said Sam, "they're the Icicles. The Scrobs are the Danes. I learned that from a Danish lad in my class at school. Anyway, we're not allowed to catch as much fish as we used to. Which means there's less fish being landed by our trawlers. Which means there's less fish on the docks than there used to be. Which means there's less spare fish going round for swapsies."

Pogsy thought about it for nearly a whole minute.

Whenever he did swapsies with any of his friends it was always like for like. Footballer cards for footballer cards. Stickers for other stickers. Sometimes, if a football card was rare, it would cost five or six other cards. The most he'd ever swapped a single card for was ten other cards, and that was for a Gordon Banks when the World Cup was on. He tried to imagine how fish swapsies might work.

Everyone liked haddock but no-one liked cod.

Ten cod for one haddock then.

Kippers were small and bony but most people thought they were delicious. So, four kippers for one haddock.

Shrimps would have to be swapsied by the bag. Two bags of shrimps per haddock.

Halibut was a big fish. But it was also dead rare. Like a Banksy. So at least twenty haddock for one halibut.

But it would get a bit boring eating all that haddock, so it would be better to swapsie one dead big halibut for ten haddock, thirty-two kippers and four bags of shrimp.

Eels would be like German money at the end of the First World War: No-one would want them. Even the biggest truck in the world filled with the most massive eels in the world wouldn't be worth the smallest shrimp in the world.

It was no wonder Mister Pearce ate what he caught. He didn't have much choice.

"Sam?" said Pogsy at last. "I've figured out how fish swapsies work. But to play, you've got to have fish to start with. If you're a fisherman, it'd be ace. But if you're not, there doesn't seem any point. You might as well just buy your fish down *Freemo Market*."

Sam smiled. "What if you did swapsies with more than fish?"

"That's too complicated." Pogsy grabbed his hair around the temples and tugged. "I'd need to take me friend Bingo with uz everywhere I went."

"Don't ever tell Dad I told you this," said Sam, keeping a firm eye on his sister, "but how it works is like this. Say a fish merchant needs a new telephone installed. Dad's bosses will charge the merchant for the phone and Dad's time to install new wires, and for the new wires too. But what if Dad had an old phone that he'd taken out of somewhere else, and some old wires he'd stripped out too? They're supposed to go down the rubbish tip, but what if he put everything in the fish merchant's office instead, on a nod and a wink?"

"Like a barrow job," said Pogsy.

"Exactly like a barrow job," replied Sam. "Except the fish merchant doesn't want to pay Dad in actual money, because that can be traced, and Dad doesn't want to take any money because, if he did and the bosses found out, he'd be in big trouble. So, the merchant pays him in fish instead. There's so much fish about, nobody's bothered about it. And yet everyone wants some. Fish is the secret currency of the docks. As long as Dad gives his boss a cut of all the haddock he makes at the end of the week, everyone's happy."

"Wow," said Pogsy. His brain felt fit to burst with all the new information. "Dad must have been doing an emassive amount of barrow jobs. If he's got to start buying fish like everyone else, he won't be happy."

"Welcome to the world of grown-ups," said Sam. "You better go get changed. And remember: not a word to Dad."

"Before I go, answer uz a question. What's probation?"

"It's when the cops keep an eye on you because you've done something wrong that's not quite bad enough to send you to prison for. If they catch you misbehaving while you're on probation, you'll be in massive troub."

"I thought it meant summut else."

"Like what?"

"Like when the gangsters led by that *Alca Pony* took over Chicago after the Yanks banned booze."

"That's prohibition."

"Oh."

Pogsy kicked off his shoes and headed upstairs. Finally, Steve's threat made sense. It wasn't a secret booze ban after all. Following their altercation, Steve had been all sweetness and light. There was no indication at all that words had ever been said. Everything was back to normal. In fact, as far as the gang was concerned, it had *always* been normal. Except it wasn't normal. Not by a long shot. Pogsy had been too shocked to call Steve out there and then in the woodyard. And after all the hard work he'd put in to getting the Treaty signed, he hadn't wanted to explode it into shrapnel in the first hour. So, he'd swallowed his anger and confusion and tried to live with it. He hadn't said anything about it the next day at school. Or the day after. He hadn't even told Ali, and she was supposed to be the one person in the world he could trust. The longer the not-saying-a-word went on, the more it seemed like the threat had never happened, to the point where he started to question his own sanity.

While he changed into his favourite tracksuit, Pogsy chuntered away to himself.

Being a Second means summut.

It's the best job in the world and Steve has no right to threaten to take it away.

There's only one thing for it.

Revenge.

On Saturday morning the three gangs all put in a good shift, trying to outbuild each other ahead of the first ever all-gang meeting scheduled for the following day. Every hour on the hour, they hunkered down while the guard came along and cast an eye over the yard. Seeing nothing untoward, he'd leave again. While the gangs moved wood around, Bigzy returned from his latest mission to catch the mystery boy.

"Pogs is right," said the little lad. "That boy *is* half-monkey. And he knows this yard like the back of his hand. The way he vanishes when he sees uz, he must have a secret hidey-hole somewhere."

"You're obsessed," said Red Top.

"I'm also the only one who's fast enough to catch 'im. I saw he's got some new kneepads to go with his elbow pads. That's how he's able to move so quick without skinning hissen." Bigzy showed off the scabs on his elbows. "Whatever shoes he's wearing, they've got super grip. He can turn on a sixpence."

"I still think he's a Tramp," said Red Top sourly.

"If he was, he'd have led them to uz by now." Bigzy shook his head. "Naw. You're wrong. He's a lad without a gang who's looking to join one."

"See what I've got?" said Reddy with an ear-to-ear sneer. He held up a battered wooden board that was singed in the top corner. "I rescued it from the fire years ago and I've been keeping it ever since, waiting for this day."

"No Girls Allowed" read the sign.

"Hang it by the entrance for good luck," said Bigzy.

Outside the den, Pogsy heard a commotion. He rushed out into the yard to see what was going on. Yeti, a lad with hairy forearms that he'd inherited when his mam had done it with an abominable snowman, was jabbering away excitedly to the rest of the Hard Nuts.

"Tell uz again," said Smiffy, beckoning The Kings over.

"I got all the way to the workmisters' hut just like Mopes dared us," said Yeti. "And guess wot? I nebbed through the winda and there on the wall at the back, behind their tea table, I spied wiv my little eye a nuddie calendar."

For the next few hours, all the gangs could talk about was nudity. Everybody wanted a look, and all the boys took it in turns to sneak down the yard and have a gander. Pogsy led The Kings' first mission, keeping to the gaps in the wood. Once they reached the hut, faces were pressed to the window. Bingo took a step back and used his 'nocs to get a better view. Feverishly, he made a note of the name of the company that had supplied the calendar. Bigzy recognised the address as down on the docks. One by one, all the boys had a good gawp at Miss November's melons.

"December's always the best month," said Bigzy, handing the 'nocs onto Weeble. "Me bruvver once had a calendar with two Miss Decembers."

"How does that work?" asked Bingo.

"You split the month down the middle!" Bigzy laughed and finger-poked Bingo in his belly. "He asked for a calendar with thirty-one Miss Decembers the next year, but the welding company that made them told him to get lost."

"Gizza look," said Squib, trying to get hold of the field glasses.

"Yer nor'old enuf," said Weeble, holding them above his head.

"I'll tell mam you looked a' a lass in the nip."

"You wha'?"

"Nuffink."

"Wha' d'you say?"

"Nuffink."

"Cum'ere, you."

Weeble and Squib began their brotherly dance of death, weaving in and out of the gang, as the older brother chased the younger one down, intent on administering a monkey-scrub.

Bingo looked at his watch. "Crikey. The security guard will be here any second."

Pogsy felt his senses switch into super-real. Every slight sound became amplified a thousand-fold. If a pin dropped, he'd hear it. Any slight movement, he'd see it. At the far end of the yard, a boy waved frantically, then dived behind a stack of wood. Pogsy heard the gate lock: *clack*. Time stood still.

Everyone froze.

Squeak.

Bigzy moved first. He shot off to the side of the hut, putting the wooden building between him and the gate. He motioned for the rest of the gang to follow. Bingo did as he was told without question. Weeble was so engrossed in punishing his brother, he failed to notice what was happening. Pogsy knocked him in the ribs. Weeble looked up, turned scarlet and, clenching his fists, let go of his brother, who ran for it.

"You startin'?" growled Weeble.

Pogsy put his finger to his lips and pointed first in the direction of the gate, then at the chosen hiding place.

Weeble shook his head violently from side to side then quickly followed everyone else.

The gang half-stood and half-crouched with their backs to the side of the hut.

Although the woodyard enclosure was laid out as a large rectangle, not all of it was accessible. Just behind the hut ran a high chain-link fence, connected to each of its side walls. Red Top had christened the smaller yard beyond the fence the *Pally Yard*. This was where planks of wood were sawn up and turned into palettes by a team of palette makers. During the week, they made plenty of noise with their electric saws and nail guns. Completed palettes were stacked up against the wall in their hundreds, awaiting use. The area was a mess of wood shavings and offcuts, and seldom cleaned. When the workmen did bother to have a spruce-up, they collected the debris in a circular metal container and set fire to it.

Pogsy felt his heart trip several warning lights. He was hiding in the one place he'd never wanted to be. Bingo pressed up against the wall of the hut, eyes closed, pretending to be invisible. Weeble mumbled profanities, continuously clenching and unclenching his fists. Pogsy watched Bigzy closely. His pal's eyes shot from side to side, calculating angles. *If he ran now, would he be seen?* Squib, who was the smallest one of the bunch, crawled underneath the hut, which was raised off the ground on a series of breezeblocks. For the rest of them, the squeeze was too tight.

They waited and waited, listening intently to the scuffle of a pair of steelies on concrete. Pogsy glimpsed a plume of cigarette smoke. A waft of burning tobacco, caught by the breeze, stung his nose and eyes. He fought the urge to cough. The security guard sang something to himself. Pogsy thought he heard the words "only had one ball".

Presently, the door to the hut rattled. A boot kicked at the wood. Once. Twice. Beyond the edge of the hut a figure appeared, clad in a dark blue uniform topped with a peaked cap. He stood facing away from the gang, puffing away. Everyone made themselves as narrow as possible and stopped breathing. The guard half-turned towards them and then stopped. He swivelled back on the spot and stared down the woodyard.

"Ooo's there?" he bawled. He took a few steps towards the nearest woodpile and hesitated. "Cum on you little bleeder, show yesen!"

Silence greeted him.

After a few seconds of staring intensely ahead, the guard shook his head, mumbled something unintelligible, flicked his fag end to the floor and stomped on it with his boot. Slowly he turned and headed back towards the gate.

The *clang* caused by the great gate slamming shut couldn't come soon enough. The moment it did, the urge to run became overwhelming. Bigzy waved his hands, begging everyone to hang fire and move away from the side of the hut towards the front, just in case the guard was checking the Pally Yard.

After a minute that felt like an hour, Bigzy stuck his head around the corner. "He's gone."

Collectively, everyone exhaled in relief. All except for Squib.

"John, you cow!" he shouted. "Don' leave uz! I can' ge' ou'! I'm ruddy stuck!"

"That was the old codger," said Bigzy. "He's a bit clueless and he couldn't catch a tortoise. We should torture him for nearly getting uz."

Pogsy laughed out loud.

It had been a close call, but there was no better feeling in the world than nearly getting caught and getting away with it. It made you feel invincible. Like Superman crossed with the Invisible Man. They'd

all be walking on air and telling tales of their miraculous escape for
weeks.

Later, once they were safely back in the den, Bingo took full
responsibility, even though it wasn't really his fault.

"I'm really sorry," he said, removing his glasses and spitting on
the lenses to clean them. "I wasn't paying attention to the time. I've
never seen a proper nuddie woman before. My dad doesn't really like
that sort of thing. And even if he did, my mum would never put up with
him having a calendar like that."

Bigzy laughed. "Me dad's got one in his garage and both me
bruvvers have as well. There's always tons of 'em about on the docks at
this time of year. Me cousin even sells 'em off his barra."

"Could you get me one?" asked Bingo.

"It'll cost you a week's pocket money."

"Ge' uz one fer the den!" Squib's hair was covered in muck and
cobwebs and his parka was equally filthy, with a brand-new tear down
one arm.

"Yer nor'old enuf!" Weeble cuffed his brother about the ear.

"Still, it's a great idea," said Bigzy, a twinkle in his eye. "I'll
ask me cousin, see what he can do."

Pogsy was late home for his tea, which earned him a telling off. He was
so busy thinking about some of the changes they'd got planned for the
den that he wasn't paying attention, which earned him a second telling-
off for not listening to the first telling-off.

He sat down to eat and quickly demolished the half-a-grapefruit
starter, with heaps of sugar on top, watching his mum intently as she
slaved over a hot frying pan. He caught a whiff of steak sizzling away in
its own juices, taunting him from the stove.

He elbowed his brother in the ribs. "The big one's mine."

"I think not," said Sam. "That one's Dad's. Yours is the really
titchy one that's so small you can't see it from there."

"Fibber!" Pogsy's tummy rumbled. "That one's yours."

There was no doubt about it: steak and chips with tinned peas
and fried mushrooms was the best a man could get. There was simply
nothing better after a hard day on a building site.

"Good luck with Ellie later," said Mum, with her back to the
table. "She's decided to stay awake all night."

"I'm seeing a man about a dog," said Dad. "It's your job to put her to bed."

"I'm out with my friends from school for our Christmas drink," said Mum, juggling pans. "It's been pencilled in on the calendar for months."

"What the ruddy hell?" Dad chewed his lips like he'd just inhaled a wasp. "You can't go out. Not tonight. Someone has to babysit."

"Babysit," said Ellie, not realising that she was the focal point of the altercation.

"This is your mess," said Mum, turning around. "You sort it."

Dad stared back, not saying a word.

Pogsy growled. All he could think about was his tea.

He was ravenous.

And he hated stare-offs.

He drummed his feet on the floor, then held his knife and fork upright, signalling to Mum to serve. But still she refused.

He wondered if begging might work.

"I'm not moving until you apologise for taking me for granted," said Mum.

Eventually, Dad mumbled sorry. By then, the steak was tough and rubbery and the chips were cold. The mushrooms, which had started out the size of dinner plates had shrivelled to the size of shirt buttons. The peas were still delicious though. They were almost impossible to ruin. Pogsy scoffed the lot anyway, even the meat rind. Then he licked his plate clean and got told off again, this time for being uncouth.

"Sam can look after Ellie," said Dad.

Mum shook her head. "He's still in the doghouse for dynamiting Armstrong's pooch."

"I'm off out anyway," said Sam. "*Cluedo* with Jimbo and his cousins."

After tea, Dad popped round to see Missis D and ask her for the favour, but she was busy and unavailable. "There's only one answer," he said. "Pat, you're coming with me."

Mum shrugged her shoulders and got on with combing her hair.

Pogsy grinned from ear to ear. Missions with Dad were always exciting, especially in the dark. And given that Dad was refusing to say what the mission entailed, that made it an extra special secret mission.

The second tea was done, he headed up to his bedroom and packed everything he thought he might need in his trusty army-surplus gasmask bag. In went his favourite penknife, some sticking plasters, a needle and cotton in case he needed to stitch his arm back on, a bottle of orange squash, some emergency biscuits, some double emergency biscuits for when the emergency biscuits ran out, a compass, a torch, and a matchbox containing three matches, five pence in pennies and his lucky troll.

Mum left home first.

In Dad's words, she was "dolled-up to the nines". Sam was the next to go. He wobbled down the road on his pushbike, which had a faulty rear light. Given that Jimbo only lived a short walk away, Pogsy wondered whether he was telling the truth, the whole truth and nothing but the truth about where he was off to.

Once Dad had the house to himself, he relaxed and put Elton John on the stereo. Even though it wasn't Glam, Pogsy sang along to "Rocket Man". Dad dressed in a padded winter coat and a red and white bobble hat decorated with reindeer, which Granny Green had knitted the previous Christmas. Ellie looked smart in a pair of thick pink tights and a parka, with a pair of Granny Green's knitted animal mittens held in place with a piece of threaded elastic. Pogsy had no idea where they were going, so chose to wear his best flares, a red and brown knitted jumper, and his favourite teddy-bear jacket. According to the weather forecast, snow was due any day. Dad's car was cold inside. Its cracked leather seats were boiling hot in summer and freezing cold in winter. Plus, the heater was broken. At night, you could see your breath and that made the mirror fog up, which in turn made Dad swerve all over the road every time he tried to wipe it.

It was a big surprise when they walked straight past Dad's MG and crossed the road to Mister Payne's house, where his Bedford camper van was parked outside. Mister Payne took the wheel, with Dad on the left, leaving the middle seat for Pogsy with Ellie perched between his legs. While the engine warmed up, they all huddled around the heater, which blew out tepid air. As there were only two seatbelts, Pogsy and Ellie were taking a chance. It wasn't a big chance though. If it had been Chip's dad driving, in his battered old Ford Anglia with overflowing ash trays and a gearstick that screeched, things would be different. But this was Mister Payne. He really liked his van and kept it spotless inside. Pogsy knew that, unlike Mister Flowers, he was a careful driver who always kept his eyes on the road. His van was usually parked in a garage around the back of his house and polished religiously every Sunday, even when it wasn't dirty. Pogsy quite liked Mister Payne, even though he didn't have a wife or any children. Mister Payne enjoyed fiddling with electronics and he was friends with Sparksy's dad. Pogsy was pretty sure that that was where Mister Payne had got his van's radio cassette player from. It certainly didn't come as standard. In fact, no-one he knew had a radio cassette player in their car. Dad's car didn't even have a radio.

"Here you go." Dad handed a couple of cassette tapes to Pogsy, to give to Mister Payne.

One was a compilation of pops songs from earlier in the year. The other had a recording of Mike Harding's "A Lancashire Lad" on one side and "Laughter with a Bang" by Blaster Bates on the other.

"You're not to tell your mum," said Dad with a nod and a wink.

"Yes, Dad," said Pogsy quickly before Dad changed his mind.

Both the original records were in Dad's *blue* pile, which was strictly out of bounds. Pogsy had sneaked a listen to Blaster Bates and knew there was plenty of swearing, but he didn't know the other artist. He was new.

"What if Ellie says summut?"

"She hears far worse from your Aunt Sandra," said Dad.

"You mean Aunt Lorna," said Pogsy.

Dad glared back, his pale brown eyes flickering with disdain. He slowly shook his head and unfolded a map across the dashboard, referring to a sheet of paper with instructions scrawled in biro. "It should take us about two hours. Provided my sister hasn't gone any battier than she already is."

"Righto, Al," said Mister Payne.

Pogsy knew the three main routes out of town by heart. One route went south to Louth, which was where Potty Gran lived. The route west involved driving past Granny and Grandad Green's house, which was somewhere near Laceby. If you carried straight on at the big roundabout, it took you to Caistor, which had the best hills in the area for sledging. Except the snow would always drift and block the road, making it impossible to reach them. Along the road, Lincoln came next. And then Newark, which had a great castle with dungeons and suits of armour. Pogsy was convinced that, if a bark-chain really could travel as far as Bingo claimed, this was the route it would take. If you turned right at the big roundabout, it took you to Barton-on-Humber and the ferry to Hull, which was always a really good day out. This was the route that Mister Payne chose. When he reached the turn-off to Barton, he carried straight on instead, towards Scunthorpe. Out of all the possible routes that they could have taken, this was the one that Pogsy knew the least well. Although it was dark and the roads were badly lit, he played *I Spy* with Ellie. It gave him a chance to keep a look out for Second World War airfields and bunkers. There were plenty around if you knew where to look. He was busy thinking of Lancaster bombers and Wellingtons, and only half-listening to Mike Harding, when the comedian started talking about Sodom and Gomorrah and "hokey-pokey penny-a-lick".

Mister Payne erupted in a fit of giggles and honked the horn twice, which made Ellie jump.

"Again!" she giggled.

Pogsy had no idea what a *sod 'em-and-go marrow* was, nor why anyone would pay a penny for a lick of something hokey. He figured it was probably a rude grown-up joke but got no further in his thought process as he spied his favourite bridge directly ahead.

"Do you spy what I spy?" He pointed to a great metal structure comprised of grey lattice-work girders that looked like a dustbin lorry. "That's *Kidney* Bridge."

"Kidney Bridge," said Ellie, delightedly.

It was really Keadby Bridge. But *Kidney* Bridge was what Pogsy used to call it when he was little, so it had become a family tradition. It was on the route to *Donkeycaster*, which was another traditional family name. By the time they pulled over in the middle of nowhere, Ellie was asleep. Mister Payne had spent the last half an hour fretting about petrol, even though he still had three quarters of a tank. Dad checked the map again and talked it through with his friend. They were two turnings past a roundabout with a bush in the middle, with a phone box on the left a half-mile back. It had to be the right place. The clock on Mister Payne's dashboard said 8.50. They were apparently early. Mister Payne drove on a bit further before turning left into a dark lay by, which was shrouded by lifeless trees and gave the impression of being a long, muddy tunnel. The further they went along, the darker it got. There hadn't been a streetlight for miles.

Dad nudged Mister Payne. "Here will do. We might as well get set up."

"Righto, Al."

"You two stay here," said Dad, picking up a torch and a crowbar, which he tucked inside his jacket.

Mister Payne turned on the inside lights and pulled the keys from the ignition. He climbed out and joined Dad around the back of the van. Between them, they opened up the doors. Pogsy hadn't considered looking in the back until now. He saw a collection of large rectangular cardboard boxes, all sealed shut, piled along the floor on top of each other, but stacked in such a way that you couldn't see them from outside. With the van's heater switched off, the temperature began to drop. Pogsy felt a chill wave emanate from the back of the van, like there was a block of ice behind his seat. While he was looking over his shoulder, a pair of headlights appeared in the distance, bouncing up and down. Dad shut the doors. The lights came closer and closer, finally stopping a few feet away.

Pogsy started counting.

Kev-a-Keegan, two-a-Keegan.

He heard voices but he couldn't really see what was going on. He felt like he was trapped in his own little bubble with his sister, who was curled up beside him. He reached thirty *Keegans*. Then forty. He clutched his gasmask bag tightly and wondered what he might do if Dad didn't come back. He had no idea where he was, nor did he have a map. He'd had one driving lesson in his life, and that wasn't really a proper drive as his legs were too short to reach the pedals. Plus, Mister Payne had the keys. He needed a better plan than just hoping everything would be alright. At the sixty *Keegan* mark he checked his matchbox. Five pence wasn't going to get him very far, especially once it was split with his sister.

Two-and-a-half pence each, to get all the way back home.

It didn't look good.

A few *Keegans* later Dad's face appeared at the window. He opened the door and beckoned Pogsy out.

"Come on down, Pat," he said. "You'll like this."

"What about Ellie?"

"She's asleep. She'll be fine."

Pogsy did as he was told, stashing his bag under the seat for safekeeping, careful not to wake his sister. Outside, beyond the wedge of Dad's torch beam, it was pitch black. The lane was covered in piles of mouldy brown leaves. Underfoot, the ground was soggy, but it wasn't going to stay that way for long. A frost was already forming. By the morning it was going to be treacherous. Pogsy exhaled, watching his breath solidify. He pulled his jacket up tight, stuffed his hands in his pockets and, kicking leaves as he went, wandered around to the back of the van letting his eyes adjust. A third vehicle appeared in the distance with its headlights on full beam. The light was so bright it hurt, and Pogsy had to shield his eyes with his hand. After a few seconds of bouncing up and down, the vehicle pulled up and the driver dimmed his lights. Two men and a lad climbed out. Jovially they sauntered over, torches in hand, and joined the two men and a lad from the first vehicle, which Pogsy could now see was a small van.

"I'm Aggers," said Dad. "The fish man. Who's Bonzo?"

"That'd be me," said one of the men from the first car in an accent that was all harsh, clicking consonants. "I'm mister fags 'n' booze, me. Me mate 'ere does perfume for the ladies."

Pogsy recognised the accent as Liverpudlian. Liverpool was his favourite football team, after all. Bonzo was all teeth and hand-talking. He had a huge nose and a bushy moustache, just like most of the Liverpool first team.

"I'm Zup," said one of the men from the second car in an accent that was broad Yorkshire. "They call us the lamb king, but any meat you want, I'm your man. Pork. Beef. Goat. Horse. Mince it up, slap it in your burgers and no-one will ever know the difference."

Zup was a colossal man dressed in an outsized padded coat. He had stubby front teeth, a bald head and ruddy cheeks, with hands like baseball catcher's mitts. Given what he was selling, Pogsy decided you wouldn't trust him to look after your pets for the night.

Without warning, another set of headlights appeared behind everyone, moving slowly along the lane. All the men, including Dad, turned around and froze. They lowered their torches and thrust their hands inside their jackets. The car slowed down to a crawl, inching ever so slowly forward until it was nearly touching the bumper of the third car. The men stood their ground, not moving a muscle. Eventually, two Pakistanis climbed out. The driver apologised profusely for being late. Pogsy stared and stared. He'd only ever seen one other Pakistani man in real life before. No-one else batted an eyelid. Not even the lads. Pogsy felt his ears blush.

"I'm Mo," said one of the new men in a heavy accent, which made his words sound like they were weighed down with lead weights.

"I bring gold watches. Gold jewellery. Gold everything for your wives and girlfriends. All the way from India."

Mo's smile was so wide it looked like a half-moon. He clapped his hands and rubbed them vigorously together.

Dad, Bonzo, Zup and Mo all shook hands with each other, then the other men shook hands too. Pogsy watched on, fascinated. Hurriedly and with purpose, Bonzo and his mate took a fold-up table out the back of their van and erected it. A pair of miner's lamps appeared, one for each back corner. The men all turned off their torches then arranged their stuff on the table. The Pakistanis didn't want anything to do with Zup's pork chops but they liked the sound of his goat, even though they said it smelt like donkey. One of the Liverpudlians had a titchy set of scales, which he used to weigh the jewellery. He complained that it was hollow. One of the Pakistanis told him his head was full of treacle. Mister Payne took an interest in a bottle of booze and had a swig, which he promptly spat out. He said it tasted like disinfectant. Bonzo shook his head at Dad's fish. Dad pointed to the yellow spots on the skin, which proved he wasn't selling catfish. It didn't take Pogsy long to cotton on to what they were doing. They were haggling. Grown-ups did it all the time in *Freemo Market*. He exhaled hard, pretending he was smoking a cigarette. It was quite realistic. The grown-ups finished their sampling and started talking exchange rates. Pogsy grinned. When it came down to it, they really were just playing swapsies.

As the real negotiations got underway, he realised that the boxes which Dad and Mister Payne had brought along were full of frozen cod. He wondered where the haddock was, and even thought about saying something. Except everyone was very happy with what Dad was supplying. Apart from Zup, who said that fish was for poofters. The Liverpudlians, who Pogsy learned were Scousers, swapped three bottles of whisky for half a pig; boxes of cigarettes changed hands for gold bracelets; cod was swapped for everything. There was one box that Dad kept a very close eye on, which was set apart from the rest of the fish, and he referred to it as his "catch of the day". Everyone was interested in the contents of that box and the bids went really high. Pogsy supposed it must be halibut, the Gordon Banks of fish. Although he couldn't be certain, he was pretty sure it wasn't a box of premium eels. There was no such thing in the whole wide world.

After a while, the two boys – who Pogsy decided were about his age – popped over.

"I'm Pogsy," said Pogsy. "Me gang's buildin' the best secret den ever."

"Ay up," said the Yorkie lad, his squiffy left eye twitching of its own accord. "I'm *Ecky*. Are gang 'ave a disused barn. We race snails, us. Or pigeons if we can wog 'em."

"Awright," said the Scouser, whose front teeth stuck out like a pair of chisels. "Me name's *Tadge*. I'm the leader of are gang, me. Are secret den's top secret."

"Leeds for champions!" bawled Ecky. "We're top o' the league and stayin' there."

"Liverpool!" shouted Pogsy and Tadge together.

For the next ten minutes they all talked football and argued about which players were the best and whose team would go down in history. As they joshed, Tadge kept on rolling up his tongue, and that, along with the teeth, reminded Pogsy of Steve. The Scouser then made a couple of outrageous claims, including one about meeting Kev Keegan down the shops. The more he watched and listened, the more Pogsy became convinced that Steve had a twin brother who'd been stolen from the hospital.

"Elland Road is easy the top ground in the whole world!" said Ecky, breaking the spell.

"That's 'cos you ain't seen the Kop," said Tadge. "You ever bin to Anfield, Pogs?"

"Not yet," said Pogsy. "But I want to."

"I'll tek yous," said Tadge. "Me bruvver's mate's a tout, 'e 'as spare tickets all the time."

Pogsy whooped. Just when he'd decided he didn't like Tadge for being a Steve impersonator, his new pal had come up trumps. "Who likes Glam?"

"We love it!" Ecky pursed his lips and nodded while his squiffy eye did its own thing.

"Us too," said Tadge. "Go on. Favourite band."

"Slade!" said Ecky emphatically.

"Noddy's the greatest," said Pogsy in full agreement.

"Get stuffed, the both of yous!" Tadge bared his teeth. "You's got your 'eads stuck up a nag's arse.

"My friend Stan..." sung Ecky.

Pogsy half-sang and half-shouted the next bit.

"Come on! Come one!" bellowed Tadge, stomping his foot. "Come on, come on, come on! Stan's rubbish and yous both knows it."

"Well Glitter's latest is rubbish too," said Pogsy.

"It's Number One though," sneered Tadge. "And it will be forever. By the time 'e's finished, 'e'll 'ave 'ad more 'its than Slade 'ave 'ad 'ot dinners. You watch."

"Slade'll—"

"Do nuthin'," said Tadge. "They're done for. Finished. All washed up, like. They ain't got no more 'its in 'em. Tank's empty. They're second best to the man."

Pogsy shook his head in disappointment. Much as he'd warmed to Tadge after the offer of tickets to see Liverpool, he couldn't possibly be mates with another big-head who worshipped the wrong star. Unfortunately, he couldn't be mates with a Slade fan who supported the dreaded Leeds United either.

It was an unfortunate end to the evening.

As the men were stashing their gear away, Bonzo offered Dad a splendiferous box of sugar.

"What would I do with *that*?" Dad looked tired.

"There's a shortage coming, mate," said Bonzo. "I 'eard it on the grapevine from me mate who knows someone on the inside. By Christmas it'll be even more valuable than petrol."

Dad and Mister Payne had a quick huddle.

"I'll have two stone," said Dad.

"Five stone minimum. Take it or leave it."

The second Scouser chimed in, "We got camping gas and candles. Twenty bottles of gas and a hundred and fifty candles should see you through the winter, mate. It's gonna be harsh, they say. Real harsh. When the power cuts start, you'll be sitting there happy as Larry while everyone else freezes 'cos they didn't see it coming. Unlike clever you. Go on, mate. What d'you say? It's for a good cause like. Keep me ma in turkey all Christmas, it will."

"Ten stone it is." Dad shook his head. "It's no wonder they call you lot *scallys*."

Pogsy nodded off shortly after they left the layby. Dad's pop tape blared away in the background, keeping Mister Payne sane. Neither he nor Dad said a word. Pogsy dozed. He imagined that while he'd been away Bigzy and his cousins had been busy and the woodyard was laid out like a football stadium. At one end the wood had been arranged into the shape of a gigantic stage. Slade were there, larger than life, playing all their greatest hits, and everyone he knew was having a great time dancing along. He humsung a few tunes, doing his best to remember all the words. Knowing his dreams, it wouldn't be long before the Daleks turned up.

He opened his eyes.

The dream was too good to let the giant pepper pots ruin everything.

He made notes of how it felt when the vehicle turned, and how long it took between each stop, remembering it for next time. Periodically he heard the clank of bottles from the back. He thought about the frozen cod. They never had cod for tea. Dad wouldn't have it in the house. He called it an insult to fish everywhere. Which meant all those boxes must have come from Mister Payne's house. Perhaps that was where Dad was storing *all* his fish now.

Just in case.

The pop tape ran out after "Power To All Our Friends" by Cliff Richard. Seconds later they reached the big roundabout near Granny Green's house. From here, Pogsy knew all the twists and turns home, including every pothole. By the time they reached his house, the clock in Mister Payne's van said it was after midnight. Mister Payne dropped them all off, then drove away to park his van in his garage. Dad carried Ellie in his arms. She looked so innocent, cuddled up asleep, clutching at Dad's jacket. Pogsy felt the cold through his jeans. As his breath left his mouth, it formed tiny icicles. Frost glittered across the ground. He heard it scrunch underfoot. He shivered, then stamped up and down while Dad unlocked the front door. Winter was definitely here and that meant Christmas was just around the corner.

His birthday was so close he could smell it.

On the way to bed, Pogsy suddenly knew what he wanted for Christmas, apart from a kiss with Ali. However, there was one slight problem. If he asked Santa, then the chances were that fatty Claus would delegate the task to Granny Green, who would get the wrong end of the stick and end up knitting something with seven legs and two armholes. Not only would it look silly, but he'd also have to wear it and be grateful.

Granny was a world-class knitter.

There was no doubt about it.

But she did love to let her imagination run wild, and that meant she found it impossible to stick to the rules. When *The Wombles* had first appeared on TV, she'd found a pattern in one of her knitting magazines and started a production line of stuffed womble toys. Her primary wombles were about a foot tall and sewn from fur and felt. She could knock out two a week and each came with a range of six interchangeable costumes. Later on, she'd downsized and created a mini-womble that was about five inches tall. At full pelt, she produced fifteen of those a week. Once Granny had got up a full head of steam, she wouldn't stop for anything, and that included fresh craft supplies. Hence, after about thirty mini-wombles, the colours changed from grey and brown to whatever she could lay her hands on. Green paisley. Pink fur. Red and purple corduroy. Tartan. The list was endless and each womble was truly unique. To begin with, her friend had done a roaring trade from her market stall down *Freemo*, but as the materials began to vary, sales had dropped off. Pogsy noticed one day that the only customers buying the unusual mini-wombles smelt of joss sticks and patchouli oil, a smell he recognised from Aunt Lorna's patchwork period when all her boyfriends had long hair, beards and round, coloured glasses.

The answer, thought Pogsy, as he pulled on his pyjamas, *was to make what he wanted hissen*. He was pretty sure he could do it. He'd watched enough *Blue Peter*. In his tired mind a plan began to form. Every Christmas, on the last day of term, all the classes in school had a do-it-yourself competition, and every year, thanks to his lucky crown, Steve won. He was an expert with a sewing needle and precise with his cutting out and gluing. In fact, he was so good at making models that everyone else had given up trying to beat him.

The leader of the gang had been dropping hints about this year's effort for weeks, and how it set a new impossible standard. His reputation was such that the playground considered him invincible.

But not this year.

Pogsy was certain that what he had in mind was easily better than whatever Steve had planned.

It was only right that his friend should lose.

He climbed into bed and closed his eyes.

All he had to do was find a decent photo to work from. It would require some careful planning. Everything would have to be measured and calculated in advance. There was no room for error, not where Steve was concerned. It had to be perfect. Once he'd worked out what he needed, he'd borrow it from Mum's sewing box. As long as he didn't ask first, she wouldn't mind.

He drifted off to sleep, convinced that nothing could go wrong.

Pogsy stifled a yawn and headed towards the woodyard. He mock-punched himself on his temples, in a vain attempt to smack Tadge's prediction out of his noggin.

Slade are done for.

They're second best and they'll never have another Number One.

He tried to imagine a world without the hits of Noddy Holder and Jimmy Lea, where his sworn enemy was the supreme ruler and everyone dressed just like him and stomped around singing his songs all the time.

It was a world of horror that he didn't want to live in, not even for a micro-milli-second.

Quickly and without fuss he scaled the obstacle course around the dens then abseiled down the inside wall, aware he was running late for the largest gang meet so far.

"All hands on deck" was something that Steve used to shout all the time, back when he was pretending to be Captain Crane. It was his opportunity to inspect uniforms and invent petty infringements, such as unpolished shoes or missing buttons, then fine boys in sweets for their misdemeanours. Not that there was much inventing to do, considering missing shirt buttons usually stayed missing and shoes were only polished at the beginning of term. This call was different though. Steve had issued it as the leader of all the gangs, in his foghorn style, and everyone was expected to be there, even the lads who weren't officially in a gang yet.

Pogsy felt his tummy clinch tighter than a razor clam.

Today was the day.

"At last," said Steve as Pogsy rounded the corner. "I was just wondering who else I could promote to Second."

Posy felt his ears fire up to orange. "Soz and all that. I was out with me dad all night." He fell in, at the front of the line, ahead of Reddy, then turned to scan the expectant faces. It was a very impressive turnout. Eleven Hard Nuts had pitched up, along with ten Wingmen and eight from The Kings. Many of the boys were armed, with an array of sticks, spears and catapults. There were probably a few hidden penknives too. He patted his pocket, reassured that his favourite stabber hadn't fallen out.

"Bigzy'll be here in a mo'," whispered Steve. "He's bringing Sarge." The leader of the gangs rested his front teeth on his bottom lip, then turned around and addressed all the lads present. "Listen up, everyone. It's really great to see you all. I know not everyone has been here before, and what we're building is something we all want to brag about. But we can't. It's dead important that we keep the location of the dens secret. We can't tell anyone, not even our brothers, and especially our sisters. If word gets out, lads will come snooping and some of those lads might be Tramps."

"If them Tramps do come sniffin', we'll 'ave 'em," said Smiffy, making a fist and holding his wart aloft.

"They don't stand a chance," added Wingnut. "Not against all of uz."

Pogsy remembered scrapping alongside Wingy and Mopes the previous summer, when they'd taken on the Old Clee Wheelers in a fight to the death. He trusted them both with their fists. Smiffy was more of an unknown. He loved to talk the talk but, when it came down to it, he always stood behind his Second. Gecko was solid enough though, and he had a heck of a punch.

Steve carried on talking, telling all the new lads about the security guards and all the close scrapes they'd had so far, especially with the old fogey who they shouldn't underestimate even though he was half-blind and slower than a snail. Then he bigged up Weeble as the toughest boy in the woodyard. Those who'd seen him ruck knew what a handful he was, and those who hadn't were the sort of boys who'd surrender the second they were threatened. Smiffy and Wingy joshed with Steve about how their dens were already better than his, which riled Steve up, but in a good way. By the time the jesting contest was over, everyone was dying to get on with building and the second they were dismissed the gangs raced to their piles.

"I like it here," said Sparksy on the short walk to The Kings' den. "I didn't think I would. But, yeah. This is what a secret den should be."

"It's quite a sight," said Gas-tank. "Unfortunately, I have to go by half ten else my dad'll have my guts for garters."

"Have you scoffed those pickled eggs that Bigzy's cousin borrowed from that job lot that fell off the back of a lorry near *Corpo Bridge*?" asked Pogsy.

"I'm saving them for after swimming next week." Gas-tank tittered to himself. "My plumbing's going to rattle like a skellington in handcuffs."

Bingo furrowed his brow. "That little twerp still hasn't got me my calendar. Apparently his cousin's friend ran their barrow into the docks and soaked everything, and I have to wait for more to get printed."

"Sounds about right," said Pogsy.

"It's not fair! There isn't much of the year left."

Pogsy looked at his imaginary watch.

Bingo was right.

1973 was drawing to a close.

A couple of woodpiles away, someone shouted. It was followed by a familiar challenge: "Halt! Who goes there?"

Immediately, Pogsy's battle senses kicked in. Reddy came beetling out The Kings' den, fists raised, followed by Weeble. Work on the Hard Nuts' den next door stopped. Lads came flying out the entrances, ready to ruck. Reassured by the size of his gang, Steve led the group of boys towards the cable-drum steps, where they joined up with the Wingmen. Sheepishly, Pogsy followed behind, his guts aching. On one hand, it was the moment he'd been dreaming of for months but, on the other, the tension was simply too much to bear.

The big lad in the bright red Manchester United tracksuit was instantly recognisable. He stood a good three inches taller than everyone else and had a smile made for advertising toothpaste. Pogsy tried not to look at the person by his side. He closed his eyes and rubbed his lucky troll. When he opened them again she was still there.

His American friend was dressed in a powder-blue tracksuit, with the jacket zip half open. Underneath, she was wearing a black top that shimmered, and on her feet she had her famous stars-and-stripes sneakers.

"Hiya, guys," she said in a soft West Coast accent. "How's it all goin'?"

"Oooo are you?" said the guard, confused. He looked at his spear, then at Ali, and finally at Sarge.

"Bigzy's gone missing," said Sarge. "We had to work out how to get in ourselves."

"He spotted a boy dressed like a monkey," said Ali, "and gave chase."

The assembled horde lurched forward and stopped behind the guard. Up close, Pogsy saw that his friend was wearing blue eye make-up and her hair was all frizzy. He forced a smile, trying to dismiss the backflips going on in his tummy.

"This is Sarge, everyone," said Steve. "He's our best runner and he can wheelie anything smaller than a forklift truck."

"And the uvver one?" asked Smiffy suspiciously.

"Ah'm Ali," said Ali. "From Texas and LA. Pleased to make your acquaintance. All of you."

"She's a Yank." Smiffy ruffled his hair into place. "Blimey. We don't get many of your types around here."

"Americans?" said Ali. "Ah suppose not."

"The uvver," said Smiffy.

Pogsy felt his ears catch fire. The flames spread to his cheeks. The urge to run away became overwhelming.

Ali looked perplexed for a second. "Ah." She showed off her perfect set of snow-white teeth. "Over in the States our gangs have boys *and* girls. Ah guess you're a few years behind."

"So, you wanna be in ar gang, ar gang?" Wingnut winked at Steve.

"Maybe," said Ali. "Ah haven't made my mind up yet."

"You can't come any further," said Steve. "Soz and all that, but only gang members are allowed to see inside the dens. Those are the rules. Sarge, you can come in."

"Not without Ali." Sarge folded his arms and looked hard at Steve.

Steve folded his tongue in half. "The rules are the rules."

Pogsy opened his mouth to wade in and defend his friend, but nothing came out, not even a fly. He thought about dashing to her side but his legs refused the command, forcing him to watch as Ali berated Steve for making up rules on the spot, then tore into the leader of the gangs for allowing Bam and Gas-tank into the woodyard. She was dead right of course. And Steve didn't like it one bit.

The rich boy cleared his throat loudly, causing everyone to turn and look at him. "Someone tell her."

"I'll say it," said Red Top. "We 'ave an important rule: no girls allowed."

"Attaboy," said Bam. "Every sailor knows girls are bad luck. The second the rule gets broken, ships sink and lives are lost."

"You're a girl-hating idiot, Alexander," said Ali.

"At least I'm not a poor tramp."

Ali strode forward until she was nose-to-nose with Bam. She raised her fist very slightly; he flinched. Pogsy wanted to wade in, but his feet were encased in fishing weights. He felt his head glowing like a red-hot coal.

"Pat," said Ali, "are you just gonna stand there? Pick a side."

Everyone turned to look at him and, as they did, Pogsy felt hundreds of eyes boring into his soul, devouring his deepest secret. Instinctively, he covered his crotch with his hands. His lips trembled. His throat felt drier than the Sahara Desert in a heatwave. He strained to force some words out – any words would do – but nothing came.

"Ah thought we were friends," said Ali.

Pogsy tried again to force out at least a single word but, against the multitude of eyes, he was powerless to form even the smallest of grunts.

"Ah guess Ah was wrong."

Bam took a couple of steps backwards. "Girls are nothing but trouble," he smirked. "They should stick to ironing."

Ali strode forward. "Say that again."

Sarge stepped between the feuding pair. "Ali, he's not worth it. Turn the other cheek."

"Seriously?"

"It makes you the better person. I came here because I thought these dens might be fun. But I was wrong. Everyone here's trespassing and damaging property, and one day they'll all get caught. I don't want to get sent to prison."

Ali snorted. "Ah can't believe Ah let y'all talk me into wantin' to be in your gang. Ah guess British boys still have a lot of evolvin' to do, especially rich ones."

Ali and Sarge let themselves out while Bam continued to make jokes about girls. The gangs watched them leave, then returned to the serious business of construction.

"You still think having a girl in the gang is a good idea?" asked Steve.

"Ali's not like other girls." Pogsy struggled to form the words, his head spinning like a weathervane in a storm.

Steve rested his beaver teeth on his lip. "What if she sprags us up?"

"She won't."

"And Sarge?"

"He won't either."

"This is all your fault, Pogs. If you hadn't invited her scrumping none of this would have happened. If they don't keep their traps shut and the police find our dens, I'm holding you responsible."

School had been trying its best to act normal and pretend nothing was untoward for weeks but, away from the formality of the classrooms, the playground reeked of excitement. The desire for presents, which was easily enough to drive boys and girls mad, had to be bottled up until the first toy advert appeared on TV. Those were the rules and Santa didn't look kindly on anyone who broke ranks.

Two days ago, things had changed.

It was magical how the grown-ups that ran the TV stations knew exactly what boys and girls needed for Christmas before boys and girls knew themselves.

And it was very mamnagimus of them to pass the information on.

While the playground lost its head and the screaming and shouting began in earnest, Ali chose to play with the girls more than normal, and whatever she'd said in private caused the girls to shoot daggers at the gang. While his friends laughed it off – especially Bigzy, who loved the conflict – Pogsy felt down in the dumps. He tried to explain what had happened to his American friend without really having the words to describe his predicament.

Soz was as far as he got before Ali turned her back and refused to listen any further.

Sarge seemed okay to begin with, but then admitted he was thinking of leaving the gang.

Pogsy begged him not to, even going as far as getting down on his knees. After much pleading, an agreement was reached. Sarge was excused from going to the den until the end of time; in return, he promised to keep its location a secret.

Steve gave the double thumbs-up.

Pogsy sighed a massive sigh of relief.

If only Ali would see things the same way.

He moped around the playground, cursing his lucky troll for running out of luck. Christmas was on the horizon and he was suddenly surrounded by boys and girls pretending not to like each other, even though it was obvious they were going to buy each other presents. He'd planned on asking Ali to be his girlfriend, even though it meant upsetting Sarge, but that outcome was now further away than Timbuktu. In class, Miss told him off for not paying attention. Later, he got a second telling off when Teacher's Pet dobbed him in for drawing rude pictures of Miss, which thankfully looked nothing like her.

Hopefully Ali would calm down after a day or two.

She couldn't stay mad forever.

The official chart rundown loomed large and Pogsy pinned all his hopes on Alvin Stardust, the black-leather-clad rock and roller, as the man to defeat the god of *Bacofoil.* Instead, the unthinkable happened.

While Pogsy tore his hair out, berating his lucky charm, Steve sang along to every word of "I Love", encouraging the girls to do likewise until Mister Cohen barged into class and demanded quiet.

"I Love" wasn't a *bad* song. But it wasn't a "Hell Raiser" either. What it was was an opportunity to sing along and that made it more dangerous than an unexploded bomb. Girls loved a singalong, and it was possible that up and down the country they'd keep on buying the record forever and ruin Christmas, along with New Year, next Easter and next Bommie Night.

Somehow the silver monstrosity *had* to be stopped.

The next day, as he left the dining hall feeling full of liver and onions, Pogsy felt someone sidle up behind him. Something was pushed into his palm. He looked around, unsure who the note was from. Nervously, he fiddled with it. Given that boys had grown out of such silliness by age eight, there was only one possibility. The best thing to do with it was to take it to the toilets and flush it unread. That way, nothing horrible could happen. Out of a mixture of curiosity and hope, Pogsy did the opposite of what common sense told him to do.

Meet me behind the pet hut in 5 minutes.

His heart fluttered.

It was from Ali. It had to be.

Cautiously, he approached the solid wooden structure where the school pets were housed. It was tucked away in a shabby corner of the playground, near to one of the main entrances to the school building. The rumour was that Gerbil was living there now, sharing a cage with the rabbits. Chip said she was kidnapping stray boys and making them bring her food. Pogsy walked quickly past the door, checking it by eye to make sure it was firmly shut. He took a deep breath and looked around for the on-duty teacher. With the coast clear, he snuck into a dank alleyway, where the school's milk crates were stacked and boys were banned from being on account of misdemeanours past. His eye was immediately drawn to a line of damp cement that ran between two layers of bulging bricks. He bent down and picked up a sharp stone, then set to, pretending he was digging a tunnel.

He felt a tap on the shoulder. His ticker cracked his ribcage open wide. He turned around, half-expecting to see Gerbil with a pair of handcuffs but hoping beyond hope that it was Ali. Instead, he came face to face with the willowy frame of his desk mate.

"P... Pollyanna."

"Who were you expecting?"

"I dunno." Pogsy shrugged his shoulders. "Gerbil."

"Don't be silly. She's nocturnal now." Pollyanna's eyes raced around in circles. "I've got a secret to tell you."

Pogsy backed off. He really wasn't sure he wanted to know a girl secret.

"Ali's pop's staying in America," said Pollyanna without stopping to draw breath. "He's working for President Nixon now, so she isn't going to see him for ages. Imagine that. Not seeing your mum or dad for Christmas and not getting any presents. It's awful. We have to start a collection. I'll do the girls. You do the boys."

"But..." Pogsy was shocked. Then he felt sad. Then he felt shocked and sad not to have heard the news first from his secret bestie.

"Everyone likes Ali," said Pollyanna. "Just do as you're told."

Later, on the way home, Pogsy spotted his American friend and raced to catch her up, blurting that he knew her secret.

Ali refused to look him in the eye. "Ah'm furious with you."

"Do you fancy coming round mine to watch TV?"

"What part of *furious* don't you understand *Patrick Green*?"

The following morning, a new note was waiting inside his desk. It simply said *Happy Friday*. A second note arrived at dinnertime, delivered anonymously by hand. Pogsy walked around the inside of the school, debating long and hard with himself as to whether he should turn up. He looked over his shoulder, once, twice, to make sure no-one was following. Sidling off behind the pet hut was nearly a habit now, and he had to admit that the sneaking about gave him a warm-tummy feeling. He conceded it *might* be linked to seeing Pollyanna, except he didn't feel excited about sitting next to her in class. She certainly ticked a lot of boxes though: she had the best hair out of all the girls, she was a fast runner, and she was good with a netball too.

Whatever the other boys thought, and contrary to the rumours, he definitely wasn't going out with her. But he wasn't *not* going out with her either. Sitting next to someone who liked you was complicated and he regularly checked in with himself to make sure he liked her back. He thought about telling her that he really wanted to be with Ali, but he was worried she'd have a fit and end up hating him. She'd had a crush on a boy in a different class the previous year and the boy had decided he didn't want to hold her hand because he wasn't ready for it.

She'd put woggums in his satchel.

Pogsy shook his head.

Having an angry girl with a monk-on as your enemy was every boy's worst nightmare come true.

He wondered whether there might be room in his life for two girls.

He felt a cramp in his gut.

What with the den, and football, and listening to Glam records, he hardly had time for one girl. It was annoying that the girl he was desperate to spend time wasn't talking to him, and the girl he didn't want to spend time with was doing one of his favourite things: sneaking around in secret.

He checked over his shoulder once more and, content he didn't have a spy watching his every move, he ducked behind the pet hut, aware that he was committing what the teachers called *suspicious behaviour*.

"I was about to give up," said Pollyanna. "What took you so long?"

"I went for a drink of..." Pogsy's nose twitched. "Hamster wee."

"That's *not* normal."

Pogsy realised what he'd just said. "Soz. I mean I can smell hamster wee. I'd recognise it anywhere."

"I've got another secret, Pat, and this one is the most important thing you'll hear this week."

Pogsy smiled his best smile.

There really was nowt worse than a girl with a secret.

The only good thing about such a situation was that girls with secrets didn't let them stay that way for long. "Go on. Tell uz."

"You like Slade, don't you?"

Pogsy nodded.

"Ruth Maddox says that they've got a new record."

"That's inposs. Ruth can't know summut about Slade that I don't."

"That's what she said, and it's out today. But you're not allowed to know. Ruth made us all swear not to tell the boys because she doesn't want you going out and emptying the shelves before her."

Pogsy felt flummoxed. "Slade need my help. I gotta go buy as many as poss."

"Which is why it's a secret." Pollyanna scrunched her lips. "You can get me one for Christmas if you like."

"Okay." Pogsy's brain whirred away at a million miles an hour. He could buy Reddy a copy too. And Sam and Dad. Everyone he knew was getting Slade's new record for Christmas, whether they wanted it or not.

"I've told you what I want for Christmas. Now it's your turn."

"I dunno."

"You've got to tell me soon, otherwise we can't be boyfriend and girlfriend."

For the last session of the afternoon, Missis Wainwright read the first few chapters of *The Magician's Nephew*, which was the follow up to *The Lion, the Witch and the Wardrobe*, even though it took place first. Pogsy thought it was pretty good, with a lot of potential, but he kept on zoning out and, rather than thinking about what he wanted for Christmas like he'd promised, he thought about Slade instead. By the end of the reading, he had to lean over and ask Bingo what had happened. Bingo being Bingo had already read the book and he jumped ahead and gave away the ending.

Pogsy laughed.

Now he knew what happened, he'd never have to listen again, which meant more time for daydreaming about Slade. There was nothing better. They had a new record out and it was supposed to be a secret but, fortunately, it was turning out to be the worst-kept secret in the history of secrets. Whatever it was, it *had* to be better than the current Number One.

After school Pogsy felt like he was balancing on the edge of a cliff. The anticipation of a new Slade record was enough to make his brain implode, but if he bought it without hearing it first, Dad would go berserk.

He'd have to buy it in secret.

When Dad came in from work, he quickly turned the house upside down.

"What a ruddy ridiculous new law!" he bawled at the world in general.

Missis D tried to make her excuses and leave but she wasn't quick enough.

"Fifty miles an hour on the roads. It's an outrage! D'you know, I was followed by a copper for miles today. He kept on driving up my bum, trying to force me to go faster than fifty-one."

"You never drive faster than that anyway," said Sam. He winked at Pogsy. "The MG would fall to pieces. And you said that the heap of junk that work gave you doesn't have any guts under its bonnet."

"That's beside the point," said Dad. "The first opportunity I get, I'm going to show the government what I think of their stupid new law to help save petrol."

Pogsy found it difficult to picture how fast fifty miles an hour was, or what it might feel like on a pushbike. He supposed that, as bikes didn't need petrol, the new speed limit didn't apply. The only person he knew who had a speedo on their bike was Sam's mate Jimbo. He couldn't see Jimbo doing over fifty, even in top gear going down Caistor Hill with the wind behind him. Sarge, on the other hand, might just make it. As long as he didn't try to pull a wheelie.

Later on, over tea, Mum said she'd heard there were coppers outside *Rammies*, checking people's shopping. "The other teachers can't decide if they're looking for Christmas bombs or hoarders."

"Crime's rampant in this town, and instead of catching criminals they're out harassing the public. I didn't vote for this."

Mum nodded in agreement. "Me neither."

Pogsy wondered whether fish hoarding was also a crime now. Not that Dad had much at home since he'd started storing it in Mister Payne's garage. Pogsy concealed a smirk. If there was such a thing as the *fish cops*, they'd definitely have speed boats with blue flashing lights and sirens. They'd likely be very busy on the lookout for haddock thieves, flatfish wranglers and kipper-nickers. He remembered Mister Payne saying something about a girl he knew whose nickname was *kipper-knickers* on the way home from the swapsie meet. It seemed a very odd way to smuggle fish out the docks.

Fish cops were still on Pogsy's brain the next morning. He was busy watching *The Virginian* starring Doug McClure, who was his favourite actor, wondering whether there was a division down the docks that specialised in halibut retrieval, when the doorbell rang. Sam and Ellie were busy playing Lego *Haunted House*. Mum was down the butchers buying gammon for tea. Dad was in the kitchen repairing the toaster that Sam had broken earlier when he'd tried to dislodge a piece of burnt toast with a knife and made it go *bang*. On the second ring of the bell, Dad stomped through from the kitchen clutching a piece of blackened crust in one hand and a screwdriver in the other. He opened the door to an inquisitive young copper. Pogsy's heart raced. He craned his neck to see if the copper, who didn't look much older than Sam, had a silver fish insignia on his helmet.

"Good morning, sir. We've had a report of petrol hoarding taking place down this street."

"Ruddy Armstrong!" Dad switched from lukewarm to boiling in under a second.

"I beg your pardon, sir?"

"First he accuses my eldest lad of making explosives. Now he has me pegged as some sort of oil baron!"

"There's no need to be like that, sir."

"Why don't you search my shed?" Dad whinnied like Doug McClure's horse. "You'll find a half-full can of fuel for my lawnmower. I assume it isn't a felony."

"You haven't seen anything then, sir?"

"I might have been sleep-hoarding. We better check."

The copper had no interest whatsoever in seeing what was in Dad's shed, but Dad insisted he take a look anyway, telling him he couldn't come inside the house with his big clodhopper boots and instead ordering him down the side passage.

"Are you getting this?" said Sam with a snigger. "The look on that young copper's face. Dad said you have to be unpredictable with the cops. I hope you're paying attention."

"Sort of," said Pogs, wishing he could draw a pistol as fast as a sharpshooter. "I'm thinking about going down the shops and buying Slade's new record."

"You're obsessed with that band. Do us a favour, will you? Look after Ellie. I'm off to Jimbo's. And get Ellie an ice pop."

"Ice pop." Ellie's bright blue eyes lit up. She held out both her hands.

"You're horrible." Pogsy glared at his brother. "You know Doug McClure's not finished killing off baddies yet."

Pogsy checked his collection of record vouchers again. He was sure he'd had three stashed away but he could only find two. Mum had one spare that she'd been given for her birthday and it was worth two pounds; she'd agreed to sell it for half-price. Sam had loaned him the money, plus another pound. All in all, he had enough for six copies of a record he hadn't even heard. A shiver shot down his spine.

What if it was another Stan?

"You're being very quiet, Patrick," said Mum.

"I'm waiting for me soup to cool." Pogsy stuffed another round of broken-up bread in his bowl. He was desperate to get on his way but, at the same time, he knew that if he let his desperation show, an inquisition would begin. "Why do they call it 'oxtail'," he mumbled, "when everyone knows it's cow?"

"I would imagine it's because the soup was named before cows were invented," said Mum flippantly.

"Then it's *cowtail* really."

"Mootail," said Ellie.

Pogsy thought his sister's new favourite game was very amusing. "Ellie," he said. "Mootail is the worst bit of the moo-moo. It's

all bony. And everyone knows you mustn't touch a mootail because
they're always covered in—"

"*Patrick!*" said Mum loudly.

The second that dinner was over, Pogsy made his excuses, using
a fib he'd spent all morning working on. "I gotta go see Bigzy. His
sister's getting a new puppy and I promised to help give it a name. I'll
be back in time for tea."

"Hold on," said Dad. "Do you know what day it is?"

"Er, Saturday. Everyone knows that."

"Patrick Green!" said Mum. "What *has* got into you today?"

"It's the second Saturday in December," said Dad. "Today's the
day we go hunting for Christmas trees."

Pogsy felt his brain split in half as his internal warning sirens
went off.

Horrible choice alert!

Quickly, he counted out the pros and cons on his fingers. Buy
six copies of a record that he'd never heard before. What if it was
rubbish and everyone hated it? What if it was brilliant and it was sold
out? He'd been waiting five years to have a go at tree-chopping and
Sam was still round Jimbo's house, which meant that there was only one
person who could help Dad. What if Dad didn't let him chop down the
tree? What if he did?

Pogsy made a deal with himself.

As long as they were all done by 4.30 at the latest, he could
chop down a tree *and* make it to the record shop. What, he wondered,
would happen if Mum spent ages looking for the perfect tree and
couldn't find it?

There was only one thing for it. He'd have to take a chance and
trust his lucky troll.

As was traditional, Dad installed a roof rack on the MG and
headed south to a tree plantation just outside Louth. Pogsy watched
Waltham Aerodrome come and go. He pointed to one of the hangers and
"I-Spied" something beginning with "H". Ellie giggled and chose
hippoplotipus, which was her word of the day. Mum and Dad sat up
front. They didn't argue once, except briefly, and that was over what to
get Potty Gran for Christmas. Apparently, she already had everything
she needed. Pogsy couldn't imagine that: having everything. In this
instance, he wasn't sure it was true. The last time he'd visited Potty
Gran's house, her living room didn't even have a telly. And her back

porch smelt of cow pats. So that was two things she needed at least: a TV and a gas mask. In comparison, he could name many things he wanted. Granted, he'd only discovered he wanted most of them in the last week, shortly after the toy adverts had begun.

Back in infant school, Red Top had reckoned that Santa could read your mind. He always knew what boys and girls wanted. All you had to do was think about a present really hard and wish for it, but it was bad luck to tell anyone. Pogsy still half-believed in keeping his wants a secret, but he'd noticed over the years that Reddy never got what he really wanted. That was why he hedged his bets by telling Sam everything. Then Mum would find out. The rest was elementary.

Mum chose the second tree they saw. Pogsy, who was rubbing his troll like crazy, was amazed.

"Are you sure?" he said, before his brain could stop him.

"It's perfect." Dad nodded.

Ellie continued to run around, pointing. She finally decided on three: the big one that Mum had chosen and two smaller ones.

"You can only have one," said Pogsy. "So make sure it's the one with the biggest branches for Santa to hang really, really ginormous presents on."

Ellie ran to the tree that Mum was standing by and tried to hug it but couldn't get close enough. She hugged Mum's leg instead.

Mum smiled. "Thank you, Patrick. Now help your dad cut it down."

Pogsy's grin took over his face. While Dad went to fetch a saw, he bounced up and down in excitement. This was the bit he'd waited so patiently for. Dad soon returned. He dropped down onto his hands and knees, made the first cut and then encouraged Pogsy to take the saw by the handle, which he did without hesitation.

Who in their right mind would turn down free saw training?

Cutting down a tree was not as easy as Pogsy had expected it to be. He gritted his teeth and soldiered on anyway, using both hands. Down at ground level, the scent of old pine needles and resin was intense. It was balanced with the smell of freshly sawn wood. The sweat began to build on his brow. He was still only a quarter of the way through and he was getting nowhere. Dad leaned on the tree's trunk to open up the groove allowing the saw to move more easily. Pogsy's arms were tired. Already, it felt like they were made of rubber. He couldn't stop now though. Ten minutes later, with the sweat pouring off under his coat and blisters forming on his palms, he finally got to say the magic word.

"Timberclaus!"

Cutting down the Christmas tree was the best feeling in the world. Pogsy shook his fists in triumph. Life couldn't ever get better than this.

Once they'd returned home, he helped Dad make a container for the tree by decorating a shiny metal pail with last year's leftover wrapping paper. They used a mixture of bricks and gravel to wedge the tree firmly in place then topped up the bucket with water. Mum, meanwhile, poured herself a large glass of sherry and set to sorting through boxes of decorations. Ellie dived in and helped. There were mirrored baubles of all shapes and sizes individually wrapped in tissue paper, coloured glass ornaments from Hong Kong, shiny butterflies with iridescent wings, and snowmen dipped in glitter. Ellie discovered Santa and his elves, and a team of eight reindeer, one with a busted antler. Pogsy blushed when he saw the state of *Blitzen* and pretended to be shocked. Mum still didn't know he'd used him to poke out a shell that was stuck down the barrel of a toy cannon last year. The tinsel flowed in reams of silver and gold, bright red, emerald green and admiral blue. There were hanging paper garlands that folded up like accordions, packets of crazy-shaped balloons, a grand glass star that sat atop the tree, and a reel of lights with bulbs shaped like snowmen. While Dad fiddled with the wiring, Mum cast her eye around the living-room ceiling. It was double the size of previous years, thanks to Dad's handiwork with a sledgehammer. She made some rough calculations out loud, declaring that she needed to put her thinking cap on. Pogsy knew what this meant: more sherry. He offered to pour her one and, while no-one was looking, took a hearty glug from the bottle. It made everything sparkle. He decided that, unlike whisky, it was a taste and a feeling he could get used to.

Mum's answer, when it was delivered, was homemade paperchains. Pogsy felt all the spittle dry up from around his tongue. His mum loved paperchains. She also loved not making them herself. Licking the glue was alright for about five minutes. After that, you couldn't get rid of the horrible taste, no matter how much orange squash you drank, and your tongue stuck to the roof of your mouth like a postage stamp for days. During the first week of December, Mum liked to organise the children in her class to make paperchains. Pogsy was convinced she did it on purpose and she was a *Satanist*, or whatever that word was for German guards who liked torturing captured British soldiers.

The only good thing about paper chains, he thought, *was that, because no-one in the house liked making them, there were bound to be loads left over.*

He considered the den.

It would look dead ace all dec'd up.

He'd sneak any spares over to the woodyard later and get the rest of the gang to do the same. Bam had been boasting about how he'd get them a tree and some Christmas cushions. Pogsy supposed that even useless rich lads had a use once a year. Even if the tree was one of those little silver tinsel ones like Granny Green had, it would still be better than no tree at all. It was their first Christmas in the new den, after all. They had to make it as cosy as possible.

Pogsy looked at the clock that hung on the lounge's stone fireplace. Ten to five.

There was something he was supposed to do.

Oh, hell.

He gulped for air.

It was proper dark out.

The batteries for his bike lights were nearly dead.

And he was drunk.

In sheer panic, he grabbed his jacket. "I gotta go see Bigzy. I'll be back as fast as I can."

"Patrick," said Mum sternly, "you haven't made a single paperchain and it's almost teatime..."

Pogsy didn't hear the rest of the sentence. He was already on his way at high speed to *Freemo Street*, to the only record shop in town he knew, convinced he could make it in time.

A thousand panicky thoughts collided in his brain, each tumbling about at a hundred-and-eighty-six-thousand miles per second. In his frantic dash to grab a copy of Slade's new record, he'd stuck to the back alleys and pavements, and made it to the record shop with two-hundred-and-forty *Keegans* to spare. Now the grown-up in charge was trying to pretend he didn't exist and shut up shop without serving him.

"I need Slade's new single," gasped Pogsy, "but I gotta hear it first."

"No' a chance," said the record man. He twitched his walrus moustache and ran a hand through slicked-back hair that was thinner on top than Granny Green's chicken soup.

"Please, mister."

"Av 'eard it twenty times already t'day."

"At least giz a clue as to whether it's any good."

"S'alrigh'. If yer like tha' sor' a thing."

Nervously, Pogsy fiddled with his gift vouchers, weighing up the odds, trying to figure out how far to go.

"Will it be Number One?"

"I prefer Wizzard mesen. Av sold loads of them today. Tha's where me money is for the Christmas spot. C'mon, lad. Stop messin' uz abou'." The man drummed his fingers on the counter. "Thirty seconds and Am off."

"Two," said Pogsy, settling on a copy for himself and one for Pollyanna. "No, three."

The man raised an eyebrow, then rung the transaction through the till. Quickly, he handed over the records and ushered Pogsy from the shop, locking the door behind him.

He stood on the pavement watching the passers-by in their Christmas hats and scarves, bags bulging with presents. Instead of feeling elated, he felt like he'd just been robbed. He tucked his records inside his jacket and joined the happy throng, trudging home, pushing his bike in front of him. He'd done what he set out to do and put his dosh where his gob was, trusting his favourite band to deliver.

Was it any good?

The worry that it wasn't consumed his thoughts all the way home.

The one thing he wanted more than anything else was to listen to his record as soon as he got in, but he didn't dare ask Dad if he could play it. Dad would insist on taking control and putting it on his turntable, and he'd ask all sorts of awkward questions, like where had it come from. Pogsy knew that, if he admitted he'd spent good money on a record he hadn't even heard, Dad would go ballistic and blow a hole in the roof. If it came out that he'd bought *three* copies, Dad would likely blow another two holes in the roof, and there was only so much damage the house could take.

He'd have to wait until everyone was out.

What if it was terrible?

Second best.

Pogsy gripped his troll tightly and tried to think only good thoughts, but all he felt was nerves. He imagined that Slade must feel the same. He reminded himself that no-one in the history of Glam had ever released a rubbish record knowing it was rubbish. Only the best songs made it onto vinyl. So Slade at least thought it was good. As long as they hadn't been drinking too much pop when they'd made it, it at least stood a chance. He wondered if Noddy had been this nervous the first time he'd listened to it. Having a new record that everyone liked must be the best feeling in the world, even better than cutting down a Christmas tree.

After tea, Dad liked to sit down and watch the evening news. Ever since the war in the Middle East had started, he'd taken to perching on the edge of his chair, lips pursed, ears primed, preparing for the worst. When a newsman from the BBC announced in a very stern voice that the fuel shortages at the country's power stations were now worse than ever and power cuts and petrol rationing were no longer out of the question, Dad raised his fist.

"Told you so!" he shouted, half at the set and half at Mum.

"Then it's a good job we're prepared," said Mum, without looking up from the book she was reading. Bingo said that *War and Peace* was the hardest, most boring book he'd ever tried to read and all the Russian names sizzled your eyeballs and gave you brain-knots.

Pogsy remembered the scallywags telling Dad that shortages were coming. He wondered how they'd known all those weeks ago. Perhaps they'd been hanging out with Uri Gellar. According to the papers, as well as bending spoons with his mind he could read other peoples' thoughts and see into the future.

Mum said it was all made up.

Like most *psychotic* powers.

That night, Dad paraded around the house attaching stickers to all the light switches, to remind everyone to switch off the lights when no-one was in the room. When Sam came home, he got a passionate lecture on following the new rules. Pogsy had already been lectured earlier but Dad gave him another one for good measure. They'd had power cuts the previous year when the miners had gone on strike. Dad hadn't bothered with stupid stickers and silly rules then. Which could only mean one thing.

This time it was going to be dead bad.

Although Pogsy only had recent experience when it came to receiving notes, he understood that the rules were they had to look as neat as possible. Pollyanna's handwriting was immaculate and she'd won gold stars for it. A poem she'd *prescribed* the previous year still hung in the school library as an example of what perfectly formed letters should look like when written in ink with an italic pen.

"This is so neat," said Pogsy, showing off his latest morning note.

"You can't keep 'em," said Reddy. "Seriously. Get rid of the evidence before your dad finds 'em."

"If it was me, I'd eat 'em," said Bigzy, rubbing his belly. "Yum, yum."

"Don' do tha'." Chip installed his serious face. "They might explode. *Mish Inposs* ink. Flush 'em."

"I'm gonna keep 'em for now," said Pogsy. "Just in case they become valuable one day."

He flicked through the notes again. The two *happy day-ers* were almost identical, as were the two *meet-ers*. The best thing to do with them was take them home and hide them in with one of the board games that he didn't play that much anymore. No-one would find them there, not even Mum.

It wasn't really a surprise to Pogsy when a new note was thrust in his mitt over dinner. He didn't turn around to try to see the culprit in action. He didn't need to. As he read the words, he was puzzled as to why the letters weren't quite as well formed as previously. The "M"s were cranky. And it said "pet shed" rather than hut. He crossed his fingers and nodded to himself.

Finally

It had taken a week but, at last, Ali had come to her senses.

The door to the pet hut was firmly closed, as were its frosted glass windows fronted by iron bars. This was a good thing, as escaped animals everywhere would cause a girl stampede, especially if they were mice or spiders. Pogsy realised that he'd never actually seen inside the hut, which meant he had no clue as to what animals the school kept.

There were gerbils and rabbits because the teachers let boys and girls take them home during the summer holidays. Tortoises were a possibility, along with parrots and guinea pigs. Moles and woolly mammoths were unlikely. One would escape too easily and the other wouldn't fit.

Pogsy retrieved the sharp stone he'd hidden under the base of the hut on his previous escapade and shuffled over to the layer of damp cement. He poked away frantically.

"Hello, *Patrick*."

Pogsy jumped out of his skin. He palmed the stone and slowly turned around, aware that the voice was not that of either Pollyanna *or* Ali.

"You got my note then." Ruth Maddox stood impassively, blocking the narrow exit. Today her hair was pinned back with a black and yellow hairband, which, along with her downturned mouth, made her look like an angry wasp.

"That was you?" Pogsy scratched his neck. "Only going behind the sheds isn't allowed."

"You like Slade don't you?"

Pogsy felt his ears turn bright red. "Er..."

"I know you do. Everyone says you're the biggest Slade fan they know." Ruth glared menacingly. "I want to know what you think of their new record. It was a *secret* last week but I knew about it because *I'm* in the Slade fan club. Now it's out and everyone knows."

"I knew too."

"Only because Pollyanna told you after I made her promise not to. So what do you think?"

Pogsy looked away. "It's okay," he mumbled.

Ruth narrowed her gaze. "What's your favourite line then?"

Pogsy's ears glowed so hot he thought his hair was about to catch fire. "I don't have to tell you."

"You *haven't* heard it!"

"I bought it on Saturday." Pogsy felt himself go properly red. He knew he was at least the colour of cough candy but it could be even worse than that. He might look like a glass of raspberry pop. "I gotta go."

"Not yet," said Ruth. "I want it to get to Number One and that's why I'm wearing my lucky headband. Whatever you've got that's lucky, you have to wish on it as hard as you can all night tonight."

Pogsy barged past, trying to put as much ground as he could between him and the evilest girl in class. She was proposing an alliance. A shiver went down his spine. It was a trick. It had to be. He realised he'd touched a piece of paper that she'd touched. It was in his pocket. If he didn't get rid of it, she had a weapon to use against him. But touching it meant he'd have a bit of Ruth on his fingers, and everyone knew it was damn nigh impossible to wash Teacher's Pet off your hands.

He headed towards the bogs.

If he used loo paper to remove the note from his pocket and flush it, he'd be fine.

It was the only way.

Pogsy quite liked his school table this year. Gas-tank was always a good laugh and Bingo ensured that everyone always knew the answers to the hard maths questions in class quizzes. Susan Grainger was clever at geography and Pollyanna was nutty for history. If he could just swap out Ruth Maddox for Ali, it would be the perfect table. During the afternoon, Ruth kept on looking at him. Inside, he felt tortured. Teacher's Pet was right. Except it was bigger than just the two of them. It involved every Slade fan, even those such as Ecky who supported Leeds United. Up and down the country they had to put aside their differences and pool their luck. It was the only way to ensure victory.

The afternoon dragged on without end. All Pogsy could think about was rushing home and listening to his new record before Dad got in. Just before afternoon break, Pogsy felt Pollyanna's hand slide under his thigh. Another note. Which meant yet another visit to the gap behind the pet hut.

"We gotta stop meeting like this," he said, making sure that the on-duty teacher hadn't seen him.

"Don't you want to be seen with me?" asked Pollyanna. "I thought we liked each other."

"It's the teachers." Pogsy scratched his neck. "If they see uz sneaking off behind the sheds, they'll do uz one, and Missis Wainwright knows my mum."

"Then hurry up and tell me what you want for Christmas."

Pogsy felt his brain freeze. It was just like the time the previous summer when he'd found a lump of ice in his ice cream and had sucked it hard rather than spit it out. "I dunno."

"Boys are *so* useless. It's a good job I worked out what you want for you. I'm not telling you though. You have to guess."

Pogsy huffed. "At least giz a clue."

"You can't eat it."

"That only leaves about a million things."

"You can have one guess a day. Those are the rules. I'll tell you if you're hot or cold. I think we should become secret confidants."

"How?" Pogsy had vague memories of his mum finding a *confidant* in a junk shop once. It was all beaten up and badly in need of reupholstering.

"We have to tell each other a secret, silly. You start."

Pogsy felt his ears fire up. It was one thing to tell Ali his best secrets but quite another to tell his desk mate. At the same time, if he only gave away a worst secret, it was cheating. "Me favourite aunt promised to try and get George Best's autograph."

"That's a silly secret!" Pollyanna laughed like a donkey under attack with a tickling stick.

"It is not!" Pogsy stuck out his bottom lip. "He's the most famous footie player in the world, so I deffo want a signed photo, but I support Liverpool and he plays for Man U, so I'm not supposed to have one. I have to keep it a secret from everybody. They can't know."

"My secret is I wash my hair three times a week with marigold shampoo."

For what remained of the day, Pogsy felt like a right dumbo. He'd traded a really good secret for a rubbish one. He wondered how such information could possibly be worth anything because, as far as he was concerned, the amount of shampoo you used was something to boast about, not hide. And besides, not a single boy he knew washed their hair more than once a week. It was unheard of.

"Ali?" he said on the way home after a long sprint to catch his friend. "How often do you wash your hair?"

"Pat! How many times do Ah have to tell you Ah'm not talkin' to you. And even if Ah was, that's not something you ask a girl."

"Is it more than once?"

"Pat!"

"Aw." Pogsy feigned disappointment. "Do you wanna come round mine and listen to Slade's new record?"

"Ah'm very, very annoyed with you." Ali's eyes shot poison arrows.

Pogsy took a deep breath. "Will you at least promise that you won't dob uz in over the dens?"

"Ah've thought about it and you're safe for now. Tell Steve that, if Alexander shoots his mouth off again, Ah can easy change my mind."

"If you do that, Steve'll chuck uz out the gang."

"Then you shoulda thought of that before you betrayed me."

Santa's secret toy factory was in full flow, making a toy every single second until Christmas Eve. At least that was the story that Sam was busy telling Ellie.

"He has thousands and thousands of elves working for him up at the North Pole." Sam winked.

"Toys," said Eli, her bright blue eyes a twinkle.

"For the whole world, and then some. The elves all work so fast you can hardly see their fingers move. Isn't that right, Pat?"

Pogsy nodded, trying very hard to dislodge the huge sackcloth-clad monk clinging to his back. Dad had beaten him home. It almost never happened, and yet today of all days it had.

That meant he hadn't been able to listen to his record and he was finding it very hard to digest.

"There are five clues that Father Christmas is on his way," said Sam. "Do you know what they are?"

Ellie shook her head.

"We'll tell you so you know for next year. But you're not to tell Mum you know. It's our little secret. Do you promise not to tell?"

Ellie nodded.

"Pat, what's the first clue?"

"Easy," said Pogsy. He lowered his voice to a whisper. "Toy adverts start to appear on TV."

When he was younger, Pogsy used to imagine that the adverts starting was the equivalent of Mister Tracy saying, *"Thunderbirds are go!"* Once the order to man the Thunderbirds had been given, it was only a matter of time until the palm trees parted and blast-off happened. It was the same with Santa's sled. All the preparations were well underway now and the toy pods were being loaded. The sleigh could no longer be stopped, not even by the evil Hood.

Pogsy continued, "If you listen carefully, those nice TV misters will tell you what kind of dolls you need and stuff."

"Tiny tears!" said Ellie excitedly, shaking her arms.

"Would you like to hear what the second clue is?" asked Sam. "It's sitting in our lounge and it begins with a 'C'."

"*Kissmas* tree."

"That's right," said Pogsy. "The second clue came on Saturday, which means that there are just three clues to go."

"Two," said Sam. "Now it's dark, why don't we go for a quick walk down the street and point out some of the changes to our little sis?"

"Do we have to?" Moving more than ten feet away from the record player was the last thing on Pogsy's mind. All he needed was four minutes alone. Any second now Dad would go to the shed. He *had* to. At the moment, he was in the kitchen with a cuppa and the evening paper, getting nice and angry with the government and topping up his rant tanks. Pogsy crossed his fingers and wished hard.

Any second now.

"Have you seen the Petherbridge's tree?" scoffed Sam. "It's a corker this year."

Pogsy peeked through the kitchen door and observed his dad. He was still on the back page, finding out how Grimsby Town were doing, which meant he hadn't even looked at the headlines yet.

"Okay," said Pogsy, notes of resignation in his voice. "Let's get our coats."

During his ten years on planet Earth, Pogsy had noticed that the nearer it got to Christmas, the more excitable the whole town became. Over the last few days, decorated trees had appeared in front windows the length of every street, bringing a splash of colour to otherwise dreary terraces. Some trees, such as Ali's neighbour, old Missis Porter's, were real but very small. Others, such as the one Missis D had in her back room, were made from green tinsel and covered with miniature presents for Santa's helpers.

Sam pointed across the road at the Johnson's tree. "They've made their own this year to save money. Can you see it's constructed from egg cartons painted green?"

"I had a good gawp on me way home," said Pogsy. "They've used sticky-back plastic and Copydex to glue it together."

"Swing," said Ellie.

Sam and Pogsy each held one of their sister's hands and lifted her off the ground, letting her swing between them.

"Look at Mister Payne's reindeer," said Sam.

The trio stopped to admire the full-sized deer in their neighbour's garden. It had a bright red, glowing nose-bulb and yellow lights in its antlers. This year, for the first time ever, it was piloted by an elf jockey.

Sourpuss Armstrong hated it, which was half the reason that Mister Payne kept the joke going, adding to it every year.

Sam pointed at the Armstrong's bay window. "What's that?"

"It's baby Jesus," said Pogsy.

As was traditional, Missis Armstrong had turned the front of the house into a real-life manger, with Mary, Joseph, three Wise Men and a doll wrapped in swaddling clothes. The rumour was Mister Armstrong hated the manger even more than the reindeer.

The door to the Armstrong household opened wide and the grumpy ex-copper emerged, dragged by his dog. She was kitted out in a homemade Santa outfit and looked immensely proud of her togs.

"Evening," said Sam. "Nice costume."

Sourpuss Armstrong stopped dead in his tracks. He looked like he'd just swallowed a fire-breathing piranha.

"Say hello to Patch," said Sam, picking up Ellie.

"Hello, Patch," said Ellie, waving at the dog.

Mister Armstrong mumbled something incoherent and shot off as his dog took him for his evening drag around the block. Pogsy laughed. He'd never thought about using his sister as a human shield before but it was very effective. His eye drifted next door to the Petherbridge's front room, where a lopsided specimen of a tree stood covered in an array of flashing lights, trying its best to hide its hunched back and roll of fat in the middle.

"The word on the street is that they stole it from the top of *Freemo Market*," said Sam. "The decs are nicked from the Heneage Road butcher's shop."

Every year for as long as Pogsy could remember it had been a similar story. Around New Year they'd dump the tree down a back alley in the middle of the night and pretend it was nothing to do with them.

The trio crossed the road and had a good gawp at Nan Eagle's tree, which was a five-foot tall fir tree decorated with bright red baubles and coloured lights.

"It's easy the best one down the street," said Pogsy.

"Agreed," said Sam. "It looks like it came straight out a catalogue."

The fourth clue that Christmas was coming wasn't far away now. Pogsy and his brother tried to explain to their sister how everyone liked to give the paper boys, the milkmen and the postmen a Christmas box for all their efforts throughout the year, except the box wasn't shaped like a box at all and instead consisted of money.

"The paper boys have to decorate their bikes and sacks with tinsel," said Pogsy. "Otherwise they won't get nowt."

"And the postie has to wear a Santa hat and say *ho-ho-ho* a lot," added Sam.

"My friend's dad is a milkie," said Pogsy. "His milk float's got a pair of antlers and a glowing nose, and the back's made up to look like a sleigh. There are even bells on the roof that tinkle every time he stops."

"That's clue four," said Sam. "Everyone goes a bit mad and gets dressed up. And that just leaves clue five."

"Christmas records," said Pogsy. He looked his sister in the eye. "You like to dance?"

Ellie nodded.

"Every year," said Sam, "there's a massive competition between all the best groups in the world to be Number One for Christmas. The record that wins helps decide how good Christmas will be. If it's a *dancer*, like last year when we got "Long Haired Lover from Liverpool", then it'll be a really good Christmas. The year before, we had "Ernie". He drove the fastest milk cart in the west. You couldn't dance much to that."

"This year," said Pogsy, rubbing his lucky troll, "it's gonna be Slade. Everyone loves to dance to Slade."

"But if it's a boring ballad," said Sam with a sly grin, "there won't be much dancing at all and Christmas is gonna be rubbish."

Thirteen: Merry Xmas Everybody

Pogsy couldn't remember ever being as nervous as he was right now.

The morning had begun with a proclamation from Steve, declaring his idol to be the best Glam star ever, and a demand that the gang kneel before his greatness. Bam had complied, along with Weeble. Everyone else had got on with playing footie. Pogsy had tried to tell anyone who'd listen that Slade were going to be the new Number One, but he only half-believed it. The rumour doing the rounds was that "I Love" was still selling like hot cakes and it would take a miracle to dislodge it.

Pogsy shook his head dejectedly. Whatever he said, it didn't really matter. His lucky charm couldn't change the contents of Johnnie Walker's envelope now.

Hope.

Fear.

Resignation.

Pogsy's belly see-sawed through all the emotions he knew. The wait for 12.45 was *eggscrutiating* agony, and when it came, there were many ears on standby, waiting for the chart rundown. Whatever the truth, there was no hiding from it now.

As soon as the DJ reached the top three, Steve started joshing around. "We all know who it is," he shouted. "Switch the radios off, everyone. There's no point in listening."

"Shush!" said Ruth Maddox. "You're ruining it for everyone."

"I'm only telling you all the truth!"

"Shush!" said the girls as one.

"La, la, la!"

"Ballsacks," muttered Pogsy. They'd missed who it was.

Everyone fell silent, waiting for the Number One record to start. When it did, Pogsy didn't recognise it. For seven whole seconds he heard music he'd never heard before. Whatever it was, it was new. And it was good. *Very good*. He didn't want to, and he tried his hardest not to, but his eyes were drawn towards those of the teacher's pet. Her mouth hung open in astonishment.

A second later, the vocals kicked in and at that moment Pogsy knew exactly who he was listening to. Nobody in the world sung like

Noddy. When he got behind a note, he whacked it up the bum harder than Kev Keegan smacking a volley. The song shot by so fast it wasn't possible to fully appreciate it on one listen, but what was obvious was that it was a belter that left not only "Stan" but also every other tune currently on the charts eating dust.

So here it is merry Christmas…

As Pogsy sung along, he was convinced that it was the finest chorus ever written in any Glam song. It was certainly worthy of the radio volume being turned up to twenty, even though the dial stopped at ten. He shed a silent tear. Not at Steve's displeasure, although that certainly helped, but at the fact that Slade had only gone and recorded the best Christmas song ever in the history of Christmas songs! He wondered how he'd ever doubted they'd do it. By the final chorus, even the girls were sing-shouting along. Pogsy bellowed the words at the top of his voice, stomping around the classroom with Gas-tank. Between them, they made so much noise that the windows shook, causing Mister Cohen to pop his head around the door to see what was going on. Pogsy didn't stop singing for a full five seconds. He didn't care. "Merry Xmas Everybody" was worth a hundred slipperings. And the look on Steve's face was worth at least six-of-the-best more.

They'd done it.

Oh, had they ever.

The next few days at school were all one massive blur spent living in the clouds. After what seemed like an eternity there was finally a new Number One and it felt brilliant.

Pogsy raised a fist in triumph.

The luck of thousands of fans combined had pulled off the inposs.

In the playground, everyone carried on as though nothing extraordinary had happened, even though they were told repeatedly to watch *Top of the Pops* later in the week, or even better still, go out and buy the new Number One. As the week progressed, the teachers put sprigs of holly up around their blackboards. One of the naughty boys in Class 4C reported that the headmaster had decorated *Old Ebeneezer*, his cane, and was giving out seven-of-the-best instead of six, as a special Christmas treat. It was surreal how all the boys and girls were going about their business, oblivious to the change at the top of the charts and the looming threat of power cuts.

Waiting for power cuts was just like waiting for Santa. Except everyone knew when Santa was coming. You could set your calendar by him. No-one seemed to know when the power cuts were coming though, not even the Prime Minister. There were rumours in the papers that he was going to make telly finish at 10.30 every night, but the most pressing rumour of all was about something called the "three-day week", which, when Pogsy thought about it, didn't make any sense at all.

Bingo did the calculations.

If every week was three days long, there'd be a hundred and twenty-two weeks in a year. Assuming the grown-ups kept weekends, that meant there would only be one day of school a week. Logically, they had to keep Wednesday as it was in the middle. Pogsy didn't mind that too much, although the idea of having swimming the day after bath night was silly. He'd rather keep Tuesday because that was when they did footie practice.

Once they'd discussed it in the playground, everyone agreed that you could always trust grown-ups to fiddle about and make things ten times worse than they already were. When the rumour of a shorter working week turned out to be true, every dad in town suddenly had a right monk-on with Mister Heath. Even Mister Wilson from the Labour Party, who was usually calm, was wearing his mardy pants. You could tell because, whenever he appeared on TV, he puffed on his pipe much faster than usual.

"My dad's more than mardy," said Steve, "he's *livid*. Our bagwash business depends on seven-day weeks to keep it going and Dad says that a three-day week is no use to man nor beast."

"The papers say he's got no choice," said Bingo.

"My dad's shops are vital to the economy and the papers are dead wrong." Steve rolled up his tongue. "They won't dare cut them off."

"Chippies are vital to the economy," said Pogsy, thinking out aloud, "because people will starve without them. People don't die from smelly clothes in the same way they die from empty stomachs."

"Come here, you!" said Steve.

Pogsy ran for it.

In his opinion, what the country really needed was *Dr Who* to come back and he was due any day now. Even the Prime Minister and his power cuts couldn't stop the Doctor from appearing on a Saturday night. Implementing a one-day week and making it a Sunday wouldn't stop the Doctor. It would just make him more determined than ever. In an election, Pogsy reckoned that the Doctor would easily beat the Prime Minister and Mister Wilson combined. If the Doctor had been in charge, the oil wars wouldn't even have started and there wouldn't be a mess with power cuts.

The days counted down.

A week after they'd come straight in at Number One, despite Steve's predictions, Slade's luck was still holding firm. Pogsy was glad that Steve was wrong. He'd been rubbing his charm so much the silver paint on the back of its head was now gone. In his opinion, the biggest threat was Wizzard, who had a record out called "I Wish It Could Be Christmas Everyday". A lot of the boys liked it but, overall, everyone agreed that they'd tried too hard to copy Slade. Even DJ Popeye thought so, and he knew more about pop singles than most Radio DJs.

The more Pogsy thought about it, the surer he became.

It was fate.

It had to be.

Christmas was a week away.

God wouldn't be so cruel as to strike down the greatest Glam song ever written on his son's birthday.

Before the best day of the year, there was the extremely important matter of the last day of term and the annual do-it-yourself competition. This year, Missis Wainwright had gone overboard and the prize was a gift voucher worth 50p. The golden rule was that whatever was made had to be assembled in the classroom and finished by 2.30 on the dot. The rest of the rules were basic common sense and the girls had got them straight away. The boys, on the other hand, had to check with Miss as to what was and wasn't allowed several times, and there were still points of contention despite the constant reminders. Ruth made a point of raising her hand and dobbing in the lads with porridge-for-brains.

Even with extra help from Miss, they still didn't get it and it was left to Bingo to provide clarification. Model kits were fine. Jigsaws weren't allowed and neither were homemade stink bombs. Plasticine

Santas and Rudolphs were acceptable, along with matchstick mangers and cotton-wool angels. For those who were thinking of sewing, it had to be done by hand. No sewing machines of any kind. On the day, scissors, glue, glitter and paper would be provided. Any other materials: bring your own.

When the competition had been announced, Steve had strutted around like a cockerel on hydraulic stilts, confident he was going to win. His track record of successes and gold stars stretched back years and the playground agreed that only an idiot would challenge him. Many boys had given up there and then. Bam was the exception. He'd said jokingly that he was going to thrash Steve into second place. They'd joshed with each other all afternoon and then again the next morning, so much so that many of the other boys took the prospect of Bam winning very seriously, mainly on account of his father's legendary money tree.

Pogsy stayed quiet.

He wanted to beat them both so badly it made his kidneys ache. There was no point in gobbing off though, as that would tip his hand. It was better to be the 100-1 outsider, just like they had in the Grand National. Someone who had no chance, who the other jockeys didn't see coming until it was too late.

As was customary on the last day of term, rather than wearing uniform, Pogsy was smartly dressed in his favourite jeans, his trusty roundies, a shirt and tank top, and his teddy bear jacket. His biggest concern was time. And spares.

If owt went wrong, he was in emassive troub.

He had to do everything perfectly.

He sat at his desk, fretting away, troll in hand, barely noticing anyone else. The second the bell rang, he dived into his specially prepared bag of tricks. He'd spent ages lying in bed at night, plotting, thinking about his project and planning each step meticulously, including what to borrow. He'd settled on cardboard as the best material for the job. Not the thin kind used in cereal packets but the corrugated stuff the large cardboard boxes that Mum brought the weekly shopping home in were made from. He'd folded one box flat and sneaked it out the house that morning, along with Mum's best scissors and some fabric from her sewing drawer.

Rather than getting stuck in, Pollyanna jabbered away about her grandma's homemade jam. Pogsy ignored her and, hands shaking, concentrated on the task at hand.

Missis Wainwright came straight over to check on everyone. She was wearing a red and white Christmas cardigan, decorated with holly.

"Are you sure you know what you're doing, Patrick?" she trilled.

Pogsy grunted.

Miss carried on, moving from desk to desk, chirping away like an electric budgerigar with new batteries, making sure that all the boys understood the rules. The teacher's pet tagged behind. When they both returned ten minutes later, Pogsy saw that his teacher's jumper was covered in gold glitter. For the first time that day, he stopped and looked up. Many of the girls in class were making Christmas calendars, like they always did. They were busily drawing their own backgrounds and painting them in. Eventually, they'd be gluing small rectangular calendars in place. On Steve's table, there was already a fountain of sticky stuff and oodles of sparkly bits everywhere.

"Crikey," said Bingo, taking a breather from the Viking longship he was constructing from balsawood and lolly sticks. "I've never seen so much glitter before. What are you up to, Pat?"

"You'll see."

Bigzy wandered over, grinning from ear to ear. "Wot'cha, Pogs."

"Wot'cha," said Pogsy.

"Me dock tower's coming on ace," said Bigzy. "I can't decide whether to paint it in before or after I build it. What does everyone think?"

"Definitely before," said Pogsy.

"Definitely after," said Bingo.

"After," said Gas-tank.

"I'd do it before," said Pollyanna looking up and flashing her eyelashes.

Pogsy felt his cheeks turn red. She was wearing falsies. There was no doubt about it. He supposed that on the last day of term it was allowed. The rules only said girls couldn't wear eye shadow or lipstick.

"Is that some sort of folded-paper dog's home?" asked Bigzy with a smirk.

"It's called *Origami*," said Pollyanna emphatically. "And it's a zoo. The orange creature here is my tiger. I'm making three more. The grey creature with the trunk is my first elephant. There'll be swans too. And lions. And zebras. But I'm going to cheat and paint those."

"Are you going to make any of those monkeys with the huge red bums like they have on *Survival*?"

Pogsy guffawed. Bingo blushed.

"You!" Pollyanna pushed Bigzy on the shoulder. "We already have one of those in class, we don't need another."

"I'll bring you a mirror so you can get a proper look," said Bigzy, ducking. He scurried off back to his table, sniggering as he went.

Pollyanna stuck her tongue out. "Good riddance!" she shouted.

Ruth glared at the little lad before returning to the calendar she was making, which had a background in the shape of Santa's head.

Pogsy checked his work one more time then set to cutting out cardboard pieces, using Mum's special fabric scissors. The ones they had at school were blunt, to prevent boys and girls from stabbing themselves, which made them useless for anything other than mangling paper. With the aid of a pair of drawing compasses he'd borrowed from his brother, Pogsy marked out two huge circles, one inside the other. He cut around the outer circle. On the inside of the inner circle he drew a series of one-inch tabs. He drove the scissors through the middle of the cardboard circle then started cutting, creating what one boy thought was a cartoon mouth with teeth. Later on, the purpose of the tabs would be revealed, but not until the last possible second. Pogsy double-checked the size of his other main component, which was a cardboard rectangle. Once he was a million percent certain it was correct, he glued and stapled a strip of cardboard along one edge, then bent the rectangle around to form a cylinder, securing the edges together with extra staples and glue which he managed to get all over his fingers. He hated using Bostick. It was too runny, you couldn't control the flow, it stuck to everything and, just like burning rubber, the smell attacked your nose and turned your brains to mush. Secretly, he hoped his dad had forgotten how much was left in the tube. From his bag of tricks he removed a length of black velvet he'd swiped from Mum's sewing box and matched it against the cylinder. Then, biting his lip, he cut the fabric to size.

Someone approached from behind. Pogsy turned around and came face to face with Steve.

"You're making a third-place hamster wheel," said Steve with a big, toothy grin. "I guess that means you've done a deal with Gerbil."

"It's a guinea pig I need. She's smuggling me one later."

"Figures," said Steve. "You'll never guess what I'm making."

Pogsy had heard it was a diorama. Other than that, he was deliberately avoiding knowing, so as not to be intimidated.

"I'm making the greatest, most realistic model of the whole Glitter Band in the world," said Steve defiantly. "And when I win that gift voucher – which I will – guess what I'm going to spend it on?"

Pogsy huffed. "Even Pollyanna's *harry garni* is better than what you're doing."

"We'll see about that," said Steve. "You can lick my boots and say soz a lot when I win, and when you do, I might just let you off. Then again, I might not. You *are* on secret probation."

Pogsy took a deep breath. "If I win, you've got to cancel it. If you win, you can put me on double secret probation."

Steve stuck out his bottom lip and perched his teeth atop it. "Fair enough. I *am* the most magnanimous Steve in the world."

Blown raspberries were quickly exchanged.

Chuntering away to himself, Pogsy put spots of glue all around the cylinder and attached the fabric. As soon as he was done, he hid it out of sight. The next step was the trickiest part of the whole operation. If anyone saw what he was doing, it would be obvious what he was making. He took out a piece of cardboard he'd prepared earlier, which had a smaller circle drawn on it, with tabs marked on its outside. A boy walked past with a puzzled expression on his face. Pogsy smiled. Everyone was still guessing at his design. He liked that. Other boys not knowing, thinking he didn't stand a chance. He wondered if Ali was interested in what he was doing. He glanced over at his friend's table, which was the furthest table in class from his own. She was in deep concentration, busily sewing together a stuffed eagle. Under normal circumstances, he'd be happy to see her win. But not today.

He checked his measurements one more time, ensuring that the tabs were sized correctly, and confident he hadn't missed anything, set to cutting out the smaller circle. As he finished, Missis Wainwright called time for dinner. He really didn't want to leave his creation unguarded in case someone sabotaged it. Carefully, he placed all of his components in a large carrier bag and secured its handles together with his bike lock, ensuring he was the last to leave. As he ran to catch his friends for dinner, he saw Steve going the other way.

"Save us a seat," said the leader of the gang.

Pogsy felt a bit sick from stuffing loads of Christmas turkey down his gullet as fast as possible then scoffing two helpings of Christmas pudding. For some reason, there were boys who didn't like Christmas pud. He wasn't one of them. He burped raisins and revelled at the thought of all the food he'd put away. He'd even managed five glasses of water. Most boys would be bursting after that. But not him. He could hold it in forever. It was part of his special superpower. And besides which, there was no better feeling than having a massive celebratory wee after you'd won a competition.

He'd just finished covering the large, hollow circle in black velvet, which was trickier than he'd imagined due to the tabs, when Gas-tank snuck into the classroom.

"Nice effort," said Gas-tank, picking up the ring and feeling it. "What is it, Pogs? Some sort of Frisbee?"

"You'll see."

"I'm making an advent cuckoo clock," said Gas-tank, showing off his hands, which were covered in cracked sheets of glue that went right into the sides of his nails. "It's got twenty-four numbered doors that all open. I'm gonna hide a goodie behind each door, then eat twenty of them straight away."

"You must have painted it before. It wouldn't be dry otherwise."

"Yeah. It feels like cheating. But Shaz and Jude are sewing together dolls from panels they spent last week knitting, so Miss can't really do me, even though Ruth says she should."

Gas-tank returned to his seat. Pogsy wasn't sure his pal was going to finish in time. But then his own creation still needed a lot doing too.

He used the compasses to draw twenty-five two-inch circles on the back of a cereal box, which he then cut out. Then, one by one, he took all the circles and stuck a paper fastener through the hole left by the compasses. He was too engrossed in what he was doing to pay attention to anyone else. It was only when Bam wandered over to interrupt him that he noticed everyone else was back from dinner.

"My table are perplexed as to your creation," said the rich boy, pulling a bemused look from his drawer of unusual expressions. He was wearing a clear, plastic apron that covered his front from neck to toe, hiding the smart tartan suit and red shirt he'd chosen for the day. "I hate to admit it but you've got me. My best guess is it's some sort of throwing game."

"Not quite," said Pogsy.

"Go on," said Bam, his voice a purr. "Let me into your secret."

"It's a..." Pogsy had to grab hold of his tongue. He'd watched Bam pull the same trick on other boys and make them spill their secrets. He'd decided he'd never fall for it, and yet he nearly had. "...I can't say. Soz and all that."

"Suit yourself," said Bam. "My scale model of the docks has issues. The sea's bubbling rather than setting."

"You need to add more plaster powder," said Pogsy.

"I can't be bothered," said Bam. "Even if it sets this second, I'll never get it painted in time. One of my model trawlers looks like it's been savaged by the Kraken."

"You can't just give up. You said you were going to win."

"Forty minutes isn't long enough. I know when I'm beaten."

As Bam returned to his table, Pogsy danced a mini-victory dance. The rich boy was dead in the water. His idea had sounded great in theory but he hadn't planned it out properly. He hadn't tried mixing plaster at home first, to make sure he knew what ratios to use. That was his undoing. At least that was what Pogsy would tell the playground later. He looked over at Bigzy and winked. Bigzy gave him the thumbs-up. Bam's real problem was the half a tin of Alka-Seltzer that had been sneaked into his plaster box during morning break. Pogsy felt bad about the prank, seeing as it was his idea. But Bigzy, the class clown, would happily take the rap if it was discovered.

Still smirking to himself, Pogsy reached inside his bag of tricks for the length of silver foil he'd borrowed from the roll in the kitchen. He felt a nest of creepy-crawlies hatch in his tummy. Frantically, he emptied the bag onto the table.

Inpossible!

It was gone.

In a panic, he looked around, searching for the thief. He'd triple-checked the bag before he'd left home and the foil was there before dinner. He hadn't imagined it. And the bag was securely locked against thieves. If there'd been a breach, the handles would be torn. Slowly the truth dawned. He wasn't the only boy in class who knew the combination.

"Steve!" he yelled angrily, marching over to his friend's desk. "You nicked my foil."

"Borrowed," grinned Steve. "I'd never steal off my Second."

"I need it back. Now."

"I've used most of it on my costumes. I knew you wouldn't mind."

Pogsy felt his brain boil. He clenched his fists. "You've sabotaged me!" he yelled.

In an instant, Miss was between him and Steve, calming things down with her hands. "What's the problem?" she said sternly.

"Steve stole my tinfoil," said Pogsy. "And I need it back."

"Pat and me have an arrangement," said Steve. "If either of us need anything from the other, we borrow it and say sorry later."

"That's a fib," said Pogsy. "He just made that up, Miss."

"Steven. Give Patrick what remains of his tinfoil."

"Yes, Miss." Steve winked. "Here you go. Good luck."

Pogsy felt the tears build inside but he was determined not to cry, not in front of the whole class. Over half of his tinfoil was gone and what was left wasn't enough to finish the job. He sat down at his desk and covered his head with his arms, cursing his stupidity. He should have known better than to trust Steve, even for a second. He always did whatever he needed to do to win, even to his friends. This was it. Without the foil, he was done for and it was too late to rush home and get any more, even supposing Miss let him.

"Patrick?"

"Leave me alone."

"I've got some foil you can have."

Pogsy looked up, straight into the eyes of Teacher's Pet. He didn't know what to say. If he agreed, he'd owe her, and having a debt to a girl was never good because they demanded that you do fifty things for them to clear it.

"If you don't want it." Ruth scrunched her lips.

"I do."

"I'll let you have it on one condition. Tell me what it is you're making."

He really didn't want to, and his entire body screamed at him for being a numbskull, but he stood up, leaned over and whispered in her ear.

Ruth's jaw dropped open. She quickly composed herself. "That's sweet," she said, "the two of us sharing a secret. I like that."

Pogsy winced.

He took Ruth's foil and, as fast as he could, covered each of the tiny discs in it, hiding them away one by one.

The last fifteen minutes were frantic.

He covered the smaller circle in velvet and glued it in place on one end of the cylinder. Then, with the aid of Dad's *Broggler*, he broggled holes in the cylinder to mount the silver circles. He had to admit that without the *Broggler*, which he'd borrowed from the kitchen drawer when no-one was looking, he'd be in deep trouble. He had no idea what the proper name for the tool was, or even what it was supposed to be used for. Dad had come home with it a few weeks ago and had been using it ever since for any job that involved poking. Pogsy suspected it had come from Buddy's junk shop, as this was the source of most of his second-hand tools. With its small wooden handle and dastardly metal spike, the *Broggler* was perfect for the task in hand. As it happened, it also excelled at removing stuck shells from toy cannons.

If only Dad had had it last year, Blitzen wouldn't be busticated.

The final job was to mount the cylinder to the large ring and add an inner felt band. Pogsy knew it was tight and, counting the seconds, he finished with thirty *Keegans* to spare. He looked up from his work to see that half the class were staring at him, including Missis Wainwright. He felt a blush start in his toes and work its way all the way to the top of his head. Inside, he curled up. What he really, really wanted to do was to stand on his chair, wave his creation in the air and yell at the top of his voice, *Merry Christmas, everybody!* But the crippling shyness he felt in front of large groups – especially groups of girls – got the better of him.

Red-faced, he sat down.

Missis Wainwright had some of the boys transport two large, flat desks into the classroom from the library and then laid out all of the creations in four rows.

At 2.35 on the dot, Grizzly Greythorpe came in to judge the efforts. He was dressed in a charcoal-grey suit with a crisp white shirt and a red tie. The class went deathly quiet. Those who were sitting stood up. If a pin were to drop, you'd hear it. The headmaster walked slowly to the front of the classroom and stood by the side of Missis Wainwright's desk. He scanned the classroom for any faces he recognised and soon settled on Bigzy. After an uncomfortable few seconds, he cleared his throat and, in a posh, plummy voice said, "Good afternoon, Class 4A."

"Good afternoon, sir," said the class as one.

The headmaster was tall and thick-set with the same hairstyle favoured by Count Dracula. Just like Count Dracula, no-one knew his first name. Chip said that if you ever discovered it and said it out loud, he'd visit you in the middle of the night and bite you on the neck. Then he'd make you live in the dungeon underneath his house. There were three missing boys who'd all heard it once by accident and had vanished, never to be seen again. They were chained up in Grizzly Greythorpe's crypt to this day, and he took it in turns drinking their blood.

All eyes were on the headmaster as he picked up a doll dressed in a homemade Santa's outfit.

Pogsy recognised it immediately. It was Susan Grainger's work.

"A very good effort."

The headmaster moved on. One by one he examined the entries on the front row close up. The ones at the back he poked and he prodded. Then came the questions. Mister Greythorpe was famous for asking questions, which he then answered, mainly because most boys and girls were too frightened of him to say a word. He held up Bam's model of the docks and asked the class what kind of weather might cause the sea to fizz? The word he had in mind was "maelstrom". No-one got it right. Then he approached Ali's eagle and wanted to know what type of bird it was. The answer was a Bald Eagle, not an American one. He pointed at Bigzy's Dock Tower and wanted to know in what year it was constructed. Nervously, Bigzy answered 1973. The correct answer, said Mister Greythorpe without a hint of humour, was 1852. He then commended the shipwright for attention to detail and wanted to know the name of the Dane who'd founded Grimsby, along with that of his son. Everyone knew the answer but no-one dared say it.

"Havelock." Mister Greythorpe tutted and picked up Steve's diorama. "This model displays outstanding costume-making skills. I congratulate the artist for a truly commendable effort."

Pogsy glanced over and caught the smug look of satisfaction on Steve's face. His belly spun around like a cement mixer, dumping concrete into his guts.

That was it then for another year.

"But after careful consideration, I declare victory to the milliner."

Pogsy looked around the classroom, trying to figure out who'd made a loaf of bread. Seconds later the penny dropped. The headmaster was holding up a black and silver hat, pronouncing it the unanimous winner, and he was asking the one who'd made it to step forward.

Pogsy froze.

For once in his life, he'd won something.

His head filled with pop bubbles that lifted him upwards. Then his mouth felt dry. Within a second, his legs turned to jelly and a set of familiar feelings took over his body.

"Excuse me," said the headmaster, "Who made this?"

Pogsy felt Ruth grab hold of his hand and thrust it in the air.

"Do come forward, boy." The head waved in a beckoning motion. "It's Patrick, isn't it?"

Pogsy wobbled as he left the safety of his friends behind him. Everyone was looking at him. He felt hundreds of eyes burning into the back of his head. "Yes, sir," he croaked.

"I believe this fine hat to be a duplicate of the one worn by the lead singer of the popular musical combo Slade."

"Yes, sir."

Ruth stuck up her hand. "Please, sir. His name's Noddy Holder, sir."

"My granddaughter rather likes Slade," said the head. "May I keep it?"

Pogsy's world exploded in a *malestrop* of fizz and confusion. He'd spent ages and ages planning his hat. He'd used up all of Dad's glue, all of Mum's fabric and the last cardboard box in the house. When Mum discovered he'd also had the last of the silver foil away, she'd likely box his ears. He'd taken so many risks to win. And there was no way on Earth he'd ever be able to make another hat as good as this one. The first one of anything you made was always the best. Everyone knew that. He felt a lump in his throat, like a vampire had a hand around his neck.

"P... please, sir..." Pogsy spluttered, forcing out the words.

"Please, sir," said Ruth, holding up her hand. "It's been made for Patrick's head, sir. For a girl, there's nothing worse than a hat that doesn't fit properly, sir."

"Please sir," said Bigzy sticking up his hand. "Pat does have a *very* big head."

Pogsy heard the splutter of suppressed titters.

His cheeks glowed like a small furnace.

"Why, I hadn't thought of that." The headmaster exposed one of his vampy fangs. He handed the hat to Pogsy. "As your head is so large, young man, you may keep it."

Pogsy's brain swirled. He saw grey spots in front of his eyes.

"Please, sir," said Bigzy. "Pat's granny is a dab-hand with hats, sir. She could make you five in under an hour, sir."

"Thank you, Wayne. I'll bear that in mind."

The ceremony whizzed by. Pogsy took his gift voucher, said his thanks and felt thoroughly embarrassed at the round of applause he received. The second the headmaster was gone, the class relaxed. Gas-tank seized the moment and, grabbing hold of the hat, which only just fit him, broke into song, belting out the opening verse to "Merry Xmas Everybody". The words he sung were similar to the ones that Pogsy had memorised, but not exactly the same.

As soon as Gas-tank reached the chorus, the whole class, with the exception of Steve, joined in.

Gas-tank looked at Miss, shrugged his shoulders and belted out the chorus again. This time even Steve relented, and seeing how much her class were enjoying themselves, Missis Wainwright joined in too. When the rendition was over and Gas-tank's back had been well and truly slapped, Steve ambled over.

"Well done, Pogs," he said. "This is a great victory for The Kings. One day soon we'll build the greatest trophy cabinet in the world in our den and your winning entry will sit alongside all the best models I've made over the years."

"It belongs on my head, not in a trophy case," said Pogsy, irritated at the thought of giving up his prize-winning hat.

"That's a shame," said Steve. "I can't possibly revoke your probation if you refuse to follow the rules. It's a nice hat too. Not that it's gonna help Slade be Number One on Christmas Day. Soz to burst your bubble and all that. With the help of my lucky crown they'll soon be defeated."

The final youth club of the year was an important part of everyone's Christmas plans and no-one wanted to miss it. Over the previous few weeks, Pogsy had noticed that the heating had been switched off earlier and earlier into the evening. Most of the boys either hadn't noticed or didn't care and kept warm by running around like idiots. Tonight the hall was lukewarm at best. The space filled up quickly with expectant boys and girls ready to celebrate.

As soon as everyone was booked in and subscriptions were paid, Missis Marsden called a meeting and made an announcement from the stage. "I'm sorry to be the bearer of bad news," she said, "but this will be the last youth club for a while. We're shut next week because of Christmas. After that, new regulations from the government mean that we're not allowed to heat this hall. Different regulations from the same government prevent us from holding meetings such as this *without* heating the hall. We're a bit stuck with nowhere to go. Once this crisis is over, I'm sure things will return to normal. Until then, have a great time everyone."

Pogsy's bottom lip stuck out nearly a foot.

"This might be the last youth club of all time," said Steve, addressing the boys. "We need to make sure we have the bestestest time ever. Who's up for five-a-side togger before the disco?"

Everyone shouted over the top of everyone else.

Steve donned his crown and put his arm around Pogsy's shoulder. "You can captain one of the teams, I'll captain the other. Foggy first pick – I'll have Chip."

Pogsy grinned. "I'll take Bam."

For ages it had been assumed that the church hall was the hall for the church and that was that. Recently, Pogsy had led a series of missions to explore the surroundings and he'd discovered that the short, antiseptic blue and white corridor that led to the loos and ended in a fire door actually carried on. He and Bigzy had snuck through the opening and found a series of smaller rooms, which were being used to store spare chairs, tables, Bibles, hymn books and general bric-a-brac. They'd kept on going, through a maze of corridors, all the way to the main church. The last door was always locked. The layout reminded Pogsy of the inside of Doctor Who's TARDIS, which he'd finally seen in colour. The Doctor was busy fighting a new monster, in a castle in the Middle

Ages, with knights and swords, but no-one had seen what it looked like yet. Hopefully, tomorrow might finally bring some answers.

Following the church Christmas fete the previous weekend, one of the rooms was now empty. It was big enough to play footie in and, after some pleading from Gas-tank, Missis Marsden relented and gave the go-ahead, provided a smaller ball than normal was used and nothing got broken. It took Bigzy all of ten seconds to hit one of the hanging metal lampshades, causing it to vibrate wildly and swing uncontrollably from side to side. Bigzy held his head in his hands.

"Soz, lads."

Bam was the next one to belt the ball too high. The lampshade shook with a violent *twang*. He let out a *snork*. By the third hit, it was apparent that the lampshades were made from the same indestructible material as Superman's cape. Either that or God was carefully watching over the contents of his house. It was certainly going to take more than a simple miskick to do any serious damage. Steve declared that hitting a lampshade counted as a goal. No-one objected. The two teams thundered up and down the small hall, slipping about on the heavily waxed floor but still managing to score goal after goal. At 18-17, with both sides covered in dirt, the game was declared a win for Steve. Chip, as expected, had scored the most goals so was named man of the match.

Everyone retired to go get some pop.

"I like playing in your team," said Bam, punching Pogsy lightly on the shoulder. "Thanks for picking me."

"You're a good player," said Pogsy. "And you pass the ball loads and don't hog it. Unlike *some* boys."

Bam nodded. "That was a really good hat you made."

"Your docks were okay too. Better luck next time."

Pogsy didn't like to admit it but, now that Bam had stopped boasting about how good he was at everything, he was much easier to get on with. He couldn't allow himself to like the rich boy though, not after what he'd said to Ali. And he'd only picked him to wind up Steve.

Pollyanna was waiting in the corridor along with the rest of the girls. Her dark-blonde hair was all frizzy for a change and it really suited her. Ruth lounged about, showing off in the Slade hat. Pogsy snorted. When he'd turned up wearing his winning creation, she'd made a point of reminding him that not only had she saved the lucky hat from the headmaster's cruel clutches, but she'd also supplied some vital tinfoil, without which it wouldn't even exist, and technically that made her a part-owner. Lending his hat to Teacher's Pet felt like surrendering a flag to the enemy but, at the same time, Pogsy was well aware that while the hat was on his head it was a target to be nicked and that might cause it to be damaged, whereas no-one in their right mind would even consider grabbing it from the bonce of the evilest girl in school.

In Pogsy's opinion, the hat suited Pollyanna much better than Ruth and he intended to tell her so later when they exchanged presents. His heart skipped a beat. The second that happened, they'd be boyfriend and girlfriend, even though they hadn't been round each other's houses for tea yet. When he thought about it, Pogsy didn't even know where his lanky desk mate lived. He supposed he should have found out by now. He vacillated. In many ways, she was just a girl who he sat next to, who he liked a bit, had held hands with once and had accidentally snogged for *half-a-Keegan* whilst under the evil influence of some very strong pop. In comparison, he'd held Ali's hand twice, been round to her house many times for tea and kissed her on the cheek for a bit more than *half-a-Keegan* with no evil pop involved. It was too late to back out now though. You couldn't tell a girl who was expecting to become your girlfriend that you'd changed your mind at the last minute, in the vain hope that a girl who never wanted to talk to you ever again might back down.

Pogsy felt very confused.

All he knew for certain was that the moment you let girls in your life, the drama never stopped.

While he was wrestling with his conscience, he caught Ruth staring straight at him with her big doey-brown eyes. She crumpled her lips. His tummy dropped a mile. She knew all about Pollyanna. Everyone did. And yet she didn't appear to care. In a panic, a plan formed in Pogsy's brain. In order to put Ruth off, somehow he was going to have to snog Pollyanna in front of everyone but Ali. Before he could do that, though, he was going to have to find something to stand on.

Ali's present ceremony was sprung on her before the disco started. Pogsy had been desperate to tell her, in an attempt to make it up, but he'd decided it might make things worse. The girls had managed to collect £2.27 between them, which was much better going than the 96p, a spare button and a custard cream that Pogsy had collected. He had no idea what the money had been spent on, and he suspected that some of the dozen presents the girls had assembled were hand-me-downs and unwanted gifts.

"Ah'm really overwhelmed," said Ali, forcing a smile, "but it's not as bad as you all think. Pop has arranged for Nan and me to fly out to Texas for Christmas, so Ah won't be alone after all. Ah honestly had no idea. Ah only found out about an hour ago."

"Three cheers for Ali," said Jude and Shaz together, leading the applause.

Hip, hip, hooray!

"Thanks, everyone!" said Ali. "You're the best."

Pogsy was happy that his friend wasn't going to be an orphan at Christmas, but also sad that he wouldn't get to see her on his birthday.

"Wot'cha," said Pollyanna.

Since he'd last seen her, his desk mate had put on some make-up and eye shadow to enhance her falsies. The light blues really suited her. "You look nice."

"Sharon and Judith helped." Pollyanna blinked madly. "I'm a bit rubbish with make-up. I saw you looking at Ali. You like her a lot, don't you?"

Pogsy nodded wistfully. "Everyone likes her. She's dead good at sports and she's clever and she's lived in America. She's like Wonder Woman and you'd have to be Batman to stand a chance. I'm more like Robin."

Pollyanna giggled. "I can just see you in green tights."

"Holy haddock, Batman!" exclaimed Pogsy, bashing a closed fist into a cupped palm. "They've kidnapped Slade off *Top of the Pops* and they plan on torturing them with tomato Cup-a-Soups."

"You," said Pollyanna, breaking out her famous donkey-bray. "You're the funniest boy I know."

They continued talking, mostly about girl stuff, such as which girl's comics were best. Ruth butted in a couple of times, nominating *Jackie*, even though it was for older girls. Pollyanna admitted she wanted to be in a pop group. Except she couldn't really sing.

"Hopefully," she said, "I'll be getting a guitar for Christmas."

"I can play the violin," said Ruth smugly. "*And* the recorder. I *might* get a guitar too."

The two girls had a good giggle between themselves. Pogsy nodded in what he thought were the right places, a trick he'd learned from watching his dad interact with his mum. Girl stuff was just so boring. It was no wonder Dad only half-paid attention. Besides, with a brain full of fish swapsies, he wouldn't have room for dresses and hairclips.

Pogsy remembered that, during the meeting with the scallywags, Dad had referred to himself as "Aggers". That must be his nickname. He hadn't heard anyone use it though.

"Why don't girls have nicknames for each other?" he asked, his thoughts cranking out through his mouth before he could stop them.

"Nicknames are a stupid boy invention," said Ruth.

Pollyanna immediately took sides. "If you get the wrong one, it hurts."

"But we all have great nicknames," said Pogsy defensively. "Thanks to Steve."

"I've heard some of the boys call you 'Pogsy'," said Pollyanna. "What does that even mean?"

"I worked it out," said Ruth. "His middle name begins with an 'O'."

Pogsy blushed. "It's a good nickname and I like it. Stephen likes being Bingo and everyone knows Wayne as Bigzy. Even Chip's okay with his name as long as no-one says it in full."

"What about Donut?" said Ruth sharply.

"Donut loved his nickname," said Pogsy tersely. "He told uz so."

"You all teased him remorselessly," said Ruth, folding her arms. "If he'd complained, you'd have teased him even more. My dad says nicknames are divisive."

"I agree," said Pollyanna.

Pogsy stopped in his thought tracks, contemplating what *derisive* might mean. He promised himself that he'd look it up later. He'd never considered that Donut might have been fibbing when he said he liked his nickname. Best mates didn't do that though. They told you the truth. Which meant that Ruth was wrong and Pollyanna was a bit dim for agreeing with her.

He shook his head.

Girls couldn't even do nicknames without turning it into a drama.

Before he said something he might regret, he was saved by DJ Popeye cranking out a tune. "That sounds like The Sweet."

Pollyanna's lips cracked wide, glistening a bright cherry red. "Last one there's a big, fat turkey with trimmings."

Quick as a flash, Pogsy gave chase, thundering after his beanpole of a classmate who, with her long legs, took two strides for every three of his. Ruth followed, holding onto the hat for dear life. Pogsy bashed into someone, almost flattened someone else, then clattered into Sarge and Ali, with all of them ending up in a pile on the floor.

"Soz," he mumbled, climbing to his feet. As he picked himself up, he caught Ali's eye. For the first time in yonkers, she didn't look away. His heart jumped. He felt a smile form. Still his friend kept on looking at him, refusing to break eye contact. Pogsy felt his ears turn red. "I gotta go..."

He caught up with the two girls and, realising he was in last place, did his best impersonation of a clucking turkey, throwing in an Elvis lip-twitch for good measure.

Pollyanna guffawed.

Inside, Pogsy felt conflicted.

Ali had looked at him funny.

It meant summut.

Perhaps she still liked him after all.

He reminded himself that he'd made a promise to do the right thing, and do the right thing he must. He'd spent ages wrapping Pollyanna's present and he'd forced himself to listen to her best stories about jam-making, even laughing at some of them. He'd also started snog training. Unlike footie, it wasn't something you could practice on your own. He knew this because he'd tried snogging himself in the mirror, only to find that it was a bit rubbish and it came with a telling-off for leaving behind a greasy smear. He'd contemplated kissing another boy but, based on what his friends put in their mouths, had decided against it. Finally, in desperation, he'd tried kissing a polystyrene head used to display fashion wigs in a store in town, but that had triggered the security guard and he'd had to run for his life.

He lamented for the good old days before this nonsense had begun. There hadn't been any of this last year when girls were aliens from outer space and boys didn't want anything to do with them.

His thoughts turned to the dens.

They were almost finished now.

After that, a gang war was coming. Everyone knew from watching films that the last thing you needed when a war broke out was a girl back home. They spent all their time worrying you might get hurt, and then they'd interfere and try to make peace. The best bit about fights was not knowing who'd win but bashing each other anyway. If girls had their way, boys wouldn't be allowed to use their fists to defend themselves by attacking first, and then fights would be no different to playing footie.

What, he wondered, was the point of that?

Fourteen: War

The moment he reached the top of the woodyard's high outer wall Pogsy knew that something was not right. In the distance, lads were yelling instructions to each other. He cocked his ear.

Excitable jest.

Stopping at the cable-drum walkway, he gazed into the distance and listened attentively. Whatever was happening, it was taking place at the far end of the yard.

He whistled a few bars of "Merry Xmas Everybody" and watched his breath crystalise. Nervously, he chewed his lips. Lads talked. There was going to be music to face today.

Hopefully, Slade would see him through.

The Wingmen's lookout, who was almost invisible, stood up and waved his arms. "Pogsy!" he yelled. "Get in 'ere. We need more climbers."

Pogsy cupped his hands to form a megaphone: "What's happening?"

"We got the monkey boy cornered."

"Where's Bigzy?"

"No idea."

It was a short hop, a trio of skips and a jump to terra firma. At ground level the air was still with a crisp edge. The sun, low in the sky, cast long shadows across the concrete floor, creating patches of black ice that were both abundant and deadly.

Carefully choosing his steps, Pogsy headed towards the den.

Everyone had their own pet theory as to who the monkey boy was, ranging from Squib's idea that he was a stranded spaceman to Reddy, who was still holding on doggedly to the possibility he was a Tramp. The truth likely lay somewhere in between and, whilst the discovery of the lad's true identity was something that needed to happen, it would, in Pogsy's opinion, reduce the speculative joshing to zero and that would make visits to the woodyard a lot more boring.

"Pogs." Red Top exited the den, clutching his trusty spear. "You timed it just right. We got the monkey boy trapped. Follow uz."

As they headed up the yard, Reddy explained that one of the Wingmen had spotted someone messing about near the hut and he'd grabbed his mate and gone to investigate. It was only once they'd got a climber up on top of the woodpiles that they'd discovered the monkey boy lying flat on the hut roof.

"He ain't got nowhere to go," said Reddy.

"Yo, Pogsy!" shouted Mopey Joe. He was sitting high up on the edge of a woodpile, catapult in hand. "I 'it 'im a mo ago. I swear."

"How many have we got?" said Pogsy.

"Me and Loggy," said Mopes. "Plus Greebs and 'is mate, and now you two."

"No-one else fancied it," said Red Top. "I tried."

"Someone 'as to get up on the roof," said Greebo. "As the best climber 'ere, Pogs, that's you."

Pogsy took stock of the situation. Mopes and Loggy had the high ground. That left a boy for either side of the hut with Reddy up front. He organised the lads to his liking then mounted the fence. Chain-link fences weren't like trees or drainpipes. The larger the expanse, the greater the wobble. He climbed, rocking this way and that, determined to confront the boy in black. Once he was ten feet off the ground, he launched himself at the roof and scrambled up. Monkey Boy was sitting cross-legged, near the centre at the back.

"I don't want to hurt you," said Pogsy quietly, talking with his hands. "In fact, I don't really want to know who you are. While your identity's secret, you're a legend. I don't want to spoil that and if it was down to uz, I'd let you go. Except the other lads don't think that way. So soz and all that, but I'm gonna have to capture you."

The second he stepped forward, the monkey boy sprang into life, dodging one way then the other, ducking and twisting, and with a well-placed foot and a push, Pogsy fell flat on his bum with a huge *thud*.

"Ballsacks!"

No sooner was the word out than the lad was gone, flipping off the edge off the roof. Pogsy stumbled to his feet. The move had caught Greebo off guard and the boy in black had skipped around him, tripped him up and was now headed towards the nearest gap in the woodpile.

"Sod me!" shouted Red Top. "'Ee's like a greased weasel. No wonder Bigzy 'as trouble."

"We've got him now though," said Pogsy. For some reason, lads in trouble always climbed upwards and often it was their undoing. "Everyone, quick. Surround the woodpile while we get more up top. Reddy, come with uz."

Certain that the monkey boy would make a dash for it along the woodpile towards The Kings' den, Pogsy chose a narrow corridor halfway along. His assent was rapid. He looked around and soon located the lad in black, doubling back on himself with a pair of boys in hot pursuit. He ducked and covered his head with his hands, not that it mattered. The monkey boy easily cleared him in a single leap. The two lads stopped and helped Pogsy to his feet, then hauled Red Top up. Over by the cable drums, more boys were entering the woodyard, presumably for the pre-Christmas get together that Steve had arranged. Down the woodpile, an odd-looking pair of boys blocked any escape in that direction.

Weeble and Squib.

"Monkey boy is dead tricky," said Pogsy, "but we've got the numbers now. He's not getting away again."

Most of the boys present gathered on the ground while the four up top spread out to prevent the lad in black making another run for it. While he didn't want to be the one to remove the mask, Pogsy knew the outcome was inevitable. The monkey boy was hemmed in on all sides. He was all out of options with nowhere to go.

"Advance," said Pogsy. "Let's get him."

While they walked slowly but surely towards the lad in black, the boy bent over and began fiddling with something near to the gap that separated the final stack of wood from the main pile.

"Anyone down there?" shouted Pogsy.

"Uz," said a voice. "Mopes."

"What's the monkey boy doing?"

"It looks like he's tryin' to make a drawbridge."

"We tried that. The planks are too short to reach the wall."

"Pogs," said Red Top, brandishing his spear, "he's deffo up to summut."

Whatever the monkey boy was planning to do with the plank he'd half-extracted, he'd finished. Calmly, he walked the width of the woodpile to get a decent run-up, then dashed towards the plank.

"It's too far." Pogsy covered his eyes, peeking through his fingers.

"The silly bleeder's gonna top hissen." Reddy shook his head, took aim with his spear and lobbed it, hoping to stop the boy in his tracks.

The lad in black shimmied to the side, dodging the projectile, and continued on his way, launching himself into the air and landing on the end of the plank which protruded for half its length. It bent under his weight and, with a healthy *twang*, flicked him upwards. He performed a forward roll and, arms outstretched, landed perfectly on one of the wall's angled uprights before turning around and blowing a kiss. Then he scurried down to the lip of the fence and vanished over the edge.

"I don't believe it," said Reddy. "No-one can do that."

"Well, someone can," said Pogsy. "And I think I know who."

"Go on."

"I gotta be poz first. Let's just say he's deffo not a Tramp."

One by one, the boys made their way towards The Kings' den. The lads who'd watched the monkey boy perform were incredulous at his cheek, while the ones who'd missed it were busy listening to Chip's account of how the lad had managed three somersaults and a backward roll through the air. The leader of the gang had the loudest voice out of everyone, and even from a distance, surrounded by wood, he could be heard telling Smiffy, who also had a pretty loud voice, what he was getting for Christmas.

Pogsy shook his head.

Any stray misters with working lugholes would easy ferret them out. It was a good job the security codger was deaf.

Other lads joined in the chatter, voting for *Cluedo* and *Monopoly*, and complaining about possible injuries from roller skates they didn't even own yet.

Someone mentioned Miss January.

Everyone laughed.

Pogsy scurried down the crevice and inched his way inside. The original chamber had been expanded extensively and was now thirty feet long and twelve feet wide. During his most recent visits, he'd put his newly acquired skills with a saw to good use and fashioned proper backs for the ground-floor benches. With help from Reddy, he'd also created a floor-to-ceiling finish for the main room, using trimmed planks and nails. Their hammering was inconsistent to begin with but they'd quickly improved. The gang flags were on prominent display for the first time in years, each logo instantly recognisable: a gold crown, a pair of white "W"s in a circle and a hammer and a nut. Across the ceiling ran lengths of paperchains accompanied by reams of tinsel, while at the far end of the room a small silver Christmas tree sat covered in red baubles. In the woodpile opposite the original access gap was a hole that led to a pair of unfinished downstairs rooms. The upstairs layout mirrored the ground floor and was seventy percent complete.

More and more boys arrived until the atmosphere inside the den was buzzing. Bigzy was last, as usual. The little lad looked totally puffed out.

Pogsy walked up and down saying hello to everyone he knew from the other gangs and nodding to the few boys he'd never seen before; studiously, he avoided eye contact with select members of his own gang.

He took a deep breath.

Someone was going to mention youth club.

Any second now.

"Hey, Pogs," said Smiffy with a wink. "What's this I 'ear about you and mistletoe?"

"Nowt," said Pogsy. He felt his ears fire up.

"The word is you snogged a donkey."

"I wasn't the only one." Pogsy glared at Bigzy, then Gas-tank.

"Ooooo..." said Smiffy. "You didn't tell uz that bit, Steve. So 'oo went first and 'oo 'ad sloppy seconds?"

Sheepishly, Bigzy stuck his hand up. "I was mugged."

"I was second," said Gas-tank. "She grabbed uz before I could scarper."

"Thankfully," said Bam, "I was able to extricate myself while Pogsy was busy playing tongue hockey."

Pogsy felt himself go fully red from temple to toe. "She's the teacher's pet," he squealed. "We've hated each other for years and it didn't cross me mind even for a micro-milli-sec that she was gonna stick her tongue in me gob."

"I counted ten *Keegans*," said Steve.

"I couldn't leg it. She had me lucky hat." Try as he might to dislike the experience, Pogsy couldn't deny that snogging Ruth had done something to his willy that snogging Pollyanna five minutes earlier hadn't.

The kiss with his desk mate had been the first time his mouth had connected with a girl's lips on purpose and he remembered it well, lasting as it had for five *Keegans*, give or take a Kevin. He'd prepared as best he could by watching a soppy Christmas film and, when the kissing had started, rather than look away, stick his fingers down his throat and pretend to retch, as was traditional, he'd studied every move in detail. As part of his on-the-spot planning, he'd chosen the perfect snog-spot by the stage, one step up, and he'd even taken Gas-tank's advice and eaten ten Extra Strong mints.

So why had she pulled away, made an excuse about babysitting her moggie and legged it into the night?

It didn't make no sense.

His kissing wasn't that bad.

"Pollyanna's gonna roast your goolies when she hears," said Steve.

"It was mistletoe," said Pogsy. "It's allowed."

"Not when you've got a girlfriend."

"Everyone knows you have to ask a girl out and she has to say yes before she's your girlfriend."

"Changin' the subject," said Mopey Joe, "where's your 'ouse-boy, Steve?"

"I 'eard he's on a chain gang," said Greebo.

"Shame," tittered Mopey Joe. "'E woulda made a great addition to the woodpile."

"What about the Yank lass 'e was wiv?" asked Smiffy, tugging a comb through his hair.

"Gone to America," said Pogsy wistfully. "Yesterday."

Bigzy took a couple of Christmas selection boxes that had fallen out the back door of a newsagent from under his coat and passed them around. Pogsy chose a Milky Way, which was known as *the goodie you can eat between goodies without ruining your appetite.*

"So, Steve," said Wingnut, chewing on a Mars Bar, "what we gonna do about the monkey boy?"

"What do you mean?" said Steve.

"We've tried catching 'im and we can't. He's too nippy. As he was the one who discovered the woodyard, we should let 'im in the gang."

"We still don't know who he is," said Steve. "We can't have an anonymous gang member."

"Dunt matter," said Smiffy. "And anyhow, we saw 'im first."

"Did not," said Wingnut.

"'Ands up, Hard Nuts," said Smiffy. "'Oo votes for Monkey Boy?"

"Wingmen," said Wingnut. "Same."

"If anyone's having him, it's us," said Steve firmly. "Except we have other new members who've been waiting longer."

"Then we should have an induction," said Wingnut with a glint in his eye.

Bingo pushed his glasses up the bridge of his nose. "We've got three on our waiting list."

"Four," said Weeble, ruffling his little brother's hair.

"Kings only," said Steve. "Who votes for Gas-tank?"

All hands shot up, with the exception of Sparksy, who was busy fiddling with a hand-held radio. Steve slapped Bigzy. "Pass it on."

The slap travelled all the way to Weeble, who cuffed Sparksy about the head fully properly.

"Ow!" said Sparksy.

"Yes or no?" barked Steve.

"Yes. No." Sparksy shook his head. Curls of unkempt black hair tumbled everywhere. He tucked his fringe back behind his tiny little ears, where it remained for all of a second. "What?"

"That's a *yes* then," said Steve. "Gas-tank, you're in the gang."

"Thanks, everyone," said Gas-tank, raising a fist.

"Next is Bam. Now he's revealed his superpower, we can vote to let him in."

"Not everyone's seen it yet," said Smiffy. "And they need to."

"Happy to oblige," smirked Bam. He dropped his trousers, whipped his willy out and waved it around like he was about to lasso a whippet. Several lads backed away. Wingnut, caught off guard, shrieked like a girl.

"Who votes for Bam?" said Bingo while the rich boy pulled up his pants.

All hands shot up.

"Congratulations," said Steve. "Bam, you're in. Now, Squib."

There was some contention on account of the little lad's age but no-one wanted Weeble offside. Pogsy counted the hands. It wasn't unanimous but it was enough.

"Well done, ar kid," said Weeble, slapping his brother on the back.

"That's us done," said Steve.

"What about Ali?" The words were out before Pogsy could stop them. He felt thirty pairs of eyes boring holes in his chest and causing his ears to ignite like a pair of small, wicker torches.

Following her visit to the woodyard, he'd seen the gang one by one and done his best to persuade them to let her in. Some were in favour, while others had stuck to the standard trawlerman response that girls, like albatrosses, were nothing but bad luck.

Predictably, the vote did not go well.

"Soz, Pogs," said Steve.

While Pogsy contemplated what bribes he'd need for the next time, the Wingmen added two to their number and the Hard Nuts one. After that, the meeting snaked off in all sorts of directions and from time-to-time Bingo had to drag it back on course. Placement of the latrines was high on his agenda, but the other gangs weren't interested in being told where to pee, especially the Hard Nuts who'd made their own arrangements. The problem was boys always developed a favourite spot and every day he'd been to visit the den, especially now there was a chill in the air, Pogsy had seen clouds of steam rising from the same patch of perimeter wall. It was the optimum location, there was no doubt about it, but come summer it was in danger of smelling like the People's Park bogs, cubicle two.

One rule that had been universally agreed upon and which had so far held was no taking a dump in the yard. A few days ago the oldest of the three de Groody brothers had had to use the emergency carrier bag, which Smiffy claimed he'd lobbed over the fence, laughing as he told the story. Later, he'd given the lad a new nickname.

Loggy.

"Comin' back to the monkey boy," said Wingnut. "What we gonna do?"

"There's an obvious solution," said Bingo. "We can make him a member of all the gangs."

"You're right," said Steve. "As the leader of all the gangs, I can do whatever I want. Everyone, who wants the monkey boy in our gang?"

A series of mini-meetings broke out, with boys arguing this way and that. Some lads thought that having a secret gang member was a great idea, while others thought that the monkey boy had to be unmasked first. The leader of the gangs listened to all the differing points of view and finally, when the conversation ran out of steam, he made an announcement.

"Listen up, everyone. We're gonna have a vote on whether to let the monkey boy join all the gangs. But he has to reveal his secret identity to me, and Wingy and Smiffy, and he can't be a full member until he does."

"Agreed," said Smiffy. "Everyone vote."

Unsurprisingly, the monkey boy made it in by a huge majority.

Bingo shook his head and mumbled something to himself.

"What is it?" said Pogsy.

"Ever since we first saw that lad, I've been trying to tell you that he moves like an ape and not a monkey."

"'Ape Boy' sounds rubbish though," said Pogsy. "And besides, what's the difference?"

Before Bingo could answer, Smiffy stood up. "We go' news. Ar gang hambushed a Tramp the uvver day."

"And we give 'im a right good threatenin'," said Mopey Joe.

This got everyone's attention, even the boys at the back.

"'E spilled 'is guts in no time and did beggin' for freedom and stuff," said Smiffy. "He told uz the Tramps' leader is a lad called JJ who arrived in Beacon Hill a few months back. He started 'is own gang, then made friends with the Wheelers and demanded they join 'im in nicking goodies from paper shops, but Sooty and Sweep refused. So JJ kicked their 'eads in and booted 'em out. The rest of the Tramps are dead scared an' they do whatever 'e sez."

Beacon Hill was further out of town than Pogsy or The Kings usually ventured. It had a nice-sounding name but there was a council estate right in the middle. Along with the town's other well-known estates, where girls could be mums while they were still at school, it was marked as a no-go zone on the Battle Map.

"The other week there was this out-of-control Alsatian that bit the Beacon Hill milky on the bum," said Reddy. "He 'ad to have stitches and a tetanus jab."

"The lad we captured said JJ's got a vicious attack dog," said Smiffy. "Mebbe it's the same one."

"The coppers didn't find the dog wot dunnit," said Red Top. "But then they refuse to go into the estate unless they're lookin' for nicked cars."

Bingo held his head in his hands while the gangs debated the best way to deal with a wild dog. The unanimous conclusion was pitchforks and airguns, although it was agreed that walking into Tramp territory armed to the teeth was likely to result in riot vans and a good truncheoning.

"We need to lure the Tramps to uz," said Pogsy.

"Then it's time to tear down the signs wot they put up around No-Man's Land," said Smiffy, raising his warty thumb.

"And wee on 'em," said Wingnut. "Foggy first. I'll lead the mission."

"Fogs go wiv," said Weeble.

"An' uz," said Squib.

"Then it's official," said Steve. "We're going to war."

"There's summut you have to do first," said Pogsy. He felt his heart jump into his mouth and his voice tremble. "Listen, everyone, I'm on secret probation for summut I did, that I said soz and all that for. We can't go to war if I'm on probation. It meks no sense."

"Probation?" said Wingnut. "It must 'ave been dead serious."

"Like snoggin' a donkey?" tittered Smiffy.

"Pogsy here called my bezzie football a shirt-lifter," said Steve quickly. "So I secret probationed him. It's all a massive joke."

"You prat!" said Smiffy, flicking Pogsy on the lughole. "You had uz dead worried there."

"Yeah," said Wingnut. "If you'd done owt real bad, we'd 'ave to get a bucket of nipper crabs and attach 'em to your goolies."

Pogsy stared at Steve. "So you're tekin' it back?"

"There's nothing to take back."

"Let it go," said Smiffy.

"Yeah," said Wingnut. "We got some weein' to do."

The gang worked their way around No Man's Land collecting every sign they could find and arranged them in a great pile. Then they took it in turns to wee on them.

The steam rose steadily.

Pogsy shook his head.

"About ruddy time," grumbled Red Top.

"Finally," said Wingnut solemnly. "We're at war."

"New rule," said Steve. "We go about in twos and threes from now on."

"No' uz," said Weeble. "A'll 'ave 'em all. By mesen."

"Am 'ard too," said Squib. "An' Am in the gang now."

"Yer no' tha' 'ard, no' ye'," said Weeble, putting his hand on his brother's shoulder. "One day mebbe. For now, yer still learnin', so you stick wi' uz."

Fifteen: Birthmas

Pogsy had difficulty deciding what was better: *feelsies, rippsies*, or playing with presents afterwards. In the end, he concluded that he preferred *feelsies* by a very small margin, followed by *rippsies* and finally *playsies*. In his house, presents that were left under the tree were always from relatives or neighbours and *feelsies* and *shakesies* of such pressies was fair game. Prodding the paper where it was taut, so that it broke, was *cheatsies*, as was using the *Broggler* and a magnifying glass. Finding a hole in the wrapping paper where the grown-up doing the wrapping hadn't done their job properly and bending the present so that you could see in – that was *detectsies*. Unless Mum caught you in the act, in which case it was *slapsies* on the wrist.

With *feelsies* and *shakesies*, you could sometimes work out what you'd got. If a present was a good one, then the excitement of knowing was better than the actual opening because, although you knew what it was, you couldn't have it. Sometimes, *hopesies* about what a present might be was better than the present itself. Best of all was when you did *feelsies* and *shakesies*, decided that a present was a pile of mouldy old rubbish but then, when you opened it, you discovered you were wrong and what you actually had was brilliant. That was known as a *jammy dodger*.

All in all, concluded Pogsy, the December 25th was easily his favourite day of the year. Not only did Santa fly overhead and open his sleigh's present-pods, filling the skies with pillowcases full of presents on parachutes, it was also his birthday. Or *Birthmas*, as it had come to be known. Naturally, there was a downside to having your birthday on the same day as Jesus and that was the prospect of going a whole year without gifts, which, come the middle of the summer holidays, was very boring, especially when a present was what you really needed to lift your spirits. There was also the problem of where to have a party. All the best places, like Cleethorpes Zoo, were shut over winter and those that stayed open were freezing, which made going out for the day a bit tricky. In previous years the answer had been to lump his official party in with Sam's, in July, and this had worked out fine and dandy until his dumpling-head of a brother had declared that he no longer wished to spend the day with a bunch of children. This year, Dad had arranged a special trip to the cinema to watch a James Bond double bill, and most of the gang were invited.

Pogsy couldn't wait.

He looked at the pile of opened presents gathered together underneath the tree. The Lord of Presents had managed to pull out all the stops this year. He'd brought Mum some expensive gold jewellery that looked strangely familiar and three bottles of her favourite perfume. Grandad Green had popped by first thing and received a bottle of whiskey for his troubles. Sam had a fancy shirt and a pair of Wrangler jeans, a BB pistol with targets, and an album by the band Yes, which he'd played after Dad had agreed to just one song. Rather than last three minutes, as was normal, it had plodded on and on, far outstaying its welcome. Worse than that, the singer had screeched away like someone had soaked his underpants in methylated spirit and set his bum on fire. Dad's highlights included a clip-on bowtie, a ratchet spanner set and Slade's new record, which he liked. Ellie had a Tiny Tears doll, a miniature doll's house and some Peter Rabbit books. Aunt Bea had bought her a set of colouring crayons, which appeared to be a great idea until the discovery that they worked on the kitchen floor.

"Elspeth *Green!*" yelled Mum, looking up from the kitchen sink where she was busily peeling spuds. "Stop that this instant!"

"Bronto," said Ellie, pointing at the rough outline of a badly drawn green dinosaur.

"Samuel," said Mum, "take control of your sister. Find her some drawing paper."

"Will do." Sam tussled Ellie's hair. "On the bright side, at least it's less dangerous than last year."

Mum took a glug of sherry. "Why's that?"

"You must remember. Aunt Lorna bought us all clacker balls. The most dangerous toy on the planet. Schools across the land banned them."

"You put all our sets in the bin," said Pogsy. "Then you made uz swear never to tell our aunt. If she asks, we're supposed to say a stray dog stole 'em."

"I was doing my best to forget." Mum returned to her potatoes.

Sam led Ellie through to the lounge, with Pogsy tailing close behind. All in all, it was shaping up to be the best *Birthmas* he could remember, even though the Paddies had tried to ruin it for everyone at the last minute by accidentally sending out letter bombs instead of

Crimbo cards. Most importantly, there was a strong rumour that Slade were the Christmas Number One. He'd find out for sure later. He settled down on the settee in his jim-jams and waited for his sister to start drawing on a sheet of wrapping paper. Once she was busy, he stretched out his legs and tickled her ear with his big toe. Ellie squealed in delight, turned away from her colouring book and jabbed him in the foot with a crayon.

He sighed.

He was eleven now and that meant his world was about to change.

It would likely never get better than this.

One of Mum's rules for the day was no eating goodies before Christmas dinner but, over the years, it had been amended to "no goodies before breakfast" and then "no goodies *for* breakfast". Pogsy eyed the two selection boxes under the tree. It was well known that the eye of Mum saw all so, even though she was a room away, stuffing the turkey and preparing a truckload of sausages, she'd know if he raided them. He made his excuses and snuck up to his room, where he'd hidden half-a-dozen Black Magic choccies in his sock drawer, borrowed the night before from a monster box that Dad had won in a work's raffle. He wished he'd memorised the flavours and weeded out the horrid ones but time had been against him.

He decided to eat two, and if one was nasty, he'd have another to compensate. If that one was also nasty, he'd keep on going. He moved the goalposts as he munched until there was only one chocolate left. As there was nothing worse than having a single horrible chocolate to look forward to, he ate that one as well, just in case, then licked his fingers to hide the evidence.

His favourite Santa pressie was the board game *Escape from Colditz*, which was based on the TV series. The game had a board shaped just like Colditz Castle with secret tunnels, disguises and even a glider. Sam had had a quick look at the rules. One player played the prison guards while the other players were the prisoners. Sam had already bagsied the Krauts. But then he always preferred the Krauts to the British. Apparently, they had the best ships, the best tanks and the best planes, and he was always buying models to prove it. What the Germans didn't have, though, was a Winston Churchill and that was why they'd lost.

To go along with the board game, Santa had thoughtfully packed the present sacks with boxes of plastic soldiers, such as the Eighth Army, some British Paratroopers, the Afrika Corps and the German Army. Upon examination, Pogsy had to concede that the German Army officers had the best pistols and the best caps. But uniforms hadn't won the war. When push had come to shove, the German's upper lips simply weren't stiff enough. That was what Grandad Green believed. And he should know. He was there, both in the desert with Monty and on the beaches on D-Day.

The second-best Santa present was an Action Man talking commander with gripping hands and realistic hair. Although there were eight commands in total, Talking Commander Kev had got a bit stuck and spent breakfast telling the family that *this is your Commander speaking*. Commander Kev looked threatening sitting in the turret of the Scorpion tank that Santa had brought the year before. This year he'd thoughtfully provided a special-operations tent for use in the garden. For now, it was still in the box. While it was winter, it made much more sense to sleep in the tank.

Pogsy took an unopened present from underneath his pillow and tossed it from hand to hand. It wasn't a record; it was the wrong shape. And if he remembered correctly, it wasn't edible, it didn't have any wheels, it wasn't flammable, it didn't have any springs or catches or rubber bands, it wasn't red, it didn't squeak or pong of eggs, it wasn't full of ink, water or washing-up liquid and it definitely wasn't a set of hand-painted racing snails.

The wrapping was first class and the handwriting on the label immaculate. In his opinion, the whole thing was a work of art.

To the funniest boy in class. SWALK xxx.

Although he was desperate to open the last of his presents, he resisted. He needed to know what was going on with Pollyanna first. If she'd changed her mind and decided that she didn't want to be his girlfriend after all, he'd hand the present back. Not that he really wanted to. A present was a present, after all.

He moped and re-hid the package.

The way that Mum managed to assemble Christmas dinner on her own was almost as miraculous as Santa's flying sled, which obviously involved jet engines rather than fairy dust, even though that was what they were teaching little kids in school these days. Post eleven o'clock, the family knew to stay well away from the kitchen and, although keeping the door closed was the safest thing to do, the suspense was intolerable. One by one, Dad, Sam and Pogsy made their excuses and snuck in for a quick progress check while pretending that they needed something vital, like a glass of orange squash.

"So whad'ya see, pipsqueak?" asked Sam.

"I used me nebber," said Pogsy, tapping his nose. "The roasters smell spuddy and the sausages deffo smell like heaven. Mum was broggling the turkey with summut pointy and she mumbled 'thirty minutes'. I hung about too long though. I was threatened with the rollie *and* the sherry bottle. The best news is nowt's on fire."

"Phew," said Sam. "At least International Rescue can stand down."

"There was a micro-milli-second when Mum was distracted." Pogsy grinned. "I nicked a prawn."

"You had a *prawn*." Dad scrunched his lips. "I need a cuppa."

"There's some cheese cubes with pineapple on cocktail sticks appeared too." Pogsy rubbed his belly. "I counted four each and one for Ellie. Mum'll easy know if you have one."

"It's gotta be worth the risk," said Sam. "I'm goin' in."

"Whoah," said Dad, rising to his feet. "Not so fast. Your mum's a perfectionist and there's always a pile of duffers that didn't quite make it if you know where to look."

Pogsy and Sam watched their dad tiptoe into the kitchen like a cartoon bandit in search of loot. Seconds later he reappeared clutching a piece of broken cheese. He was followed by a missile that struck him squarely on his bald patch.

Sam jumped up and arm outstretched caught the largest fragment of the projectile in mid-air. He sniffed it with interest. "Stuffing."

"Giz a chomp," said Pogsy.

Sam popped the misshapen ball in his gob and chewed. "It's delicious. Your bit's on the floor."

Quick as he was, Pogsy was still slower than his sister, who reached the remnants first. "You won't like it," he spluttered.

Ellie's bright blue eyes shot out moonbeams as she giggled and put the crust of sage and onion in her mouth.

Pogsy felt his belly rumble. "I'm starving to death and it's all your faults."

Ellie spat out a bit of chewed food into her hand and offered it around.

Pogsy shook his head. There was starving and there was *starving*, and as it turned out, he wasn't that *starving* after all.

One of the best things about living in a closely packed terraced street was the ease with which one could spy on the neighbours. Over the years, Pogsy made a point of discovering who liked to have family over at the major celebrations and who liked to spend the day visiting relatives. To be sure he was up to date, he'd had a look down the street first thing and everything was as expected, apart from one small detail.

"You look quite the dandy, Patrick," said Missis D. She was wearing a smart red dress with white trim; it looked like she'd had her hair done too for the occasion.

"Thank you, Missis D." Pogsy smiled, stretching his lips and exposing a host of teeth. "Mum found uz the suit and me gran did the alterations. It's just like the one Noddy Holder from Slade wears. I made me lucky hat mesen."

"Well done," said Missis D.

"Missis D," said Pogsy. "Do you have a key to Nan Eagle's?"

"For emergencies," said Missis D. "Why do you ask?"

"Her curtains are open. She always shuts them if she's away."

"You're right," said Missis D.

"Foggie come too."

Walking down the street in his brand-new second-hand suit, Pogsy felt like he was worth a million pounds. He waited while his neighbour retrieved her spare key; all the while she mumbled something to herself that sounded like the Lord's Prayer. Apparently, it was a good defence against burglars, especially the ones who lived just across the street.

"If it *is* a break-in, I'll run and get me dad," said Pogsy. "Even though he thinks I'm mad and making stuff up."

Missis D narrowed her gaze.

"They *were* shut yesterday. Honest." Pogsy considered letting on about his ongoing spying mission on Ali's house, which had begun the day after he'd first met her, but he knew from experience that grown-ups could be funny about that sort of thing.

Missis D approached the house and stuck her face up against the window. Content that there was no movement inside, she unlocked the door and opened it a few inches. "Anyone there?"

The sound of movement from the living room caused both Pogsy and Missis D to take a step backwards. They looked at each other with a mix of fear and trepidation. Missis D opened her handbag and withdrew a silver-plated fish knife, while Pogsy fiddled frantically with his pocket-stabber.

"Bang! Bang!" said a girl's voice. "If Ah was a felon, you'd be dead."

"Alison *Eagle*!" Missis D's voice had an edge like a flint axe. "Don't you ever dare do *that* again."

"Hiya, Pat." Ali was dressed in a long black dress with a gold belt. Her hair was frizzed up and she was wearing powder-blue make-up around her eyes. "Happy birthmas."

"But you're in America," stammered Pogsy.

"Things kinda didn't go to plan."

"And your nan?" asked Missis D sternly.

"She's ill in bed with flu." Ali looked away. "And Ah couldn't go without her."

"I better see her," said Missis D, marching up the stairs. Shortly she returned, confirming Ali's diagnosis. "Nan and I have had a chat and we've agreed you can't spend Christmas Day here. We'll take care of Nan. You're to come round Patrick's with me."

"Ah'd hate to impose." Ali tilted her head sheepishly.

"Nonsense. There's plenty of food. You'll be perfectly welcome."

"Me mum never turns anyone away," said Pogsy. It was a lie but he couldn't think what else to say.

"Swell." Ali wrinkled her nose. "Ah'd like that very much."

Christmas dinner was an event that Pogsy had always taken for granted. Mum was responsible for making it happen and she loved to do an extensive shop down Rammies just before the big day; he liked to go with her, to ensure there was plenty of pop in the trolley. He realised, while they were busy pulling crackers, that in all the years he'd accompanied her, she'd never bought a turkey. Slowly it dawned on him that turkeys, like fish, had a value. Turkeys only ever appeared at Christmas and that made them extra rare. He remembered the swapsie

meet and the man from Yorkshire, who'd mumbled a lot and pulled
Dad's leg about real blokes only scoffing meat. If that was true – and it
was a doubtful claim – then turkey dealers would likely demand fifty
haddock a piece. As this year's turkey was bigger than normal, it must
have cost Dad a fortune. Something like thirty haddock, a halibut,
twenty bags of shrimps and forty kippers.

Ali insisted on saying grace before everyone ate, and she
finished with a little prayer: "For those less fortunate than ourselves this
Christmas Day."

Silently, Pogsy said a little prayer of his own, for Weeble and
his family, who probably had the most *mimiscule* turkey in existence,
likely no bigger than a sparrow, at a cost to Mister Pearce of over a
million eels.

"Amen," said Ali. "Thank you so much for invitin' me over,
Mrs Green."

"A pleasure," said Mum. "Tell us again what happened with
your nan?"

"She got real sick a few days ago." Ali smiled. "Ah decided Ah
better stay here and nurse her back to health. We moved our flights to
Friday."

"I wish my boys were as grown up as you are," said Mum.
"Unfortunately, Elspeth is the most responsible of my children."

"That's not true," said Sam.

Pogsy nodded in agreement.

Ellie giggled in delight.

The family tucked into dinner and ate and ate and ate until
Pogsy thought he was going to burst. From time-to-time he paused and
looked at Ali. Each time, she blinked back. He scoffed some more,
accidentally-on-purpose took a gulp from Dad's glass of *Liebensraum
milk*, got told off, slurped some pop and continued shovelling in grub
until he reached the point where, rather than drooling for turkey, he
groaned at the sight of it. Lasciviously, he eyed up the sausages wrapped
in bacon; he managed to ram another one in on top of the three he'd
already had.

His tummy whined, *No more.*

He continued, albeit at a slower pace, until he'd almost cleared
his plate. A third of a sausage winked at him, splashing away in a pool
of gravy that also contained half a roaster and three Brussels sprouts.

This year, he'd managed two whole sprouts, which was a new record for the vilest of all vegetables.

Leaving half a roaster was a crime. Not quite as bad a crime as garden creeping and stealing toilet rolls from outside loos, but close. In the gob it went, followed by the remains of the sausage.

"Another sprout, Alison?"

"Thank you, Mrs Green, but Ah couldn't possibly."

Pogsy sat there while the plates were cleared away, feeling a little unwell.

Burp!

"Patrick!" spluttered Mum.

"Soz." Pogsy felt his ears burn hotter than the sun.

"Right. Who's for Christmas pudding?" said Mum. "Potty Gran made it. And she put a silver sixpence in the middle this year. Whoever finds it gets to keep it. Provided they don't choke to death first."

"I should take a plate of food round Nan's," said Missis D.

"I need a breath of fresh air," said Sam.

"And I need to walk me belly off," said Pogsy.

"Ah'll come too," said Ali.

"Twenty minutes," said Mum. "Don't go far."

Pogsy, with Ali in tow, followed his brother down the garden. "I ate the most sausages this year," he shouted.

"It's a marathon," replied Sam, "not a sprint. Mum cooked forty-two in total. I know because I counted them. Dad had five, you had four, I had three, Ali had two and everyone else had one each. That leaves twenty-five. Between now and when they run out, I'll eat more than you."

"You know Dad always gets there first."

"Well, neither of us will beat him, but I'm certainly having you. I already beat you on stuffing and roasters."

"And sprouts."

"We drew on sprouts," said Sam solemnly. "We both ate just enough to stop Mum moaning but not enough to turn the house into *Trumpton*."

Pogsy sniggered.

Ali shook her head. "Boys and their asses."

"Pat's been saying for ages that you're dying to see your pop," said Sam, looking at Ali. "If you're so grown up, why didn't you fly to America on your own?"

"Ah guess Ah'm just too responsible," said Ali.

"It's true," said Pogsy, closing ranks. "Ali's the most sensible girl I know."

"Thanks, Pat." Ali folded her arms. "Pop's real busy right now, workin' on an important plan for the President to help end the oil crisis, so he won't mind."

"That's tricky Dicky, right?" said Sam.

"Only his enemies call him that," said Ali pointedly.

"The number one rule of fib club: if you're gonna fib, make your fibs small and believable." Sam shook his head in disdain. "The President of the United States of America. Really?"

"Really," said Ali rolling her eyes. "Boys can be so stoopid."

After dinner was finished and he'd burnt his tongue half to death on a silver sixpence that everyone knew had been deliberated planted in his pud because it was his birthday, Pogsy made sure that the TV was turned up extra loud for *Top of the Pops*. He tried his best to enjoy the show, but the wait for Number One was even more *eggscrutiating* than the wait to hear Slade's latest hit. As each song was introduced he rubbed his troll like crazy, then closed his eyes and touched his lucky hat. Before long, his nerves felt like they were made of mushy peas.

"I heard a rumour," said Sam, with a nudge, "that Wizzard have snuck in and nicked it."

Pogsy jumped out of skin, convinced his poor heart was done for. He grabbed Ali's hand and held it tight.

"Or it could be the New Seekers," joked Sam.

"Stop it!"

Finally, after twenty-five minutes of agony the Christmas Number One was revealed and it began with a familiar seven second introduction.

"Yes!" Pogsy let out a cheer and kissed his hat. He'd made a promise to himself to study all of Noddy's best moves in order to copy them, but his promise lasted all of seven seconds, after which he danced around the room like a maniac. This set Ellie off and she insisted Ali join her. Missis D had a go too and even Mum and Dad had a bit of a jive, which, according to Chip, was a dance that had once been popular a hundred years ago. Sam remained seated throughout, pulling faces.

While the grown-ups made themselves presentable for the Queen's speech, which they watched every year without fail, everyone else retired to the kitchen.

"What did you get for your birthday?" said Ali.

"Me best pressie is a brand-new second-hand bike that Dad got uz. It's cherry-red with white muddies and it's even got ten gears. Santa brought some cowies, which Sam'll help uz fit."

"It sounds great."

"It came from Buddy's," said Sam. "Betcha."

"Who or what is a 'Buddy'?" asked Ali.

"According to Mum he's a pervy old gypsy who likes to pinch ladies' bums."

"'Is junk shop is full of dead good stuff though, like Second World War bayonets and helmets," said Pogsy defensively. "And he has bags of old Lego and boxes of Action Man gear that you can't get anymore."

"And," said Sam, "he looks like a grandad troll crossed with a wizened baby. You wouldn't trust him to look after your piggy bank."

Pogsy tittered. The bushy grey hair, squat face and wide nose, along with a single front tooth, didn't do Buddy any favours. Plus, his breath had a sour smell to it, which Bigzy said came from homemade whisky. Anything that came from Buddy's had a musty smell to it, a bit like Gerbil after she'd spent too long in the pet hut and it had to be thoroughly scrubbed before it was allowed in the house. "So what if me bike came from Buddy's. It's ace and the weather'll disinfect it eventually."

"Hey, you two," said Sam. "Look after Ellie. I'm off round Jimbo's."

"Mum said you're banned from seeing him today."

"Tell her I've taken the dog for a walk."

"But..."

It was too late. Sam was out the back door and on his way.

"What do you wanna do now?" asked Ali.

"I thought you were dead mad at uz and stuff, and never wanted to talk to uz again."

"Ah changed my mind."

Pogsy took a deep breath. "Let's wait until it gets dark. Then we'll get our torches, put on our climbing gear and sneak off to the dens. I wanna say soz and all that for not sticking up for you that time."

"That sounds kinda dangerous."

"Ali..." Pogsy tried to look his friend in the eyes but couldn't. "There's summut you gotta know. The gang had a vote and they won't let you in for being a girl. It's dead unfair what they did. That's why I wanna show you all the dens. It's our revenge."

Ali laughed and shook her head.

The pair pretend-played *Escape from Colditz*, making up the rules while they waited for the skies to go dark. Then they made their excuses and popped round to Ali's house to check on Nan. Pogsy kept an old black tracksuit hidden in the bike shed out the back and he collected it on the way along with Dad's torch. Once they were round Ali's, they changed clothes and snuck out the back way, moving along the alleyways until they were a safe distance away. Then they crossed the road, re-entered the alleyway system on the other side of the street and doubled back on themselves.

"Ay, you," said a voice from the shadows.

Pogsy jumped out of his skin.

"You be'er no' be nickin' on uz patch," said another voice.

Pogsy recognised the dull growl. It was the eldest Petherbridge brother. "Come on," he said, quickening the pace.

Although Ali had visited the den previously, she was unable to recall where the handholds and footholds that gave access to the top of the wall were located. Pogsy took the lead and pointed out each of the bolt shanks in turn. When he reached the top, he lay down and extended his arm to assist his friend. Quietly, they skittered along the wall, arms outstretched, moving by feel, then dropped into the woodyard using a pair of knotted ropes. Pogsy pointed to each of the dens in turn and whispered how it was bad form to go inside without an invite. They took a looksee anyway, switching on their torches to get a better view. Both rival dens were taking shape but had a long way to go. Finally, Pogsy showed her inside The Kings' den, highlighting each of the major construction challenges they'd faced, bigging up Bingo who, with the aid of a huge book on civil engineering that he'd borrowed from the library, had overcome each one in turn.

"We're building a crow's nest next. It'll even have an opening hatch that's camouflaged so the misters will never know." Pogsy smiled. "I love making dens. It's the best feeling in the world."

"For a bunch of stoopid boys you're certainly industrious," said Ali. "How ever did you find this place?"

"You remember the last time you were here, when Bigzy went chasing that monkey boy? He's the one who showed uz. Officially, we don't know who he is, but I've got a good idea."

"Who?" said Ali.

"There's one of our gang who's never there when he is."

"That's real curious." Ali laughed, showing the dimples in her cheeks. "It's a lovely, clear night. Let's lie down on the roof and gaze at the stars."

Pogsy felt the chill through his trackie bottoms; he did his best to ignore it. With Ali following, he clambered up onto the roof. The surface wood was damp and slippery to the touch. The pair found a spot above the den and lay down together.

"That's Orion the Hunter," said Ali. Pogsy followed her finger towards a set of stars rising in the east.

"I only know the Plough. It's that one up there. Its handle points to the North Pole or summut. My brother's forever looking for that rubbish comet with his mate's telescope." Pogsy scratched his neck. "Ali. That story you told about stayin' to look after your nan. Was it true?"

"Kinda," said Ali, "but there's more. Ah heard Nan tellin' her friend that Mom had invited herself over for Christmas and Ah just know she'll get drunk and cause a scene, and Ahm so over that."

"Can't your pop just tell her no."

"Mom has a way of persuadin' him to back down. And if he doesn't, she'll threaten to divorce him, take custody of me and take me away somewhere where he'll never see me again."

Pogsy felt totally out of his depth. The only experience he had of parents splitting up was Red Top's mam and dad, and in his case his mam didn't want anything to do with him or his brothers. "That's horrible," he said at last.

"Ah hate her, Pat. She's nothin' but trouble. When she finds Ah'm not there she'll cause a scene and probably call the cops. Ah should call Pop real soon, before we go back to yours, but Ah'm frightened. Will you hold ma hand while Ah do?"

Pogsy felt his heart thump against his rib cage. "Yeah."

"Thanks." Ali leaned over and planted a kiss on his cheek.

He felt his face light up the woodyard. "Before, when I said I wanted to snog you, I thought I was gonna be the best snogger in the history of snogging, but now I'm not sure, not after Pollyanna ran off."

Ali laughed.

"It wasn't funny."

"Teacher's Pet is the most devious girl Ah know. She told Pollyanna that you pick your nose and eat the boogers."

"That's *disgust*. I'd never do that."

"You do it at home, in secret, so no-one sees you."

Pogsy slapped his forehead. "That explains everything. Except why Ruth stuck her tongue in me gob if she thinks I eat boogers."

"Because she knows you don't."

"She's evil." Pogsy shook his head. "If I deny it to Pollyanna, it's just gonna make it look like it's true. We split up before we even went out."

"Confession," said Ali. "Ah haven't kissed Sarge yet."

"But... That's inposs."

"He said he wants to be engaged first, and Ah haven't said 'yes'."

"Then we *could* snog each other and it would be okay."

Ali nodded. "Avoidin' Mom is only half the reason Ah stayed. The other half is you. Ah like you a lot, Pat, and Ah had to patch things up with you just in case Ah don't come back and Ah never see you again. After what happened, Ah thought you didn't like me anymore."

"I've said soz for that," said Pogsy. "And I'll say it a million more times if I need to."

Ali continued. "Ah saw how you were that day when your hat won the competition. You turned bright red and froze to the spot, just like when you didn't stick up for me."

"I've always bin like that," said Pogsy. "It's just summut I live with. It's why I can't be the leader of the gang even though I'm better than Steve. No one else has it. Me mum just tells uz to stop being stupes and pull me socks up."

"There's a lot of folk suffer from the same thing. It's called *Scopophobia*. In the States we have pills that can make you better."

"So I just gotta take a tablet and I'll be normal and then I could be in charge of the gang? That sounds ace. Can you get uz some?"

"Ah'll try. Ah wanna do whatever Ah can to help fix you."

"Thanks, Ali. You're the greatest."

Ali leaned forward. Pogsy did too.

Their lips met.

Finally, *Kev-a-Keegan, two-a-Keegan*, his dream had come true.

Sneaking about without being seen was one of Pogsy's favourite pastimes and it was something he considered he excelled at. Over the months, he'd imparted all of his best sneaking about knowledge to Ali, such as always dress in black and hide your identity whenever possible, even though, unlike Bigzy, he didn't have a single proper disguise to his name. One day, when he was older, he hoped to employ a fake nose and a fake beard but better made than the joke ones that the toy shops in town sold.

"We'll sneak in the back way. Remember, we got distracted playin' *Buckaroo* and lost track of the time."

"Gotcha."

The second the back gate's hinges squeaked, Pogsy knew his plan was in tatters. His mum had retired to the kitchen, as she often did on Christmas Day, for cigarettes and booze, and through the mucky windows, she didn't look at all pleased.

"*Patrick Green*," she said loudly, opening the door "where *have* you been?"

"Round Ali's." Pogsy felt his ears catch fire.

The kitchen was laced with thin wisps of grey smoke, which meant Mum had only just got started. Give her another hour and you'd need a knife to cut your way out.

"There's someone here to see you," said Mum.

Pogsy stumbled through to the lounge, followed by Ali and Mum. On the sofa sat his aunt Lorna dressed in a long, white, fur-trimmed coat with huge white PVC platform boots, eyeing an empty drink.

"Aunt Lorna!" screamed Pogsy.

"'Ello, ar Pat," said Aunt Lorna, rising to her feet for the obligatory hug.

"Grandad said you were coming over tomoz."

"Well, I'm 'ere now. You remember yer Uncle Leon?"

Aunt Lorna had had so many boyfriends over the years that Pogsy had lost count of his uncles. Most of them had lasted a few weeks at most, but Uncle Leon was still there, hanging on for dear life. He was the smartest dresser of the pack and he was wearing a light brown and pale yellow plaid suit with the widest lapels this side of Pluto, a crisp white shirt and a mustard-yellow tie with brown cross-hatching. Unusually, his dreadlocks were tucked away out of sight, hidden under a floppy black hat.

Pogsy gave his uncle a fist-bump handshake sort of thing, which he'd learned the last time they'd met. The final move involved slapping backs of hands and twisting thumbs together, which was difficult to get right given the huge difference in hand sizes.

Uncle Leon chuckled, showing off a set of pearly white teeth. "Nice one, Pat. You remembered."

Pogsy nodded. "I taught one of my friends and we practised loads. This is Ali. She lives a few doors down and she's from America."

"Pleased to meet you," said Ali.

"The pleasure's all mine," purred Uncle Leon.

"Why don't you pour Uncle Leon another drink?" said Dad.

"Can I?" said Pogsy excitedly. "It's rum and ice, and Aunt Lorna has Coca-Cola in hers. I know where everything is and stuff, and how much rum to put in."

"I'll help you," said Mum loudly, grabbing Pogsy by the arm and shepherding him back towards the kitchen. She waited for Ali to catch up then closed the door. "Uncle Leon's here to discuss business."

"What business?" said Pogsy, feeling intrigued.

"Business that's none of your business."

"I bet it's got summut to do with swapsies."

"The rum's at the back of the bottom cupboard on the left," said Mum.

"Ah'll help," said Ali.

Pogsy dug deep within the drinks cupboard and, as he did so, he eyed up the bottle of sherry at the front. He glanced over at his mum. It was too risky to take a full swig. "Uncle Leon's summut to do with music. Is he swapping records for fish?"

"Patrick Green! I said no nebbing."

Pogsy tugged at the sherry bottle's cork and coughed as it dislodged. "Can Ali and me have Coke?"

"I suppose. Remember it's ice first, then rum, then Coke."

"Yes, Mum."

Between them, Pogsy and Ali retrieved four glasses and lined them up, filling each to the brim with ice cubes from the freezer compartment atop the fridge, giggling as they worked. All the while, Pogsy willed his mum to leave. Instead, she fiddled in her handbag, withdrew a packet of ciggies and lit one up.

In went the rum.

It would be simps to sneak a drop into his own glass but he'd tried rum before and it was truly horrid, even worse than gin. Instead, Pogsy winked at Ali, put his finger to his lips, pretended he'd forgotten something, blocked his mum's view with his body and poured a glug of sherry over the ice cubes in his glass.

She'd never know.

"Sherry and ice?" said Mum. "That's not at all suitable for a ten-year old."

"I'm *eleven*," spluttered Pogsy.

"Still. I better have that."

"But it's Coke. You hate Coke."

"Keep on digging." Mum shook her head. "You'll burrow all the way to China one day. Now give that here."

Pogsy lamented to himself and made faces at Ali. It was so unfair the way that Mum knew all his best plans before he'd even thought them up. He finished making the drinks and hurried back to the living room, a glass of rum in each hand. Uncle Leon liked his ice cubes to resemble miniature icebergs, whereas Aunt Lorna wasn't fussy as long as there was plenty of booze.

"That's a wicked drink you make," said Uncle Leon taking a sip. "You can come be a bartender in my club any day."

"Really?" Pogsy felt his ears turn pink. "Can I?"

"Manchester's a long way away," said Mum.

"I can stay with Aunt Lorna." Pogsy turned to his Aunt. "And Ali can come with uz too."

"I'm not sure about that," said Aunt Lorna. "While I remember, 'appy birthday, ar Pat."

"Happy birthday," echoed Uncle Leon, reaching inside his jacket and withdrawing a card, which he handed on. "I got you something extra special this year."

With trepidation, Pogsy stuck his little pinkie into the corner of the envelope and wiggled it about to dislodge the gum, then expertly, he moved his finger in a clockwise motion opening up the card. It was a picture of a footballer with the number "11" on his back. "Thanks, Uncle Leon. I've never seen one like this before."

"Take a look inside."

Pogsy grinned. "It's George Best's autograph. Betcha."

Opening the card revealed a signed photograph. However, it was not the signature that Pogsy expected to see.

"What do you think?" Asked Uncle Leon.

"I..." Pogsy felt the tears well in the corner of his eyes. There was no doubt who the photo was of, and there was no doubt that the subject had signed it. It was probably worth loads. Fighting the urge to rip the photo to shreds, stamp on the tiny pieces and then set fire to them with a flamethrower, he tried his best to remember the manners his mum had taught him. "It's okay. I suppose."

"Leeds United are your favourite team, right, Pat?" said Uncle Leon with a wink.

The anger at being the butt of the joke boiled over. "You know what I think of Leeds and now you've only gone and brought a picture of their captain Billy Bremner into the house. Out of all the Leeds players he's the one I really can't stand. In fact he's me worst footie enemy. Grown-ups say you should keep your enemies closer than your friends, but they don't have a clue what they're talkin' about. Only someone who's bonkers in the nut with a blancmange for a brain would invite their worst footie enemy in on Christmas Day."

Uncle Leon laughed out loud and slapped his chest with his palm. "Priceless!"

"It's 'orrible. You brought summut my enemy touched into the house then made uz touch it and now I've gotta drink disinfectant. You're the worst uncle in the world and you've ruined my perfect day."

"You're mean," said Ali to Uncle Leon, trying not to laugh.

"I'm truly sorry," said Uncle Leon apologetically. "He was in my club the other week and I couldn't resist."

Aunt Lorna reached inside her gold-coloured handbag and produced a second card. "I 'ope this makes it up to you."

"George Best!" said Pogsy. "For real this time."

Aunt Lorna's mouth crinkled at the edges. "Don't be disappointed or owt."

"It is though," said Pogsy. He looked to his auntie, then with great suspicion at his uncle, his mum and finally his dad. Slowly it crossed his mind that another wind-up was in progress. If a joke worked once, grown-ups always tried it again. Profanities were muttered as the envelope was prised open, although, really, he didn't want to open it at all. This time he was presented with a plain gold card. Slowly, he opened it and looked through half-shut eyes expecting it to be something even more awful than the previous photo, such as a set of autographs of the whole Leeds United team.

Instead, he discovered something miraculous.

He felt the tears return again. Only this time they were tears of joy.

"Gotcha!" giggled Aunt Lorna. "I met 'em doin' a show before Crimbo. Smashin' bunch of lads, they were."

"Show me," said Ali.

It was a black and white photograph of Slade, fully signed by the whole band in black ink.

Dave Hill's autograph was easy to spot. Jim Lea's dodgy "J" gave him away, which meant that the remaining scrawl belonged to Don Powell, the drummer. But the biggest autograph of all was that of Noddy Holder, who'd written: "To Pat. It's Xmaaaaaasssssssss!!!"

Pogsy tried to think of something to say but words eluded him. Nothing had prepared him for this. He was holding in his hands a thing of beauty that everyone in Slade had touched, which meant that he had all of Slade on his fingers and he could never wash them again. The only thing he could think to do was to hug his Aunt Lorna, followed by a hug with his uncle.

Compared to the photo, all of his other pressies paled into insignificance. It was without a doubt the *jammiest dodger* in the history of *jammy dodgers* and the best pressie he'd ever received in his life. One that he fully intended to treasure to the end of his days.

"Thanks, Aunt Lorna and Uncle Leon," he said at last. "I've got a brand-new second-hand bike and a brand-new second-hand suit, and the luckiest hat in town. It's Christmas Day *and* it's me birthday, Ali's agreed to be me girlfriend, Slade are Number One and my gang has built the best secret den ever. Now this! I've changed me mind. You're the best aunt and the best uncle in the whole wide world and today is easy the *bestest* day of me life."

Epilogue: Queues and Pees

Early on Saturday morning Pogsy set to work on his new bike, determined to finish the planned modifications as quickly as possible. Even though he was eleven now, Dad still didn't trust him to use tools on his own. He had to admit anything beyond basic maintenance, such as reseating a chain or applying oil, was outside his comfort zone and he remembered all too well the time he'd gone round Reddy's to borrow a spanner and fit new brake blocks on his own; he'd done the job so badly the blocks had worked loose and caused a traffic incident with a bread van when, out-of-control, he'd sailed blithely across a road junction unable to stop. Instead of going back to apologise, he'd decided to keep on going all the way to Bigzy's house, where he'd had to beg Bigzy's older brother for help.

"I still don't get why you're destroying a perfectly good racing bike," said Sam, scratching the side of his head.

"Because no-one has racing bars anymore," replied Pogsy, removing the last of the racing tape.

"Except cowies are only useful for knocking over old ladies."

"And for wheelies."

"You could have reversed the racing bars for that." Sam loosened the bolt on the steering column and jiggled the racing bars out the hole.

"No-one does that anymore."

Sam inserted the new bars and tightened up the bolts, encouraging Pogsy to fit the brake levers on his own.

"I saw you sneaking out last night with that astronomy book you got for Christmas. Were you watching comets get undressed again?"

"We did actually manage to see it last night."

"Joanne Dowling's bum-titty-bum? I bet you did."

"Shut up, pipsqueak!"

Sam gave chase around the edge of the square lawn in front of Dad's shed, until eventually he caught his brother and put him in a headlock. Pogsy screamed loudly and thumped his brother on the bum. Ellie wandered into view, followed by Mum. Sam administered a quick head-scrub then let go.

"We were just talking about *Colditz*," he said sheepishly, looking at Mum. "We can play it while you and Dad go out on New Year's Eve."

"Samuel *Green*!" Mum brandished her special medium-range death-stare, which was known to turn kittens to solid granite at twenty paces. "You're still a *long* way away from being trustworthy. That's why we've arranged for the three of you to stay with Granny and Grandad for the night."

"Do I *have* to?" moaned Sam.

"You're *not* staying around Jimbo's house, so don't even think about asking. He's the reason you're in this mess. Now play with your sister. I've an appointment with Mister Benson and Mister Hedges."

Ellie ran towards Pogsy, arms outstretched. He caught her and lifted her up, spinning her around.

"Again!"

He did as requested, holding his sister tightly by the arms.

"Again!"

"I'm done," said Pogsy, following a dizziness-inducing spin. "I gotta go test the cowies. She's all yours."

He left Sam tossing their sister up in the air. Slowly, he wheeled the bike towards the house, getting used to the width of the handlebars. They were just narrow enough to fit down the side passage that led to the road.

Sam was right: old biddies didn't stand a chance.

Pogsy tucked his flares into his socks, mounted the bike and set off on the first of two very important missions. Once clear of Dad's van, he pulled a wheelie; the front wheel lifted with ease, exactly as he'd hoped, and he kept it up for nearly a second. By the third attempt, he'd managed two seconds, and before he'd reached the main road, he'd set a personal best of *Kev-a-Keegan, two-a-Keegan, three-a-Keegan, Kev.*

Bigzy's house was only a short ride away. It was located at the end of a terrace street that ran parallel to People's Park, next to a plot of derelict land that Mister Bignell had requisitioned for his own private use. Every now and then, according to Bigzy, a neighbour would complain loudly and threaten to smash the fence down. Within half an hour, fifteen cousins would turn up, jeer at the neighbour, flash their bums and wee on his car. The matter would then be laid to rest until the next time Mister Bignell or the neighbour got drunk.

The Bignell compound was a junkyard comprised of old car parts, pieces of engines, puddles of oil and chemical spills. Plants knew better than to try to grow in the toxic wasteland. A few had tried over the years but they didn't last long. Those that succeeded had three heads and soon evolved legs, which they used to scuttle off sharpish.

Pogsy's route took him past a run of local shops, where he practised wheelies until, eventually, with a huge, toothy *whoop*, he managed five *Kevs*. He let out a cry of triumph, surprising a line of customers queuing outside a general store. A sign in the window proclaimed "Flour 2lb Max." Across at the butchers there was a different queue, and a further one at the grocers.

"Wot'cha," said Bigzy opening the gate to the compound. "Nice push iron."

"Birthday pressie," said Pogsy.

"One of me cousins has just dropped off a couple of bike frames. Giz 'and stripping 'em."

"Soz and all that, but this is a quickie. There's summut I gotta say and you gotta swear on your budgie's grave not to lie to uz."

"You know uz," said Bigzy, scratching his neck. "'Onest Bigzy. From a long line of 'onest Bignells."

"I think you're the monkey boy."

Bigzy spluttered like an old car backfiring. "You're jesting, right?"

"Whenever I've seen 'im, you're not there."

"Pogs. You've heard all my best stories about chasing 'im and the time I nearly caught 'im fair and square. Then there's the time Ali and Sarge came to the den. We all saw 'im at the same time."

"Ali says it was just you."

"That's stupes. She spotted 'im first."

"It *is* you."

"Cross me heart and hope to die, it's not. I'm dead close to figuring it out though. I've asked around all me cousins to see who they know who's an acrobat and I've narrowed it down to two lads."

"Are either of they called Wayne?"

"Pogs! 'Onest, it's not uz."

"You're the best climber I know and the fastest runner too. It's the only explanation as to why I couldn't catch the monkey boy that time: it's you."

Bigzy screwed up his face in frustration. "Well, I dunno what to say then. Are we still mates?"

"Course we are," laughed Pogsy. "The jest is on uz lot for not gettin' it quicker."

"Except it's not uz, Pogs. I swear."

Pogsy shook his head. He'd been sure his pal, who had a reputation for being a world-class fibber, would break under the pressure and spill his guts like he usually did. Except he hadn't. The joke, it seemed, had plenty of life in it yet.

The route to Donut's house was seared into Pogsy's brain. He'd walked it and ridden it so many times he could do it blindfolded with both hands and both legs tied behind his back. Donut lived close to Mister Mortis, in one of the posh houses just off Weelsby Road. It was definitely a well-to-do area, because all the roads were called avenues rather than streets. He was pretty certain that Donut's dad was involved in oil. Like everyone else who lived in an avenue, he had a nice car that was only a few years old.

In comparison to the Chopper, the new bike handled like a dream. Mum was forever twitching about boys on bikes being involved in accidents, but there was only one main road to cross, and at ten in the morning Pogsy counted two cars. The gang would sometimes play a game that involved winding up motorists by pretending to pull out in front of them but, with hardly any drivers on the road and no friends to impress with his antics, it seemed a waste of time.

Clouds snuck across the sky like thin grey fingers trying to throttle the sun. Every once in a while, the sun won through, only to be stifled again seconds later. Even in the drab December light, the houses down Donut's avenue managed to look fresh and clean. It was unusual that his friend hadn't been in contact. But then he'd quit school in an unusual way. He'd left it until the final week of the summer holidays to tell everyone that he wasn't coming back. This wasn't too odd in itself. Every year, one or two boys or girls left school because their dads moved away to different jobs. This was balanced out by a couple of new boys or girls arriving, due to all the factories opening up on the Humber

Bank. It was the first time an actual member of the gang had gone though. What made the revelation such a shock was that no-one had seen it coming. Normally, boys moaned a lot for months before they left. And there was always the obligatory "For Sale" sign that went up outside their house. With Donut, none of these clues were present.

Pogsy leaned his bike up against the side wall of Donut's house, like he'd done many times before, and headed to the back door. He knocked three times, using a special *tappity-tap* pattern that he and Donut had developed between them. Missis Prince answered in her usual jolly tone, almost singing every word of her greeting. She was a roly-poly mum with blonde curly hair streaked through with grey, which shot out in all directions. She wiped her hands on her purple apron, which proudly proclaimed the wearer to be the *Best Cook in the World.*

"I'm sorry for the mess," she warbled.

Judging by the flour all over the kitchen surfaces, the bowls in the sink and the lovely aroma of warm butter, she was baking again. Possibly it was her famous chicken pies. Most likely it was a cake. Pogsy licked his lips. Missis Prince was always making something. She was an expert at it.

"Is Do... Chris in?" asked Pogsy. "I heard he's back for Christmas."

Missis Prince ushered Pogsy inside. "He likes to be called Christopher now. Christopher! There's one of your friends to see you."

Pogsy's heart jumped into his mouth. He realised he wasn't sure what to expect. It was Chip who'd alerted him to Donut's reappearance after he'd been spotted in town the other day. Chip had spun a tale about him being the size of a Sherman tank and needing support wheels to remain upright.

"Hiya," said Donut, grinning from ear to ear.

"Wot'cha," said Pogsy, looking his friend up and down. He saw immediately that this version of Donut was taller than the previous version. And his fingers weren't quite as pudgy. His belly was smaller. And he wasn't breathing so hard.

Donut had always been a tubby boy. He wasn't a supersize porker, but he was certainly a fatty. He couldn't run for toffee and he was always last in any race, well out of puff before he reached the finish. He was terrible at kicking a football, terrible at bowling and terrible at batting too. When it came to sports, the only thing he was any good at was being in goal, but he wasn't really much good at that either.

What he did excel at was knowing everything about TV shows and films. Pogsy found his imagination to be quite incredible, and that was why they'd become friends. Until Donut had joined the gang, other boys used to pick on him because of his size. That had stopped the moment Pogsy put him under his protection.

The biggest change by far, though, was the short-cropped hair.

"In case you're wondering," said Donut, "my asthma's gone."

"That's good," said Pogsy. "Are we off to your bedroom?"

"I thought we could stay downstairs," said Donut, leading the way to the front lounge. "Dad's out with my sister searching for flour, even though we've got a cupboard full."

"Okay." Pogsy took a seat. "What's your new school like?"

"It's hard, Pat." Donut closed his eyes. "Very hard."

Pogsy thought his friend was about to blub; that was something he was *really* good at, especially after an accident that involved falling over. "What sort of hard?"

"Dead hard. They make you get up at six in the morning every day, even at weekends. Then you have to do running and press-ups. There's porridge for breakfast but it has salt in it. And we're not allowed to have goodies or cakes. But I can run a bit now. More than I used to be able to. I managed a mile before Christmas."

"Wow," said Pogsy. "Do they make you play in goal like we used to?"

"We're a rugger school. Where I am now, the PE teachers say that football's for girls."

"I just got me first full Liverpool kit in the sales."

Donut smirked. "I guess that makes you a sissy then."

Pogsy laughed. The old Donut would never have dared call him out. He supposed it was an improvement.

"I got *Escape from Colditz* for Crimbo. And Slade's autographs and a new bike from Buddy's for me birthday. I even managed a four-sec wheelie on the way here. D..." Pogsy paused. "There's summut I have to ask you. Do you mind being called 'Donut'?"

"*No.*" Donut screwed up his mouth, then his face. "Actually, yes. I didn't mind at the time, but I'd mind now. I'd been a *donut* all my life, it's all I knew. But when I started at my new school where no-one knows me, I decided to be plain old Christopher Prince. Donut couldn't run. But Christopher can. Or at least he's trying to. When someone thumped Donut, he beeled his eyes out. But if someone thumps Christopher, they get a thump back."

Pogsy mock-punched his friend to test the assertion. Donut grabbed his fist and held it tight.

"Pat, don't. No-one does that to me anymore. I'm not hard, Pat. But I'm not soft either. After you weren't there to look out for me, I thought I was going to get my head filled in every night. That was when I learned that it's better to stick up for yourself and get hit than do nothing. I used to be scared when other boys threatened me. Now I'm not. There are even boys who are frightened of me now."

"Have you got a new best friend?"

"I'm working on it. What about you?"

"Reddy asked uz." Pogsy scratched his neck. "I had to say yes. Those are the rules."

"I don't mind. Red Top's a good choice."

Pogsy talked to his friend about TV and films and comics, and all the things they used to have in common. Christopher said that comics were for little kids. And since he'd turned eleven, make-believe wasn't something he played anymore. Pogsy talked about school, and winning the do-it-yourself competition, and how Steve was still the class gob, Bigzy the class clown and Ruth the main teacher's pet, just like every year.

"It doesn't sound like I've missed much."

"Well, there is *summut*. I've got a girlfriend now." Pogsy felt his ears turn red. Donut's face did likewise. "She's American. Her name's Ali and she lives with her nan a few doors down."

Pogsy told his friend about how Ali had stayed in England at Christmas because her nan was ill, but really it was because she didn't want to see her mom, and then when her mom had discovered where she was it had almost caused an international incident with a kidnapped minor. She'd calmed down eventually but there'd been tears all around.

"Ali's convinced her mom's gonna keep her in the States. I went to the station with her and her nan to say goodbye and stuff, and even had a few snogs. The thing is I'm worried I might never see her again."

"I can't really help you there, Pat. I dunno much about girls and there aren't any at my new school. I know they're more complicated than boys and when they say one thing, they mean another. And they think they're really clever, much smarter than us. Sometimes I think they might be right."

"I just hope I'm wrong, that's all. I've never had a girlfriend before. I'd hate it if it was over after two days."

"I heard you've got a new den."

"That's the big secret I was saving until last." Pogsy screwed up his face. "Who told you?"

"I overheard Steve gobbing off. I was in that department store in top town getting some new school togs and he was in one of the other changing rooms. There was another lad with him but he was whispering and I didn't recognise his voice."

"Great. I bet the whole town knows about the dens now."

"There's something else. I heard him mention you. He said, 'Pogs tried to keep the dens secret from me because he wants to start his own gang, but I knew his every move thanks to my spy.'"

Pogsy felt his guts drop like a paratrooper stepping out of a plane.

"You best be careful. Someone's out to get you."

At that moment, Missis Prince came through with a wooden tray bearing slices of cake. Pogsy watched as Christopher turned them down. He could see his friend wanted one. As in really wanted one. But he held his ground and didn't give in.

Pogsy had two to make up for it.

Shortly after that they said their goodbyes.

Missis Prince gave Pogsy his friend's new address and he promised to write, even though he'd never written a letter in his life. Except for thank-you notes to aunts and uncles, although his mum told him what to say. He made a note of Christopher's birthday. December 3rd.

"I'll write and tell you what happens with Ali," said Pogsy, wheeling his bike down the drive. On the road, he pulled a wheelie lasting for three *Kevins*, all the while chuntering away.

Perhaps there was a good reason why Donut hadn't been in contact.

He wasn't Donut anymore.

He pedalled away, thinking about all the things Christopher had said.

There was a spy in the camp.

Someone was reporting everything back to Steve.

He scowled.

Teacher's Pet telling on you was one thing; a spy was much more serious.

He thought about who'd been there when he'd first discovered the woodyard. It couldn't be Reddy; they were best friends. Bigzy had been his mate forever and Bingo was a scaredy cat who couldn't lie for toffee. Weeble only did stuff to your face, never behind your back, and Squib was too titchy and in the wrong year.

Pogsy felt sicker inside than the last time he'd overdone it on three tubes of sherbet fizz.

Someone he trusted was a spragger.

What if it was Wingnut or Smiffy who'd said summut to Steve before they'd signed the Treaty?

Perhaps one of them had tried to sabotage everything.

Except they'd both been happy with the deal.

All Pogsy knew for sure was that he couldn't trust anyone anymore, except for Ali.

She was in the clear.

Everyone else was under a cloud of suspicion.

Granny and Grandad Green lived in a three-bedroom semi-detached house just outside town. Although Pogsy had visited their new place many times he'd not stayed over before. Their previous house was within walking distance and he hadn't stayed there much either. He'd once overheard Mum say that when the boys stayed with the grandparents it took a week to get them back under control.

Pogsy couldn't remember getting *that* out of control.

Grandad liked to talk about the war and he enjoyed a good war film. He firmly encouraged bayonet and grenade practice in his back garden, with plenty of shouting. He could be a bit mardy sometimes, especially when his shrapnel wounds were playing him up. You always knew when he was feeling down though because he'd retreat behind a war book with a bottle of whiskey. Granny was really kind. She always had plenty of sweets and biscuits and, unlike Mum, she didn't put a limit on how many you could eat. If you wanted to run around screaming and stay up late drinking pop, she let you do that too. She even let you write rude notes to Santa, telling him to stuff his rotten presents up his jumper.

Unusually, the drop-off fell to Mum. From all the cussing, Pogsy gathered she no longer felt safe driving the old MG, mainly due to the lack of seatbelts for Ellie. Sam said she'd told Dad to get a new car but so far he was refusing, so she'd started referring to the MG as the *clapped-out-old-banger* or the *cow-with-wheels*, which Ellie repeated as *wheelie cow*. Mum made sure that Ellie knew this only applied to Daddy's car and cars that looked like Daddy's car, but every now and then Ellie pointed out the window and said her new favourite words anyway. Aside from the freezing-cold seats with jarring springs, the lack of safety features, the general rust problem and the heavy steering, Mum was also unhappy about the amount of fuel in the tank, which registered just above empty. The car was so old it didn't have a locking petrol cap and Dad said there was no way he was leaving it parked in the road with a full tank in these uncertain times.

Mum huffed.

On the way to Granny's, she stopped at the garage, even though there was a ten-car queue, and bought three gallons of petrol and a packet of cigarettes, for what she said was her own peace of mind.

Pogsy spent the remainder of the journey wondering what Granny was knitting these days. She was still selling wombles, but nowhere near as many as before, not now there were proper stuffed toys in the shops. The advantage of Granny's version was the interchangeable clothes and the possibility of creating a brand-new womble. The girls at school all liked Orinoco the best and didn't want to change a thing. What Pogsy wanted Granny to make was a soldier womble with a helmet and rifle. Despite his best efforts, Granny had yet to knit *Normandy Womble*, whose costume consisted of an ammo belt scavenged from the beaches on D-Day, a gas-mask case instead of a wombling bag, and a pair of binoculars. He also had camo-fur, which made it impossible to spot him hiding in a bush.

Upon arrival, Ellie was first out the car.

"Gran-gran!" she shouted, running to hug Granny's leg, while Florence, Granny's elderly Pekinese dog, watched on, wagging her tail excitedly.

"Elspeth!" Granny's voice grated Pogsy's ears. Whenever she got excited, she sounded like an air-raid siren.

"Hello, Lizabeth," said Grandad. "Alan not with?"

"He has some important business," said Mum, handing over a packet of something wrapped in newspaper.

"This is nowt," said Grandad stroppily. "Sign o' the time, eh?"

"I'll get the kid's stuff out the boot," said Mum. "They've brought enough books and games to cobble dogs with."

From past experience, Pogsy knew that Granny loved welcoming visitors into her home and plying them with cup after cup of milky tea. Once she had them captive, she'd tell tales about her time working at the hospital. He was never sure which hospital, as the locations kept on changing. Gran only worked part time now, but she'd spent years and years running up and down wards, saving people's lives. Most of her best stories involved tropical diseases that no-one had ever heard of that did horrible things to you. Her best stories all ended with something dropping off, and she made you guess which bit it was.

As soon as *wheelie cow* was unloaded, Grandad took to his chair and slumped in the cushions with a look of contempt on his face, puffing away on a roll-up. Within less than a minute, he'd accrued Florence by his feet and a black and white cat with a missing ear on his lap.

One-ear must be new, thought Pogsy.

But then Granny was always getting new cats.

It was one of her hobbies.

He watched his grandad blow smoke rings. The burning tobacco did a great job of disguising the whiff of cat food emanating from the kitchen.

Puff... Puff... Puff...

Grandad's sandy hair was thinning on top. He had just enough grey strands criss-crossing back and forth for a combover. He also had freckles around his hairline, and ears that were almost triangular in shape. His nose had a bit of a bulb at the end, which Mum claimed was down to drinking too many cups of tea.

"That's what you'll look like one day," whispered Sam, administering a quick dig to the ribs.

"I will not!" Pogsy realised he was screaming. "Soz, Grandad."

Puff... Puff... Puff...

He feared his brother was right. According to Granny, he had the same colour hair as Grandad had had at his age. The stupid-shaped ears ran in the family. Dad had inherited them, along with Uncle Gordon and Aunt Lorna. Then he'd passed them on, but somehow Sam had got Mum's ears instead. Dad had the nose but not the tea bulb, although he was working on it. Based on his Grandad's looks, Pogsy swore he wasn't going to start drinking PG Tips anytime soon.

Mum fussed about making sure Ellie was comfortable while Granny moaned about the queues at the local supermarket, the grocers and the bakery. Periodically, she pumped Mum for information about Dad's goings-on. Mum gave nothing away.

While the grown-ups gabbed, Pogsy took the opportunity to go on a cat hunt, although really he was checking for his favourite auntie. He counted two downstairs and four on the beds upstairs. There were bound to be a few spares hiding in the wardrobes too. Granny never seemed to know exactly how many cats she had. People brought her rescue moggies all the time and, once one went into hiding, she'd forget about it. Then there were the cats that belonged to neighbours that hardly ever went home. If they purred, Granny bribed them with a comfortable bed and, according to Mum, better food than she fed Grandad.

Mum bade everyone farewell, promising to return by teatime the next day. The second she'd gone, Sam arranged the *Colditz* board.

"Zo, Grandad," he said with a wink, "tell us about ze Germans."

"I'll tell you this much," said Grandad, "The only good Kraut is a dead 'un. I don't know what they teach you in school these days but I didn't spend five years of my life fighting the Jerries only to give it all up for nowt. It's despicable, us joining the Common Market. Midnight tonight it happens."

Pogsy had heard of the Common Market and he knew it was happening soon, but it didn't mean anything to him other than it was likely a market for things that were common. Bikes were common and so were footballs but, according to Dad, they weren't going to get any cheaper. Which made the whole thing rather pointless.

"It's all that Ted Heath's fault," said Grandad. "The best hope we have is for an election and Wilson getting in. He's promised to take us straight back out again."

"Tell us about D-Day," said Sam. "Pat's not heard the story."

Grandad motioned for Granny to take Florence for a walk along with Ellie, who clutched an orange corduroy womble tightly in both hands. Once they'd left, he cleared his throat and popped a Liquorice

Imp into his mouth. Sam and Pogsy looked at each other and made choking-to-death faces, refusing Grandad's kind offer of one each.

"On the day war broke out, I joined the Royal Lincolnshire Regiment, 2nd Battalion. Gran was busy having your dad at the time. I waited until he was a few days old then went off to training camp, where I met the best bunch of lads I've ever known. Spent the next five years with 'em. Me best mate, Nobby, got run over by a tank. And Cyril the Squirrel lost an arm to shrapnel. But that's another story. Who can tell uz how many beaches there are in Normandy?"

"Five," said Sam. "Gold, Juno, Omaha, Sword and Utah."

"Very good," said Grandad. "Me and the lads landed on Gold beach at eight o'clock in the morning. We'd been up since five, checking our weapons and drinking tea. The army knew how to brew a proper cup of tea, let me tell you. I've never had tea like it, before or since. The Brew we called it. We drank as much of it as we could because, once you're in foreign parts, you never know where your next cuppa is comin' from. By the time we hit that beach, the entire company was busting for a piddle. There were bullets and shells flying everywhere. The air was thick with smoke and the explosions were so loud you couldn't hear yesen think. Our ships were shooting up Kraut gun emplacements, our planes filled the sky and our subs torpedoed owt that moved. The bombs and shells rained down thick as shite all day. Even with all that lot goin' on, all me pals could think of was their bladders. When you get shot it all comes out. Men to the left of me wet themselves. Men to the right pissed their pants. Before long, we were pinned down, nearly out of ammo. 'Well,' I said to mesen, 'Someone's gonna have to do summut to break the deadlock.'" Grandad paused to roll another cigarette.

"What happened?" asked Pogsy.

"I might have been out of bullets but I wasn't out of pee. I zig-zagged across the sand and ran at the nearest pillbox and luckily I made it in one piece." Grandad spun the packed cigarette paper in his thick fingers, licked the gum strip and finished his rollie. Slowly, he lit it. "The second I reached that pillbox I whipped me cock out and let loose. It was like trying to control a ruddy firehose! I peed up that wall as high as you like and the tea kept on coming. I peed so high it went straight through the observation slot, with such ferocity that it blinded two German gunners. 'Englander swine!' they shouted. 'Ach! Ve cannot see!' With their machine gun out of action, Lofty snuck up behind uz, lobbed a grenade in the hole and blew 'em both to kingdom come. Others saw what we'd done and joined in, and pretty soon we'd cleared a path off that beach. They make no mention of it in the history books, but tea won the war for us that day."

"Wow," said Pogsy, putting two and two together. Not only had he inherited Grandad's ears, nose and hair, he'd also inherited Grandad's bladder.

"Is that where you got your Luger?" asked Sam.

Grandad nodded. "I had one, Lofty got the other. I used mine all the way across France. It's the best ruddy gun the Germans ever made. The British Army only lets officers have pistols as a rule but they turn a blind eye to captured weapons."

Grandad reached over and poured a glass of Christmas whiskey from a bottle that was already half-empty. He offered a tot to Pogsy and Sam. They settled for fizzy pop instead. Grandad kept on talking about the war and the fight across France until teatime, when Granny cooked up cold turkey, egg and chips.

Unlike at home, Pogsy kept his lucky hat on to eat.

"Are you working tonight Grandad?" asked Sam. "I remember you moaning about being on shift last year."

"Stuff that! I got mesen a new job with better pay and better hours. Don't yer dad tell you nowt?"

"He likes to keep us in the dark." Pogsy winked at his brother.

"I'm doing security near you now," said Grandad. "At that new cold store. I can tell you a tale or two about that place, believe you me."

Pogsy felt his ears turn bright scarlet; his heart stopped. "Such as?" he croaked.

"I shouldn't really. But seen as you're family, there's summut very odd going on. Someone's been leaving bottles of piss outside me office. And the other day there was a carrier bag full of shite on me door handle."

Sam tittered while Pogsy slinked down in his chair.

"It's not ruddy funny! I've never seen owt like it, not down the docks or on the beaches on D-Day. To top it all, there's a thief who dresses in black and creeps around at night. He might be a terrorist."

"Do you think he's the one doing the defecating?" asked Sam trying and failing to keep a straight face.

"All I know is that if I get me hands on the bleeder wot dun it, I'll kick his arse into the middle of next week."

Pogsy didn't understood the fascination with New Year's Eve. You went to bed one year, got up and it was the next year. But apart from that, nothing changed. Granny said they could stay up until midnight and watch telly if they wanted, but he persuaded Sam to play *Colditz* in the kitchen, guiltily staying as far away from Grandad as possible. Every few seconds he thought about the dens and the horrible things they'd concocted to do to the *old codge*. Evidently, plans had been put into action. Ellie went to bed at eight, clutching her new orange toy. Sam called it a day at eleven, after two rounds of sandwiches, a pork pie, some cheese triangles, a slab of Granny's iced Christmas cake and two glasses of orange squash.

"Sam," said Pogsy as they both lay in bed. "What did you do with those After Eights I saw you nick from Mum's new box?"

"They're for breakfast," replied Sam. "Go to sleep."

"I can't. What's your New Year's *Revolution*?"

"It's a resolution. Something you swear to do, no matter what. It's like a pinkie promise. I've got two resolutions. The first is to get better at blowing things up and the second is not to get caught doing it. I'm fed up with Mister Armstrong smirking at me all the time. I'll show him."

While Pogsy considered what his top-five resolutions were, old one-ear jumped on his bed and stood there purring, looking at him. He gave the cat a quick pat, which it seemed to like. It padded up and down and settled on his belly.

"Me first resolution," he said, "is to pee up a pillbox and get it in the gun slot, just like Grandad did."

"You do know that's made up," said Sam. "It's just old army tales."

"I believe him," said Pogsy. "I could do it. Weeing ten feet up walls is my superpower."

"As if."

"I reckon he peed his way to Berlin," said Pogsy. "That's what I'd do. I'd pee in bunkers and down tank barrels, and gun barrels, and even on a Messerschmitt if I found one. Historians would know which way I went by following the trail of wee."

Sam switched out the light. "Night."

"You haven't heard my second resolution yet. That night I went to *Donkeycaster* with Dad, when he was doing swapsies with the

Scousers, he had a special box of fish labelled 'Catch of the Day', which everyone thought was really valuable. I'm gonna find out what was in it."

"That's easy. Halibut."

"Except a halibut wouldn't fit. That's why I think it was turbot."

"If you're looking for a really valuable fish, you should consider monkfish. It's one of the rarest fish of all. It's also ugly with a big mouth."

"Like you then."

"It's better than being a sprat with big ears. I'm intrigued now. I want to know too. Let's have a competition to see who can find out first."

"Done," said Pogsy. "Me third resolution is to find out what the rules are for being eleven."

"There aren't any," said Sam. "Goodnight."

"But there must be. There were rules for being eight, rules for being nine and rules for being ten."

"That's where they stop."

Pogsy scowled to himself.

How was he supposed to know if he was too old for playing Action Man and reading comics if there weren't any rules?

He scowled some more.

The *Dandy* and *Beano* were definitely for little kids, but not *Valiant* or *The Amazing Spiderman*. They were for teenagers, which meant he was reading above his *actual* reading age. *Shoot!* was for boys *and* teenagers. Famous footballers wrote stories in it and there were tales about the most important football games in the world, from people who were there, who saw all the goals go in. 1974 was a World Cup year; *Shoot!* had said so. But it wasn't due to start for ages, and England weren't even in it because they'd only gone and lost to Poland.

"Who do you think will win the World Cup?"

"West Germany," said Sam, "obviously."

"I reckon Holland."

"What do you even know about Holland?"

"They have windmills, tulips, bright-red cheese and clogs and I'm goin' there next year on a school trip. And Mister Flowers, who knows loads about footie, says that Holland are really good."

"Your greasy-haired mate Chip Pan Head's old man?"

"He hates it when you call him that. It's *derisive*."

"Listen at you with the big words.

Pogsy was pretty certain that if the Dutch footie players wore clogs with studs, like Chip claimed, they weren't going to win anything, but he kept quiet about that bit. He thought again about what Donut had said and his *propisterous* claim that footie was a game for girls. While he knew very little about rugger – other than they had some very rude songs and the players liked to bite each other's ears off – football was a game of skill. The idea that girls could play it and be any good, and score real goals, was just ridiculous.

Everyone knew that.

Granny's spare bed wasn't as comfortable as his own. The blankets were thinner too. He rolled over, which disturbed old one-ear. The cat adjusted itself. There was one last thing to do before sleep. It was a silly ritual but he'd done it every night since Christmas Day. Ali's face popped into his brain. She was his girlfriend now. He thought about his best snog with her and tried to remember how it felt, pressing his lips against her lips.

He remembered the counting.

The second *Keegan* was the most important. That was where a kiss finished and a snog began, and you had to start breathing in and out through your nose. During the snog he'd had with Pollyanna, he'd held his breath, which was why he'd had to stop at seven *Kevs*. Which was silly because he could easy do twenty *Keegans* underwater. His actual record was eighteen but, if anyone asked, he always said twenty.

Thanks to Ruth, he'd worked out the breathing bit and managed to set a record of twenty-five *Kevs* with Ali. He wondered what happened if a snog went on to fifty or even a hundred *Keegans*. He had no idea officially how long it was before a snog became something else. He decided that 1974 was the year he'd find out.

His fourth resolution, which he didn't tell Sam about, was to find out which of his friends had said something to Steve.

Unmask the spragger.

And once he knew who it was, he'd mell their head in. It was as simps as that.

Resolution number five was trickier and required careful planning. He was going to scare the pants off Bigzy by telling him Grandad thought he was a thief and a terrorist and thus unmask him as the monkey boy.

Something in the back of his mind chimed in.

The words belonged to Bingo, the cleverest boy in school.

"Sam. What's the difference between a monkey and an ape?"

"Not this again! We've had this conversation before and the answer hasn't changed since last time."

"Giz a clue."

"You've seen the film *Planet of the Apes*. How many monkeys were in it?"

"I dunno."

"If there were monkeys in it, it would have been called *Planet of the Monkeys*, and it wasn't. Goodnight."

Pogsy thought about the film, which he'd really enjoyed, especially as it starred his favourite actor, Charlton Heston.

The orangutangs were in charge, and they were led by Doctor Zaius. The troops were gorillas that could ride horses, and they were led by General Urko. Finally, there were the scientists led by Cornelius. The monkey boy definitely wasn't a gorilla, nor was he an orang. Which left a chimpanzee. Except the gang wouldn't call him "Chimpanzee Boy"; it was too long. They'd call him "Chimp Boy" instead.

Except they wouldn't.

They'd shorten it to Chimpy.

Pogsy took a deep breath. Then another. Finally, he slapped his forehead.

How had he not seen it?

He laughed out loud.

The stoopid boys had chucked Ali out The Kings and then voted to let the monkey boy into all of the gangs. She'd played the biggest jape in the history of japes on the lot of them, time and time again.

You really couldn't get much more stupes than that.

Perhaps Donut was right.

Perhaps girls really were smarter than boys.

Perhaps, if boys let them try, they'd even be good at footie.

"Night Sam. See you in 1974."

Sam laughed. "Not if I see you first."

(Pogsy and friends will be back in 1974)

Acknowledgements

Thanks to my wife for encouraging me to finally write down the tales of my time growing up in Grimsby. Whilst all the characters in this novel are fictional, the places they visit are real. Or they were in 1973.

Further thanks to those who helped along the way with their suggestions for the composition of the gang, the language of the times and the fashion tips. I'm especially grateful to the retired fishermen who shared tales of their times at sea, the realities of the Cod War(s) and the layout of the docks — which have changed beyond recognition since the early 1970s.

I'm too young to remember 1973 in full (honest!) but I do remember Glam Rock and the huge effect it had on my musical tastes for years to come. I most certainly remember Christmas 1973 and Slade's ascent to the top of the charts. That song rocked my world and still does. It reminds me of what Christmas is all about — family, friends, dancing and making merry. We didn't have a lot in those days, so we made do with what we had and made the best of the worst of times. Family and friends will see you through. They always do.

Whilst I haven't lived in Town for some years, I still have fond memories of the place. You know what they say — you can take the lad outta Grimsby, but you'll never take Grimsby outta the lad.

My home town — I salute you.